The Greatest Story Ever Told

A TALE OF
THE GREATEST LIFE
EVER LIVED

Other books by Fulton Oursler

BEHOLD THIS DREAMER!
SANDALWOOD
STEP-CHILD OF THE MOON
POOR LITTLE FOOL
THE WORLD'S DELIGHT
THE GREAT JASPER
JOSHUA TODD
A SKEPTIC IN THE HOLY LAND
THREE THINGS WE CAN BELIEVE IN
THE PRECIOUS SECRET
A HISTORY OF PROTESTANT MISSIONS

The Greatest Story Ever Told

A TALE OF
THE GREATEST LIFE
EVER LIVED

by

Fulton Oursler

GARDEN CITY, N.Y.
Doubleday & Company, Inc.

PRINTED IN THE UNITED STATES

I have two friends, man and wife, who in their lives, privately and professionally, exemplify the teachings of Jesus Christ more truly than do any others I know. Their modesty prevents me from recording even their initials, but to them I dedicate this imperfect work in affection and gratitude.

FULTON OURSLER

Preface

THIS is the story of Jesus. It is a chronology of events from the betrothal of Mary and Joseph to the days after the Resurrection, and the episodes are taken from the four Gospels. What is imaginative in the narrative is largely detail to fill in chinks left open in the Bible accounts; nothing has been included that did not seem a reasonable assumption from the records.

In writing anew the wonderful life of Jesus, the author has had but one thought in mind, and that was to induce readers to go to the Gospels and hear the story at firsthand. It was Rabbi Solomon B. Freehof, of a great Jewish temple in Pittsburgh, who said to me at dinner one evening that the unspoken scandal of our times was the hidden fact that Bible-reading had been largely given up in America.

Later, as I traveled around the country and talked to many different kinds of men and women—fellow passengers in Pullman and day coach, stenographers, lecture committee chairmen—I made casual allusions in conversation to biblical passages. I soon discovered that references which in my boyhood were clichés of front-porch talk had no meaning whatever for these later companions. Even such obvious phrases as "Thirty pieces of silver" or "The talent buried in a napkin" or "The angel that troubled the waters" left many listeners with blank stares. Yet when I explained the meaning, their interest was clear; a sample from the great history invariably roused the appetite for more.

These experiments helped me to come to a long-considered resolution. Ever since my first visit to Palestine, in 1935, I had been tempted. A tour of Galilee, Samaria, Judea, and Transjordania had evoked again in me a deep interest in Christianity which had filled me up when I was young. Now, after twenty-five years of contented agnosticism, I was stirred up again. I began to read various chronologies by which Catholic and Protestant theologians had sought to straighten out the apparent confusions and contradictions in the Gospels. This book follows none of the established time and sequence formulae but draws from several, in what seemed to the writer the most natural and probable line.

The book is not offered as an explanation or an interpretation. It is rather an attempt to tell, faithfully, just what the four Apostles, Matthew, Mark, Luke, and John, assert to have happened in those thirty-three years of the life of Jesus. It is, further, an effort to state the believing Christian's understanding of the meaning of those years. There is no intention here to rationalize or to hunt out a symbolism. While sometimes dramatized, the story is completely faithful to the literal statements of the text.

While I was still at work on the manuscript I found myself on a sponsored radio program negotiated for me by a producing agency of which Mr. Waddill Catchings was chairman. During this association of more than three years I became well acquainted with Mr. Catchings, and in 1943 I suggested to him that the manuscript on which I was working would provide stirring material for a radio presentation of episodes in the life of Our Lord and dramatizations of the Christian teachings.

Where many another radio producer might have been frightened off, Mr. Catchings was attracted at once. Together, in many conversations, we explored the difficulties. Could we please both Catholics and Protestants with such a presentation? Would those of other faiths protest? Could any sponsor be found to take the risks implied in those questions? Would the general public be shocked at the sound of an actor's voice impersonating the Master?

To these and many other problems we felt eventually that we had found the solutions, and soon Mr. Catchings began to approach possible sponsors. Here our path was for a time full of discouragement. More than once, after prolonged negotiations, we had reason to believe that a contract would be arranged, only to have the plans fall through at the last moment. But never did either of us lose hope. This confidence was justified when, through the efforts of Mr. Catchings and the bold enthusiasm of Mr. James H. S. Ellis, head of Kudner Agency, Inc., the Goodyear Tire and Rubber Company expressed an interest. Mr. Paul W. Litchfield, head of the firm, wanted to be shown how our plans would be materialized in actual performance.

It had seemed to me from the first that the parable of "The Good

Samaritan," with its deathless dramatic action and its basic lesson against intolerance, would make an ideal beginning. Here, in a most exciting story, was the Christian teaching on racial hatred.

Accordingly a script was prepared. Step by step I outlined the story and my friend, Henry Denker, took that skeleton and with dialogue and sound effects clothed it with exciting life. Then Mr. Marx Loeb, radio dramatic director, began to assemble a cast of Broadway actors. All of us—Catchings, Ellis, Denker, and myself—sat with Loeb, listening to brief recordings of scores of voices, picking not only the actor to portray Jesus, but all the other figures in "The Good Samaritan." And Mr. William Stoess was enriching it all with his special arrangements of music.

Yes, Mr. Litchfield said, when he had listened to the recorded performance of our experiment; yes, he believed in it thoroughly. But he had one reservation: Could we do as well in all the shows to follow?

"If you can do one more show as good as the first, I will be convinced," he said.

For the second experiment I selected the parable of "The Unmerciful Servant." Mr. Litchfield heard it and signed the contract. To his everlasting credit let it be said that while spending near to a million dollars a year on the program he refused to take any of the time for advertising. Because the laws require it, the name of the sponsor must be mentioned at opening and closing. So one hears: "The Greatest Story Ever Told—presented by the Goodyear Tire and Rubber Company." That is all, until it is repeated at the close.

The program began in January 1947. Since then, week after week, Sunday evenings at 6:30 P.M. over the network of the American Broadcasting Company, we have presented "The Greatest Story Ever Told." Many of the half-hour dramas have been original stories—modern parables if that is not too bumptious a term—but illustrating always some text from the New Testament. The plots for these I brought to Denker and he, with skill and inspiration, transformed them into vivid scripts. But also we frequently drew our material straight from this book, notably the five weeks of the Nativity scripts and the three episodes at Easter. The mood and method of this book have always been the basis and spirit of the radio program.

Each script was read, corrected, and approved by Monsignor Joseph A. Nelson, of St. Patrick's Cathedral staff in New York; Rev. Dr. Samuel Shoemaker, rector of Calvary Protestant Episcopal

Church; and Rev. Dr. Paul Wolfe, minister of the Brick Presbyterian Church, New York. With them has been associated Mr. Otto Frankfurter, brother of Justice Felix Frankfurter of the United States Supreme Court. Nothing has appeared on the programs without the approval of these four.

There have been no clashes; the program has gained in favor ever since it began. I cite one of many collateral miracles: In the spring of 1947 the General Tire and Rubber Company, a competitor of Goodyear, took page advertisements in newspapers throughout the country urging the public to listen to its rival's radio program. The Christian influence makes itself quickly felt. A little leaven leaveneth the whole.

With much help and counsel I have told here the great story once more—the story of the greatest event in human history. For once upon a time and long ago it actually happened, according to the faith of true believers, among which the author counts himself.

God, who had fashioned time and space in a clockwork of billions of suns and stars and moons, in the form of His beloved Son became a human being like ourselves. On this microscopic midge of planet He remained for thirty-three years. He became a real man, and the only perfect one. While continuing to be the true God, He was born in a stable and lived as a workingman and died on a cross.

He came to show us how to live, not for a few years but eternally. He explained truths that would make our souls joyous and free.

This is the story of Jesus—the greatest story ever told.

Contents

Book Three

THE PREPARATION

Book Four

THE FIRST YEAR

Book Five

THE SECOND YEAR

Book Six

THE THIRD YEAR

The Greatest Story Ever Told

A TALE OF
THE GREATEST LIFE
EVER LIVED

Book One

A CHILD IS BORN

Chapter 1 THE MAN WHO WAITED

PEOPLE in Nazareth said that Joseph was like his great ancestor, the favorite son of Jacob. It was true that the carpenter of Nazareth, with his small golden beard, so different from his black-haired neighbors, was a dreamy, quiet-spoken man, looking more like a scholar than a craftsman.

His uncle who brought him up had taught the orphan boy his trade. With those great knotty hands of his Joseph could build a house or a fence, fashion a chair or a bench, hang a door, mend a wheel, build a new plow or yoke. On the high street in Nazareth, his little shop with its earthen floor had a clean, constant smell of shavings and sawdust. In the back was a cot and near by a grate on which Joseph, the bachelor, cooked simple meals. On long evenings he would sit on his heels at the open door and sew a rent in his smock or stand outside and breathe deep of the cool air. Later, by the yellow flame of a rush burning in an oil lamp, he would read for hours from borrowed scrolls.

The golden-bearded Joseph with the prematurely bald head was called a visionary because he refrained from gambling with travelers of passing caravans; he avoided tavern women, and found his pleasure in good talk with a few neighbors. Among Nazarenes these were queer habits, for generally they were a rowdy lot.

This town lying hidden in the mountains was near a post on a busy trade route between Europe and Asia, so there was often excitement in the neighborhood, a tide flowing back and forth of camels and baled merchandise—pungent fragrances and spicery and rainbow silks of the East, skilled manufactures of the West, wines and oils, the barter and trade of Alexandria and Damascus. At night caravans often rested in the fields, and the rocky hillside gleamed with golden tongues of camp fires. The townsfolk got their news from those travelers, and day and night lived in an atmosphere of the new, the strange, and the exciting. They were rough men, these merchants and camel drivers, and the people of the town were rough, too, ready to take offense, ready to brawl, to gamble and haggle—ready for anything!

Late one afternoon Samuel of Cana stood in dark silhouette on the threshold of Joseph's shop, at the end of the Street of the Coppersmith. The young merchant was tall and powerful against the fading light.

"The Lord be unto you," he said politely.

Joseph put down his hammer, separated his bare feet which he had been using as a vise for a board, brushed sweat from his forehead with the back of his hand, and grinned at his friend.

"And peace be with you, Samuel. Come in. Your chest of good Galilean oak and sycamore is finished and I am about to eat. Join me?"

"No, I have just eaten at home. But thank you."

The giant Samuel sprawled on the shavings litter of the floor, while Joseph, forsaking chisel, adze, and saw, squatted on his bare heels and spread out a repast of bread and curds and a cup of milk.

"Who fixed you such a dainty meal?" asked Samuel suspiciously.

"When a man is an orphan and has no wife, he must learn to do for himself."

"You are lonely, Joseph?"

"Sometimes."

There was a moment's pause as the carpenter smeared his bread with the curds.

"I have a cure for loneliness," murmured Samuel, a gleam in his inkberry eyes.

Joseph chuckled with private amusement.

"I can guess!" He laughed.

"No," Samuel cried vindictively. "I've long ago given up trying to make an adult out of you, Joseph. No amourettes, no little love affairs for you! Of course you don't know what you're missing, but that's not what I was thinking about at all. My thoughts for your future were elsewhere."

"Where then?"

"Jerusalem!"

"Are there not enough carpenters in the big city?"

"Carpenters, bah! Joseph, don't you ever have a thought beyond your work?"

Joseph blinked self-consciously.

"Why, yes, Samuel, I think about many things that have nothing at all to do with my work."

"What, for instance?"

"Oh—the law."

"Bah!"

"Bah!" repeated Joseph with a wag of his bald head. "Bah is not an argument, Samuel. It is a noise."

"It has a meaning just the same. It means that I and many like me are tired of being taught about the patriarchs and the judges and the prophets—the history of Israel. We are tired of more than that. We have had enough of being ruled by foreign powers; we are all slaves, run by Herod for the benefit of Rome, and what has Rome to do with us? We want to be free!"

"Oh," said Joseph. "That again! Better lower your voice, Samuel."

The danger was real. Roman spies were everywhere. It was folly to take part in political discussions, with the police listening, holding the downtrodden people in a misery of fear. One learned not to speak ideas aloud. In the last century there had been a series of hapless rebellions in the land; fierce and fanatical men still roamed the hills of Galilee, striking at Romans when they dared. Some of the best of the young men of the province, healthy and strong ones, enthusiastic ones, had perished in those feeble and foredoomed revolts—thousands of patriots dying for Israel during the one hundred years the Romans had held Israel. Not only Galilee of which Nazareth was one of the chief towns did they hold, but Judea, too, with Jerusalem, the golden capital. All the territory that once had known the valor of Joshua, the power of David, the wisdom and glory of Solomon was now paying tribute to the Emperor Caesar Augustus.

Ah, Samuel could tell Joseph, conditions were getting much worse. Rich and powerful men of their own nation were collaborating with the invaders, fattening their fortunes by betraying their own people. How long must they endure slavery with treason thrown in? Did Joseph realize that in every village young men were once more plotting to throw the Romans out and make the people free? Why would Joseph not join?

Ever since Joseph could remember impetuous youths in Nazareth had been planning a secret, melodramatic resistance against the Romans, but it never came to anything more than talk.

"Don't you love your own country?" prodded Samuel reproachfully. "Aren't you one of us in spirit, at least?"

Joseph's smile was quizzical. Poor workman that he was, he belonged to the house of David and his line ran back, clearly indicated in the scrolls of the Nazareth synagogue, all the way to Jacob who was of Isaac, who was of Abraham; and farther than that, even, to Seth who was of Adam, who was of God.

The smile deepened as he patted the knee of his impetuous friend. This revolutionist really did want to save Israel. But how? By uprising, by blood, by death. In the holy books prophets had promised liberation—salvation for the people who had known the terrors of war, the slavery of Egypt, the wanderings in the wilderness, the captivity of Babylon, and now the Roman occupation. But salvation was to come, according to these ancient writers, when a messenger was born, the long-promised Messiah, who would lead the nation to peace. Joseph believed his books, therefore a good man must not turn to blood and death to hasten salvation. And Joseph was well aware that every son of the house of David was being watched.

"But have you heard the news from Jerusalem?" demanded Samuel, impatient of books. "I have been talking to some camel drivers who arrived only this morning. King Herod has murdered more of his family—he has already murdered one wife, as you remember—and every day of his life he kills our own innocent and helpless people, according to his whims. As a sensible man, how can you depend on promises made hundreds of years ago, when today——"

"When today," Joseph interrupted, "the God of Israel is still the same Lord. We must rely on him, and, Samuel, don't let me hear you say *bah* to that, for that would be blasphemy."

"Bah!" insisted Samuel fiercely. "Go and report me. Let them put me to death for blasphemy—I would rather die than live like a slave."

Joseph stood up, brandishing his saw over his head, but his grin belied the violence of the gesture.

"This saw is a tool without soul or conscience," said Joseph. "It can be used to cut open a Roman's skull, or it can help make a cradle for a Nazarene baby. That's up to the man who uses it. Every man has tools; the whole world would be better off if we used them for peace rather than war."

"You mean that we should go on submitting to unspeakable Herod —and Rome—and do nothing?"

As he spat out these contemptuous words, Samuel scrambled to his feet and confronted his friend.

"The ruin of our people," Joseph retorted, "has always been to depart from faith and depend on their own powers. We know that a deliverer will come—and we've just got to wait."

"Do you think the Messiah is coming tomorrow—perhaps the next day?"

"Who knows?" asked Joseph simply. "Violence, revolution, all these secret schemings are tricks learned from aliens who have forty gods, and all forty are not enough, and any one of them too many, to give them peace."

"I would still like to know," persisted Samuel, "whether you expect to live to know the Messiah."

Joseph chuckled. What a fanciful idea!

"A workman like me know *Him?* What would a poor carpenter know about such great affairs? No, I look forward to a quiet life."

"And lonely, Joseph. You said so."

Joseph waggled a great forefinger amiably.

"Not at all. I do not expect to be lonely forever. Like any other man, I want a wife in my house . . ."

"And children?"

"Many, I hope; a houseful; I would enjoy them."

Samuel's burning eyes softened a little.

"Well, I hope you find the girl of your heart, my friend. She will never have to fear a thrashing from the gentle kind of husband you will make her."

Joseph did not seem to be listening. He stood very thoughtful, with a touch of sadness in his manner. His eyes were on the doorway; he was staring out into the street as if he were expecting some wonderful vision. Only his right hand, huge and flexible, reached out and seized the other by the elbow.

"I have already found her," he confided. "She is very young—and very different from all other women in the world."

"Come out of your trance, Joseph, and tell me how this girl is so different."

"She is not as any of the others are; that is all I know how to tell you. Look, Samuel, I was sure of it—she is coming toward us now. See her, with the empty red jug on her head?"

Samuel strode to the doorway and shaded his eyes with his hand.

"Don't stare," admonished Joseph severely.

"I will admit that her walk is more than ordinarily graceful," announced Samuel over his shoulder.

"Everything about her is more than ordinary," murmured Joseph, taking a place near to the hulk of his friend, who nearly filled the doorway. The carpenter's head was turned to one side, and he was looking under the upraised arm of Samuel, and there was still that distant look in the blue eyes as if he were enraptured by the strains of music.

The shadowed street was almost empty as a girl came toward them down the narrow pavement. Dark hair framed the pale face above the light blue mantle and the intense blue eyes set so wide apart. She walked in grace.

"Joseph," said Samuel, lowering his voice, "there may be something in what you say. That girl is somehow different. Yes, she *is*. Can it be the expression? It is most unusual; it is, why . . . look . . . it has me stammering, man . . . it is . . ."

Samuel lowered his hand.

"Never have I seen such serenity on any face," he acknowledged. "It gives me, my friend, a strange sort of feeling."

He looked after the girl searchingly as she passed, eyes straight before her, arms lifted gracefully, fingers spread against the red water jug.

"What can it be that sets her apart?" the merchant fumed. Then he shook himself and with forced heartiness turned into the shop again.

"No wonder you won't go with me to Jerusalem," he barked. "Tell me, has that maiden promised . . ."

Joseph sank dismally on the bench.

"I have never even spoken to her," he admitted.

With a boisterous laugh Samuel walked over and laid a hairy hand on the bald head.

"Shy as ever, Joseph," he teased. "You have to pluck up your courage, boy. You're not too young, you know! And the bucks of this village are not blind. Don't be losing time."

Joseph looked up with an air that gave a sudden strength to his face.

"I am not afraid," he said quietly.

Samuel snorted loudly. It came to him then with a sense of obscure annoyance that the gentle people of this world are a strong and obstinate mystery. There was conviction in the words of Joseph.

"At least tell me one thing. You don't know her parents?"

"Not yet. They have just come here from Jerusalem."

"Have you never learned her name?"

"Her name?" Joseph looked up. "Oh yes, I know that."

"Tell me, then, before I go."

"Her name," said Joseph, "is Mary!"

Chapter 2 THE BETROTHAL

FOR this night's negotiations Joseph had made great preparations. Behind the curtain at the back of his shop he scrubbed all the sweat from his stocky body. The muscles of Joseph were strong as those of any Nazarene bully. He could put his shoulder under a Roman axle and lift a broken chariot from the mire. Thoroughly he cleansed himself and trimmed his beard and washed the sawdust out of the stiff tangles of his curls. Carrying a gift of Damascus sweets, he set off through the crowded Street of the Coppersmith.

Now Joseph turned to scan the crowded street. There, up and down, in an unending stream, a noisy crowd of men and women tramped in the ooze of the unkempt thoroughfare. Unruly Galilean workmen, some in sandals but most of them barefoot, and all in a hungry hurry, so it seemed, shouldered and elbowed their way home as if rudeness with them were a purpose in life. The air was clamorous with insults in a variety of languages—Greek and Roman for the strangers and piercing, passionate tones of home talk—a frenzied fluency of Aramaic Chaldee. The babel of all three tongues mingled with the bleating of lambs and goats, the hoarse sneezing of camels, and the soft, incessant clonking of their desert bells. And everywhere, underfoot and in corners and doorways, homeless scavenger dogs were snuffling for garbage.

Just at the edge of the town, about a mile from Joseph's workshop, on a shoulder of a hill stood the house of Mary. It was somewhat more substantial than the average dwelling and much more charming to the eye than the shacks of sun-dried bricks in which lived so many of the valley people on the floor of Sharon and the great plain below.

Mary's home was made of the mountain stones. It was covered with plaster, and the white half-ball dome at the top had a square terrace all around it on which fruits and vegetables were drying tonight. The flooring of that dome-shaped roof was on a slant to pour the scant rain down into a rocky cistern in the rear; the parched land of Palestine hoarded every raindrop.

The door opened into the one large chamber of the house. The house's mighty walls were of rough-dressed stones, four feet thick to keep out the heat, and smoked by old fires; in the hollow height of the roof pigeons cooed and fretted in the dark. At the rear was a high platform that was really the family home—an elevation of masonry ten feet above the entrance on the ground floor. It was raised on stone arches and reached by a steep stairway—the heart of this household, where the family ate, slept, and lived.

Near the front opening the ground floor was cluttered with the family's livestock: sheep and goats, a rooster and his hens. When the family had company overnight Mary had to sleep on this floor level, near the warm animals, and she always enjoyed the adventure.

Joseph was greeted at the door by Joachim. Inside were Anna, Mary's mother, and a strange woman he had never seen before. This was Elizabeth, kinswoman of the family.

Once, sometimes twice a year, they had a visit from Cousin Elizabeth, daughter of Anna's much older sister. Between Mary and Elizabeth there was a difference of more than forty years; it was like being cousin to your own grandmother. Most of these forty years the older cousin had been married to a country priest in a village not far from Jerusalem; his name was Zachary, and the town they lived in was called Ain Karim.

Cousin Zachary was even older than his wife; his back was so stiff that he found it hard to stoop over and trim his toenails. About the aging pair there was a settled feeling of taut dignity, as if they had dutifully made friends with sorrow.

They were very poor, and the village of Ain Karim where Zachary labored in the synagogue was small and obscure. There he served the townspeople, married and circumcised them, advised and buried them—a busy and peaceful life. Elizabeth had arrived with news. Soon Zachary was to be pulled out of his obscurity. To any little village priest the honor might come. Now Zachary was called again, after years, as a priest of the line of Abia, if you please, to celebrate the sacrifice at the holy place, in the Temple of Jerusalem.

"You tell me this? Great news indeed!" Anna closed her eyes and remembered the glory and the magnificence of the great temple. That good old Zachary should wear the white-and-yellow robes and the blue tassels before all the worshipers and send up smoke to the very nostrils of Jehovah!

"Oh, Elizabeth, aren't you happy?"

"Yes, my loved one, I am very happy."

Joachim entered and cleared his throat.

"This is Joseph," the husband announced awkwardly. "He comes to tell you how much he loves our child."

Anna sank to the floor and crossed her legs and shook herself from side to side and made a sad, low, crooning sound as if an adumbration of sorrow had fallen upon her.

"Mourning," exclaimed Joachim reproachfully. "There should be no sadness in all this."

"You are right! I know it—I know!"

Anna lifted a tear-stained face.

"I trust your judgment, beloved. I do not mean to make sadness. I am sure Joseph must be a fine young man because he has so touched Mary's heart that she is really foolish in her thoughts of him—beautiful, foolish thoughts of love and pretty dreams. I want Mary to have happiness. To know deep love and kindness and sweetness as we have always known it, Joachim. I am sure you know best."

Joachim spread out his arms, palms to the roof.

"Then why is she crying?" he demanded of the universe.

"I don't know. I really don't know. We are an unusual family, Joachim; we have strange feelings at times——"

"You have been dreaming?"

"No. It's just a fear—like a pain in my heart that portends something and won't go away—as if our Mary will know too great a misery because of this. The feeling has been there ever since I saw her this afternoon come home from the well. They had seen each other there. I don't know what I fear, Joachim. All I know is that there is pain, this foreboding . . . something that makes me deathly afraid."

She made a hopeless gesture and scrambled to her feet.

"There! I will have done with such feelings. Bring in the young man," she said in an altered voice. "He is very determined, as you say. And he does have a handsome beard. One has to admire that."

The worry in her heart was lessened when Anna met Joseph for the first time. Later she admitted to her husband that the carpenter made a good impression the moment he came through the door. Such devotion as Anna had for her child carries with it a kind of prescience: she divined something warming and good and trustworthy in the awkwardness of the workman; in his placating smile she sensed a guarantee of honor. As she led the visitor up to the household platform, it came to Anna that Joseph was a gentle but very strong man.

There was a certain ceremoniousness in the beginning of the interview: the drinking of a traditional cup of hospitality, passed from hand to hand, and an embarrassed discussion of weather, of crops, and of burdensome taxes. Then they came to a complete stop, and after a silence Joseph blushed and said bluntly:

"I love your daughter Mary. I saw her on the first day you moved into this town. I have seen her every day since, except that sad time when she was ill with a cold and you kept her in bed."

"You knew about that?" gasped Anna, then turned her head suspiciously. She had heard what the others had not—the distant tinkling sound of young laughter. Where was that Mary? She had gone to the roof with Cousin Elizabeth. Wherever she was now, she was listening. Anna remembered that she, too, had listened when Joachim had made his formal call upon her father.

Joseph told them how he was the son of Jacob Heli, who had died long ago and who was the son of Matthan, and that the book of his generation carried his family back to Abraham.

"All this I have inspected in the scrolls at the synagogue," Joachim told his wife. "He is the son of Abraham and the son of David."

"Mary is also of the house of David," nodded Anna.

Joseph further explained that the uncle who brought him up had been dead for three years; the suitor stood alone in the world, without aunt or uncle, brother or sister or cousin.

"I am lonely and I want Mary to be my wife. I have come to espouse her, if it will be your pleasure to have it so," he finished, a little frightened of the high-sounding words.

Anna and Joachim exchanged nods, and the mother walked with dignity to the door leading to the open roof.

"Mary!" she called.

And presently Mary, light blue mantle over her shoulders, came barefoot into the room and stood before Joseph. Elizabeth followed and put her arms around Anna. The father took the young man's hand and placed it in the hand of his daughter, and gave them his blessing.

The future bridegroom thanked the mother and father but kept looking at his promised one; so young and strong and dreamy was Mary that night.

"You are espoused," said Joachim.

"You are betrothed," said Anna.

"Peace be with you," said Joachim and Anna.

"And the Lord be with you," murmured Joseph and Mary.

Tomorrow all Nazareth would have the glad information. Why, thought Joseph, as he laid his other hand over hers, this is almost as official as being married. In this province of Galilee, and indeed in all Palestine, once a couple were engaged, only the most serious circumstances could justify man or woman in breaking off.

And Joseph chuckled at the ridiculousness of the notion—that he could ever be minded to break his engagement with Mary!

Chapter 3 THE UNKNOWN MESSENGER

OF COURSE Joseph was invited to go along with the family to attend Cousin Zachary's proud occasion in the Temple.

The prospect was tremendously exciting. In all his life Joseph had never been more than ten miles outside the town of Nazareth, and now, at last, he would behold the city and the Temple—a lifetime experience!

One brisk day in the Palestinian spring Mary and Anna mounted rented donkeys, and Joachim and Joseph, reins in hand, started off, leading them on foot, for the three-day journey to Jerusalem. It was a journey of contentment all the way, free of accident or misfortune—a time of long talk among the four. After that experience Joachim and Anna loved Joseph as if he were their son; the family ties were bound before the marriage in the intimacy of their trip down the great southern road, until at the close of the third day they came in view of the capital.

"Oh!" gasped Mary, whispering in Joseph's ear. "This is all so magnificent."

With the double delight of a country boy on his first long journey and a well-read man who knew the history of where he was and what he was seeing, Joseph beheld Jerusalem. The sight of the mustard-colored walls, the bastions and indented parapets, the battlements and towers roused in the carpenter a kind of tranquil ecstasy—the state he had sometimes known in prayer.

Soon, less exalted, but not less interested, they passed through the gate and made their way down the noisy darkness of the roofed streets, stepping gingerly to avoid the filth of the paving stones and lifting their noses helplessly. The reek and feculence and foulness, the unutterable stink of the Jerusalem streets, were in their nostrils even as they stared at the ivory and gold glories of Herod's palace on the western hill, his amphitheater for games and his castle, Antonia, named for his great chum, Marc Antony.

A broad area, this place of the Temple, with its still unfinished colonnades. The eyes of Joseph bulged. Its great rectangle was at least four hundred yards the long way and three hundred yards east and west—a vast plant of worship and sanctuary and market place for ecclesiastical supplies. As they came nearer to it Joseph began to see signs warning Gentiles to keep out of the inner courts on pain of death.

Now they were entering the outer and lowest court, first approach to the sanctuary where Cousin Zachary was to appear in his hour of glory, chief performer at the sacrifice just before sundown. Already thousands of worshipers filled the rectangle within the five gates of this mighty edifice with its courts and double galleries, its marble pillars fifty feet high, and its roof made of blood-red cedar from Lebanon.

Mary's heart was filled with wonder; she had the odd feeling that she had been here before. Actually, as a very little girl she had been brought here by her parents, but she had been too young to remember it. Yet today everything seemed vaguely, frighteningly familiar—the outer square, cluttered with tables of the money-changers; the clamor of people counting their coins, and the brattle and brangle around the cattle stalls where shrill voices of bargaining men and women mixed with the cooing doves and the bleating of lambs destined soon to die in smoking sacrifice.

Without delay Anna and Elizabeth and Mary proceeded to the

Court of the Women, beyond which they might not go. Joseph and Joachim, mounting the farther steps, paused at the entrance to the inner court to take it all in. The rays of the evening sun poured down fiercely on their heads; the service was soon to begin.

And now Joseph had arrived at the very spot where David had built the altar and where Solomon had reared the wonderful Temple that had stood here for nearly 400 years until it was destroyed by Nebuchadnezzar. The imaginative workman from Nazareth was almost swooning with an awesome feeling that blanched his face and tightened the muscles by which he swallowed.

For this present Temple at Jerusalem was a symbol to Joseph as it was to all the people. When his enslaved ancestors had at last straggled back from the captivity in Babylon they had been able to build themselves only a poor substitute on the site of vanished glory. That second temple, too, had passed, and in its place now stood the most magnificent of all three—a gift to the people from their detested ruler, King Herod.

A gift of appeasement it was, but it failed of its purpose. No tyrant in history ever was more hated than Herod was hated by the people who worshiped here. He was not of their blood; he was an Arab from Ashkelon, a tribal warrior, ferocious enough to win many a battle, shrewd enough to be an expert politician, but no true king of theirs.

By turns Herod had tried being cruel and kind. Having despoiled their treasury, and with the very money he had filched from them, he built this magnificent house of God. The people took his new Temple to their hearts but they barred him from entering any part of it.

Joseph reflected on all that had come to pass here—since the Babylonians sprang down like wolves, sacked the city, and left it, as they boasted, "a haunt of jackals"; of all the other wars that had oppressed the capital, and the thirty-eight sieges of Jerusalem. It did seem to the country carpenter that there was something in this city of immortal and indestructible destiny.

There would always be a Jerusalem, he thought, as long as Jerusalem remained true to the ideals of those altars of old, when the people were free under their own kings.

But would that time ever come again? Now that, as his friend Samuel had said, the very leaders of Israel played a secret game with Herod?

On one side of the high altar before them sat a short, watchful man with a goatlike beard, a priest in his early fifties who kept his eyes fixed on a small doorway. As Joseph looked at this little man he felt for a moment the pang of a curious presage; he forgot all about Cousin Zachary in the contemplation of this grim figure. Suddenly he heard an irreverent chuckle close to his left ear, and, turning, beheld the incorrigible and yet friendly face of Samuel, the merchant, the revolutionist. Samuel winked elaborately and turned a lowered thumb toward the grim figure on the altar and whispered:

"That man you were watching is Annas! Famous and mighty Annas! It is very unusual for him to be at such a service as this."

To the provincial workman from the north the name meant little, but Samuel, with a baleful glance up at the altar, explained that Annas was the High Priest of the Temple; then Joseph felt very much awed. But the gossip, shaking his head and still further lowering his voice, insisted that Annas was not a godly man at all but a mere politician; in fact, he did not even believe in a future life nor in the resurrection.

"The important thing about Annas," whispered Samuel, "is that he is the political boss. It is Annas who bargains in secret with Herod and then comes out and tells the people just what to do. His enemies say that he has betrayed his own people for years."

It was Annas, Samuel declared, who controlled the banks and set up the money-changers at their tables in the Temple; he also owned the concessions for the selling of birds and animals for the sacrifice. The money-changing and the selling of doves and lambs were two branches of the same business; in controlling them, Annas and his crew bilked everybody and through their cheating became among the richest people in the world. A powerful friend, an implacable enemy, a man with a long tooth—that was Annas, the High Priest.

"I wonder," Joseph was thinking, "why I feel so afraid of this Annas?" He looked around, but Samuel had vanished. The young revolutionist had strange comings and goings.

Even from far off Joseph could see the iceberg-blue eyes of Annas, and wondered if those glittering eyes ever melted or if that straight, hard mouth could ever relax in a tender smile. It was strange, indeed, that Joseph should feel warned of Annas. What had a little peasant carpenter to fear from the High Priest of the Temple?

"Ah," sighed Joachim, "there comes Cousin Zachary now. Joseph, look; that is he! Cousin Elizabeth must have sewn that wonderful robe for him!"

Why, old Zachary looked young in his fine raiment. How erect he stood in the gorgeousness of ceremonial robes, stiff and straight and chin up for all his seventy years. A bright gleam was in his fading eyes as he lifted his arms, a sign that the people were to cleanse their hearts with prayer in readiness for the rubric of the sacrifice, the performance of his sacred office. Standing beside the altar of unhewn stone, Zachary closed his eyes, and all the people prayed.

Of the thousands praying in the rectangular courts only Cousin Elizabeth knew of one special intention this old priest would be including in his prayers this afternoon. But Joseph could guess from what Mary had already told him. Zachary's faith was tenacious and humble; some of his relatives called it fanatical and preposterous that though he was past his threescore years and ten he still asked God dutifully every day that Elizabeth and he might have a child.

Now the priest turned and faced the congregation. Hanging from a chain in his right hand was the censer from which silver smoke plumed upward, and the sweetness of burning spices was carried on chill winds blowing from the desert of the Dead Sea. All priest and servant of the living Lord, Zachary held his censer high and let the south and east winds carry off the smoke while he began to mount the twelve steps, one for each of the tribes of Israel. Lifting the temple veil with his left hand, he disappeared into the tabernacle, the little holy place, where minor priests came closest to the presence of God.

With bowed heads and closed eyes the crowd waited. For a long while there was no sound, not even a cough. Then, presently, Joachim opened one eye and glared at the altar. What was keeping Zachary within? No one was to be seen on the platform except the grim, observant figure of Annas. Joachim gave a puzzled look around at Joseph. Zachary had already stayed much too long in the holy retreat. Something must be wrong. There was not much for him to do in there; the priest was to stand only for a moment in silent prayer. He must look up at the golden candlesticks and down upon the cakes made of wheat and barley with oil of honey; upon the twelve loaves of the showbread he must look and then, in a prolonged moment of silence, he was supposed to swing the censer three times. After these actions were performed Zachary was meant to back out of the holy place, face the reverent multitude, and offer up the final prayer.

By now five minutes had gone by and there was still no sign of Zachary.

"Something is strange," Joachim murmured to Joseph. Had the old village priest fallen ill in his hour of glory? Did anyone dare go to see, past the veil and into the holy place?

Then suddenly Zachary came out in a wild rush from the sanctuary, and something very serious was wrong with him—the whole multitude could see that. Swaying dizzily down the twelve steps, he staggered to the rim of the open part of the altar. As Zachary tottered there, Annas, the High Priest, leaped forward and put strong arms around him. In the stillness of the sunset air they could all hear the crisp voice of Annas asking for an explanation. But Zachary, cheeks pale, eyes glittering, hair mussed, could only stamp his right foot and wave his arms in frantic movements, pointing to his open mouth as if he had swallowed the mystery and therefore could make no sound.

There was nothing to be done but for Annas to leave him standing there by the altar of unhewn stones while he, as High Priest, took over the service, made the final prayer, and dismissed the people. Then and then only could Elizabeth get out of the Court of Women and beat her way to the outer square where Joachim held Zachary waiting. The old wife sheltered her man in her arms.

"We're going home, Zachary," she murmured. "Don't weep. Don't try to talk. We will go home now."

Not until they were back home in Ain Karim and the curious villagers had been shooed away, leaving the weary little family to themselves, did Zachary divulge the facts. He sat at the table, motioning for parchment and quills; Zachary would talk with them by writing; the first great fact was that he had been stricken dumb.

"*Ah! Ah!* For once in his life he could celebrate the sacrifice in Jerusalem and he was stricken dumb!" Elizabeth sobbed and groaned; surely they were under a curse of God.

But Zachary admonished her with uplifted finger. His glaring eyes seemed to remind her that this was not the first time in the history of the earth that a man had been stricken dumb. There were much more important matters.

"Ah! Ah!" cried Elizabeth, "my husband is right; my husband is always right. What has he to tell us?"

Slowly, and forming the inky characters with great exactitude so that his meaning could not possibly be mistaken, Zachary wrote on the parchment:

"I have been listening to an angel!"

When she read these words, Elizabeth gave a low moan and began pacing back and forth, beating her fists against her temples and sighing disconsolately. Zachary had not only been stricken dumb; he had gone mad. See what he had written. Ah! Ah! It was blasphemy. Tear it up before someone reported it to the High Priest; a man could be put to death for such dangerous thoughts.

But Zachary rose up, too, and stood in the way of his wife so that she couldn't go on pacing up and down and crying; he was dumb but he was not deaf; he heard it all and it made him impatient. Writing again, he declared he was still master in his own house. Let her call him mad if she pleased, but would she first have the kindness to receive what he was trying to tell her; what the angel said? Stop the tears! Would she listen?

The house of Cousin Elizabeth was a noisy place just at that moment; everybody except the scribbling Zachary seemed to be talking at once. Anna was trying to comfort Elizabeth, and Joachim was taking his stance in the middle of the floor to speak his mind.

"Since when," Joachim reproached them, "has it been madness to believe that angels can talk with men? Are we to deny the Scriptures of Moses? And since when, Anna, have you forgotten, or you, Elizabeth, that we have always known that ours is a remarkable family? Since our great ancestors we have had strange dreams and always obeyed the will of God. Does Zachary look mad to you, Elizabeth? Let us be quiet and ask him what actually happened in there!"

Zachary lowered his head gratefully to the towering and suddenly authoritative figure of Joachim. He sank wearily in his chair; he was an aging man and it had been a day to try the stoutest nerves. He pointed again at the line he had written:

"I have been listening to an angel."

The others nodded solemnly. The priest picked up his pen and wrote again:

"I entered the sanctuary. A figure was standing there. He stood with folded wings and looked at me. I was terribly frightened and almost dropped the censer. My brain felt numb. My body was cold. My knees . . ."

"I can guess how you felt, beloved," urged Elizabeth. "But did the angel speak to you?"

Zachary nodded emphatically.

"Then please write what he said."

Zachary bent over the parchment and his hand moved faster and faster:

"He spoke in a deep tone unlike any voice I ever heard, and he said: 'Fear not, Zachary. Your prayer is heard!' "

A chill went down the spine of Elizabeth; her thoughts whirled. Could it have been the secret prayer that Zachary had made just before he mounted the twelve steps? She bent over and saw that the old man was still writing; still quoting the winged messenger.

" 'Your wife, Elizabeth, shall bear you a son.' "

Elizabeth began to weep again, and Anna and Mary with her, while practical Joachim, his hands clasped, leaned over Zachary's shoulder reading word after word as the old priest scribbled on, now in a frenzy of writing:

" 'And you shall call his name John.' "

"John!" cried Elizabeth. "John! John! That means the gracious gift of God!"

Zachary nodded to her. His face was still white as the parchment under his hand; his chin bobbed up and down in confirmation. Yes, they were to have a son and they would call his name John. And he wrote again:

" 'And you shall have joy and gladness. Many shall rejoice in his nativity and he shall be great before the Lord. He shall drink no wine or strong drink and he shall be filled with the Holy Ghost . . .' "

Zachary's hand stopped, the same question agitating all. What could be the meaning of that strange phrase? A baby coming to them. The very thought made Elizabeth put her hands against her breasts and croon aloud. But what could those queer words mean: the boy was to be "filled with the Holy Ghost"? None of them knew.

It was all hard to believe, yet look at Zachary! That guileless and pious old man, who scorned lies and pretense, could not be acting a part. And how would anyone err about seeing an angel? Zachary was dumb and that must be a sign. Why was he not permitted to speak?

Zachary still had to tell them the answer to that question. Entreating them with shaking hands to be quiet and to hold back their questions, he went on writing his account. The angel had not finished when he said that the man-child, John, would be filled with the Holy Ghost. He went right on speaking in that same bass, unearthly voice, to predict that the son of Elizabeth and Zachary would grow up to bring many of the people of the country to the worship of the Lord their God. More, the angel declared that John, who was yet to be born, would have the spirit and power of the ancient prophet Elias. At this the others could keep quiet no longer.

"Do you realize what you are writing there?" gasped Elizabeth.

"The coming of a prophet!" murmured Anna. "I told you we are a strange family. We always *were* a strange family."

"Wait until it happens!" replied Elizabeth cautiously. It was plain to see that she felt it necessary to remain skeptical. But the speechless priest was writing furiously:

"I mean what I say. Every word of it. I saw the angel. I heard his voice. Once and for all I insist that you remain quiet and hear the whole story."

Silence again as he continued:

"The winged messenger with whom I held this interview finished his first remarks with these words: 'He shall turn the hearts of fathers unto their children and the incredulous to the wisdom of the just, to prepare unto the Lord a perfect people.' "

The priest looked around him at the strained faces and shrugged.

"Then I felt a little better," he wrote, "because I recognized the quotation. It was from the Book of Malachi, the last of our prophets. But here I made a serious blunder. Since the familiar quotation made me feel more at ease, more like myself, I suppose I lost a little of the awe I felt. I am afraid I was a little disrespectful to this angel. At least I plucked up enough courage to speak for the first time and asked him a question. I spoke with great humility but I felt I had a right to know, and so I simply asked: 'Whereby shall I know this? For I am an old man and my wife is advanced in years.' "

"And what did he say to that, Zachary?" The words burst uncontrollably from Elizabeth.

"He answered me at once," wrote Zachary. "He simply said that he was Gabriel."

Gabriel! Their faces paled with fear at the very idea. Gabriel was the celestial messenger who had visited the prophet Daniel—one of the four archangels of the heavenly host.

Zachary nodded solemnly; sensed their awe.

"That is what he informed me," Zachary continued writing. "He told me that he stood before God habitually and that he had been sent to the holy place just to bring me these glorious tidings. But his manner was much more serious and reproving now, let me tell you. He had not liked my doubts. I felt sure of that by his manner. He told me that I was not going to be allowed to talk any more. 'Behold, you are dumb,' he said to me. And he said I was not going to be allowed to speak again until the day when these things come to pass 'because,' he added, 'you have not believed my words.'"

And Zachary dropped his pen, looked helplessly around him, and pointed to his open mouth, while he grew red in the face trying to make a sound which would not come, not even a groan.

"Did he say anything else?" breathed Elizabeth.

Her husband shook his head and wrote again:

"I closed my eyes and prayed a moment. When I opened them again, the angel was gone. That was when I staggered out of the holy place and found that his words were already proved true: I could not speak."

Had the old man dreamed these things in a vertigo, a sudden stroke? Such things had happened within their experience. With all the faith in the world Zachary might be imagining the whole story. Elizabeth insisted on calling the flea-bitten physician of the town who prescribed a purgative and a diet of warm barley soup and figs. Moreover, the patient must remain flat on his back for three or four days. Of course the doctor was not told the Temple story; that was for the ears of the family alone. Soon after the doctor left Zachary fell into a deep sleep.

Late into the night the others talked the marvel over. Elizabeth found it hard to believe it was anything more than the phantasy of a sick and tormented mind. Anna was puzzled. Joachim stubbornly remained the believer. In the face of the realism of the womenfolk he argued mystically: such visitations were not uncommon in the olden times; why should people assume, then, that the age of miracles had passed? Was there ever a time when people were more in need of miracles?

Joseph kept his own counsel, and no one asked Mary what she thought. In their eyes she was still a child whose views were not sought in family counsels. But before they went to bed Mary said to Elizabeth:

"Cousin dear, you have prayed a long time. I believe in your prayers, Elizabeth. Why should we be surprised if God has heard them and will answer them? Why not wait and believe?"

And that, as time was soon to prove, was the wisest thing said in the family that night.

Curiously, though, the next morning there was not much talk about the mystery of the priest and the angel. By unspoken agreement they avoided the topic. Human beings, when confronted with the strange and inexplicable, have an immediate instinct to get back to the accustomed and the normal. We do not hug our miracles close; we put them hastily away, preferring the commonplace to live with. It is as if some compulsive hand wipes clean the wall on which the handwriting appeared.

At breakfast Joachim and Anna and Mary and Joseph talked about the weather and the crops and the taxes, and Joachim decided they must be starting home that afternoon.

Even on the return journey they spoke only once or twice, and that briefly, about Zachary's experience. More and more they were relieved to put the whole matter out of their minds. But when they were all back in Nazareth and Mary carried a hot lunch down to Joseph at the door of the carpenter shop, she sat with him there, in wood chips and sawdust, her bare feet tucked under her skirt, light blue mantle tossed back, and they talked together.

"Do you believe it will come true, Joseph?" Mary asked, as if this were the moment when she would be told how she should think about it thereafter.

Joseph was slow to reply. He leaned his bearded chin on his palm and stared off into vacancy, as if there were some hint in his heart that the words he spoke now might someday bind him like a vow.

"Zachary is a good man. He wrote clearly and distinctly; his thoughts weren't confused or wandering; he didn't ramble like a drunken man. He should trust a messenger from God."

"Oh yes, Joseph. You saw that he was as rational as you or I."

The frown left Joseph's face and he turned to her fondly.

"Look at it this way," he argued. "Zachary is not only dumb; he is also committed by a prophecy to prove himself a man who has talked with an angel, or else one who has a delusion. There is no escape from that. Either he and Elizabeth are to have a son or he has told a demented tale. No man in his right senses would put himself in such a position with his wife and relatives unless he believed it with all his heart and soul. Now would he, Mary?"

And Mary, sighing with admiring happiness, said: "No, Joseph. Why hadn't I thought of it that way?"

And she rejoiced at how fortunate she was to be engaged to a man who saw things so clearly and so wisely. After that conclusion they had themselves to talk about. Over the months the exciting episode receded in their minds until one day, by caravan messenger, a note was brought to Anna.

"Peace be with you, my beloved one," Elizabeth had written. "God has heard our prayers, indeed, and the promise of the holy archangel is fulfilled. Anna, my darling aunt, listen and tell Joachim and dear Mary and that fine young man, Joseph—listen, beloved—at my age I am going to have a child!"

Chapter 4 NO DREAMS TONIGHT

AT THE close of the day's work Joseph sat in the back of his shop and emptied a palmful of coins from a crock taken down from a tall shelf. Farthings and pence and two gold pieces he had there—a fragile fortune, but it would soon be enough. Ever since he had first seen Mary he had saved every mite against his wedding day, which would not be long.

"Almost enough for everything," he congratulated himself. "And my wife won't have to skimp and scrape."

Wife! What a magical word for a lonely man.

"Tonight," he resolved, "I will tell the family that we do not have to wait any more."

It was spring in Nazareth and the warmth of April was in Joseph's heart. The green hillsides all around the town were spread with little blue and yellow and crimson flowers, their petals richer than the incredibly bright carpets that came in bales on Arabian camels. You could even taste the flower sweetness in the wind blowing through the door of the shop.

It was good to step abroad after the long day's work. Good to feel himself a living part of the town. A Roman soldier strode arrogantly by, leading an officer's white horse, a pampered animal fed only on barley and chaff. But Joseph did not hate the Roman; he did not hate anything in this soft April dusk. His heart was happy. Through the gloaming and the untidy crowds he made his way with confident haste. Now and then the carpenter was saluted by a customer—a farmer, a shepherd, a blacksmith—and he relished every greeting with a sense of peaceful security. To be known and liked gave him a sense of belonging—a feeling of maturity. Soon he would be a married man and a householder in Galilee; a workman with a good trade, a home, and a family; a part of the very backbone of the community.

Oh yes, he knew now that in Jerusalem sophisticates looked down on the countrified Nazarenes, yokels with a ridiculous northern accent. Travelers whose broken wheels he mended told how in the stadium shows of the capital comedians often imitated the rude ways and provincial dialect of the Nazarenes and that a favorite jest on the Jerusalem streets was the question: "Can anything good come out of Nazareth?"

But Joseph, with all his fellow townsmen, felt that the people of Jerusalem were unnatural and overcivilized. Anyway, he was proud of his home town and expected to be very happy there with Mary and children and work. What more could any man ask? Let Samuel have his Jerusalem and his revolutions too.

A psalm of David came to his lips as he marched on through the crowd. Everywhere around him were noisy people, enveloped in their own errands. Once he passed a knot of excitable citizens surrounding two old rabbis, all talking at once. For a hasty moment Joseph's lighted lantern lit up their beards and caps. Dark-skinned men, some with oily curls, tall bodies wrapped in street-stained robes, they were engaged in a sidewalk arbitration. A husband who had been penalized demanded to know the precise kind of meat offering he must bring to the synagogue for his atonement. A bereaved father complained that he had been overcharged by the funeral minstrels. Men and women and children all in a clamor about their own affairs! But their numbers grew less as Joseph trudged on, and the streets thinned and the crowds fell behind.

Just ahead of him was a lane, and at its turning was the house of Joachim and Anna, white dome ghostlike in the dusk. At one side of it ran a staircase that led to the roof, and looking up there Joseph saw Mary. She had a lantern in her hand and she was bending over, collecting dates and figs that had been spread out to dry in the hot sun. Knowing his footsteps, she straightened up and waved her hand.

Then Joseph passed into the house with the freedom of one who feels himself already a member of the family. Anna was busy over an earthen pot filled with live coals; she would spread the outside with freshly kneaded dough and the heat would bake it into bread. Joachim strode forward, the two men bowed ceremoniously, and the younger man kissed the father's beard.

"Welcome the more for coming early," said Joachim heartily.

Joseph seated himself beside the older man and plunged at once into his business. He had saved his money, he had improved the living quarters behind the house, he was ready to buy a goat and hens and a rooster; he wanted his wife. Why should there be any delay?

"Who makes delays?" demanded Joachim.

The carpenter glanced uneasily at Anna.

"No, Joseph," said Mary's mother, looking over her shoulder as she patted the dough. "I will not stand in your way. I know now that you love Mary and that she loves you. There is really no sense in waiting. I am forced to agree with you about that; it will be better so. Have you fixed a date in your mind?"

"I want to marry her yesterday," jested Joseph, and they all laughed. "But no, I have not fixed any date. I want to talk with Mary after supper tonight. I would like it better that way."

To this Joachim made no comment, but his glance was a little puzzled. In his married life he made all the decisions; at least Anna had succeeded in making him believe so.

Later, in the damp darkness of the Nazareth road, Joseph and Mary strolled and talked. They were full of their plans and felt a little awed by them. Completely occupied with a dozen small and enchanting details about their wedding, they were oppressed that soft evening with no foreboding. The clover-laden night winds carried no warning of what was in the air, and once, when the pair stood silent together and looked up at the lean and golden scimitar of the new moon and the hiving, glittering stars, and all earth seemed hushed for them to listen, they did not hear the faintest rustle of a wing.

Minds and hearts filled only with their personal plans, it was late when they were ready to say good night, but they had come to a decision. Within three months they would be married. Joseph would have liked it earlier but Mary pointed out that there was still sewing to do and a few more shekels her father wanted to accumulate, she knew, to fill out her modest dowry. Three months would not seem so long, now that the date was fixed.

"I hope I see you early tomorrow," said Joseph when it was time for him to go home.

"Very early, Joseph. When I go to the well for the morning water," she promised.

Their hands clasped and they parted. Joseph strode off bravely to his carpenter shop; he flung himself down on his pallet with a happy sigh and buried his head in his arms and thought how fortunate he was among Nazarene men; how happy he was and how much happier he was going to be. Soon he fell asleep. Sleeping, he dreamed only of the slight, inconsequential phantasmagoria that all men dream of: Mary's blue mantle blowing in the clover-laden wind and Mary's dream-laden eyes.

No grand dreams, such as his ancestors, the prophets, had known in olden days. No foreseeing of what was on the way, marching in a mighty silence toward the earth. And no more than Joseph did Herod the Great and his kingdom of Judea with him, nor Cacsar Augustus in his Roman palace, dream that night that the world was about to roll another way. None even to feel one cosmic hint that near at hand was a social and moral revolution, coming without harp or cymbals but in the deep soundlessness of this night. . . .

Early the next morning Joseph awoke to know that something had gone amiss. He heard a pounding on the door and his name being shouted. As he opened sleepy eyes he beheld Joachim standing, pale and distrait, distracted hands uplifted.

"Peace be unto you, Joachim," Joseph muttered, embracing him. "What is it? Tell me, what is wrong?"

"The Lord be with you, Joseph," groaned the father, laying a heavy hand on Joseph's shoulder. "Listen, my son. Mary has disappeared."

Chapter 5 HAIL, MARY!

MARY, the young betrothed, the blue-eyed, black-haired girl who loved Joseph heart and soul had fled Nazareth because within five minutes after she had said good night to her beloved her life, her body and soul, had undergone a change.

It was an experience shattering to the very roots of her being. For hours after it happened she was unable to speak; she could scarcely breathe. It was so inexplicable, so dazing and frightening that for the time she could not force herself to tell her mother or father or even Joseph.

How could she ask them to believe that she had actually known such a wonder?

Yet she *had* known it. Without one instant's preparation she had walked into it, immediately after that tender good night at the gate. Joachim and Anna had been chatting up on the roof; they, too, had much to talk about. The hens and rooster were perched and fast asleep; the dog was out barking behind the garden, and the sheep and goats were dozing.

Feeling a little chill, for the night was damp, Mary had crossed the lower floor inside the house and mounted to the inner terrace. As she went up the steps to the platform she realized that she was not alone. A tall figure was standing near the farther wall!

A stranger. An odd and altogether different stranger! Because he seemed to stand in light where there was no lamp, and a kind of silvery mist enveloped him as if the light were his cap and gown. Mary opened her mouth to speak, to demand who he was and what he wanted there, but he anticipated her with an unexpected greeting.

"Hail, Mary!"

The voice was kind and fathomlessly deep; such a voice as Mary had never heard before—bass and yet tender.

"Full of grace!" the voice continued.

Hail, Mary, full of grace! She felt embarrassed and even more frightened.

"The Lord is with you. Blessed are you among women."

She folded her hands and she knew then how she was trembling in every muscle. The stranger saw.

"Fear not, Mary."

She bowed her head. She must not be afraid. She knew she could trust this deep and tender voice. But she could not still her quaking. She closed her eyes and listened to the astounding words this stranger was speaking. She had found grace with God. She would conceive in her womb and bring forth a son.

She too! That was akin to the message that had come to Zachary for Elizabeth. Cousin Elizabeth was to have a son and his name must be John.

"And you shall call his name Jesus!"

"Jesus! He will be my son. Jesus! Jesus, son of Mary! I shall bring him forth and hold him in my arms and sometimes I shall give him to Joseph to hold too!" Her mind was a place of wild, birdlike thoughts; yet she must listen to all that the stranger continued to tell her: her son Jesus was to have the throne of David, his father—

"And of all his kingdom there shall be no end."

Then came her instant need for reality. The very human impulse that had made Zachary question his angel and lost him his speech as penalty now possessed Mary, too, for there was in her, as in us all, an insatiable necessity for the actual in the midst of the marvelous. Who this stranger was she did not know; yet the maiden who heard his words felt bound to question him.

"How shall this be done?" she asked in a whisper. "Seeing I know not a man?"

But there came no frown on the austere and shadowy face of the stranger. Instead, in the starry blaze of his eyes she read only compassion. He took a step nearer and she saw the folded wings and knew him for what he was.

His voice lower and deeper still:

"The Holy Ghost shall come upon you. The power of the Most High shall overshadow you and therefore also the Holy which shall be born of you shall be called the Son of God."

Mary felt stifled, suffocated, as she heard these incredible words. She to be the mother of a son who would be called the Son of God?

How could one little Nazareth girl take all that in?

The voice of the stranger was lowered into an intimate whisper:

"Your cousin Elizabeth . . ."

He paused until she nodded, and then he went on:

"She also conceived a son. In her old age! This is the sixth month with her that is called barren. Because with God nothing shall be impossible!"

This was the reality she needed. For the angel had spoken truth as she knew it. It was true about Elizabeth. Well, then . . .

She looked up at him plaintively, her eyes half closed, her words coming so softly that she could barely hear herself speak.

"Behold the handmaid of the Lord. Be it done unto me according to your word."

As if by incantation the angel vanished; one instant he was there, gone the next. And Mary, swaying and murmuring, crossed the floor and sank to her knees and lay upon her pallet and closed her eyes and wept and prayed. Too much to understand! She wanted to scream for Anna and throw herself into those strong, stout arms and cry to her mother what had just happened. But she could not bring herself, even in the first agony of that hysteria, to risk certain disbelief. They thought of her as still a child, anyway. They would say she had imagined this thing because Elizabeth was having a child and Zachary had said he saw an angel.

Mary lay there quietly while Joachim and Anna tiptoed down from the roof. They went to their bed after their prayers. But Mary could not sleep. She stole up from her bed after two hours of restlessness; she wrote her mother a note, made herself a bundle, and set off alone down the long road.

There was one other person in the world to whom she felt she must first confide the experience.

She was walking to Cousin Elizabeth.

Chapter 6 WHAT A ONE, THINK YOU!

"WELL, Joseph?" demanded Joachim, something like truculence in his voice. "Now you've heard. What do you say?"

Joseph shook his head slowly and turned to the washbasin. From a jug that Mary had filled with water for him only the night before the carpenter poured a splash into the basin and dashed a handful on his face. He wet his hair and beard and, panting a little, dried himself with a bundle of hay.

"Mary had a good reason," was his answer. "Be sure of that."

Joachim's face softened.

"She must have had," he agreed. "But can you imagine what it would be? This is an unheard-of thing, Joseph. A girl does not run off from her parents."

"And from her espoused one."

"And, of course, from her betrothed," Joachim agreed. "Why, only last night you two were setting the date for the wedding. Do you suppose she got a little giddy; overexcited, I mean? She is a very young girl."

"No, not Mary," declared Joseph firmly. "There was never another so composed as she. As serene. And," he added with an eloquence of words not usual in him, "unshakeable in her purposes. She loves me. She is going to marry me. Last night we made great plans. Something happened after I left her, I am sure of that; something good; we must believe when we do not know."

But the same thoughts were in both minds. The great southern road was long and difficult.

"If," sighed Joseph, answering his own doubts, "she had wanted me she would have called me. And God will protect her," he added, his voice breaking.

Joseph's faith was fully justified. As one under special protection Mary traversed the weary distance. She had walked only a few miles when a small caravan overtook her and offered her a donkey to ride to the next town. Most of the whole way she was carried by kindly strangers; three successive nights she found shelter with friendly travelers glad to share with her their hospitality. In her bundle was food enough but she need not have brought it along; everyone offered her food.

Brooding she was, all the way; the wayfarers were struck by a feeling of special separateness that distinguished her. One of the least of them, a bearded old tatterdemalion who had journeyed east and west on the backs of camels for more than forty years, a rakehell from the Damascus bazaars, gave her a cup of flavored water late one night and whispered:

"Where have you found such peace?"

There was no mirror for Mary to study; it would be days later before the peasant girl would notice for herself the pallor that was coming to her face and neck, arms, and the backs of her hands, like cream over strawberries; the blood-red natural color of strength and youth was giving way to some newer and purer force taking possession.

Without a mirror she realized that something had taken hold of her and changed her. She felt as if she were a new person, a stranger who—keeping all previous memories—was nevertheless different; a mixed awareness of glory and humility. She felt small and weak and yet powerfully protected. She walked with a new assurance in which there was not pride but a profound sense of participation in the universal flow of life; kinship with all nature. The sap rising in the twisting trunk of a sycamore tree was also in her blood; the very sight of dewdrops on the morning grass seemed enough to slake her thirst; the warmth of the sun itself was stored within her being and shone from her as well as upon her from the sky. Not a glisten in the eyes of a weeping child but became a part of the love in her thoughts, and the singing of birds, the softness of winds, the good taste of milk, everything good and useful made a unity in her, a oneness, a celestial unwearying sense of belonging.

This was the way she had felt ever since the Annunciation of the Angel. These were her sensations, waking and sleeping; her thoughts were simple and almost like the thoughts of someone else: ideas hatched on some distant star and only vaguely related to present place and time. And this was so, even while thoughts of reality persisted; they were of Anna and Joachim a little, and of Joseph a little more. How could she tell him? What could she say to him? Cousin Elizabeth must advise her.

The image of Cousin Elizabeth was uppermost in her mind and sustained her through the seventy-five-mile journey. It was nearing sunset of the third day when she found herself four miles east of Jerusalem, back in the tiny suburb of Ain Karim; ahead only a short way was the squat house of Zachary and Elizabeth, and there was her cousin, six months big with child, sitting on the dooryard stoop.

Now Mary had come all the long distance to Elizabeth, not because she doubted the angel but because she believed in him. Only for a moment during the shadowy interview had she questioned the message. There was never again a doubt in her mind; she had acted on the message with prompt faith. Yet even the trust of Mary was startled at the confirming greeting she received.

"Hail, Mary!" cried Elizabeth happily.

The elderly and pregnant woman did not seem at all astonished at seeing her young cousin. The stern face was flushed with pleasure as she got to her feet and waved both hands, and as Mary came nearer she cried out:

"Blessed are you among women!"

The dusty figure of Mary stopped short in the road. Those very words she had heard before—from the angel!

"And blessed is the fruit of your womb!"

"You repeat the angel's words to me, Cousin Elizabeth. How did you know?"

Elizabeth embraced her, and then whispered:

"For look, as soon as the voice of your salutation sounded in my ears, the infant in my womb leaped for joy. And you are blessed because you have believed, because those things shall be accomplished that were spoken to you by the Lord."

With a sob of relief Mary flung herself into the arms of Elizabeth. For what seemed an eon, an incalculable period of time, she stood there quivering in that comforting embrace. Then, speaking very softly, she uttered the words of her Magnificat, all unaware that the world would sing those words and pray them for thousands of years, but pouring them out for the first time in the consolation of her communion with Elizabeth:

"My soul doth magnify the Lord; and my spirit hath rejoiced in God my Savior. Because He hath regarded the humility of His handmaid; for behold from henceforth all generations shall call me blessed. Because He that is mighty hath done great things to me; and holy is His name. And His mercy is from generation into generations, to them that fear Him."

As at last Elizabeth led her into the house, she whispered:

"Do you realize that you are pregnant already?"

Mary's eyes entreated her.

"I have not known a man." She trembled.

"Of course, beloved!"

For the first time tears rolled down Mary's cheeks.

"You believe me. You know," she quavered. "But how can anyone else ever believe me? Will not Joseph be sure to think . . ."

"What would any man think in his place?" asked Elizabeth. "But God, Who has shown us these things, will surely show us how to talk with Joseph. Come in now. You are tired and dusty and hungry. No more deep talk until you have rested."

So Mary had a good rubdown by Elizabeth, who was a practical nurse and often helped the sick of the village. With strong, well-oiled hands she rubbed Mary's arms and back and thighs and eased them of travel aches and pains. Then, having washed the feet of her guest, she gave her bread to eat and cool goat's milk to drink and bade her lie down. Almost before she closed her eyes, Mary was asleep.

The kindness with which she was received on her arrival never once wavered in the months that followed. In her advancing pregnancy Elizabeth was not strong enough to do the housework and so Mary remained to be a maid to her until the child was delivered. At once she wrote notes home, explaining this as her intention. She also told her mother that she had passed through an experience of which it was impossible for her to write. When she came back to Nazareth she would confide everything.

To Joseph she sent a dutiful and tender note, telling him that the time was soon coming when she would explain to him why she had to leave so suddenly. No mention of the day they had set for their wedding; indeed she did not dare to speak of their marriage at all. For Mary was perfectly well aware that any man might refuse to believe her and cast her out. This was her only source of unhappiness in those first three months. She was busy, she worked hard, and she retained within herself that supernal sense of universal belonging, of general participation with earth and stars in the mystery of life.

She remained in Ain Karim until the great day when pains of the womb brought Elizabeth moaning to her couch. The midwife and Mary succored her through long and weary hours of labor until at last her child came into the world. As the angel had predicted, a man-child, more than ten pounds in his birth weight, screaming of voice at the age of one minute he was, and red and wild-eyed and with a look of outrage at the behavior of the world on his broad and wrinkled little face.

And, true even to the last prophetic accent of the angel, Zachary immediately found his voice again. For the first time in nine months the village priest could speak. Friends and relatives and neighbors clamored around him, exclaiming at the wonder and drowning out his own long-postponed tones, refusing to listen to him but rejoicing at the top of their own lungs that Zachary could talk again, which he could not, not until they quieted down and gave him a chance.

When he was alone with his family, Zachary wonderingly repeated the words of his neighbors:

"What a one, think you, this child shall be? For the hand of the Lord was on him."

And delighting in the musical resonance of his own tones he raised them an octave and cried out:

"Blessed be the Lord God of Israel."

Later, when baby John was washed and rubbed with ointment and his already unruly hair smoothed with a little oil, Mary carried him in and laid him in the arms of his father. On the rugged face of the priest there was a look of almost juvenile delight as he gazed down upon this child of his old age.

"John!" he murmured teasingly, as if the child should already know his name. "John, our gift from God! John!"

Perhaps there was a touch of sadness in his voice. Perhaps Zachary was oppressed with the realization that he had not much longer to live; that he could not remain another lifetime on earth to guide the career of his little son. But he consoled himself that this was probably a saint he had brought into the world. The wildest, roughest, toughest, and bravest of saints! Even from his little boyhood John would be different; he would not play as other children. Shunning companionship, he would be drawn to the gaunt, parched gullies that go down to the desert, and the steep, blistering hillsides of the Judean wilderness. John would even turn aside from the spice-flavored lentils of his mother's kitchen; he would refuse goat's milk, and grow up to prefer locusts and wild honey.

The baby, less than two hours old, nestled peacefully now in the arms of his old father while Mary looked down, pale and smiling, upon him. John was to know less than most men of love and merciful tenderness, yet he was to open the gates for the coming of love into the world.

Chapter 7 WHEN HALF-GODS GO

SUDDENLY Samuel, the trader, returned from Jerusalem and called on Joseph.

"I think," the carpenter said, "I notice a change in you, Samuel."

"No, I am just the same."

"Let be, then."

"Please, Joseph, what kind of change did you think you saw in me?"

"Well, then, if you will not be offended . . ."

"I promise not to be."

"Your speech has changed, for one thing. You no longer sound like a Nazarene."

Samuel grunted smugly. Far from being offended, he was flattered.

"Of course," he agreed. "In the big city they laugh at the way we talk. Some of them can even tell a man from Lower Galilee from a man from Upper Galilee just by his accent. In Jerusalem you soon learn to talk as other educated persons do."

Joseph nodded, not without admiration. Like most country people, he disliked the vices of the metropolis, yet he took a certain proprietary pride in its vastness and busyness; he liked to think that he understood the best and the worst about the great place.

"Is it only my accent that has changed?" asked Samuel carefully.

Joseph shook his head slowly.

"It is a little more than that. When you lived here in Nazareth you were a merchant and you acted like one, even when away from your bazaar."

"And how does a merchant act?"

"Very politely, Samuel. His voice is low and trustworthy—if it were not, the customers would distrust him. And there is a kindly look in his eyes . . ."

Samuel began to laugh.

"And I come back looking like a criminal, is that it?"

Joseph again shook his head.

"You don't look like a ruffian at all, Samuel. But you do look hunted. And furtive! And frightened!"

Samuel instantly became serious.

"There is never a moment when I am not in fear of my life. Go on working, Joseph; no reason for you to lose a day's earnings because I am here. But let me talk to you a little while you do your sawing and chiseling. The last time I talked to you, I thought I knew all about the wickedness of Reb Naamaan. But now . . ."

"Who is Reb Naamaan?" asked Joseph innocently.

Samuel cupped his hands around his mouth and whispered in his friend's ear.

"King Herod. We never dare mention his real name when we talk. The sound of that name in your mouth will bring a spy to your elbow instantly; if they misunderstand you, it may cost you your life. So we never mention him except in code. Joseph, his deeds would shame a tiger."

"More beast than man, then?" asked Joseph in a sad tone. He put aside his tools and sat down for a moment on a sawhorse.

"Oh, don't underestimate him," cried Samuel. "He is a brilliant leader . . ."

"Herod? You call such a man brilliant?" asked Joseph, thoroughly shocked.

"The truth must be told even about Beelzebub himself. Herod has brains. He has a kind of military genius. And he has bravery. But he has the hardest heart, the most unused conscience this side of Sheol. He and his ghastly sister . . ."

"You mean the one they call Salome?" asked Joseph hesitantly.

"The same. They work together in a kind of satanic partnership to increase the misery of our people. Imagine! He is fifty-nine years old, with nine wives . . ."

"Nine wives!" groaned Joseph. "Nine wives, indeed."

"And only God knows how many concubines," snarled Samuel. There was a moment's silence and then Samuel came nearer Joseph, towering above him, and clamped both palms on his shoulders.

"Joseph," he cried, "hasn't the time come for you to change your mind? How goes it with you? The last time I was here you were mooning about marrying some girl you had never met. But I see by the look of the premises that no one lives here but you. You're still a bachelor. Her father refused you, then? Come with me to Jerusalem . . ."

"She accepted me!" protested Joseph, leaping to his feet. "We are to be married in a few days."

"A few days. You mean that?"

"Yes. We set the time almost three months ago today."

"Then where is she? Where is the excitement? Where are the wedding preparations?"

Joseph looked distressed.

"You see, Samuel," he explained, "she has a cousin who has not been in the best of health. She went to see that cousin. I am expecting her back any day."

"You're still hard to figure out," Samuel grumbled. "But look here, Joseph. I am with a caravan that rests in Nazareth tonight. We are taking, along with our merchandise, a troop of Roman minstrels who will make a tour of eastern cities, singing the Roman songs. Come down with me this evening to the camp fire. Let's have supper together. And sing a few songs for old time's sake. And talk more about our affairs. Will you do that?"

Sunset found Joseph at the camp with his friend by a small fire of dried twigs. They ate bread and cheese and listened to the roistering voices of the minstrels, who sang to the accompaniment of a stringed instrument on which the musician played with little padded hammers. One sang an ode of Pindar, the lyric poet of Greece.

Another chanted of Dionysos, god of wine and the drama, who had changed his name to Bacchus and made himself a Roman. Pagan songs, yarns, and dithyrambs about the gods of Rome and how they mated with mortal women, breeding half-gods who always stirred up a lot of trouble in the world.

"Now you're hearing something," gloated Samuel. "Not those sickening old psalms. Did you hear that song of the god and the woman?"

"Yes. These men are simply pagans, worshipers of false gods, in whom they do not really believe, anyway. But their gods are *not* real. Their stories *are* false. They are just inventions. The singers themselves laugh at them."

"Of course, Joseph. And does that not have a personal meaning for you?"

"I do not follow, Samuel. You must speak clearly."

"Didn't you tell me a year ago that you would not fight for the freedom of the people?"

"I remember."

"But do you remember what reason you gave me?"

"Certainly. I said we must put our trust in the promises of God."

"And He promised to send a deliverer, wasn't *that* it?"

"Right."

"Who was to be God's own son, and born of a virgin? Am I not now quoting the prophecies?"

"Yes, Samuel."

"And it is on those very prophecies that you were relying?"

"Yes."

"Well, then——"

Samuel crept forward. He was lying on his stomach, his vast legs lost in shadow, but his face, resting in his palms, was reddened by the fire.

"Can't you see, Joseph, that it is all just an old wives' tale—told in every language? Every silly religion teaches the same thing. You talk to the Indoos from India and the Iranians from Persia. Or, for that matter, talk to the Greeks. They all have the same story of gods having children by mortal women."

He paused, and when Joseph did not speak, he prodded his friend: "Don't you see?"

"See what?"

Joseph was showing unexpected stubbornness.

"That you are making your decision on a fairy tale. You are believing in a universal nonsense."

Joseph leaned forward, and now the light was on his face.

"In universal truth," he replied with the same tranquil conviction that always annoyed Samuel with its force. "Even though some people worship these false gods, and believe in myths, the Messiah will not come just for our people, but for all—for everybody!"

"What's that, Joseph? Watch yourself. You will be uttering a blasphemy."

The two men laughed, but Joseph finished what he had to say.

"God is not just a little kingling like Herod. Not just the God of our people alone. He is God of every people; of every human being living in this world. No matter what others believe, I am sure the Messiah will come not only to us, but to the Romans, the Indoos, and Persians, as well as everybody else."

Samuel clucked his tongue.

"I think that is both nonsense *and* blasphemy." He sighed. "There's something rather pretty about it though. It would be glorious if anybody could believe it."

"Our people have believed it for a long time."

"Oh, I know. I went to school as well as you, Joseph. I'll admit that I wasn't so interested. I remember that God made the promise to redeem the race of Adam, after the flood."

Joseph cut in earnestly:

"Was there ever a time in history when we needed the Messiah more?"

"This Messiah has become an obsession with you," objected Samuel. "And with too many other people. It is what is holding us back. I will admit that we need a leader. I went to Jerusalem to join the revolutionary movement and was ready to put my services at the command of someone who could use them. But I could find no real leader of the resistance. That is what we have to have. We want a superior military genius. Do you expect your Messiah to be a great general?"

Joseph shook his head.

"I fear," he smiled, "that you are incorrigible. You want a soldier Messiah. That is so he can attack Herod, throw out his soldiers and the Romans. A puny country like Palestine against the empire of Rome! That is a man-sized undertaking, even for a messiah. But still not enough for you. After he has thrown out the foreigners, put Herod and his supporters to death, he will then have to tranquilize our own people, and unify them. After a military genius, you want next a Messiah who is also a political master. Before long you will be asking for a great financier too!"

Joseph laughed softly at his own words.

"Perhaps not you, Samuel, but a great many expect the Messiah to be all those things and more, and I fear that they will be greatly disappointed because I do not think he will be any of them."

"And what do you think he *will* be like, then?"

In the waiting silence a driver, suddenly befouled by the beast he had just fed, screeched a malediction on the whole tribe, and swearing that when God had finished designing all the other animals, he made camels from the scraps. And then before Joseph could answer Samuel a hand was thrust from the darkness behind him and tapped the carpenter on the shoulder. Startled, he turned swiftly, looking up into the face of Joachim.

"Peace be with you," the young man breathed, aware of sudden fear.

"And the Lord be with you, Joseph. I came over here to ask you to come to your shop. Mary is there, waiting for you. She says she wants to talk with you at once. Alone."

Chapter 8 JOSEPH DREAMS A DREAM

ON THE wooden table the rush lights were lit and fluttering, and the shadows were like jumpy phantoms on the white plaster of the wall. Mary was standing before the door, and the lambent yellow flames of the candles inside were playing over her face in shivering light. But the sportive light only showed clearer to Joseph how much Mary had changed; she looked like a phantom of the girl he remembered.

She was so pale now that she might have been a specter, not of the dead but the living. She whose cheeks had been ripe orchard red with the warmth of health; whose strong arms could swing the household baskets, heavily burdened, and take pleasure in her own strength; whose stride was young and free and full of the energy of earth, was now a wraith of her former self, yet she had grown taller. There was a primrose pallor in her skin. Especially the enlarged glow of her eyes startled Joseph—it summed up the mystical, frightening change in her.

"Mary!"

"Joseph!"

"Peace be with you!"

"And the Lord be with you."

"Beloved, are you ill?"

"Beloved, don't come nearer to me. Not—just yet. There is something I have to tell you."

He stood, straight and tall, twisting his cap nervously in knotty fingers, his brow heavily creased.

"Say it at once, Mary, beloved, whatever it is. I am listening."

"Then, Joseph, beloved . . ."

"Yes?"

"I am with child."

If the world had broken into two parts and dropped away into bottomless space, her words could not have sounded more unlikely. She had spoken softly; all her talk was soft, with a new and dignified strangeness and sweetness which he noticed vaguely and wondered if, having been away from Galilee, she was losing the country accent of the people, like Samuel, but it was more than that: it was a new and singular dignity in her voice and the remote music of it, the authority in it.

Mary with child!

Joseph stood, unmoving; the fingers stopped playing with the cap; it was as if he had fallen into a catalepsy. Mary running off. Mary staying away. Mary coming back. Mary with child.

"Joseph!" she faltered. "Speak to me."

"But you have not known me," he spoke in a far-off whisper.

"I have not known man."

"But you say you are with child!" he cried, and in his wounded tone was the pain of a man who cannot believe his own anguish.

"Yes, Joseph."

"Whose child?" he groaned.

"Not the child of any man," she answered, her pale face clear before him.

"What is this you say?"

And he mumbled her words, repeating them twice over, trying to grasp the incomprehensible.

"It is from God," she insisted. "It is not from man but from God.

The angel Gabriel, who came to Zachary, came also to me. Elizabeth's child is born and he is a man-child and his name is John, just as the angel declared. And now I am the handmaid of the Lord and shall be the mother of the Promised One!"

"Mary! Do you know what you are saying?"

"Yes."

"If the elders hear you, they will have you put to death."

"Still it is true, Joseph."

He threw his cap to the ground and flung himself after it on a pile of chips and sawdust.

"Tell me this strange thing," he invited glumly. "I shall listen and no more interruptions."

Step by step Mary rehearsed for him the incredible proceedings From the moment when they had bidden each other good night she took up the story: the meeting with the stranger on the inner terrace of her home, the annunciation, the folded wings, the vanishing of the angel whom she knew to be Gabriel. She explained why she could not come at once to Joseph, nor to her parents; she felt only Elizabeth would understand. And Elizabeth had understood; in fact, Elizabeth had learned of it all in advance in a dream and had greeted her with the same salutation as the angel. She had remained with her cousin until John was born; had conceived and of the Holy Spirit. She was a virgin and she was going to bring a child into the world.

And then there was a long silence. At last Mary said:

"You are thinking deep thoughts, Joseph."

"I am thinking," muttered Joseph, slowly scrambling to his feet, "it is a curious thing that no angel came to me."

He exhaled a vast and hopeless sigh.

"Surely I have a right to be shown the truth of this matter!" he cried. "Am I expected to take this shocking story casually? I have no wish to quarrel. The Lord knows that I have loved you, Mary, with all my mind and all my heart and all my soul. I have no eyes for any other—only you. Since I first saw you, my whole life has been shaped around you. I counted on you. But if this thing has happened, why is it that no angel reassured me? Is that so unreasonable? Don't I count at all?"

She wept. It had not occurred to her that he had been neglected by the angel. But it was true. Joseph had only her word for what had happened. And that was a great deal to ask of any man.

"Have you told your mother?"

"No; nor Father, either. I felt I must tell you first."

Joseph went to her slowly and she noticed how his shoulders were bowed, how sagging the line of his small golden beard, how stricken his eyes. A wave of mothering pity went through her; she wanted to gather him in her arms and croon to him.

"I must think," said Joseph. "Tomorrow we will talk more."

"Then peace be with you, Joseph."

"And the Lord be unto you, Mary."

He heard the rustle of her mantle as she gathered its folds around her and walked, face toward the starless sky, out of the shop and into the Nazareth night.

That was a dark night for Joseph. Sleepless he lay with misery darkening his soul; he tossed back and forth on the straw pallet, groaning in disappointment and grief, beating his fists against the rough walls; he was ready to scream to the top of the city's heights, yes, and to the invisible stars. Tearfully he recited old psalms and prayers, hoping to quiet the storm in his heart. What was it his lovely betrothed asked him to believe? That a virgin was to have a child; that she was still as pure and innocent as he had known her to be the day they promised each other to be husband and wife. She asked him to accept God as the sole Father of her son. Then she was asking him to believe something even more irrational—that their son—no! not his son, but hers—was to be the Deliverer for which the people had been waiting for thousands of years; that Mary was bringing into the world the Messiah. With a shudder he remembered the Roman songs of the travelers around the camp fire:

Lord, God of Hosts, bring peace to my soul!

But peace seemed far off. In the gentle soul of Joseph stirred a new possibility—a way by which he might escape from this anguish; he might run off with Samuel and join the revolutionary movement and forget Mary and the child. Forget by learning how to kill.

These were momentary notions. They were not welcome to Joseph's spirit. He admonished himself: he must be wise and calm in the disaster. He would not raise a scandal. There must be no disgrace. Joseph was minded to put away Mary privately. That was by far the best way. Somehow things could be managed without gossip. There was always a way to manage that, in Nazareth as everywhere else in the world.

When she came home, he would marry her. He would ask no

more questions, raise no more doubts, accept the situation and stand by her; he still wanted her. And then, having decided all this, Joseph broke into stormy sobs and the little moans of a man's heartbreak.

His face was wet when at last he fell asleep.

Like his great ancestor, Joseph, son of Jacob, the young carpenter of Nazareth dreamed a dream.

It was not a vivid, waking experience, such as Zachary and Mary had known; it was a man's dream in his sleep, but it was so real, so complete that on him it had all the effect of reality. In the dream the angel of the Lord came to Joseph too; spoke kindly to him, almost paternally, and told him not to be afraid to make Mary his wife; that the child had been in truth conceived of the Holy Spirit, that the name of the child was to be Jesus, and that he was to save the people from their sins. Then the dream ended.

Slowly Joseph wakened. The darkness all around was so deep that it was as if he lay in the womb of grief. Eyes open, staring into black vacancy of space, Joseph found himself muttering a prophecy from old Scripture–the words of the great Isaiah:

"Therefore the Lord himself shall give you a sign. Behold a virgin shall conceive and bear a son."

And then Joseph turned a little cold at a new thought that rushed upon him. He would marry Mary, yes, and help bring up her supernatural son.

Joseph did not know it, but even as Mary changed, so he was changing now; changing into a great man. He could do that because he possessed what is called the gift of faith. He would marry Mary. And he would be her most chaste spouse! Lying there in the immeasurable dark, Joseph renewed his betrothal vows.

Chapter 9 COMMAND FROM ROME

JOSEPH watched over his young wife with ever-deepening and guardian concern. And Mary, with unresting love for Joseph, cooked his meals and scrubbed and mended his clothes, never tiring of keeping that little house and shop shining and clean.

It had been a very simple wedding in Mary's house; afterward, Joseph, arm around his bride, led her down the long and muddy street and proudly through the open door.

From their first moment alone together they knew perfect companionship. Theirs was a marriage based on the yearning of soul for soul, unbound to the earth; they were profoundly in love, so that they felt closer than any union possible to mere bodies, knowing a richness of delight that lay beyond the reach of flesh.

They worked all day; they visited with Joachim and Anna and neighbors and friends in the evening; at first they went on a few outings with friends. To the town they seemed a normal and ordinary couple.

But when they were alone together, they often talked of the wonder that had altered their lives.

How very curious, Joseph sometimes found himself thinking. While all Israel was in trouble, the people hoping and praying for the promised Deliverer, Mary was carrying in her womb a miraculous child.

"Ah, if it should really be so, Mary——"

"God will show," she whispered, hushed and scared. "We must wait!"

Only that afternoon new tales had come from Jerusalem of the scheming of Herod to lay new taxes on the backs of the people.

"How can we pay?" a traveler railed. "We are starving already. Our herdsmen tend lambs that they cannot eat. We are all undernourished. More, now, this Arab king is thinking about."

How had he heard about Herod's secret plans? The traveler winked at Mary and Joseph. The workers of revolution had ways of finding out everything that was going on. Their spies scrubbed and dusted in the very bedchamber of Herod and his wives. Watch and see!

And then this same traveler told of how he had visited recently with Elizabeth and Zachary. He gave a great account of their little son John. That was the strongest boy baby he had ever seen; his little hands had incredible strength, and he could already walk, long before his time. But so far John had not uttered a word.

Not long afterward Joseph learned that this visitor had known what he was talking about—the news came just when Joseph had begun to worry about Mary's condition. The village midwife and Anna both agreed that the time was not far off for her child to be born, and Joseph was insisting that Mary must not do any more housework; she must lie down a great deal and rest. He had all a young husband's terror of the first ordeal of motherhood.

It was then that the word spread through every street in Nazareth of a new fiat from Rome: there was to be an empire-wide census. The word had an ominous sound in Israel; the people had an ancient, almost superstitious aversion to being counted.

But the orders for this colossal undertaking came down straight from the Emperor himself; an imperial command from Caesar Augustus: every one of his subjects was to be enumerated.

"And for what?" asked the little dyer in his shop down the street from Joseph. "Why? Because they are going to increase the taxes and no one must get out of paying."

Get out of paying? Joseph laughed. You could get out of the world quicker than that. The Romans by their land tax took one tenth of every man's corn and two tenths of his grapes and fruit. And then there was the poll tax; one per cent from everybody. And all the other taxes. Now, more!

Soon the news was blazoned and proclaimed throughout all the provinces. Jerusalem, it seemed, had been ignored in making the arrangements; Caesar Augustus did not trust his puppet, Herod. From the throne the word came that the people of Israel were to be counted as an all-Palestine group, under the management of the ranking emissary in the area, Cyrenus, governor of Syria. And Cyrenus had already announced stern penalties for any person living in Palestine who did not obey this positive and authoritative command.

The most disturbing fact to Joseph was that it meant a long journey for him when he felt he was needed at Mary's side. To remain in Nazareth and be counted was impossible, because under the ruling each person must be registered in the city headquarters of the tribe to which he belonged. For Joseph, that meant he must go all the way down to Bethlehem.

"Not only you," he was told by one of the elders of the Nazareth synagogue. "Your wife must also go to her rightful headquarters to be counted."

Joseph's incredulous look was full of sudden fear.

"How can Mary go?" he protested. "Don't you know she is going to have a baby any day?"

"What do Romans care about Jewish wives or babies?" the elder returned with a shrug. He did agree, at Joseph's urgings, to make an appeal; to see if an exception could be made in this case. The answer came back swift and certain, "No!"

They must leave at once to be in Bethlehem on the appointed day!

Bewildered at such inhumanity and injustice, Joseph scarcely heard the clamor of talk around him; in the synagogue there was sorrow in many a heart. "We were counted once by Moses; why should we be counted again?" Not much logic in the question, but no one was feeling logical; they were thinking with their nerves, with their emotions, above all with the galling sense of power exerted by empire's force upon them.

Later, Joseph talked long with Mary about it. He reminded her how, in the second year after the flight from Egypt, Moses had mustered the tribes, all except the priestly caste of Levi, who were exempted from military service and taxes. From then on, according to those tribal divisions set up by Moses, their ancestors had marched, pitched their tents, and made their offerings. And ever since the branches of family trees had been faithfully preserved in or out of captivity, under generals, kings, and judges. Some records in the Nazareth synagogue and the family traditions made it clear that both Joseph and Mary must go to Bethlehem, because that was David's city, and they were both of the house of David.

"Why should it have to be?" demanded Joseph, who was profoundly shaken by the danger to his young wife. "Our priests have their own way of arriving at these things and it is good enough. When they want to count, they have only to add up the passover lambs and multiply by ten."

"And why by ten, Joseph?" asked Mary, delighted as always with his knowledge.

"Because from ten to twelve persons may eat a passover lamb. Then we have to make an allowance for the lepers and the other unclean outcasts. But we know pretty accurately just how many of us there are. This journey to Bethlehem! Oh, Mary, I am afraid . . ."

But Mary smiled confidently.

"Joseph, my beloved," she said, "remember what the angel said to me?"

" 'Do not be afraid, Mary!' " he quoted.

"And what did he say to you in that dream?"

"The very same words."

"Then we should not be afraid. And there is something else. I have been listening to the Scriptures in the synagogue; the rabbi does not know how eagerly, Joseph. There are prophecies."

"About the Messiah, Mary?"

"Yes. That he was to be born in Bethlehem. Had you forgotten, Joseph?"

He gasped.

"No, Mary—I had *not* forgotten. It confounds me now to realize . . ."

"Should we be afraid, Joseph?"

"No, Mary, my beloved. We shall go to Bethlehem."

The next morning they began their journey.

Chapter 10 THE LONG JOURNEY

FROM Nazareth it is a distance of seventy-five miles to Bethlehem of Judea. For Joseph and Mary and Anna and Joachim—the aged father and mother also had to go down to be counted—that made a three-day journey. The two women rode on stubborn little Galilean donkeys, while their men trudged alongside and held on to the reins.

They went by the way of the great pilgrim road, running north and south, crowded with other families, on donkey and traveling afoot. Wayfarers by the thousands cluttered the highway, all leaving their homes because the Emperor of Rome had said that they must. Resenting the edict, most of them, nevertheless, made a holiday of the excursion; friendly bands kept together and camped and cooked and at night pitched tents around wood fires; they slept on blankets spread upon the ground.

During the heat of the day they sang lustily from the psaltery: the brave and happy songs of David; several men had brought along little harps and plucked at the strings as they marched. So it was not a lonely journey and Mary did not suffer. Her light blue mantle was tucked back like a high collar rising behind her head and the wind played with her hair; she was pale and her face was much thinner, but her eyes were quiet and she remained very still; not once did she join in the singing; she seemed to be listening and waiting.

Joseph tried to beguile her. Only once before had he ventured from his home town, and he had an unaccustomed traveler's eagerness to find out all about the places through which they passed and then to tell his wife what he had learned. Casting a learned eye on the fertile fields and orchards that lined the road, he recounted what farmers had told him of prospects for the harvest. But soon the farms were left behind and their way led through rocky Galilean hills and red earth weathered from the hard limestone of the highlands; the fields now were like deserts broken with fragments of black stone.

"Mary, beloved, we are coming near to Shiloh."

"Is Shiloh a big place, Joseph?"

"Not so very big. Except in history. The teacher in the synagogue says it was there that the mother of Samuel came to pray for the gift of a child."

"Ah, she certainly had an answer to her prayers. We must keep on praying like that, Joseph."

"Yes, we must."

And a little later:

"Now we are coming into Gilgal."

"Gilgal? I have heard the name. What happened there, beloved?"

"That was where Samuel judged our people more than eleven hundred years ago."

"It seems too far off, that time, to be real."

"Yes. I suppose history is always like that to modern people like ourselves."

With Mary sitting on the donkey and Joseph pulling at the bridle rein, they passed through the tall defile of rocks that was known in legends as the Valley of Tears. They laughed their way through its gloomy shadows; Anna had driven up and was riding abreast of her daughter, and now old Joachim began to tell stories of his boyhood.

They talked, too, of the great events of old that seemed as near to them now as the historic regions they traveled—Gibeah, where once was the palace of the fierce and arrogant King Saul; and not far off Bethel, where Jacob made his prayer and the backsliders sounded their cymbals before the golden calf.

"And there," added Joseph thoughtfully, "Amos made his prophecy—of the Messiah!"

Hearts were lighter the third morning because they expected to reach their journey's end before nightfall. Joseph was apprehensively watching his wife all day; he had been wakeful during the night and heard her sighing in dreams, and he kept praying constantly that they would get safely to Bethlehem.

"Bethlehem!"

A shout went up. Throngs of the pilgrims began to sing the psalms of David again and others, tired as they were, danced with joy in the dust. But a most solemn feeling came over Joseph when he saw the white roofs and greenery of the little town. He took Mary's hand and they looked together; slanting golden light on white plaster houses topping the green hillsides, where flocks of sheep were grazing drowsily.

This was the city of their tribal ancestors. And Mary recalled the old story of how the great millionaire Boaz came down this very road on his camel one day and saw a poor woman moving about in his field. The reapers had long since gone, but this lovely and hungry young woman was laboring for spillings of grain they had left behind them on the ground. Ruth and Boaz! They were among the ancestors of Mary and Joseph!

The pair rested on the road for a few minutes as they gazed upon the serene landscape, the tall spurs of the hills, the wheat fields, the olive clumps, the fig trees—and many other trees tall, strong in their green reach against blue sky and puffy white clouds.

"Those trees are wonderful, are they not?" asked Mary. It was her way of being casual in these last desperate hours. She knew he had a carpenter's eyes for such things and easily named for her the poplars and live oaks, the pines, the firs, and the tamarisks.

"Are those the ones you told me were cut down for the ships?" asked Mary.

"Right, my beloved. They are used for masts and keels; the Mediterranean Sea is full of such things from Bethlehem."

And as they renewed their steep climb into the town Joseph kept determinedly talking. He had noticed a tightening of his wife's hands, a whitening of knuckles.

"The child must be coming," he told himself. "I will get her to a bed as quickly as possible. Meanwhile I will try to keep her mind busy with other things."

And so he chattered on about the noble respect in which all men held this city of their ancestors. It was from here that Saul had set out to find his father's cattle and laid the foundation of the kingdom. Here Jesse, son of Obed, son of Ruth, had pitched his tents, and here his youngest boy, David, had watched his sheep; David the poet, the soldier, the king, had lain on these same grassy hillsides and heard the morning stars sing together.

Presently a well-intentioned traveler tried to join in the travel lecture of troubled, anxious Joseph. Blandly this talk-hard seized Joseph by the wrist.

"Over there!" he pointed. "Where the olive groves meet with the road? That solid little building of small rocks with the white plaster roof. See it?"

"I see it!" acknowledged Joseph, with the sigh of a man who has other matters to see to.

"That is one of the most ancient sights in the world. Inside there is a great boulder, all shiny smooth—worn that way by the kisses of women for a thousand years, my friend—women who weep and wail."

"Why do women kiss and weep in that place?"

"Because it is poor Rachel's tomb!"

Joseph shuddered and drew his wife quickly away from this morbid stranger. He had forgotten that it was here the great tragedy had befallen Rachel; here she lost her life in giving birth to Benjamin.

Now they entered the streets of Bethlehem, and the press of pilgrims was so great that the pair could scarcely move forward; no one would even listen to Joseph when he asked the way to a hotel; one urchin laughed in his face at such a question. Five hostelries they tried but all were filled up. Joseph kept on doggedly; he forced his way through the door of the last tavern and demanded to talk to the host.

"My wife is ill," pleaded Joseph. "Her baby is about to be born."

The innkeeper was a stout and grumpy man with an enormous stomach. He had rolls of fat under his chin, and little dumplings hanging under his eyes, and oily gray curls.

With red hands clasped in front of him, he gaped at these four Nazarenes, and it seemed to Joseph as if all mercy fled from his little eyes. For a moment he said nothing; then he curled fat fingers around his mouth and bawled hoarsely:

"Sarah!"

His wife, just as stout as he was—she might have been himself in women's clothes—came shuffling from the back of the house.

"What you want?" she demanded, hoarse voice a replica of his own.

"Look at this woman."

"Which?"

"The young one, not the old one."

"I see her, yes."

"Is she having her baby now or is this a scheme to get lodgings?"

The greasy wife leaned forward, hardening the creases in her neck.

"This one," she announced, voice even hoarser with fright, "is having the baby now. I know. I have had ten."

"Please," implored Joseph, "for the love of God——"

"Don't you realize," growled Sarah, "the place is full? All Bethlehem is full. There's not a bed in the town tonight. But she can't have a baby here on the floor. We've got to do something. Gabriel!"

"Hah?" answered the innkeeper obediently.

"There is one warm and comfortable place where we haven't put anybody yet."

"Is there now? Where? Just where?" demanded Gabriel.

"In the stable!"

"The stable!" echoed Joseph miserably, and Anna put her arms around Mary. But the young wife looked gratefully at the innkeeper's wife.

"You are very kind to think of it," she said. "A stable is warm. And it will be like home, because often I slept downstairs with the sheep and the goats." She turned to Joseph. "These people would surely take good care of their animals. And we will be alone there."

She turned quickly back to the old woman.

"You will not rent it to anyone else besides us?" she pleaded.

"No," smiled Sarah slowly, with a reluctant chuckle. "And I will help you. God knows we women have got to help each other."

The stable was in a roomy cave that extended under the whole building of the inn. Joseph held Mary's hand as he led her down twisting stone steps to an earthen floor; in his free hand he held a lantern that threw against the rough walls the magnified shadows of Anna and Joachim and Mary and himself.

"Where are we going to put her down?" cried Anna distractedly.

Heaving and puffing, the stout Sarah came clumping down the stairs behind them, and after her Gabriel, puffing even louder than his wife, both clasping fresh bundles of straw. They laid a bed against the inner wall, which was warmer and not so damp, and they brought linen and a coverlet and a pillow for Mary's head.

Then Gabriel and Sarah had to leave them, for business was brisk upstairs, but both of them paused to give a hoarse: "God be with you tonight!" As their footsteps died away the four at last felt relieved, if only to be alone. Anna helped Mary to undress, and then she went upstairs in search of jars of heated water, while Joseph stood near brooding.

"Why do we have no sign now?" he was asking himself. "Where is the angel? Why doesn't Anna hurry back?"

Anna soon came back with the water. She briskly exiled Joseph and Joachim through a rear door in the stable, bidding them to stay out until they were sent for. It was dark outside, the night air moist and cold.

Meanwhile Anna, with the wisdom of old wives, urged Mary not to lie on the straw but to get up and walk. Mary obeyed. Back and forth in the stable she walked, amid the braying of donkeys and bleating of sheep, her nostrils filled with the sweet, pungent odors of barley and oats and hay. To and fro she walked.

And Joseph was trudging up and down in the dark area behind the stable. Again and again he tightened and then loosened the frayed girdle around his travel-stained robe. He fingered the pouch that held his store of coins and wondered whether he had enough money to see them through. The hours dragged on. Joachim had sat down on his haunches and soon fell asleep. But Joseph walked on like a man in a nightmare, waiting, praying until at last and suddenly he heard the sound—a child's first cry.

In the dimmish light he knelt beside the bed of straw where Mary lay, pale and weak but wide-eyed and with a small, brave smile for him.

"See!" she murmured.

Joseph was on his knees. Mary held out firm hands, lifting up her son, wrapped in Grandmother Anna's swaddling clothes—lifting him up adoringly, the fate of the world reposing in the chalice of her hands.

Even in the first instant of seeing the child Joseph was aware of something extraordinarily different about him. Somehow he knew that this newborn baby, whose face was not red and crinkled but smooth and white, and whose expression was of such potent innocence and affection, had come into the world to get nothing and to give everything.

Chapter 11 SHEPHERDS AT THE BACK DOOR

MARY had fallen asleep, and there was quiet in the stable. Anna and Joachim made a bed for themselves, far back in the shadows. And Jesus, the baby, lay asleep in his first bed, which was the food box of the donkeys and the cows—a manger which the foster father had hastily filled with fresh hay and barley oats that smelled sweet and clean.

For Joseph, sleep was impossible. His mind, his very soul, was too tremulous and excited. Again he paced in a kind of march around the stable, stopping regularly to see that Mary and her child still breathed, which they did, quite naturally. There was glee in Joseph, a sacred rippling joy in his blood, a bounce to his muscles; his only regret was that he had no one to talk to. Joseph in that dark hour could have poured out his heart in rapturous conversation.

"The oddest thing about it," he told himself, in the absence of any companion, "was the feeling I had when I looked into that little fellow's eyes. I seemed to have known him all my life. He wasn't a stranger!"

Was that a special fact because Jesus was a special child? Because, after all, Joseph was not the child's father, and even now he did not allow himself to forget it. Yet he felt a tender closeness to the baby, deeper and truer than fatherhood itself. He still felt baffled that there was no further sign.

A long time had passed while Mary carried her baby, with no reassurance from supernatural beings. Nine months since the angel had stood with folded wings in the Nazareth house; the day of the Annunciation. After that the dream message had come to Joseph; then silence; months of commonplace reality. Was it not strange that the baby had been born without some demonstration? Here was the child; where were the angels?

He listened for a rustling of wings and heard only the sleepy bleat of a yearling lamb. That, and presently a low rumble of distant voices, the shuffling of feet outside the house and, at the lower back entrance of the stable, the knocking of a staff.

With a gasp of concern that Mary would be awakened, Joseph

hurried to the door. Unfastening the latch, he opened the upper half of the door, then put a finger warningly to his mouth. A group of bearded faces were staring in at him. One man held up a lighted lantern. Behind them was still the night, dark and clear, with the sparkle of unaccountable and extraordinarily brilliant stars. Joseph had not seen those stars until now.

"Peace!" breathed Joseph. "This is no time to make noise."

"The Lord be unto you," returned one of the men in a low, placating voice. "We have not come to make any trouble at all."

"Who are you, then?"

"We are shepherds from the hills outside this town. We have been tending our flocks."

"The hour is late," insisted Joseph firmly.

He would have closed the door but the speaker held up his staff.

"Wait. Only one question. Has a child just been born in this place?"

A quiver of alarm passed through Joseph. Was something wrong? Their papers not in order, perhaps? Had they broken the law in taking shelter in the stable? No one ever knew what queer laws might be declared by King Herod.

"Why do you ask, shepherd? How is it your business about a child?"

"Don't be afraid of us, man. We are friends."

"Well, then—yes. A child has been born here."

"Only a little while ago?"

"True. Within two hours."

Low exclamations came from the bearded mouths of the shepherds. They turned and patted one another on the back and one of them whispered:

"It is true, then."

And the first speaker laid a kindly hand on Joseph's shoulder.

"Tell me—is it a man-child?"

"It is."

"And could it be possible that you have laid the child in a manger?"

"Yes," answered Joseph, feeling the tears gather in his eyes. "There was no cradle, you see. The town is overcrowded; there was nowhere else I could take my lady . . ."

"Then God be praised!" murmured the shepherd fervently, and the others muttered agreement in their beards.

"Listen, man," cried the one with the lifted staff. "We five men have just seen a marvelous sight. An unbelievable sight. And it has to do with you."

Marvelous sight! And unbelievable. Hope sprang up in Joseph's thoughts.

"Believe this thing we tell you. We were all tending our flocks tonight, minding our own business. The night was clear, air cool, stars bright, everything going along just as usual. Suddenly Jonas here interrupted our talk and pointed at the sky."

"That I did," confirmed Jonas. "There was a great big bright light in the sky and the shape of it like an angel bigger than the world. And I heard a voice . . ."

"We all saw the light," declared the first man. "And we all heard distinctly that voice from the sky."

"What did the voice say?" asked Joseph eagerly.

"It told us not to be afraid."

"Yes. It always begins that way. And then?"

"And then it said it brought us great news. The Savior of the world was being born. I remember the very words; how can I ever forget them? 'For this day is born to you a Savior who is Christ the Lord.' "

"Christ the Lord," whispered Joseph.

"Yes, friend. That's what the voice said. It told us the child was being born right here in this town and that we would find it, wrapped in swaddling clothes and lying in a manger."

Here another shepherd pushed himself forward.

"You can never imagine what happened then," he broke in excitedly. "The whole heaven seemed to open up. The curtain of the stars was split like a tent, and through the opening we saw a host of angels that filled the sky and they were all singing at the top of their voices . . ."

"And do you know *what* they were singing?" demanded Jonas, again interrupting. "The words were: 'Glory to God in the highest and on earth peace . . .' "

And then the shepherds seemed to lose their tongues. The sound of their own story seemed to subdue them. Strong, out-of-doors men, who smelled of grass; practical men, and yet they had told the story with something of the frenzy of poets. Now came the reaction.

Their leader lowered his lantern and sighed deeply.

"Of course," he said with an apologetic air, "we can't expect you to believe all this."

Then his eyes flashed open and he looked straight at Joseph.

"But it is true," he averred, as if he were taking an oath, "I saw it. I heard it."

Joseph wrung their hands. He believed them utterly, as they went on to tell how they forsook their fat-tailed sheep and ran into Bethlehem. Of every dark straggler on the streets at such an hour they had asked questions. Where could they find the newborn baby? And when they found this house then they must know if it were lying in a manger. Someone had sent them to the stable of the inn.

The tale of the shepherds brought peace to Joseph. The sign had come at secondhand, which was better. These men, panting and out of breath and sweaty, full of strength and humility, had seen the gates of another world open up and had heard singing from on high, the heavens rejoicing at the birth of Mary's child. Humble workingmen of the fields were the first to come and visit the newborn Jesus.

Joseph received them with open arms and one shepherd after another kissed his beard. On tiptoe they followed him as he led them straight to the manger, where they looked down and then knelt beside the sleeping figure of Mary's son.

Soon they were gone, and Joseph resumed his unsleeping vigil. But now his heart was calmed. The sign had come. In his mind's ear he could hear the unnumbered hosts of the servants of God, singing to the ages: "Peace on earth to men of good will."

Chapter 12 TWO PIGEONS, PLEASE!

"JOSEPH, my friend, are you going to have this child circumcised?" asked Samuel, who had come to the stable when at last he had found out where the family stayed.

"But of course. Why not?"

"You yourself say that he is not born like other children."

"That is correct. But whatever is done that is out of course of natural ways is not to be done by me, Samuel. I love this child more than I love my own life, but I must remember my place. I am only his foster father. And I have thought a lot about that, Samuel. It is a terrific responsibility for an ignorant carpenter like myself."

"Not so ignorant," interrupted Samuel, with a loyal shake of his rough hair.

"Mary and I have made up our minds," pursued Joseph, "to bring Jesus up very carefully and the very best we know how. Everything that should be done will be done."

"Fine, Joseph, but . . ."

"So of course he will be circumcised. I am going to follow the law of our people with him in everything. Scrupulously. The law says that every little boy baby must be circumcised on the eighth day of his life. That doesn't mean the seventh or the ninth."

Samuel gave a little snort.

"The eighth day, and not the seventh or the ninth," he scoffed. "Why would such meticulousness be important to a great gentleman like God, who runs the whole world?"

Joseph shrugged.

"I haven't the faintest idea," he admitted calmly. "And I doubt if I could understand, even if someone explained. But I do know what is written in the scrolls—and that's enough."

Samuel squinted at his friend. He loved this gentle carpenter, and yet there was something in their chemistry that was opposed; the boisterous Samuel was impatient of all obedience. He did not want to hurt Joseph, and yet something urgent in the heart pressed him on to bait and heckle.

"And, no doubt, Mary will be purified?" he asked?

"Why not?"

"Why should any woman have to be purified of motherhood?"

"Be careful of blasphemy!"

"Bosh! For seven days a woman is supposed to be unclean after her baby is born. There is no other word for it than bosh. You have to wait three and thirty days while she is allowed to touch nothing that is hallowed—and a lot of other silly rules."

"We obey them," said Joseph crisply.

"But, Joseph. Isn't it still true that you think the Holy Spirit was the father of the child?"

"I know it is so."

"Was that sin?"

"No."

"It was sinless? Your wife was still a virgin when this child was born?"

"Before God, yes!"

"Then, if she is sinless, why must *she* be purified? Answer me that, Joseph?"

The husband of Mary laid his hand on the shoulder of his friend and smiled patiently.

"It was not our doing that the law of nature was altered so that this child could be born," he answered simply. "We could not have done that if we wanted to. We are not lawmakers and therefore we cannot be law changers. Our business is to try to understand the laws and obey them, not find out the reasons for them, not try to make exceptions for ourselves. I haven't brains enough to fathom God, Samuel. And pardon me, old friend—neither have you. So we just act according to our lights."

And thus according to their lights Jesus and Mary and Joseph and Anna and Joachim left the stable under the inn on the eighth day after the Nativity and rode their donkeys six miles up the steep heights that led to Jerusalem. The air was warm and a pleasant breeze was fluttering through the abundant sunshine; the hills were green, and the trees moved gently, and the world looked beautiful to the mother with her child in her arms.

Their eyes were turned upward to take in the great glory of the capital, the proud city of walls and towers on its bold south promontory of the bleak limestone ridge.

"Think of it, Mary," remarked Joseph. "Some of the old residents I talked to in Bethlehem have never seen this great city, so near at hand. Think of that! Living so close and never bothering to go over and see."

"I think Nazareth is a very much pleasanter place," Mary answered.

With this the others agreed. They said that Jerusalem was a great place to visit but they would never want to live there. But the height and sweep and power of the great city stirred their imagination, willy-nilly. As they came up from the gorges, the ravines and gashes in the earth, the gullies and deeps of old geological catastrophes and the walls of the city came more plainly into view they felt again a surge of pride in such a big place.

Now they were approaching the level of the high, irregular city wall; it was the color of a yellow cat, its great tawny stones piled, course on course, thirty feet high. As far as the eye could see the wall continued, with its eight gates and sixty watchtowers each guarded by Herod's cutthroats. They entered that morning through the Sheep's Gate. In the shadow of the archway Mary looked down into the baby's face; his eyes were open, and there was a focus to their gaze—an intelligence that startled her; it was as if this baby mind understood his first entrance into Jerusalem, and that he would come here again, and more than once, and at last to tragical ends!

But the baby's eyes soon closed and he dozed off, unmindful of worldly wonders. The others looked about them with eager interest, seeing the white arches of the stadium, called the xystus, where young men were encouraged by Herod and the Romans to strengthen themselves by athletic drills for prowess in battle.

"Jesus must never be a soldier," was the instant prayer in Mary's heart.

And she turned quickly from this gladiatorial training ground to the theater where heathen plays were produced. All manner of filthy drama was shown there, its intellectual degradation matched only by the physical filth of the streets. The gentle country folk were bewildered anew at the violent contrasts in poverty and riches on every hand; great houses and mud hovels; wide plazas and dark curling streets full of disease and crime, and high on a nearby terrace, close to the Temple itself, the dazzling palace of Herod and its three military towers, filled with the soldiers of the apprehensive king, who more and more lived in fear that the people would rise up and give him his just deserts.

Samuel had told Joseph about the lavish iniquities of that palace; of the king's couch, made of gold and ivory and white velvet; of his wives and concubines and maidservants and manservants and cooks and minstrels and dancing boys and the unending round of entertainment in its halls and peristyles and banquet chambers.

The four grownups on their mission of devotion saw the signs of wealth and pleasure on one hand and also the want and teeming discontent, unwashed pavements slippery with mortal slime and excrement, lying at the base of the rich people's glory; there was barely enough water to drink in this Jerusalem and palaces where vice played all day and all night and lanes where hunger and leprosy crouched together.

They were glad when they reached the outer gate of the Temple area and found a little knot of relatives waiting to welcome them:

Zachary, joyous and very talkative beside the radiant Elizabeth, who had brought little John in her arms. Strutting forward and back, they found also the mocking but very friendly and companionable Samuel.

It was not the first time that Elizabeth and Mary had met since the birth of Jesus; three times in the last week Elizabeth and Zachary had made the journey over to Bethlehem. Now they all moved inside the Temple walls with happy faces and halted in the outer court to buy their ritualistic offerings. And here Mary looked to Joseph, wondering what he was going to decide.

According to the law they could purchase a one-year-old lamb for a burnt offering and a young pigeon for a sin offering, or Joseph could choose the less expensive course of buying two turtledoves or two young pigeons, depending altogether on his conscience and his purse.

Feeling that he could not afford anything better, for Gabriel and Sarah had charged them plenty for the use of the stable, Joseph decided to buy two plump pigeons. He picked out one and Mary the other, and Joseph carried them in his hands as he proceeded toward the inner Temple. Looking about him, Joseph felt again that sense of belonging and continuity of race and history of which this Temple was the symbol. Herod might have paid for it, but the people's architects designed it, the people's labor built it, and here the people drew to themselves apart from tyrants and overlords; here they remained most peculiarly themselves, uncontaminated by any intrusion from the outer world. And here, in spite of Roman armies and puppet Arab king, they persisted in adhering to the last meticulous detail of their faith. Within earshot of Herod, who was not deaf, they came regularly not only to praise the Lord, God of Hosts, but to entreat Him to deliver them from their conquerors. That was the principal prayer raised in the Temple their oppressor had built for them.

But as Joseph and Mary were about to cross the court, where the offerings would be turned in and ceremonies performed, there came a startling interruption.

Mary, with the sleeping Jesus against her breast, was walking a little behind Joseph, when a shadow fell across them; a withered figure swayed out from under a pillared archway; a purblind old man tottered before them in the sun.

"What's he want?" asked Samuel hastily.

But Zachary, the priest, who knew his way about the Temple, lifted his hand reassuringly.

"Don't be worried," he said, out of the side of his beard. "It's only Simeon. Everybody around the Temple knows old Simeon. He's harmless."

"He's old enough all right," agreed Samuel.

Indeed, Simeon was so decrepit that it seemed a wonder he did not fall apart, from sheer inanition and decay.

"He is a devout and just man," remonstrated Zachary, "and he tells everybody that once he was visited by the Holy Spirit. The angel promised him that before he died he was to see the Messiah in the flesh."

Samuel looked warily at Zachary. The priest's face was set in an ivory calm. The others stood back while the tall, ragged figure of Simeon crept nearer, toward Mary and Joseph with the child.

There was a moment of curious silence as he halted and lifted up his hands and croakingly thanked God. At last, he groaned aloud, he could be allowed to die. A chill ran even in the spine of Samuel when he heard that prayer. The whole group stood still, as other persons came hurrying down the courtyard; a crowd collected, all watching as Simeon leaned forward and his emaciated face of a thousand wrinkles came close to the young mother.

"This child is set for the fall!" he gasped. The sunken eyes gleamed again straight at Mary. "And for the resurrection of Israel," he went on huskily.

His bony right hand raised, the lean, misshapen forefinger pointed crookedly at the mother's heart.

"And your own soul a sword shall pierce!" he predicted.

As tears gathered in Mary's eyes, he added:

"Out of many hearts thoughts shall be revealed."

Now Simeon swayed back, waving both hands haplessly, as if saying farewell to a life he had never enjoyed; as if this moment were a tremendous relief to him and he was glad to lose himself in shadows.

Before anyone could speak, there came a new voice—the sound of crying—and out from under the same arcade appeared a woman crawling on her knees.

"She, too, is incredibly old," muttered Zachary. "Even older than Simeon. Her name is Anna. For eighty-four years she has been a widow. Since the day the Temple was built she has never left it."

"And what is *she* saying?" snapped Samuel.

"Listen!" said Zachary.

Anna was struggling to stand up in front of Mary. Looking down into the face of the sleeping child, she found her voice, so clear that even the dying Simeon could hear what she was saying:

"Here, indeed, is the deliverer of the people!"

Chapter 13 THE KING AND THE CHILD

Of course dark-brown Herod heard of these matters. Ever since Zachary had been stricken dumb on the altar there had been rumors of queer happenings in Jerusalem, and Herod's spies, hearing everything, reported all the gossip, including whispers from the north that a virgin of Nazareth was going to have a baby. The shepherds, too, had naturally babbled about their supernal experience. When, right out in the courtyard of the Temple, old Simeon then declared the child to be from God and promptly died, after having conspicuously and publicly waited so many years, and when the old crone Anna added her testimony, Herod quite reasonably began to feel vexed.

"Is the king going to arrest us?" asked Joseph, when Samuel told him about it.

"Very likely, I'm sorry to say," grunted Samuel. "This Herod is now afraid of his shadow. But he is a lot more afraid of a rival to his throne. And that's what he is likely to consider your child, if he takes the stories seriously."

Spies of the revolutionary movement, still working as servants in the Herodian palace, had heard with their own ears and seen at firsthand exactly what had happened. First the agents of the king, diligent every day, reported the strange stories, but had to admit that the tales were vague; they had learned nothing circumstantial, not even the names of the father and mother. Rumors had been distorted and multiplied and spread in profusion; some had it there were twins, others that it was a girl child; so far, thank God, Herod did not know that Joseph the carpenter of Nazareth and Mary his wife were the ones he sought, nor that they were still quartered with the child in a Bethlehem stable.

Herod had a turbulent scene with his spies.

"What kind of service is this?" he roared at them. "Get me facts!"

They came back with alarming facts. Three wise men from the East had arrived in the capital. They had no caravan; merely four camels, the extra beast loaded with bales and boxes which they kept ever near them at the khan. Gossip said they were kings, traveling incognito.

"Three strangers and four camels at the inn," Herod said to his spies. "What kind of men do they pretend to be? Merchants? Ambassadors with gifts for me? Or what?"

"They are called magi," the spy reported.

"What are magi?"

"Magi are wise men," was the answer. "Yet these three do not seem to be so very wise. They have gone up and down Jerusalem from the stadium to the Temple, saying nothing wise at all but instead asking questions of everybody."

"What questions?"

The spies gulped and flushed and cleared their throats.

"What questions, fools? Speak up or I'll have you flogged."

"They are asking about the birth of a fabulous child who is to take the throne of Israel. They say they have seen his star in the east and have come to worship him."

With armored fists Herod struck the two men down. He kicked them with his boots. He screamed and ranted and ordered them carried out and put to death. He drank two goblets of foaming wine and ordered music and dancing girls and Egyptian singers and dancers, and then as soon as the music began, he cleared the apartment of them with one scream of mortal rage. Gasping, he lay on a couch for an hour, fanned by a tamarisk boy, who was a spy of Samuel's resistance group.

Later, when he felt calmer, Herod talked with Nisus, his secretary, who knew more about magi than the spies.

"They can do wonders, those people," Nisus declared.

"Sorcerers?"

"Holy men in their own land. Priests of Eastern occultism. They are capable of understanding the past and of foretelling the future."

"So!" exclaimed Herod, and the tone came from the belly. "Bring Annas and the chief priests and the scribes to me."

But when these worthies responded, he decided to talk with Annas alone. They understood each other.

Even in those early days Annas, already the political boss of Jerusalem, was hated by the people because they knew he had sold out to Herod and Rome. If a revolution were ever successful, Annas, leader of the forty richest families in the land, would have been the first to be put to death. The people well knew how he had come to terms with tyrant and invader. He had asked Herod: What does the Empire want of Palestine? Taxes and tranquillity was the answer.

"Taxes we will get for you, tranquillity we guarantee"—such was the bargain Annas had made. "Only we must keep order ourselves, and we must collect the taxes."

Then Annas and his friends hired the collectors and taxed the people almost double, keeping the unjust half for themselves. They had their own secret police to ferret out rebellions and punish upstarts. Annas and Herod perfectly well understood each other.

Herod began the interview with a crafty grin.

"Annas," he said, "I have been having a dispute with some of my friends in court here. I sent for you to settle it."

Annas spread his palms toward the ground and inclined his head forward.

"I hope I can help your brilliant majesty," he replied with composure. He had no fear of Herod, but he was careful to observe every detail of court punctilio. "You have only to command me," he added, in court etiquette. "My very life is in your august service."

Herod laughed. He always relished flattery and servility, even when it was purely formal; he fed on adulation, though he had not tasted many sincere compliments.

"It's about your religion."

Annas sucked a hollow tooth.

"Your Majesty is interested in our religion?"

"Of course I know nothing whatever about it. And I don't want to learn, either."

"No, Majesty?"

"All I want is to settle a dispute. Is it true that you have scriptures that predict the coming of a deliverer of your people—a Messiah, as you call it?"

"Majesty, that is correct."

Herod, who had the bulging eyes of a hyperthyroid victim, leaned forward, truculent and roiled.

"You realize that can mean deliverance only from my royal authority," he snarled. "You realize that is sedition?"

Annas turned his head to one side and smiled composedly through his goatlike beard. He appeared quite unperturbed.

"Majesty," he said, "you will forgive me if I correct a tiny mistake. These prophecies were made about the time of our captivity. When we were in Babylon. Hundreds of years ago."

Herod sat back a little relaxed.

"But your people still go on believing in them," he complained.

"Some of them do," agreed Annas, with disarming frankness. "But, Majesty, is it not the same in every religion? The ignorant take things literally. Why undeceive the stupid masses of people—especially if it keeps them on their good behavior? No intelligent person believes in any of the wonder stories of the old Scriptures, and certainly not in the prophecies."

"Don't you, as a priest, believe in them, Annas?"

"No, sire. I am a Sadducee. We don't believe in such things. We don't even believe in a future life or a resurrection."

"Neither do I," barked Herod irritably. "We live today, we die tomorrow, and that's all there is. Anybody who believes anything more is a fool."

"Precisely, Your Majesty."

Annas was hoping they would not have to pursue the conversation, but apparently Herod was still not satisfied.

"Was there anything said in those old books of yours about where the Deliverer—— There was some title for him, too, wasn't there?"

"Yes, sir—the Christ."

"Ah, yes, that's the term I heard. Was there anything said about when or where the Christ was to be born?"

Annas heaved a sigh and scratched his head. His confession was thoroughly honest.

"Yes, there was, Your Majesty, but I am sorry to say I have forgotten it. That should show you how important it seemed to me."

"Well, couldn't you have it looked up for me?"

"At once."

"Then come to me at the same hour tomorrow and give me place and date. Have I made myself clear?"

"Perfectly, Your Majesty."

No sooner was Annas gone than Herod commanded that the three wise men be brought to the throne room.

For this interview he arrayed himself in his kingliest robes to impress the savants and rulers from the lands beyond the Euphrates. A frontlet of diamonds and rubies gleamed on Herod's forehead, the diadem of Judea, and from it rose a tufted egret that was like a little rainbow springing from his gray hair.

It was a curious meeting. The august travelers from the East behaved admirably before the king, observing all the proprieties of a throne-room audience. Then, rising, they announced their names—Caspar, Melchior, and Balthazar.

Herod looked upon them with a blandiloquent smile, affable and suave.

"We are curious to know," he told them, "why it is that we are honored by a visit from such great dignitaries."

They told him very simply that they were following a star.

"A star?" repeated Herod. His spies had mentioned something of this, but vaguely; there was the court astrologer, Marto, waiting now in the rear. Herod beckoned to Marto.

"Listen to this carefully, Marto. Was it a large star, friends, that you followed here?"

The Magi nodded. It was a large star, in the east and very bright. They had been following it for many days.

"Would you know what it is, this star, Marto?" demanded the king, chafing at having to go on pretending to be amiable.

Marto explained that there had recently appeared a most remarkable conjunction of Jupiter, Saturn, and Mars—a condition that would not recur in more than a million years. But that fiery display had faded away more than a week ago.

"Then you three have seen a star that my astrologer has not found," reflected Herod aloud. The wise men said nothing.

"Well, at any rate, what do you say this star portends?"

The Wise Men were very wise, indeed, because they merely shook their heads and said they could not tell fortunes. But did they not know what it meant for the future of Israel? No, they could not be sure of anything in the future; the star led them on, that was all.

"But," persisted Herod, "what do you expect to find under this star?"

Then Balthazar told him.

"A child," the old traveler answered, closing his eyes.

"A child?" Herod's voice was creamy with interest. "And what about this child?"

Melchior answered that they were not free to talk until their errand was complete.

"Very well, then," growled Herod. "Where do you expect to find him?"

"Bethlehem!"

"Bethlehem. Such a place?"

Again they shrugged. They could only follow the star. With the coming of night they would resume their journey. Herod saw that it was useless to bring mere force against wisdom, and turned a cunningly smiling face upon the three.

"Then this is what you must do," he dissembled. "Go find the child and then come back and tell me and I will go worship him too."

Lifting a sweating hand to his brow, Herod allowed them to depart. No sooner were the doors shut behind them than he gave the signal to his spies; they were to follow the Wise Men and search everywhere else besides; find the child that had been born under a magical star.

But in the darkness of that night Caspar, Melchior, and Balthazar, with their extra laden camel, eluded Herod's pursuers. The Wise Men rode by an inside lane, on to Bethlehem, as if there was nothing in the world of human cunning that wise men had to fear. They found the town, the inn, the stable. They knelt, and their eyes were full of worshipful glory as they gazed upon Mary's baby.

Then the Wise Men embraced Joseph, kissed his beard, and bowed ceremoniously. Having bestowed their gifts, they departed from the stable, but not to return to Jerusalem. The waiting Herod was never to see them again. Having bedded down at another inn, all three Magi went promptly to sleep and dreamed the same dream. Because of that dream, they rose in the middle of the night and got away on their camels, completely outwitting several searching bands from the palace. By another way they headed for their own country and so, obedient to their own vision, they jogged out of history, never to reappear.

It was a night of dreams powerful in meaning. The visit of the Wise Men had come at a time when Mary and Joseph felt troubled and bewildered, for this was the night of the day that they had carried the baby to the Temple.

The incidents of the morning had been shocking to the simple-hearted family, and the terror of those two encounters lingered—

the old man Simeon squeaking down the long range of pillared arches that at last he could die, having seen the face of the Savior of all the people of the world. And after Simeon, the fasting and praying widow of eighty-four years, Anna, who had crept out of the shadows of a marble pillar and called him the Redeemer.

The dream that followed in Joseph's sleep was even more upsetting.

Once again the foster father of Jesus found himself face to face with the same bright angel that had come to his bedside in Nazareth and told him to marry Mary without distrust, for the child in her womb was miraculous. This time the bright angel gave Joseph new instructions:

"Arise, and take the child and his mother and fly into Egypt; and be there until I shall tell you. For it will come to pass that Herod will seek the child to destroy him."

But how? How get to Egypt? It would take money to travel so far, and only a few coins were left.

It was a most tormented Joseph who stood in the dark stable thus early in the morning, accepting to the full the stern warning of his dream—yet penniless to obey.

What to do?

Almost instantaneously he learned there was nothing needed for him to do at all; the money for the long trip to Egypt was already provided. For now he saw, moving toward him in the gloom, the bent figure of his father-in-law. Joachim, too, could not sleep. So he had busied himself usefully, unpacking the gifts the Wise Men had left for the child.

"Flasks of perfume," Joachim whispered to his son-in-law. "Frankincense, the most perfect of all; an ointment made from olive oil, sweetened with spices, fragrant gums, odors of pressed flowers, and in the second package, another stuff called myrrh—they told me it was an aromatic gum taken from a thorn tree!"

Joseph laid a hand on the shoulder of his father-in-law.

"Joachim," he sighed, "we have now to think of other matters."

"And this third gift," the old man rumbled on, "is the smallest and the heaviest of all the Wise Men's bounty. Guess what is in this bundle, Joseph?"

"What, Father-in-law?"

Joachim shook the package and a heavy clinking sound echoed to the vaulted roof of the cave.

"It's gold!" whispered Joachim. "They brought us frankincense, myrrh—and gold. They must have known we would need it!"

"Glory be to God. Praise His Holy Name," gasped Joseph, and fell to his knees.

Chapter 14 KILL THEM ALL!

HEROD was livid when he learned that the mysterious Wise Men had escaped his clutches.

Which way had they gone? His spies galloped all the roads. Down through Jericho and across the plains of Transjordania; up through the northeastern provinces, through Samaria and the two Galilees, and on through Syria to the distant east. Which way?

Outriders with spears were charged to bring back the Wise Men but came home empty-handed. It was then that the fears of Herod broke like an explosion in his soul; he was lost in a demoniacal panic.

"In spite of hell I will find this miraculous child!"

That was the one frenzied thought that batted around in his brain. The one clue he had was that the child was supposed to be in Bethlehem. But crowded Bethlehem was full of babies. How find the right one?

A horrible notion occurred to him, and for a cautious instant even Herod hesitated. No. He would better not try that idea! After all, he had already been rebuked seven times by Rome for his cruelties. In the old days Rome had never been afraid of cruelty, but now, apparently, there were limits under this peaceful-minded Augustus. The one thing the dun-skinned Herod cared about was his throne. Because the child was a menace to his reign, he meant to get rid of it. But he must act carefully. Or must he? Was he the King of Judea or was he not?

"I have always been strong—and now what does it matter? I am an old man. Soon I shall die. No. No. I have a long time to live yet. I will be sitting on my throne when this upstart child has a beard. No. I am not going to die soon. I must get rid of this child. He must never live to grow a beard!"

His face blanched at his own scheme. But terror smoked again in his brain, and fright was roaring in his ears. A queasy turn of his stomach set him trembling and sweating with weakness. He clapped red palms together. When his captains came, he spoke to them crisply, briefly, firmly, his right fingers scratching at the poniard in his belt. It was his last resort, but if it had to be, it had to be.

"Do all as I have told you!"

Those captains had to go out of the palace and lead troops to Bethlehem to do his atrocious bidding. They surrounded the city, occupied the streets, rushed into the houses with drawn short swords and uplifted spears. By the order of the king, they cut to death every boy baby in the town. Not one of those holy innocents was spared—only the infant Jesus.

And that was so only because Joseph and Mary and Jesus obeyed the messenger and had already left behind them the city of this massacre. They had bade fond farewells to Anna and Joachim. Then Joseph put mother and child on the donkey's back, their precious goods, the gifts of the Magi bundled and tied to the sides of the little beast. Staff in one hand, Joseph seized the donkey reins with the other and in the middle of the dark the family started out from Bethlehem.

Before them lay the Sinai Desert where for forty years their ancestors had wandered after the escape from Pharaoh.

They were taking the road back to Egypt.

Book Two

A BOY IN NAZARETH

Chapter 15 BY THE NILE

HEROD'S SPIES sought them even in Egypt. Had anyone seen a bald-headed carpenter with a small golden beard turning silver and his blue-eyed dark-tressed wife, little more than a child herself, with an indescribably lovely infant whose smile was like the warm light of the sun? More than once these spies came uncomfortably near, when their trail led them past the stone obelisks set up by Cleopatra in the gilded city of Heliopolis; there the Nazareth family had settled. Some day those obelisks would be set up in Paris and London and New York and Constantinople and other great cities then not even thought of, for unborn eyes to see stone monuments that Mary and Joseph and the baby Jesus had also seen.

The family learned, too, that there was an intense and senseless dislike of their people in the land. Joseph and Mary learned about anti-Semitism in Egypt.

At the very time when Jesus was taken there some of the haters of the race in Alexandria were reviving a vicious old lie. They spread the tale that all the children of Israel, who had been led by Moses into the desert, were nothing more nor less than lepers; that was the only reason why Pharaoh had let the people go. In this atmosphere of ancient and persistent racial hostility Mary and Joseph, displaced persons of a very long time ago, had to care for the little son.

Surrounded by such hatred, Jesus learned to lisp His first prayer —in a pagan town, committed to the idolatry of a whole gallery of mythical gods. During the first years of His life He lived among Egyptians parading before gigantic stone images of Ra, the deity of the midday sun; Isis, the mother; Osiris, the father; Horus, the son; before horned bulls of holiness, too, and the sacred cat of Bubastes—in the very midst of such ignorance and fear the baby

Jesus was taught by Mary, His mother, crooning at her cradle, to say:

"Hear, O Israel! The Lord, our God, is one God!"

Their new home in Heliopolis was some ten miles away from the Pyramids; here there was less prejudice than they had found in Alexandria. Whenever he had the time, Joseph, who had obtained work at his trade, sought out travelers from Palestinian provinces, hoping for news from home. None of the news was ever good; the excesses of Herod grew worse.

Thus nearly two years passed before Joseph had another supernatural experience, but at last it came.

Once more the angel interrupted their quiet lives with a sign from the other world; one last dream for Joseph, a vision with great news, the angel declaring:

"Arise and take the child and go into the land of Israel. For they are dead that sought the life of the child."

They are dead! *They* meant Herod! He was king and spoke plurally of himself as "we" this and "we" that, and of him the angel spoke plurally, too, in proclaiming the end of him.

With no question in their minds Joseph and Mary, the most perfect believers in history, obeyed the directive. From his sleep Joseph sprang up and began to pack at once. Taking the child and mother on a donkey, he turned again to the gray and yellow desert that lay between them and home.

Chapter 16 HEROD'S LAST NIGHT ALIVE

As THE long desert days passed and the little family drew nearer to their own part of the world, other travelers in wayside camping confirmed the news.

Yes, Herod the Great was dead—and what a death!

"He must have been mad to kill all those babies in Bethlehem," one wayfarer remarked. "Their bodies had scarcely begun to rot in their graves before their murderer had to follow them in death. You can have no idea what it has been like in Jerusalem the last two years. His own son tried to poison Herod. Did that news reach Egypt? And how Herod had him killed?

"Oh yes, we have had evil's own time of it. Secretly the whole population of Jerusalem was praying every night for Herod's death. And every day there were old women's tales of birds squeaking in the rafters of the palace; vultures winging lower, as if nosing a feast that was soon to come. Omens—everybody was whispering about omens.

"The servants in the palace, of course, kept the rest of us constantly informed. So we know that Herod suffered the most awful agonies. There was a slow fire inside him that seemed to get hotter and hotter. Queer too; it gave him a vehement appetite. He couldn't stop eating. But his entrails were ulcerated and the worst pain of all was in his bowels. So he would eat, and then soon began to scream, and that went on many times a day. His feet were swollen with bags of a transparent fluid that settled there and squashed as he walked; it got so that he could not put his feet down.

"And what a time the king had breathing during that last year! The stench of his breath filled the palace and he snorted all the time. Every now and then he would have convulsions. And here was the singular part of those convulsions: they gave him an inhuman kind of strength, so that he could fling strong men across the room and break skulls against the walls.

"Yet almost until the very end Herod still tried to believe that he was going to get well again, as he had so often done before. He had a hundred doctors from every part of the world. He did everything they told him to do, some of those things being silly and ridiculous, but nothing helped. Only a few months ago he was carried on a litter all the way beyond the river Jordan and bathed himself in the warm baths at Callirrhoe. Another time they lowered his entire body in a vast vessel full of oil. He fainted then, and we all hoped he was dead. But the servants' screams of joy at his supposed death brought him back to life.

"That was when he began to fear that nothing could save him. So for a little while he began to be kind. He gave orders that every soldier should receive a bonus of fifty drachmas. Much larger sums, of course, he gave to the commanders and to his friends. But later he seemed to go out of his mind again; he screamed and ranted against our people and then finally hit upon a most hideous and horrible scheme against us which he at once put into execution.

"One morning he called in his prime minister and gave orders that all the principal men among our people—two hundred of the

Jewish leaders—should be arrested. He ordered workmen to put up a great fence and make a camp inside and in that barracoon, that concentration camp, he caged them alive for a while. But that didn't satisfy him; he changed the orders and had them confined in the hippodrome at Jerusalem. And when the prime minister asked what he intended to do with those two hundred prisoners, all scholars and leaders of our people, Herod told the prime minister to get out. He sent for his sister Salome and her husband Alexis, and this is what he said to them, as taken down behind a curtain by one of our own:

" 'My sister and brother-in-law, I shall die in a little time, so great are my pains; death ought to be cheerfully borne and to be welcomed by all men. But what troubles me principally is this: I know that I shall die without being lamented. Because I have always done my duty as a king, no one is likely to weep for me when I am dead. There will be no mourning of the people. They all hate and despise me and will rejoice at my passing. So, curse them all, I have formed my own plan to outwit them. The minute you see that I am really dead—and make sure of it, sister—act swiftly and discreetly. Let no one know that I am no longer living. Keep my death a profound secret. Call out the soldiers and send them to the hippodrome. Kill every Israelite leader that is imprisoned there. Slay all two hundred without allowing one to escape. Kill them! Then all the people of this wretched country will mourn and weep for their own that we have killed, and when that lamentation is well started, then you can announce my death. And what can they do about it then? I will have had sorrow at my death! Is it not a good scheme, sister?'

"That, my friend, was how it was! Five days later the rapacious King Herod died. But not before he had caused the death of his own son Antipater. He died, but the captives in the hippodrome were not slain, according to his instructions. His people did not obey that last command, that wicked thing, fell, barbarous, hideous. His rule of thirty-seven horrible years is at an end. People say that he stole to his throne like a fox, ruled like a tiger, and died like a dog. A man he was of great barbarity toward all men equally. He was a slave to his passions. His reign was one of plunder and rapine. Yet fortune favored him for a long time. I wonder why?"

Joseph and Mary shuddered with horror at the awful end of their powerful enemy. They listened to vivid descriptions of how he was carried on a golden bier to be buried in high state on the ridge above Jerusalem. The air along the route was full of talk of politics and state affairs and what would happen next in the capital.

From another traveler they learned that Herod's will had been opened; the last will, indeed, for in his illness Herod had torn up his previous will, written a new one, torn that up, and written another new one which he died without a chance to destroy. The effect of this will was to make Joseph at once alter his plans.

By his final testament, a compromise in his palace of conspiracies, Herod carefully broke up the little jigsaw empire he had put together in a long, arduous lifetime. To his son Archelaus he bequeathed Judea with the precious title of king. The troops had given Archelaus homage as soon as the will was read, now all the world knew he was the new ruler in the capital. But not of Galilee! To Herod Antipas, another son, Herod bequeathed Galilee, with Perea, and with the title not of king but of tetrach.

What would life be like in Jerusalem—or any part of Judea—under the new king? Joseph had often heard that of all the sons Archelaus was most like the wicked Herod. He decided not to settle in Judea as he had been planning for the last two years to do. Who could say whether Archelaus in inheriting Herod's throne had not also inherited his fears which had led to the massacre at Bethlehem? Already the gossip of desert caravan men was that Archelaus had gone to Rome to have confirmed by the Emperor his succession and crown under the will of his father—and already, while he was gone, some of his friends had tried to do him in.

Mary and Joseph, crossing the sands of Sinai, took counsel together on these reports and decided not to settle near Jerusalem, as they had thought of doing, but to go back to Galilee, back to Nazareth, where Joseph had a good trade as a carpenter.

Thus the period in their two lives of the supernatural, of wonder and danger and flight and strangeness came to pause. For Joseph that period was never to be renewed. Nearly thirty years of peace and quietude lie before mother and son, sheltered from the world, before the signs will come again, multiplying and beckoning them into danger.

By that time Joseph will have passed on.

Chapter 17 BEHIND THE MASQUERADE

WHEN Jesus learned to toddle, he followed His mother around the house and sang with her at her work. He played with chips of wood and little boats that Joseph carved for Him. He had a companionable smile, sharing every moment in unspoken felicity, and yet from infancy He took time out to be alone, for what seemed reveries and daydreams.

Time to pause, bread in hand by the open door and look knowingly into the sky and the soaring, creamy clouds. To lie in the field on a dewy morning, and press the cool, moist grass against His cheek. To listen at the night window as if the very wind spoke in whispers that only He could understand; to smell Mother's hand, kneading the dough, and to taste, in long, slow mouthfuls, the cool innocence of a cup of milk.

There was in the child Jesus from the very beginning an acute sharpness of all the organs; His were the first perfect faculties since Adam, and by them and through them He received a fulness of sensation not known to those around Him. The sounds He heard, the colors He saw, smells and tastes and feelings were rapturous with a completeness and intensity, an ecstasy even, possible only to the mortal whose soul and body are perfect to receive the gifts of nature.

"He sees more than we do, no matter what He looks at!" Joseph would muse, and Mary would smile, as if to answer:

"And why not?"

Nor was the mother surprised at the friendliness the birds and animals showed Him, nor that He was tender and full of concern, even for ugly little red worms; His sympathies at home with all living things.

Nevertheless Mary and Joseph saw to it that Jesus was strictly instructed in the stern school of Shammai. Sitting on the floor of the synagogue, Jesus was taught from the beginning the Scriptures and the prophets of His people. In His home teaching Mary and Joseph proceeded with awe-filled and secret care. They depended on the grace of God to show them how to bring Him up. He must be taught His lessons. His manners. His skills. So mother and foster father prayed for light, and meanwhile they had their own resources of kindness and common sense.

But often they were baffled.

"I don't know what to think sometimes," Joseph confided one night when Jesus was fast asleep and they were preparing for bed. "Already He looks far beyond our little town."

That was after Joseph had dutifully tried to impart to the boy a sense of old tribal closeness, of intimate and binding family loyalty. Somehow, although He remained silent, Jesus seemed to be nourishing richer and larger loyalties. It was not that the boy seemed far away from His mother and foster father or His relatives; it was, instead, that He showed a friendliness, a willingness to be affectionately close to everyone else too. That broadness of affection was new to Joseph.

But when the carpenter talked to Mary about it, her serenity was undisturbed. From the first she meant to hold on to a complete assurance in the supernatural destiny of her Son. She could never forget how He was conceived, and how born.

Nevertheless, strict rules of family life were completely observed in the household. They faithfully obeyed the laws. Like all their neighbors, they would rather be stoned to death than eat unclean food; they kept to the letter the Levitical ceremonial laws, just as they observed conscientiously all the customs and festivals, days when they might labor and days when they might not. They recited prayers and sang psalms; their lives were consecrated to an exact fulfilment of the Pharisees' regulations. Thus Jesus grew up in an atmosphere of regimented duty where the things one was allowed to do, could not do, and must do, were regulated almost from hour to hour.

On the Sabbath, for example, in the house of Mary and Joseph, one could not light a fire or put one out. A man could not peel a fruit. A woman could not knead her dough. A boy could not wash his dog. A girl could not plait her hair. An old man could not tie a knot in a string. No one could write or cross out what had been written. All was forbidden, except, of course, that a man could go to the help of a bogged cow or a trapped sheep.

Jesus obeyed those laws as a child, but in spite of the grim regime He enjoyed His boyhood. He was lean and strong of body, fleet of foot, unafraid of climbing heights, especially the blunt shoulders of Mount Tabor, only five and a half miles from the town, or of descending into hillside caves; He could shout as loud as the next boy and laugh as gleefully. No matter what happened, He was never known to snivel or accuse, to cry and run at the nose or complain. But Jesus had no taste for triumph. If one thing set Him apart from His playfellows, it was a lack of interest in the rewards of competition. He loved to run, but He cared nothing for a racer's laurel. He would contend in boyish trials of strength but took no pleasure in lording it over His defeated partner; there was joy enough in the mere exercise; joy in the full use of life forces—and what good the trophy?

That was true also in His studies, in which He effortlessly excelled. His friends hated the whole idea of school, but boys in Nazareth had to go whether they liked it or not. Nearly two thousand years ago education in that hillside town was already compulsory, and there was a Nazareth school board that saw to it that no child played hooky after he was six years old.

Invariably Jesus read quickly and easily the scrolls the teachers lent Him, mostly the works of Moses and the prophets; it was as if He already knew the Scriptures and now refreshed His memory. In a short while He knew the writings by heart. Ask Him a question out of Leviticus or Deuteronomy and He could answer it instantly; as Josephus was later to write of most boys and girls of that day, "It was graven into the very soul."

Sometimes Joseph would take Him on a picnic to the top of the highest hill above Nazareth and show the little boy the whole circuit—that, Joseph explained, was the meaning of the word "Galilee" —fifty miles from north to south and thirty-five miles from the seacoast to the boundary line. As they looked out to the distant blue of the Mediterranean Sea, Joseph would point to the long crouch of the Carmel ridge and thence on around the horizon to the peaks of forbidden Samaria. Yonder, in a vast declivity, lay Joseph's favorite vista, the broad sweep of the plain of Esdraelon, carpeted with wild flowers to obliterate the bloodstains of its ancient battles. They could see far into the Jordan Valley, all the way to Gilead and, turning the other way, behold the Sea of Galilee, the mountains of Lebanon, and the snow like a chain of pearl around the high throat of Mount Hermon.

Tired of the grand sights, and of recalling the tales of how Gideon defeated the Midianites and where Saul and Jonathan died together, Joseph and Jesus would open Mary's picnic box and munch awhile, and then lie supine on the grass, forgetting the wide scene of gray rocky hills and green pastures, forgetting the storied past; lying on their backs, they would know the communion of silence which is a strong binder of the affections of men.

But in His daily life Jesus was also looking around Him; he was learning a great deal through His own observations. Already He was beginning to challenge in His own thoughts the tyrannical power exerted by the religious authorities. The people of Nazareth had to be constantly running to the synagogue for advice in the simplest of household affairs. Whatever one wanted to do must be done only on the advice of the priests and with their consent; they settled everything. As a Nazarene lad Jesus was supposed to perform, promptly and obediently, any task set Him by a scribe; He must carry the fellow's bundles, run his errands, water his donkey, sweep out his dirt. The mild eyes of Jesus betrayed no insubordination; His thoughts, in those years of boyhood, were never spoken—except once! And that was some years later on.

Jesus also found the religious services prolonged and tiresome. Everybody had to stand during interminable prayers—petitions to God in which the same thing was said over and over again. The day was to come when Jesus would teach a simple, noble prayer of His own in which there would be none of those "vain repetitions" which so wearied Him as a child.

Actually for Jesus, as for every Nazarene boy of His time, the synagogue was the school of life. There was very little of the world that one could know outside one's own household and synagogue. But the still very young Jesus saw through the imposing masquerade of ecclesiastical services to the atrocious fact that all too often only the letter of the law was being kept while its living spirit was being droned away.

By supernatural insight, His alone, He was looking already beyond the boundaries of family, of village, town, and nation, and beholding a world that should be one world, one home for people and all the people, children of God.

Chapter 18 JESUS BARABBAS

THE boys of the village liked to talk everlastingly about deliverance of the nation from foreign tyranny. At heart they were all little revolutionists. Their games, like cowboys and Indians of today, were of Zealots and Romans, patriots and tyrants. On street corners, around fires in the field, on the steps of the synagogue, their elders too—peddler, shepherd, everybody—talked of a king who was to come one day and free Israel by force of arms. But Jesus showed scant interest in the boys' games of revolution though He heard every day about the crimes of government.

And indeed the years of His childhood were no improvement for Israel over the sway of the late King Herod. The acute misery of the people brought about a rebellion in Galilee when Jesus was eleven years old.

That abortive uprising began and ended in the town of Sepphoris, only four miles away from Nazareth. There was a patriot called Judas of the forbidden Zealot party, and he led a desperate crew—of whom Joseph's old friend Samuel was a vigorous lieutenant—on a madman's enterprise. Those were the days when the secret counsel ran through the province: by blood and sword "the holy simpleton," Judas, was going to save everybody, free everybody from Roman tyranny. "No Lord but Jehovah" was the rallying call; "no tax but to the Temple; no friend but the Zealot." So Judas, the Galilean, raised an army of rebels, a rag, tag, and bobtail valiant crew who, following his bidding, raided the king's armory in Sepphoris and then began to march. Soon enough the Roman colonial troops, under General Varus, cut the army of Judas to pieces, and Sepphoris was burned to the ground.

Jesus would always remember the smell of the cremated city which filled the nostrils of Nazareth. Those inhabitants of Sepphoris who did survive the fire were sold into slavery.

That was a time of panic for the Nazarenes: Judas beheaded on the field of battle, the rebel soldiers in flight and hiding, perhaps in his own cistern. All the neighbors of Joseph had stood on the heights and watched in despair the fury of Roman punishment. Two thousand men, suspected of complicity in the schemes of Judas the Galilean, were crucified in the open country—two thousand crosses with hanging victims—between Sepphoris and Nazareth. Those two thousand crucifixions—some of the victims men He had run errands for —were among the early memories of the boy Jesus.

In the midst of such civil clashes there was the gravest anxiety in Joseph's mind, when one day a long-bearded stranger in Syrian dress walked into the shop and whispered a name. Then Joseph knew the stranger was Samuel in disguise. Samuel, who had survived the broken rebellion and escaped the Romans; Samuel, who now, very casually, dropped in to tell of new, even more desperate plans.

"King Archelaus is worse than Herod but not so smart," Samuel told Joseph late that night as the two stood talking in hushed voices near the front door. In the dim light Joseph looked at his old friend with misgiving. Formerly Samuel, wild as he was, his blackholly eyes full of rebellious zeal, had always in his voice a ring of idealism. Now he sounded tired and disillusioned.

"Have you heard the news, Joseph?"

"What is it now, Samuel?"

"The new king's cruelty has stirred up the people so that they have sent a committee to Rome—secretly, of course—to complain against the puppet ruler to the real boss—the Emperor!"

"The Emperor!" Joseph repeated, and clucked his tongue. He was no politician, but he knew enough to realize that great Caesar Augustus on his throne would not be pleased at such reports. Already he had mastered the world; now he meant to keep it in order and, as he had said, wherever possible in an atmosphere of intellectual liberty. His ambition was to make Rome a light to future history. And it was true that before Octavius, now called Augustus, had come to power, the old republic had been torn with dissensions. As Emperor, he had healed the hatreds, and for forty-five years he had reigned in comparative peace while Virgil composed his epics, Livy wrote his histories, and Ovid the *Metamorphoses*.

What, then, Caesar was likely to ask, was all this disorder in the land of Israel? He was certain to be most majestically annoyed, was he not?

"That is just how it turned out," agreed Samuel. "The committee is back and we know now what is going to happen."

It seemed that the Pharisees on the committee had leagued with envious relatives of Archelaus and fell at the Emperor's feet to report vastly exaggerated accounts of the only disturbances left in his empire.

"This will never, never do!" complained the Emperor angrily, according to Samuel's reports. "I am going to see to it that after this there shall be peace in Palestine forevermore."

"That is an admirable idea," agreed Joseph ironically. "How can it be done?"

"By order of the Emperor, the king will be banished and we will get a new one!"

"A new one! Another one? Is that a remedy? Why cannot the Emperor learn that peace in Palestine can come only from God?"

"From scribes?" scoffed Samuel. "Like Hillel, you mean?"

"Alas," Joseph said, "Hillel is no more."

One of Palestine's earnest seekers after peace, the famous Rabbi Hillel had died only a few weeks before. His maxims were quoted in every synagogue. Once he said to a Gentile who had sought to understand the laws of God:

"That which is unpleasant to you, do not to your neighbor. That is the whole law and all the rest is but its exposition."

"Dead or alive," the insurgent Samuel retorted, "Hillel was of no help. He counseled peace. There can be no peace. It is as I have always told you—Israel must fight, fight to the death. The trouble has been that we have had no leaders. Well, at last I am going to become a leader. Joseph—your hand.

"I am going away from Nazareth and you will know me never again. My old self dies tonight. I shall haunt the caravan roads, pounce and rob and plunder—and slay when I have to; I shall stop at nothing to finance a new rebellion. My old name is forgotten; Samuel is no more."

The brave lift to Samuel's chin, now exposed by moonlight, was slightly adolescent. He saw himself, like any small boy, a rogue, a picaroon adventurer, a patriot. And Joseph saw that nothing could be done about it.

"Alas, my old friend, will nothing stop you from this craziness?"

"Nothing, Joseph. Someday the people of this land will have to choose between your views and mine."

"Your new name? Have you chosen it? What will it be?"

"I have chosen it. Only you may know—because I can trust you. My new name will be Bar-Abbas!"

"I commend you to God, Bar-Abbas!"

"To freedom, if you please! And, Joseph,—kiss the little Son for me. Tell Him I have also taken *His* name. Hereafter I shall be known as Jesus Bar-Abbas!"

And Samuel rushed down the road. Joseph was never to see him again. But Mary was to see him in the darkest hour of life.

"If he would only put his trust in the promises of God," murmured Joseph. "In the Messiah. And yet, he did ask me to kiss our little boy!"

Chapter 19 WHERE IS MY SON?

MEANWHILE, in His school and in conversation Jesus heard more and more of the Messiah who was to bring freedom to the people:

"A prophet like unto me will the Lord raise up to thee."

Writers and haranguers at the crossroads constantly assured the tax-ridden people that the long-awaited Christ would soon be with them. The most popular book at the time, one that Jesus often heard discussed, was by an unknown author and was called *The Praising of Enoch*. It emphasized the old promises of deliverance. More than once Jesus was to mention the book as He preached through Palestine. This and the prophetic book of Daniel were the best sellers of His boyhood.

Everywhere men were quoting from the prophets to anticipate just how the Son of God would come to earth.

"There will be a great star in the heavens to announce His birth," said one.

"He will be born into the line of the house of David in Bethlehem, but He will live in Galilee," said another.

Naturally Joseph and Mary had told Jesus of the three Wise Men who brought Him gifts and said that they had seen His star in the east and had come to worship Him. Also He knew that He had been born in Bethlehem and that Joseph and Mary were both of the princely house of David.

But very early in life Jesus learned what the people were expecting from their Messiah, and He knew that they were wrong. There was coming to them no Savior with supernatural genius for war and government. No Messiah was to lead them in revolution, free them and make them in turn masters of the whole world. God would not send His Messenger to earth merely to rally the glory of David and Solomon. It was in vain that the people waited for such a Messiah—a trinity of patriot, general, and king.

Already more than one man had falsely proclaimed himself as the expected Messiah. Jesus heard much talk of one called Thedeaus. The Jews demanded a sign from the pretender, so he boldly led them up to the Mount of Olives and commanded the walls of Jerusalem to fall down. When the walls stood firm, Thedeaus was left alone.

Such adventures merely emphasized the people's need for a real leader; there was a slow ferment in every heart, a turbulence, an anguish, that threatened to turn into mass hysteria—and that would be restrained by Roman spears.

Such was the state of the world, of the Roman empire, Judea, Nazareth, when Mary and Joseph decided to take the twelve-year-old boy on a visit to Jerusalem for the Passover. Year after year the family made this journey, but this was the first time they would take Jesus with them.

In Jerusalem again Mary's growing boy looked around Him, fascinated by the splendor and the squalor of palaces and slums, the penury in the midst of magnificence, and especially the beauties of the Temple, with its walls of cedar and marble. As He walked with Mary and Joseph through the Gate that was called Beautiful, Jesus carried a few coins that His foster father had given Him: mites and pennies knotted in the hem of His robe; with these copper pieces the boy paid His own way into the Temple courts.

That was when Joseph explained to Him about money in the Temple. Because Judea was a prisoner state and occupied by legions of the Imperial Army, only empire money, coins bearing the head and sign of Caesar, could be used for buying and selling. But the older Jewish coins, by special concession could be (and must be) used within the area of the Temple. When one came to the ancient promontory to worship God, one carried with him the coinage of Rome, but while one was still in the outer area of the Gentiles, the forecourt outside the sacred precincts, one must make an exchange of that silver into Jewish money.

"And," the gentle Joseph added sadly, "a man invariably loses money on the transaction. For this Roman piece he gets less than half in the people's own money, because he has to pay the agio, the premium for changing cash; that is how the money-changers around the Temple get rich! Men like Annas and his friends!"

But why did anyone need money for obligations in the home of God? Why? For to buy sacrifices! One had to pay for doves and lambs, for burnt offerings on the altar. And for these little birds and beasts one was charged five times what they were worth. The profit of that also went to Annas and his friends.

On learning this the Boy Jesus became very pensive. And what thoughtful mind could fail to remember that this city of dreadful contrasts in human existence was the birthplace of Jeremiah—that great prophet to whom the boy felt so close; that singer and saint, who could look into the wrongs of the state and then lift his gaze straight into heaven. And Jesus could remember also the persisting legend that Jeremiah, having been proved right to the people he tried to save, was exiled into Egypt to die a martyr. The world has a way of punishing its friends.

By this time Jesus and His father had crossed the outer court. And still the Boy was remembering, too, that Isaiah the prophet had also once walked these streets, telling the people: "Cease to do evil; learn to do good; seek justice, relieve the oppressed; judge the fatherless, plead for the widow . . ."

Toward the northwest corner of the court there was the terrace, divided into three parts or elevations, one for His mother and the other women, another for the men and boys like Joseph and Himself, and, closest of all to the Sanctuary, a court for the priests. That was where thirteen years before Zachary, now dead, had been stricken dumb. The boy Jesus counted the twelve steps down which the dumbfounded old priest had fled, and admired the gilded doorway and hanging on its gilt rod, the veil of the Temple, a many-colored curtain woven in Babylon during the captivity. Gold spikes on the flat roof reflected the glitter of the sunset, and just over the doorway was a gleaming bunch of golden grapes.

Wherever Jesus looked there were priests. On that very day twenty thousand of them were registered in the Temple and got their living from it. The place swarmed with men in ceremonial costume—Levites with pointed caps and large pockets in which they carried the books of the law; Pharisees with their broad philacteries and deep white fringes on purple gowns; solemn Essenes in white robes—and with them from Galilee and Judea and the land beyond

Jordan crowds of earnest believers who came to buy lambs or pigeons and lay them on the altar to be burned; women after childbirth, sick people after recovery, grateful men and women and those who hoped soon to have cause to be grateful—Jewish Parthians and Medes with close-cropped beards, Elamites, the dwellers in Mesopotamia and Cappadocia; Israelites from Egypt and Libya and Rome—uncounted hundreds and thousands of them. Bargains were being struck, greetings exchanged, psalms sung; genuflections—all day long, the smell of burning flesh, the smoke of incense.

Jesus was gripped with this spectacle of color and noise and movement. The voice of the Temple choir, the sounding trumpets, and the music of the sweet-stringed harps of old King David softened the intensity of His dark eyes. He watched the people kneel and worship and heard the phrases of the priests and the intoned responses of the congregation; presently there was in all their hearts a mystical sense of communion as they sang the Sixty-sixth Psalm:

> "I will go into thy house with burnt offerings: I will pay thee my vows,
>
> "Which my lips have uttered, and my mouth hath spoken when I was in trouble . . .
>
> "Blessed be God, which hath not turned away my prayer, nor his mercy from me."

But why did they burn the animals? Why did they imagine God would be pleased when altars bled and smoked? Why did the poor have to spend their money to buy animals? Why must they buy them only from the priests? What did the priests do with the money? Did not such absurdities detract from the dignity and goodness of the Idea of God?

What was it that Amos, the prophet, had said?

> "I hate, I despise your feasts. And I will take no delight in your solemn assemblies. Yea, though you offer me your burnt offerings and meal offerings, I will not accept them; neither will I regard the peace offerings of your fat beasts. Take thou away from me the noise of your songs; and I will not hear the melody of viols.
>
> "*But let justice run down as water, and righteousness as a mighty stream.*"

Why had no one carried on the fight for the realities of religion that old Amos had begun years before?

Seized suddenly with a great warm rush of zeal and a surge of such questions, Jesus stood up, while Joseph remained praying with closed eyes. Burning with eagerness, the twelve-year-old strode into an offshoot shelter of the inner Temple where the Fathers of Israel sat with the rolls of Scriptures around them and debated the texts of judges and prophets. A circle of admiring intellectuals was listening in awestruck silence.

Into this ring of professors of the sacred teachings walked the boy from Galilee and His tongue was on fire with the questions He now put to them. He seemed eager to learn from these sages, but they recoiled from His honest inquiries.

Were ever such questions put to these brains before? Never, never! He was not there to higgle and dispute about trifling matters. The savants of the law listened first with scorn and irritation, then with incredulity, with astonishment, friendly, but with awakening alarm. Who was this radical child that dared to question and challenge the recondite technicalities and the established order of a thousand years? And why did He continually seek to bring these scholarly minds back to the troublesome problems of human behavior?

Day and night came and the fifteen men still tried to answer the questions of this unknown stripling. New judges took the place of weary elderly ones, and the debate went on with the unwearying lad.

It was impossible by logic or tergiversation to dislodge Him from the simplicity of His position; He merely kept reminding them of the beauty of their own neglected teachings, quoting every now and then from the magnificent simplicity of Micah, the prophet, when he demanded:

"What does Jehovah request of you but to do justly, and to love kindness, and to walk humbly with your God?"

The new recruits to this famous debate had taken no note of the passing of time until Jesus, looking over the heads of His antagonists, saw the pale face of Mary. Tears glistened in her reproachful eyes; for the first and only time since He was born she seemed not to comprehend.

"Son, why have you done so to us? Behold, your father and I have sought you—sorrowing."

At once Jesus made His farewell to the groggy teachers; even the newest arrivals were worn out with the unwonted exercise He had given their brains. Around Mary's shoulders He wrapped the cloak of deeper blue that she wore now, and took her hand and led her toward the gate, and as they walked together, she told Him what had been happening while He was immersed in his first mental joust with order, custom, and the way people have always done things.

It seemed that Mary and Joseph had started on the journey back to Nazareth, feeling sure that Jesus was following with a troop of other Nazareth boys. But when they began to search for him, Jesus was not to be found. That was why, as soon as the sun was up, Mary and Joseph turned their faces back toward Jerusalem. There, at last, after weary search, they found Him arguing the law with the elders!

Looking into Mary's eyes, Jesus said with a tender smile:

"How is it that you sought me? Did you not know that I must be about my Father's business?"

Did she not know? Why should He think she would know? And then Mary remembered that dark night when she had fled Nazareth. When the supernatural had awakened her, she could not call mother and father and hope for their comprehension of her incomprehensible experience—in the conception of this child. Did you not know, Mother?

For that moment it was Mary and Joseph who felt like children and Jesus their instructor. But only for that moment—then He was their boy again. With an impulsive gesture He embraced His mother and kissed the gray and golden beard of Joseph. They had no further cause to worry. All the rest of His youth Jesus obeyed them. Mary watched Him grow up into strong manhood, advancing in wisdom.

Chapter 20 STRANGE WORD FROM THE SOUTH

For eighteen years, until Jesus was thirty, He and Mary lived in Nazareth. In that long period of obscurity Joseph died, and so did Mary's parents, Joachim and Anna. For His mother and Himself Mary's son earned a living carrying on the work in the carpenter shop.

As a young man He was a solitary figure in a boisterously sociable community. What He saw in Nazareth was a miniature of the whole—sorrow and bitter poverty and bewilderment and oppression. He saw the people exploited by their own leaders, betrayed by their own flesh and blood, despoiled by thieves in high places, and ordered around by superstitious old men who split hairs over rules and regulations. Yet He saw, too, that the men and women of Nazareth had fortitude and courage. They had hopes and dreams. They had good instincts as well as bad. He not only pitied them but loved them. Humanity was worth saving!

The day was coming, as He had known from the beginning, when He must drop His carpenter's tools, leave mother and home, and devote the remainder of His life to bringing light to the bewildered and frightened. No one else would or could offer them new life of hope, in this world or the next.

Thus long before He left the shelter of Mary's home Jesus saw Himself in opposition to the priestly classes, the rich and the powerful, who used religion for their own ends. The clash was sure to come. His fate was sealed the day Jesus began to look around Him and do His father's business, which was to bring light, to expose the darkness of evil to the light of truth, and to teach the poorest man the rich meaning and possibilities of life.

And what would He tell about the meaning of life? The reason for it? He had listened to the talk of oriental travelers through Nazareth, chattering about Nirvana, the denial of individuality. From them He knew the Vedic holy books of India, and the Sutras, and tales of their sacred Mahabharata. As they believed, one human life was like a drop of water falling into the ocean; men are still assuring other men of that same fallacy, and other men are still believing it; all identity to be lost, a man being nothing. Jesus would recall to them the truth. Man, individual man, with his infinite capacity to know the bliss of growth, the joy of action, the wonder of beauty, was the creature to whom He would address Himself; to man, who had immortal individuality.

So the maturing Jesus, now nearly thirty years old, and brooding on the tribulations of the world, was ready to offer it joy. No dreary servitude, but a new way of living, a great search to be entered upon to find the kingdom of God. Not the kingdom set up by overthrow and revolt and independence; not the sort of thing Samuel, His foster father's friend, now called Jesus Barabbas, would hope for, but the Father's kingdom, not of this world as yet but one to be brought here by love. Of such unbounded capacity would the subjects of that kingdom become that man or woman could ask what they would and they should have it. All that men and women of good will had ever hoped and dreamed of good could come true.

Not the shadow but the substance. Only they must first seek the truth and the truth would make them free. And that was a freedom where men were just to other men, kind to their fellows, loving and brotherly, adoring God, their Father. Such freedom in which war could not exist. Not only a world of one God but of one family with God as its Father. Let man love God first and then his fellow men; that summed it.

The torment of the world all around Him made clear how urgently the message was needed. What respect could the people of Galilee feel for the national life when they beheld their tetrarch, Herod Antipas, stealing his brother's wife and making her his queen? That recent and shocking indecency was doing more than rousing indignation; it was causing people to lose heart, to ask if anything mattered any more.

In the high hills around His home Jesus the workman slowly dreamed into objective form the message He had been born to deliver. Now His heart was on fire with a dangerous purpose. He had reached sturdy manhood; His hair was long and soft and golden brown and hung around His shoulders; He had His mother's glorious dark eyes; His muscles were strong from hard work. His face was paler than the skin of most men. . . .

Suddenly a strange word came to Narazeth—word of a strong man from the wilderness of Judea, a man who was preaching in various towns down south and blessing people by dipping them in the water of the Jordan River; a new man named John.

"That John," the widow Mary told Jesus, "is your own cousin; he is the son of Zachary and Elizabeth."

And the same John was telling great crowds that he was the herald, the forerunner, preparing the reception for the Savior of the world!

His message was that the Messiah was coming at last.

Book Three

THE PREPARATION

Chapter 21 THE VOICE IN THE WILDERNESS

JESUS was profoundly moved by what He learned about His cousin John.

The story was brought down by traders from the capital how John was creating a furore, not only in Jerusalem but in all the countryside. The old-age child of Zachary and Elizabeth had grown in thirty years to be a giant. From birth John had been strong and powerful, as Mary well remembered. During childhood he had been brought to Nazareth on occasional visits, but in early manhood, after his father and mother died, the youth had vanished. For years his relatives heard little about him, although there were reports that he lived in a rocky cave in the blistered valley below Jerusalem near the Dead Sea, and that he ate only locusts and wild honey.

Now, suddenly, he had emerged as a public character, and already he was suspect in the eyes of the Temple police. Perhaps that was because he was different from ordinary men. Around his loins, so Jesus was told, John wore a girdle made from the skins of wild beasts; his cloak was of camel's hair, and his own hair and beard were long and tangled. Bronzed arms upraised, John would stand day after day on the outskirts of towns and shout to the crowds that the time had come for the people to repent of their bad lives.

To people who had neglected and then virtually forgotten the stern ideas of the prophet Isaiah these words of John had a startling sound.

"Do penance!" he shouted. "The Kingdom of Heaven is at hand."

His audiences were not quite sure what he meant by the Kingdom of Heaven. But they knew, well enough, that they had plenty to repent of. To their amazement this wild-haired John was not accusing merely the poor, like themselves, alone, as the priests and the scribes had generally done. No, John, fearless, fiery apparition from the desert, laid about him on *all* sides, sparing no one; not mighty Caesar who reigned in Rome, nor Pontius Pilate who was the Emperor's official agent in Jerusalem—not even Herod Antipas, the cruel son of the great Herod, and builder of Tiberius, whose title was Tetrarch and who still ruled the province of Galilee, after thirty years of discord.

Such effrontery as John's made sensational news even in the cynical streets of Jerusalem. From out of the capital great crowds streamed, toiling down steep and rocky defiles, out into the parched and desert plains, to listen to this new man's voice crying in the wilderness.

"You offspring of vipers!" John shouted imprudently at the arriving hordes. "Who has warned you to flee from the wrath to come?"

Instead of getting angry at the abuse, many of them lifted their robes and waded into the water, doing just as he asked—which was, as a sign of penance, to submit to baptism, a cleansing rite in which remorseful men were splashed and blessed.

More than one of his puzzled followers had asked John if he were the expected Christ, the promised Deliverer and Savior of Israel. His answer, repeated around camp fires of resting caravans and over bake stoves and cook pots in a hundred towns, was:

"I, indeed, baptize you with water. But there shall come one mightier than I the latchet of whose shoe I am not worthy to loose. He shall baptize you with the Holy Ghost—and with fire!"

When these tales were talked over in Mary's kitchen, she was reminded of the words of Isaiah, the favorite prophet of Jesus:

"A voice of one crying in the wilderness; prepare ye the way of the Lord; make straight his paths . . ."

It was when He heard these tales of John that Jesus sighed, laid down His carpenter tools, and after a tender farewell to Mary started off alone, on foot, going from Galilee to the wilderness—to see for Himself.

For most of the journey His way led him along the same road that He had traveled with His mother and Joseph often before. After days of lonely trudging He came to a desolate region: bare mountainsides and limestone ravines where nothing grew; ancient rock tombs everywhere; pebbles and broken stones, emptiness and death. Hurrying on, He reached the lower part of the Jordan Valley, welcome sight with tamarisks, reeds, and willows. Near the bank of the narrow muddy river He saw a crowd of people in a trap of silence as they hearkened to John. Harsh and distinct, His cousin's voice resounded in the hot, dry air:

"And now the ax is laid to the root of the trees!"

Without difficulty Jesus made His way to the front; presently He stood calmly before John. For the first time since boyhood the cousins were face to face; John hulking, vociferous, sweating with earnestness; Jesus, taller, gaunt, and pale, in perfect tranquillity. A long moment and neither spoke, while the crowd watched curiously amid a low buzz of speculation. In that historic meeting—though doubts were later to assail the mind of one—both Jesus and John were sure. They knew their mission; knew, too, that they were doomed men.

In a voice so low that only John could hear, Jesus said that He had come to be baptized by his cousin. John was shocked.

"But it is I who ought to be baptized by you," he objected. "And you come to me?"

Jesus lifted His head and replied with a disarming smile:

"Permit it to be so now—for so it becomes us."

Then John bowed his wild head, that head so soon to be severed, and the two cousins walked together into the tumbling Jordan. There Jesus submitted His body to the rite of baptism—that perfect body that was soon to be nailed to a cross.

When the simple ceremony was over, Jesus, looking up through dripping eyes, saw a white pigeon flying over His head, hovering, pausing, with fluttering wings. The bird lighted on His shoulder and in it He knew that the Spirit of God had appeared to Him. Many in the watching crowd asserted that they heard a voice from heaven say:

"This is my beloved son, in whom I am well pleased."

This brief ceremony over, Jesus pressed John's hand in farewell. Telling no one what He intended to do, He made His way alone back into the wilderness. He was both led by the Spirit of God and driven by it; impelled and compelled to a great and lonely test. This parched and arid place was to be His place of testing; here, with red-tailed buzzards wheeling overhead, He was to endure a hideous experience none the less frightful because He deliberately invited the trial upon Himself.

On a hillside He found a cavern and there He made His solitary camp. His sole reason for retreating to this grotto was that He must become acquainted with human suffering and temptation. He had to know them at first-hand and altogether before He could begin His work which John had just welcomed. He must overcome temptation Himself—as a man, not as God—before He advised other men what they must do.

That was why Jesus made His way into this gigantesque waterless region one day to be called Quarantaria—an inchoate place like a piece of creation begun but not finished; abandoned by all except fanatics and madmen and a sect of queer ascetics called Essenes who had no property except in common in the dead lands where they lived—a mountainous expanse of stone ravines, blistering hills, and beds of crumbling shale, where no birds ever roosted except the birds of prey; a lonely, scorched, and gloomy place fit only for panthers and wild boar.

Here Jesus forced upon Himself a grueling discipline of fasting and solitude. For forty days He remained there eating nothing. And during those forty days the little home at Nazareth and the blessed face of Mary His mother seemed very far away.

It was only after those forty weakening days and nights that Jesus was subject to the ordeal of temptation. Not until He was faint and exhausted did the temptations come—at a time when He felt weakest, most lonely, and friendless.

He stood on the height with evil itself. Around Him lay a scene like the panorama of the world: near at hand the dead yellow rock baked in the merciless heat of this forsaken valley, down which, in clear view, a lion stalked a stag. Off in the southern distance lay the plain of Zoar and Sodom and Gomorrah, fit backdrop for this bitter temptation. To the north the hills of Moab behind the poisonous mists rising out of the Dead Sea; sand and gravel casting up heat; torrid air and vicious smells, desolation—and to the heart of the man Jesus was offered now all the beguilements and blandishments and cajoleries that have, since Eden, plagued the human race—uttered more often than not in quotations from the Scripture; Satan is a great repeater of God's words.

Why not abandon His great mission to help the suffering people? Why not think, instead, of Himself? After all, did the Son of God have to go on with this unnecessary farce? He who had the power to bring a feast ready to hand if He but gave the word! And another thing—why remain a lonely, obscure man, a carpenter about to turn wayside preacher? If the miraculous signs of His birth were to be trusted, then He had the power of God, and all the world would have to serve Him, and He would know such titanesque glory as no conqueror in history had ever known—not Darius, Alexander, Caesar. All mankind would adore Him.

Why not?

His answer He drew from Scriptures of long ago:

"The Lord, your God, shall you adore and Him only you shall serve—not in bread alone does man live, but in every word that proceeds out of the mouth of God. Get you behind me, Satan!"

In his deliberately weakened condition evil had not been easy to resist. No temptation ever is. But now Jesus, who in addition to being really God was also a real man, had experienced the torments that come to men. And He had banished the temptations by the example of sheer devotion.

When the torturing forty days were over, haggard Jesus walked slowly back toward the Jordan River. It was good to come out again from the hot region where Cousin John had spent most of his life; good to feel the bracing, invigorating wind blowing on His perspiring face as He trudged nearer to the river. Dates in His sunburned hands, He walked as He broke the long fast.

His cousin John He found preaching to crowds even greater than before. As Jesus stood on the fringe of the multitude and listened to the crowd's chatter, it became clear that in Jerusalem the authorities were already deeply disturbed about John the Baptist. He could pick up what the Temple politicians had been saying:

"This John is a violent man who at any moment may incite the people themselves to violence."

"He mocks our authority; he reviles Pharisees and Sadducees as hypocrites."

So, it seemed, the priestly leaders had just appointed an investigating committee. A deputation had been ordered to go down to Bethania, beyond the Jordan, where John was currently preaching, to ask certain questions. Their hope was that the Baptist's answers would form the basis, later, of an indictment against himself.

So here were the members of the committee now, near the very elbows of Jesus; their leader coldly facing John and demanding to know whom he claimed to be. And John, who saw instantly what was bothering them, answered:

"I am not the Christ."

"What? Then are you the reincarnation of the old prophet Elias?"

This, because the people had a prophecy that Elias the prophet was to return from death, reincarnated just before the coming of the Messiah.

"I am not!"

"Well, who are you, then?"

"I am the voice of one crying in the wilderness"—thus, by quoting an old prophecy, he identified himself as the herald of the Christ to come.

But he baptized, which was a ceremony supposed to cleanse men of sin. How dare he do that if he were not the Christ?

"I am baptizing with water. But there has stood one in the midst of you . . ."

John paused. His bold and searching gaze had picked out the pale face of Jesus. There was a moment of utter stillness. Then John resumed:

". . . whom you know not. The same is He that shall come after me. Who is preferred before me! The latchet of whose shoe I am not worthy to loose!"

The glum deputies from Jerusalem shook their heads and departed, shoving against Jesus without a glance in His direction and unknowing whom they had jostled. The crowd again engulfed John, and Jesus went on His own way.

Chapter 22 NEW FRIENDS

The next morning Jesus took a walk and came face to face with the Baptist. At the sight of his cousin, worn and thinned from desert hardship, John threw up his hands and murmured:

"Behold Him who takes away the sins of the world! This is the Son of God!"

That day and the others that followed Jesus lingered, watching John and listening to his speeches and talking with him in lonely walks at night. But soon came a bright morning when the two were to part, never to meet again in this life.

That was when John was standing with two friends, a young man with the Greek name of Andrew and the other a good-looking northerner, also called John. These two Galileans rented boats in a fisherman's guild at Capernaum, also called Copharnaum, on the inland sea. Good friends they had been since boyhood, yet no chums were ever more unlike. Andrew was a sturdy, hardheaded man, proud of his sound business judgment. On the other hand, John was excitable, imaginative, and full of curiosity. He had a stormy nature, too, and those who thought him over-gentle or effeminate were preposterously mistaken. A day was to come when John, feeling that Jesus had been insulted, would plead with the Master to call down fire from heaven upon His foes.

This Andrew and this John were frowning and puzzled as they stood talking with the Baptist. For some days they had lingered in the neighborhood, listening attentively to all John had to say, but this was the first time they had ever spoken to him privately.

"You are fishermen from the North Lake?" John asked in surprise. "Why did you travel all this long way—just to listen to me?"

Andrew put it very succinctly:

"We earn very little money and most of that goes for taxes. We can't even afford to eat the fish we catch in our own nets. A dog's life is better. What can we do? Jump into the sea and end it? Then someone tells us a man is preaching down south, near Jerusalem, and that he has the secret of a happy life. A desperate man will try anything . . ."

And here the Galilean gave a wintry smile, as his companion added:

"So we tried you!"

"And have I helped much, John?"

At the directness of the question the two fishermen were embarrassed. Before they could find speech the ragged Baptist pointed over their shoulders, where Jesus was walking toward them; he whispered to the two bewildered fishermen:

"Look! There is the real Lamb of God!"

This was a profound utterance, which his two groping inquirers fully grasped; it was an immense tribute to Jesus. As the Lamb of God, He became the living reality of which the Passover lamb was a symbol in the religion of Israel; by the same token, fulfilling the prophecy of Isaiah and Jeremiah. It was a statement to stun the two men.

"I saw the Spirit of God descend on Him when I baptized Him with water," testified John. "He it is who baptizes with the Holy Ghost. This is the Son of God!"

There was no mistaking the urgency in the Baptist's words. Perhaps no odder pair ever stood together than Andrew and John that morning: fishermen away from the water, and from their nets and hauls; concerned only with the hard mystery of the world and the misery in their own lives. Not philosophers and mystics, they were interested less in truth than in their daily problems; these two practical young men from the Capernaum beach were consumed with a desire to find out whether it was worth while to go on living the hard life which was all they knew. Instead of imparting to them some magical secret, or merely telling them to return to their work in Galilee and lead pious lives, the Baptist pointed to the approaching Jesus and described Him as the Lamb of God. That might even mean the Messiah!

More, he prodded the two young men to follow this stranger, now walking past and on toward the end of town, if they wanted to learn the true meaning of life.

With hasty and grateful glances the Galileans hastened after the lithe figure, already crossing the sunlit square of Bethania. At the sound of overtaking footsteps Jesus slowed down and looked over His shoulder; then, halting at once, He turned and faced them. They saw a lean, clean-washed man of thirty, pale but muscular, with a brief golden beard and flowing yellow-brown hair and immense dark eyes. He laid a hand on Andrew's shoulder and smiled at John.

"Looking for someone?" He asked. His winning manner told them that somehow He understood their plight—disheartened men, almost completely discouraged. In the springtime, now that the rains had ceased, they had tramped a long way with their still-unanswered questions: Was life worth living? Why toil and die in a world without any visible purpose or sense to it? Was life only the tragic, mixed-up mess it seemed to them?

Jesus, looking through space and time, could foresee the fate of this earnest young Andrew—one day to be tied like a letter "X" to a blazing cross; that would be in Patras. The future of John, too, who, in old age, was to behold visions and write the Book of Revelation.

To this pair of confused men Jesus spoke with bold directness, explaining that He was planning a tour of all the Palestinian region —a long series of roadside discourses to the people, trying to answer just such questions. He would need helpers immediately, but He did not want hasty enthusiasts who might abandon Him just as hastily. Not quick converts but firmly convinced ones were necessary. Before inviting them to be the first to join His mission He would require long discussions and debate with them; hours, even days of sharp questions—as many as they could think up. He insisted that they must use their brains; He would not accept obsequious assent to His ideas but logical, innermost conversion, because He was not merely asking them to give Him a part of their time. He needed their lives! Their souls! So they must make sure. In the end, if they believed in His message, they could join together and look for other disciples.

To all of which the fishermen repeated their words:

"Master, show us where you live and we will go there with you right now!"

"Come and see!"

Jesus led the way to lodgings in one of the temporary booths outside the town, and from the twilight of the crow to the twilight of the dove, as dusk and dawn were called, the three sat together, and never before had John and Andrew heard talk like His.

Again and again Jesus insisted that they must question Him thoroughly. They were perturbed men, out of balance, full of a frustrated sense of insecurity and injustice. When He spoke of a free, new vision of kindness and sacrifice, the overwhelming sweetness of His personality struck their hearts like lightning. Under the spell of His power they were quickly convinced, but Jesus refused to accept their hasty conversion. First they must try Him out, face Him with every doubt, confound Him if they could—for they must feel not only His love in their hearts, they must, He reiterated, also be logically persuaded. He wanted their good sense as well as their faith, because for the work to which He would attract them a man must be so sure (as well as enraptured) that he would leave home, family, life itself to follow in His steps. A convert must not only have the gift of faith but logical conviction as well.

If they could think of no more doubts, He would point out the objections they had overlooked. Night and day they asked and listened and asked again—but there came a time when they could think of no more to ask. They accepted all that He had offered them, knowing, too, that even sterner phrases of the truth would come later.

Even so, they were enthusiastically ready to join Him. They felt immensely thrilled and impressed. There was no arrogance in this teacher's manner and no formality; already in those brisk hours they had come to feel as if they had known and loved Him of old.

Andrew posed a final question:

"Master, all that you propose for the world, a life of sacrifice and inner communion with the Father in heaven, sounds wonderful to us. But have you come to change the law of Israel?"

Jesus shook His head slowly.

"No, Andrew, I come, not to change the law, but to fulfill it!"

Instantly the two fishermen turned to each other. Did He mean what that answer might hint? That He was the Messiah? He had not said so. They did not ask; their hearts were burning now with a great exhilaration; merely being with Him had filled them with a sense of peace.

"Master," said John, "we shall go with you in this undertaking. You have warned us that these ideas are dangerous. Let them be so! They are worth dying for!"

Later Andrew confided that he had a brother that he would like the Master to meet, and ran off to find him. Meanwhile Jesus and John discovered that they, too, were blood cousins—strange as it seemed, this younger John was the son of Zebedee and of Salome, who was a grown-up sister of Mary. Until this time the cousins had never met.

Busy washing big, clumsy feet at the town fount, Simon the elder brother of Andrew looked tired and exasperated. He was a tall, broad, bulging man with robust shoulders and a rugged, healthy beard; eyes bright and fierce; face perpetually disgruntled.

"Simon!"

"Hey? Oh, so it's you. Laggard! What makes you heave and grunt so, Andrew?"

"I'm out of breath, that's all, Simon. We have found Him! And I ran all the way to tell you about Him!"

"Who has found——"

"John and I."

"John and you have found what?"

"I hesitate to say it, but I actually believe we have found the most wonderful new teacher in the world. He knows the answer to every question you can think of."

"What are you blabbering about now, Andrew?"

"We have found a Messenger of God. I am sure of it."

Simon milked his beard and shook his bald head and wrinkled his freckled nose.

"Don't believe a word of it," he growled. "You two strike me as getting sillier all the time. First you run after John the Baptist. You think *he's* the one. Then he tells you in plain words he is not. *Now* you fasten on somebody else—"

"Come and take a look for yourself."

Simon finished drying his enormous toes. He knew that Andrew was a careful man, and a conservative, often keeping Simon himself with both feet on the ground.

"All right," he yielded, "I will go with you and set you right!"

It was dusk when the two brothers came to the booth where John still sat listening to Jesus. As the great hulk of Simon filled the entrance and his shadow—a shadow that was one day to heal diseases—fell at the feet of Jesus, the Nazarene's face seemed to light up in richer welcome for the bald and bearded fisherman. Again the Master of timelessness with inner vision could perceive the future: lighted gardens in Rome and a cross turned topsy-turvy, with this same impetuous, baldheaded, square-bearded braggart, crucified head downward and burned alive.

Jesus embraced him enthusiastically, exclaiming:

"You are Simon, son of Jona! But you shall be called Peter."

All were stunned at this extraordinarily friendly reception. The Master spoke with immense feeling in His simple words, as if He meant much more than He was saying. Simon, to be called Peter, and his brother Andrew, and John their friend, all waited for Jesus to say more.

Chapter 23 THE CATERER IS AMAZED

But after that greeting Jesus changed the subject. He proposed that they set out together and He would explain His message to them during the journey; since they were all natives of Galilee province, they would all walk home. To this the three were glad to agree. But the long trek up the stony northern roads had hardly begun when their number began to grow. The first recruit was a friend of Andrew, a wayfarer like himself with a Greek name, Philip, whom they overtook on the highway.

This shy, thoughtful Philip, although he had been born in Capernaum, had lived for most of his life in a watering place called Bethsaida. Now he was determined to get out of the town—once a simple port of fishermen, it had lately become a resort for carousing Romans, and no decent native could tolerate the open drunkenness and roistering lust and lawlessness of the soldiers.

Jesus welcomed the young fugitive with instant approval, and Philip not only agreed to join the party and hear about the new teachings and the plans for spreading them, but he offered to try to enlist another friend. Begging a free ride on a passing camel, he hurried some miles forward until he spied the friend who was named Nathanael Bartholomew lying under a fig tree and staring at the sky. The skeptical young fellow was wondering what a philosophic man could possibly do with his life in a land of oppression like this one.

"Nathanael!" called Philip, forsaking his mount. "We have found a most wonderful teacher. He is so wonderful, he might even be the man Moses promised. And the one the prophets promised too!"

"Really, now!" mocked Nathanael with a noisy snort. "Wonderful, wonderful. Well, gullible, who is he?"

"His name is Jesus."

"Yes, and from where does this Jesus sprout?"

"From Nazareth."

"From Nazareth?"

"Yes!"

Nathanael's laugh was lazy and patronizing.

"Can any good thing come from Nazareth?" he jested.

"You better come and see!" ordered Philip, yanking his old playmate unceremoniously to his feet. And he forcibly led Nathanael down the road, until they caught sight of the approaching Master.

"Look!" called Jesus, waving to Nathanael from a distance. "An Israelite indeed, in whom there is no guile."

All the others smiled, as Jesus added:

"Before Philip called you, when you were under the fig tree, I saw you."

Nathanael blinked. He *had* been under the fig tree. But that was miles beyond, where Jesus could not possibly have seen him. He stammered:

"Master . . ."

But Jesus put a friendly arm around him.

"Because I said to you that I saw you under the fig tree, you believe!"

His bearded chin toward the sky, he calmly promised:

"Greater things than these you shall see."

Once again Jesus had seen far beyond, not merely the present time and immediate space, but into the future of this Nathanael Bartholomew, the son of Talmai of Cana, in Galilee—the future in Arabia Felix where this innocent and simple man, who always considered himself a skeptic and a sophisticate, would one day be flayed alive; and nearly a score of centuries deeper into the future, when his bones would be venerated in the Church of St. Bartholomew on an island in the Tiber.

But on that faraway day in Judea Nathanael Bartholomew could not see an hour ahead; he only felt convinced he had found this greatest and truest friend, and that was enough!

When, with his five new followers, Jesus came back home to Nazareth, He found His own household in a happy dither. It happened that a daughter of friends of Mary was getting married. The family lived in the village of Cana, Nathanael Bartholomew's home town, and Mary was planning to go over to help in serving the feast; in the midst of her scurrying Jesus and His new friends reached the house. Eyes shining, the gray-haired mother gave them all a welcome. Although Peter, Andrew, John, Philip, and Nathanael made a handful in the little home, whatever Jesus did was right in Mary's eyes; His friends were her friends, and she made room for them.

More, she suggested they all come with her to the wedding. So, although the newcomers were a little weary, they all walked five miles more down the highroad from Nazareth until toward sunset they came into Cana of Galilee. Then, as now, it was a mere formless jumble of stone houses and mud huts; a few gardens of the well-to-do, with cypress trees and olive groves. The narrow streets were overrun with burnoosed men straddling camels, veiled women on donkeys, and underfed children, scales on their eyes, scabs on their faces, carrying lambs upside down by their forefeet through streets of noise, filth, stench.

This evening there was a great stir of elation because of the wedding. Jesus did not often attend parties of this kind; He was too thoughtful, too studious, too solitary for such festivities. But tonight He had a happy time. He and the five disciples put aside all their intricate discussions and enjoyed themselves like everyone else at the happy affair. The fun was at its height when Mary beckoned to her son.

Quietly the mother whispered a story of their hosts' sudden embarrassment. More guests had come than had been expected—Jesus and His five friends among them!—and now the wine was about to give out just when the festivities were at their peak; the caterer was in despair.

"I want more wine!" squealed one curly-haired guest, holding up a large, wide-mouthed goblet—a beaker which he turned upside down.

Jesus took His mother's hand, His face full of a meaning tender and intimate. There was a note of challenge in His voice as He addressed her in the respectful phrase of that day:

"Woman! What is that to me? And to you? My hour is not yet come."

All around was song and laughter. In the corner where mother and son talked there had come suddenly, startlingly, one moment of significance for all the rest of history—a moment in which He, the son, and she, the mother, were partners. Do you realize, He was really saying to Mary, what it will mean if I do as you ask? You are asking me to show before the eyes of men and women, merely for the success of this convivial affair, the unlimited power of Almighty God. If I do what you ask, if I show this power, do you know what will happen? The story will fly over the land. All privacy, all quiet, all further time of preparation will be gone. My ministry must begin immediately. And when that happens, I take my first step—and you go with me—to the cross. All this that wedding guests may have more to drink?

She knew His thoughts, she, who kept so many things in her heart. She knew that by woman death had come into the world, and she believed that she had been given Eve's second chance, through this son, to bring salvation. For her, as well as Him, this was the moment their faces turned to Calvary.

Both knew what it meant. Their handclasp tightened; then she turned away, and went to the waiters, and told them:

"Whatever He tells you to do—do it!"

Jesus turned and walked to the back of the room. There He found the six stone water pots which were a part of the furnishings of every well-appointed home where frequent religious purifying ceremonies had to be held. Beckoning the attendants, Jesus asked them to fill the jars with water. Puzzled but polite, they did as He requested, filling the pots to the brim. Next, at His direction, they dipped up some of the fluid in a ladle. Then they screamed and shouted. The color had changed! The water was red! Indeed, it was no longer water at all—it was wine!

The hired caterer rushed up, tasted the wine, glared around him furiously, and swaggered up to the bride's father. What, he wanted to know, was happening here? Any sensible man served the best wine at the beginning of the feast and then, when everybody had had plenty to drink, he would serve the inferior stuff. But this late wine was the best the steward had ever tasted in all his forty years as a caterer in Galilee.

Soon everybody in the room was talking about the wonderful wine, but Jesus and His disciples, in deep, reflective silence, were already walking back to Nazareth.

Chapter 24 THE WICKED QUEEN

THE following day Jesus and His mother set out with His disciples to visit their home town of Capernaum and meet their relatives and friends. Again they trudged the five miles to Cana and then continued on, down and round a mountain with two humps, where one day Jesus was to preach His greatest sermon.

And still on they trudged, past many of the bloodiest old scenes of Israel. Yonder were the caves of Endor, where Saul crept to have his future told by a witch. On, far below the level of the sea, where beside the lake of Galilee stood Capernaum.

A great sight on the day they arrived, this lake port, seething with energy, overrun with men and women of all nations. Mother and son looked around them, startled and interested and a little sad at all the scurry of the place. It was a town rich, busy, and corrupt, one of the chief stations on the great route from Damascus to the Mediterranean ports of Egypt; a market where silver hordes of fish were carted through the streets, where wine from climbing grape arbors stained the bare feet of farm girls, and there were so many olive groves that a man could take a bath in oil. Through its high streets the caravans moved north and south, and one could buy and sell wheat and silk and ivory; well-paid artisans walked through the bazaars with hands stained blue from the indigo dyes made in next-door Magdala.

When Jesus and His mother came to Capernaum with the five new friends, the city was called the Queen of the Lake, the Majesty of Galilee. In rich glory it stood below desert mountains of yellow limestone, but immediately behind the town the hillsides were covered with a profusion of fruit and nut and fig trees and red blooming oleanders.

Here the bluff, excitable widower Peter became a guide, just to show Jesus and Mary around. First, Peter brought the Master and mother into his own home—a one-story structure surrounded by a courtyard—and presented his mother-in-law, a feeble old lady. Peter, the widower, took good care of her.

And of course Peter knew the whole fifteen-mile length of the lake with its almost unbroken ring of cities and towns. He had fished this lake water all his life and now he introduced Jesus to other fishermen, showed Him on the beach the miles of drying and mended nets with the little lead weights—the very same kind of nets and weights are used at Capernaum to this day—and showed Him, too, how the fish were pickled in barrels and sold to the merchants of Caesarea and the Syrian Jews.

But more than lake and town and synagogue with Roman pillars Jesus saw on this first visit. Most important, He perceived that this crossroads of the east and west worlds was a strategic place from which He could speak to humanity. Here in this metropolis of travelers where men were forever in the midst of excitement and talk of new tricks of government, great events of war, crimes of Rome, and scandals of Jerusalem, here was a perfect platform, an incomparable rostrum from which to utter a message that would be carried to the farthest places.

That was why Jesus there and then decided that Capernaum was to be the headquarters of His work. He would make it His own city, the home center from which He would carry out His Father's work.

Yet, having made this decision, He did not at once settle there. There were more immediate tasks back home in Nazareth: first, long days of talk and explanation to His first five disciples. In those beginning days Jesus took time to get acquainted with the hard, logical Andrew; the thoughtful, almost cynical Nathanael; the eager, goodhearted Philip, and the always loyal, but explosive, quick-tempered Peter. They and John must be taught slowly, molded to work together, before others could be added to the company. And all must begin to understand the deeps of the startling ideas they were soon to hear Him preach.

In those days they were just beginning to feel acquainted with Him, to relax within the warmth of His unbounded charm and understanding, to know Him as friend and brother as well as leader. At this time they did not suspect the vastness of the differences that separated Him from them. Some hoped that He might be the Messiah, but doubted it more than they believed. Sometimes they thought of Him as a great teacher, even a divine messenger, a little lower than an angel. That He was the Son of God, part of God, God himself as an expression of a Holy Trinity they did not, for a moment, dream. Not until He came back to them from death would they fully realize the being that He really was. Jesus could have told them; He kept His secret, and only gradually over the next three years He initiated them into those mysteries. Had it been otherwise, they would have been too awed, too paralyzed with dread, to have known Him in His human nature and so learned from Him the tasks they must one day carry on alone.

Those, the best and most tranquil days Jesus and His friends were ever to know, came to an end all too soon. Presently they must start back all the way to Jericho, for there were rumors that John the Baptist was getting himself into serious trouble.

With the five Jesus left Nazareth, and they began again the long trek down to the edge of the desert. There they made a little camp and observed for a while the excitement that was growing around the courageous preacher. Day by day word of what John was telling the crowds was being brought to Herod, the tetrarch and puppet ruler of Galilee. And day by day John's hints about the tetrarch's marriage made his adulterous queen more enraged. Finally one afternoon John thundered explicitly to Herod's astounded and frightened subjects:

"It is not lawful for him to have his brother's wife."

When she heard about this, Queen Herodias demanded of the king that John at once be tortured and put to death. But Herod dillydallied; he was politically wise enough to realize that it would be folly for him summarily to execute so popular a man as John had become. But he had to do something or lose his stolen wife, so a few days after Jesus and His followers reached the desert the king's soldiers suddenly rode up and seized John and dropped him into a dungeon.

And then, most curiously, the little Herod Antipas—dissolute, drunken, and singularly free from decency as he often was—began to take a curious interest in his prisoner. For some obscure reason the brave, uncompromising man from the desert fascinated the soft-skinned ruler on his tinsel throne.

Often at night Herod would slip away from the lacy boudoir of dreaming, exhausted Herodias to go and talk with the man he had chained in a pit. Undoubtedly the king feared John, and he certainly could not understand the moral indignation that made him preach such indiscreet and indelicate sermons, yet something in the mystic's words stirred him, brought him a little light—like a door that opens just a crack.

The more Herod Antipas listened to John, the more thoughtful and melancholy he became; the more he realized that John was a just and good man, and thus the more to be feared.

It was then that the queen, who had a cunning brain, decided that she must get rid of John the Baptist.

Chapter 25 THE WOMAN AT THE WELL

ONCE John was arrested, Jesus and His five friends started back toward Galilee. Guided by an inner voice, the Holy Spirit, the Master startled the others by His decision to go home by way of Samaria.

Here, indeed, was a shock. Decent citizens avoided that province as they would a colony of lepers. The feeling of the Galileans against Samaritans was so deep and malicious that a mere glance from one was an insult, cause for a fight. That old feud between people of identical ancestry went back hundreds of years to the time when the Samaritans fraternized with invaders, when collaborationists married and intermarried, and forever since they had been held in revulsion by all patriots of Israel. The ancient hatred made trade and peaceful intercourse impossible in modern times.

Yet the land of the Samaritans was fair and could have been much more richly developed, with prosperity for many, native and stranger. The soil was fertile; it had more water than the southern part of the country because the limestone had not yet absorbed most of the springs. In the valleys the rich black earth was often flooded over. The Samaritans planted great fields of wheat, raised fine vegetable gardens and luxurious orchards, but no outsiders liked to buy their grain or vegetables or fruit. Good Jews would walk far out of their way to go around Samaria. Only Romans befriended them.

Jesus led His five followers straight to this forbidden province, fifty miles north of Jerusalem. Once within its borders He did not rest until He had reached its most historic spot, the well of Jacob, at the eastern base of Mount Gerizim, where the earliest of Israelite patriarchs had worshiped. This was the land which Jacob had given to his son Joseph. Everyone thought of this spot as the oldest well in the world and near by, so the devout piously believed, was the actual grave of Joseph.

By now the five disciples knew when Jesus desired to be alone and so they went on, a mile and a half, into the town of Sichar, or Shechim, as it is known today, to buy provisions for the evening meal. And knowing the fierceness of the feud, they were wondering what kind of reception they would get from the Samaritans.

Meanwhile Jesus sat in a reverie on the stone rim around the old well. Presently a woman came toward Him with a jug slung over her shoulder, a green hood thrown back from her head. As if she did not see Him at all, she busied herself tying a rope to the handles of her vessel and then lowered it into the darkness of the well.

"Give me to drink," said Jesus suddenly.

With stunned deliberation the woman pulled up her dripping jug of water and set it on the stone. Then she turned to him blankly. Plainly he was not a Samaritan; this stranger was a Jew. She well knew how people in Jerusalem said, as a slang phrase in the streets: "We know you are a Samaritan and have a devil." She knew, too, that it was forbidden of a God-fearing Jew to ask help of Samaritans or to receive food or water from them: "He who takes bread of a Samaritan is like unto him who eats the flesh of swine." He might make a friend even of a Gentile but never a Samaritan. In bewilderment she answered:

"How do you, being a Jew, ask to drink of me, who am a Samaritan woman?"

Jesus turned His head thoughtfully. The same old racial prejudice and fear! From boyhood He had been familiar with this mad and senseless hostility between His native Galileans and the Samaritans who lived next door. They fought like rival robber bands. The Galileans pillaged the Samaritans and the Samaritans ransacked the Galileans, each attacking the other from ambush. And the old quarrel was forever encouraged and egged on by debauched governments of both provinces.

"If you would know the gift of God," said Jesus, "and who He is who says to you, 'give me to drink,' perhaps you would have asked of Him."

The consternation in her deepened. *She* ask water of Him? Jesus nodded.

"And He would have given you living water."

The words "living water" thoroughly puzzled this buxom, vital peasant full of the swaying and shapely magnitude of sex. Putting the back of one hand to her cheek, she said:

"Sir, you have nothing to draw water with and the well is deep. From whence, then, do you get your living water? Are you greater than our father Jacob, who gave us the well and drank out of it himself, and his children and his cattle?"

Leaning forward and speaking confidentially, He replied:

"Whoever drinks of this water shall thirst again. But he that shall drink of the water that I will give him shall not thirst forever. The water that I will give him shall become in him a fountain of water springing up into life everlasting."

She smiled incredulously.

"Sir, give me this water that I may not thirst."

"Go call your husband and come here," He suggested.

Those words flustered her. With a toss of her head she replied:

"I have no husband."

And now the voice of Jesus was so low she could scarcely hear Him:

"You have said well, 'I have no husband.' For you have had five husbands. And he whom you now have is not your husband! You have said truly."

The woman leaned against the parapet of the wall, both hands grasping the stones.

"Sir," she gasped, "I see that you are a prophet."

Then, as if to placate a dangerous man, she reminded Him that He should be merciful to her, because the patriarchs, common great ancestors of Samaritans as well as His own people, had worshiped on this mountain. Her face was growing paler, body trembling. It was a relief when, after a long pause, He spoke to her:

"Woman, God is a spirit and they that adore Him must adore Him in spirit and truth."

She whispered:

"I know that the Messiah is coming who is called Christ. When He comes He will tell us all things."

Jesus stood up and looked at her and said:

"I am He who am speaking to you."

She stood and looked at Him dumbly, for she had heard the great secret that He had not yet told His followers. There was a sudden noise behind them—Peter, John, Nathanael, Andrew, and Philip—back from town, their arms filled with bundles of food. On seeing them, she concealed her face, forgetting her water jug, and ran off into the city, where she told everyone she met that the Christ, the Messiah was out at Jacob's well.

Jesus, seeing the packages in the arms of His friends, astonished them quite as much as He had startled the Samaritan woman when he shook His head, as if reproving their headlong interruption, and said:

"I have meat to eat which you do not know."

"Has someone else brought Him something to eat?" they wondered. Throwing an arm over the shoulder of Peter, most baffled of all five, Jesus said simply, as one spells out a word to a child:

"My meat is doing the will of Him that sent me—that I may perfect His work."

He was going on, explaining to them that the harvest time of His work would not be long, when they heard a great sound of voices. Crowds of Samaritans were surrounding them; they had heard the story of the woman at the well and were trooping out to see the man she said was the Messiah; they would judge for themselves.

So much did they approve His teachings that the Samaritans pleaded with this unknown Nazarene not to leave them. They made Him their guest, asking Him questions of ethics and human behavior, while they offered Him oval cakes of wheaten flour, which was their favorite bread, and bowls of meat stew with a most savory smell, and milk and wine. They washed His feet in the ancient form of their hospitality. And Jesus taught them and, with them, His five new companions.

The Samaritans, who were no fools, asked searching questions, and what He taught them sounded very new and radical. If He was the Messiah, how did He mean to improve the condition of the world? Wherever one looked, one saw intolerance, cruelty, misery.

Did Jesus offer Himself as the hope of the distressed?

And He, hearing these questions from the Samaritans, lingered with them two days while He told them of the Kingdom of Heaven. What He taught them was a new Testament, a perfection of the old law, brotherhood of man for man, for all were children of the Father; an end of old grudges and blood feuds and hatred; forgiveness the answer to racial and religious strife; love to heal all wounds. This lesson of tolerance was His first public teaching.

Chapter 26 WHAT HAVE WE TO DO WITH YOU?

THROUGH the cool sweetness of a May morning Jesus led His band of five men down the highroad from Samaria back into Galilee. The tingle of new forces of the season filled their veins; there was a feeling of fresh and adventurous life in the spring creep of the land tortoise across the road and the squonking flocks of storks and cranes flying overhead.

They had come to a halt, for a little rest, not far from Nazareth, and beggars and curiosity seekers had gathered around them, when a shocked silence fell suddenly; all movement ceased, and the unclean mob stood rooted in fear.

A rich and powerful magnate had suddenly appeared among them. His breast was decorated with a pendent disk covered with watery-blue aquamarines, black opals, and emeralds. The very smell of the aristocratic oil in his ringlets commanded their bent heads; they were in the presence of wealth and authority. Through the path they instantly opened for him the nobleman strode forward. But as the crowd peeked and turned their heads, they observed that the stranger's face was pale, his eyes moist. His words were incredibly humble.

"I have heard," he began without parley, "strange reports of you —a carpenter of Nazareth. There is a tale of a fountain of wine you caused to spring up at Cana. And another tale, which has gone before you, of how you read the mind of a disreputable woman at Jacob's well. Such reports have given me, a despairing man, hope. I need help. I come from Capernaum; my son is there—very ill. Please come down and heal my son, for he is at the point of death."

"Unless you see signs and wonders, you believe not," Jesus replied with a testing glance at the rich man.

"Lord, come down before my son dies," pleaded the father, breaking into sobs.

Jesus closed His eyes; this man's tears were real. Softly He spoke:

"Go your way! Your son lives."

As the rich man looked up, there was no doubt, but only hope in his face. His eyes spoke his gratitude as without another word he turned and with outstretched arms flailed a path for himself through the crowd and ran down the open road. The five disciples were speechless; Peter's brow knitted in wonderment. Not until later would those dubious disciples learn what had happened.

The next day, as the ruler was still making his way down the steep roads to Capernaum, he was met by servants coming up to greet him, and with news. His son lived!

"Praise God! At what hour did he get better?"

"Yesterday, at the seventh hour, the fever left him."

At the seventh hour! That, as the father knew, was the exact hour when the carpenter from Nazareth had told him: "Your son lives!"

This healing was a master stroke. It fixed the attention of the whole region on Jesus. Everybody heard of it; as He returned to the metropolis by the lake, throngs of people were frantic to see and hear Him. At once He was invited to make a series of public talks. Crowds packed the rectangular Capernaum synagogue with its illicit Corinthian pillars; they hung on to His words, but many with ears cocked for error. And sophistry! These fishermen and merchants and workmen were well instructed in Moses and the prophets.

After the reading of the Torah, the attendant handed Jesus the scroll, and He repeated the prophetic words:

"The spirit of the Lord Jehovah is upon me, because Jehovah has anointed me."

And many were restlessly aware that they felt in the living presence of knowledge and felicity and power when He began to speak.

"Repent and believe." This the burden of His message, preached now for the first time publicly before crowds. Soon afterward He began to travel around the lake, from town to town, synagogue to synagogue. It seemed to the people that He was boldly proclaiming startling new truths, yet much of what He taught came straight from their own religious books, which they knew well, or had thought they did, until now. The difference was that He showed them a richer meaning of their own texts, bringing new light on old laws and prophecies, as well as flaming new promises.

Finally, and with Mary happy to be with Him again, Jesus came home to Nazareth. Not to the carpenter shop now but to the synagogue.

He came there to recall to people who had known Him all His life ancient doctrines, and especially the hard, strong advice of Isaiah, the troubled servant of the Lord, who praised the constructive power of suffering—truth so hard for anyone to understand. On the Nazareth platform Jesus quoted to His fellow townsfolk from Isaiah:

"The Spirit of the Lord is upon me, because he has anointed me to preach the gospel to the poor; he has sent me to heal the brokenhearted, to preach deliverance to the captives, and recovering of sight to the blind; to set at liberty them that are bruised."

That day the townspeople were all deeply impressed, and complimented Mary for raising such a gifted son. He was not yet so famous or controversial a figure that they hated Him. Not until later were they to turn on Him, but when they did, it was to be with murder in their hearts. Now it was with a feeling of peace that Jesus and His five disciples walked the long road back to Capernaum, where two deeds performed in public still further increased His fame.

The first occurred in the synagogue. There Jesus was being heard by ever-growing crowds, enchanted by the power of His delivery, the rich conviction in His voice, the force in His pliant and fortunate gestures; more and more He held them as under the spell of a storyteller. Not as the scribes and the rabbis, not with droning voice and mechanical utterance, with mere repetitions was He talking to them, but with a natural skill greater than the technique of

Roman actor or Greek orator. In every address He startled them with the completeness of His knowledge, the depth of His assurance, the intensity of His desire to pass on hope and courage to the oppressed.

This promise so vitalized every lecture He gave that He had already become the principal topic of conversation. Women, picking lentils in the field, praised His kindness to all who told Him their troubles; hucksters sitting at the market place, just within the city gates; dark-skinned traders, with earrings, stacking their bolts of silk and baskets of linen; day laborers sitting idly in the shade and waiting to be hired—all sorts of men and women admired and trusted Him. Housewives at their ovens, leavening sweet dough with sour; the miller throwing chaff and grain against the morning breeze with his winnowing shovel, so that the wind would blow away the chaff and the good grain would fall to the ground; the husbandman in his field praying against locust and grasshoppers, the trappers in the hills, seeking partridge and fallow deer and keeping a wary eye out for stray bears from Mount Hermon—all Capernaum, at its daily jobs, talked about Jesus.

How, they soon asked themselves, could anyone doubt, after that insane man had rolled on the floor of the synagogue last Sabbath?

Jesus had been talking when suddenly a man in the crowd began to scream. Running up to the front, he fell writhing to the floor. It was shocking to see him contorted in his ghastly spasms; the spectators shuddered. Many knew the man, and a chill of repulsion came over them because they believed he had a devil; believed that some spirit, unearthly and unclean, possessed his body, making him two persons in one frame. That, they thought, was why he rolled at the feet of Jesus and shrieked:

"Let us alone! What have we to do with you, Jesus of Nazareth? Did you come here to destroy us?"

And then, oddly changing from plural to singular, as if only his real self spoke, the sick man finished in a frightened gasp:

"I know who you are—the Holy One, of God!"

Without a second's hesitation Jesus spoke sharply and decisively, commanding something vicious and unclean within the man:

"Hold your peace and go out of him!"

That moment the illness ended. The exhausted man lay quiet as a sleeping child. Who was this Jesus? Even the skeptics wanted to know more of this powerful personality who commanded evil spirits.

No wonder the people talked.

And right after this episode Jesus performed another strange deed—in the home of His close friend, Simon, called Peter.

Chapter 27 PETER'S MOTHER-IN-LAW

In those days Peter was not too popular in his own household. He had been tagging around the south provinces, listening to John the Baptist, and now taking up with Jesus and neglecting the fish business. He who had always been a hard-working family man had become a dreamy, thoughtful fellow, whose boat was splitting at its seams and whose nets were dry. This did not make for peace in Peter's home.

Just at this time Peter's mother-in-law fell ill—not merely down with an aging woman's pains of the moon; no mere sick headaches or cramps, but seriously ill, with a glaze over the eyes, dryness in the throat, cheeks flushed, forehead burning—a painful agony of fever. It was an epidemic illness, that fever, often prevalent in the low country after the first rains of autumn.

Naturally Peter at once called in a physician. This man, like many others of his craft, had a wise look, usually said nothing, but placed his hope, daily renewed, on the pharmacopoeia. Four hundred years before the Greek Hippocrates had founded a sensible medical science. But oriental charlatans clung to most outlandish remedies. Prescriptions consisted of the ashes of a charred wolf's skull, heads of mice, eyes of crabs, owl's brains, salt of vipers' sweat, frogs' livers, elephant lice—from these resources were the simpler doses compounded. Kiss a mule on the nose and cure a cold! Frogs cooked in vinegar would take away a toothache! For rarer troubles the doctor would turn to the foam of wild horses, mothers' milk, and the urine of unweaned calves. Did Peter's mother-in-law have colic? Let her swallow the drip of rabbits! Dysentery? Pulverized horse teeth for her! Troubled with her bladder? Then she must partake of the kidneys of an ass mixed with a little scraping of mouse's fat.

But none of their weird prescriptions had helped Peter's mother;

all febrifuges and other medicines efficacious against fever had failed to still the rising fire in the old woman's veins.

When Simon returned home, just after the Master had healed the demoniac at the synagogue, his mother-in-law was much worse; Peter felt sure she was dying. The ex-fisherman did not wait, but rushed back to fetch Jesus. Andrew and James, John and Nathanael stood in the doorway as Jesus passed in and went directly to the bed and touched the mother-in-law's hand. She turned away from Him, hostile at first, then looked back with a bewildered air, not knowing how to account for the instant change in herself. Until then she hadn't thought much about Jesus. She had been sick. Now she was well! Strong enough to get out of bed and minister to all six of them.

By sunset of that same day the whole town heard about it and the house of Peter was mobbed. The narrow streets before it and behind, the alleys and the broader highways were choked with sick people. They hobbled on crutches and crawled on their knees; old men were toted on the shoulders of their sons and old women cradled in the arms of husbands who staggered under their weight; children hastened and soothed by mothers and fathers, they all came clamoring. Some had pains and fevers, boils and cancers and leprous sores; minds that were like the stables of wild creatures, full of lust and hate and blood thirst. They were crippled and humpbacked and blind, they were dumb and tongue-tied.

Upon them all, one after another, Jesus laid firm, cool hands. He blessed them, not with a solemn face but with a bright expression, even a chuckle, especially for the youngsters. Not one was left with boil, or fever, or speechless mouth. The cripples were uncrippled, the hunchback now had a straight spine, the dumb could speak and shout his thanks, the blind could see the Master's pleased but perspiring face. And others who, like the man in the synagogue, fell down in their writhings, were released and they, too, in their ecstasy cried out:

"*You are the Son of God.*"

That was when brow-knitted scholars in the synagogue began to read again the prophecies in old, neglected scrolls. One, with a little shiver, pointed out to his companion an ancient prophecy of Isaiah:

"Land of Zabulon and land of Nephthalim . . . the people that sat in darkness have seen a great light . . ."

Capernaum was on the borders of Zabulon and Nephthalim!

And a second scholar pointed to another prophecy of that same neglected Isaiah:

"He took our infirmities and bore our diseases."

No wonder all Galilee talked! No wonder the crowds assembled so that for a brief spell Jesus had to seek renewal for Himself in a retreat to the desert. But not for long; finding solitude was not to be so simple. After curing old and young of diseases, He was not to be left to Himself. Word passed swiftly that He had left town; they feared He might never come back to Capernaum. The gathering crowds stormed Peter's house and demanded to know. Some hint they got because, dropping flax and seedlings, merchandise and family wash, they rushed out to seek and find Him on a rocky ledge some miles farther toward Damascus. Soon He was again surrounded by a sweating, unwashed delegation, entreating Him to return.

The Master explained that He must first visit other cities around the lake; assured them all that He would return and sent them on home. In the towns He now visited He repeated his first Capernaum program; He taught in the synagogue, and healed the sick. The tales of these healings were carried into Samaria and Judea, and He was already being talked of as far south as Jerusalem.

The story that seemed to create the most wonder was not about healings, however, but the tale of a draught of fishes.

The Master, as many now called Him, had been beleaguered by a listening crowd, pressing so close to Him that He was forced to the very edge of the lake. Near by were two fishing boats, with oars, mast, and little sails. Fishermen stood ankle deep in the water, washing their nets, but their baskets, made of wicker and rope work, were empty. Others were gathering murex shells, washed in by a storm, to sell to the makers of Syrian dyes.

Jesus saw that one of those ships belonged to His stormy follower, Peter. Waving a hand to the impatient crowd, the Master clambered into Peter's boat. Would the sailors pull out a little farther into the water? Thank you, Peter! Now the impetuous, over-eager throng must keep its distance. Jesus had a little space for Himself, and, sitting quietly in Peter's boat, He finished His talk. When the crowd began to disperse, He turned again to His friend:

"Simon, launch out into the deep and let down your nets for a draught."

Peter heaved a patient sigh. He had begun to feel one needed a great deal of patience to deal with this calm, pale, unruffled Jesus. Very politely the bearded fisherman made a protest. Clearly the Master did not realize . . .

"We have fished all night and have taken nothing."

But the Master did realize it! Indeed, that was why He had made the suggestion.

So Peter called his helpers and they did as Jesus had advised them. No fish all night long, no fish for all their tough, hard work in the dark—they were completely discouraged. But now look! Look in the full glare of morning light—silver pounds of flopping, wriggling, squirming fish, bulging the nets until the ropes broke. They had to call partners from another ship; they filled both holds with the catch and even so the ships wobbled and nearly sank with the weight of their cargoes.

"And there is a meaning to it," whispered one fisherman to another. "Don't get discouraged; keep on fishing!"

So they told the story from Nain to Bethany, but not all of it. For the gossips did not know the new self-doubt that overwhelmed the heart of Peter, the shamed fisherman, who, weeping at the memory of his own skepticism, pleaded with the Master:

"Depart from me, for I am a sinful man, O Lord!"

The others stood by watching—Andrew who was Peter's brother, and James and John, who were their partners, and Nathanael. They heard, as well as Peter, the quick, eager reply addressed to them all:

"Come after me and I will make you to become fishers of men. Fear not!"

That settled it as far as these five were concerned. They had seen and heard everything. This was their definitive call and they answered it, even though already warned it was a pathway to death. No more fishing except for men!

They left the boats with Zebedee, the father of James, waiting only for a moment while their leader healed a wayside leper. They started out, ready to follow Jesus all the way to Gethsemane.

Chapter 28 THE FIRST CLASH

FROM then on the first five disciples were constantly at His side, serving and helping when He would let them. They saw Him heal and exorcise and teach until they feared He would faint with fatigue. At such times He would invariably go off by Himself to a desert spot; from such brief sessions of solitary prayer He would come back invigorated, as if within the space of an hour He had concentrated the benefit of a rest cure or a whole summer's vacation.

The five friends could not restore themselves. They were tired out when finally Jesus had completed His tour of the lake cities, but He came back to Capernaum the very image of strong, magnetic health.

And Jesus was going to need His strength, for a long struggle was now to begin, never to be relaxed until the end.

It was, in fact, on His return to Capernaum that He first clashed with the public authorities. They were agents from the Jerusalem Temple, sent down to make an official report on the wonder-worker, and the emissaries sat in the synagogue with the doctors of law and looked anxiously at the crowds this unknown Master was attracting. Yet why should they feel distrustful? What they heard from Jesus, as He preached that day, was sound orthodox doctrine; He uttered no heresy. If that was what they feared, their long trip was a waste of time. But later in the day events heartened the flagging hopes of the spies.

Jesus had entered a private home and sat in an upper room, answering questions from a group of scholars. The Temple agents were there, too; they had orders to follow Him everywhere and miss nothing. Suddenly, overhead, they all heard a disturbance. Much annoyed, the master of the house climbed up to the roof. Who was making the racket? What he found there was a family, a wife and four sons, carrying a father, deathly ill.

The sick man's wife pleaded with the outraged householder. Her aged husband had caught a strange disease; without warning his whole body had lost the power of movement or sensation except for an intense internal suffering. They said, the wife and the sons, who had carried the sick man to Capernaum, that no doctor in Galilee knew how to cure paralysis. More, they knew that the old man's death must soon follow.

That was why, in desperation, they had lugged the sick man a weary distance here. Once arrived, they still could not get to Jesus. The human crush around the synagogue had been too dense; no one, sick or well, would give way for them. Later He entered this house of a friend and sat talking with them in an upper room. So the pilgrims dragged the bed and the sick man around to the back of the house next door. No crowd there! Up a narrow flight of steps they carried their burden to the roof. One of the sons ran off and came back panting with an armful of ropes.

These ropes they now attached to the corners of the bed, which was only a pallet or mattress filled with cotton and straw.

Their purpose was clear. They wanted to lower the sick man through the opening in the roof, deposit him in front of the Master, and implore His mercy. All very touching, but the irate householder was ready to order them off the premises when the pale, upturned face of Jesus stopped him; that glowing gaze was full of command.

"Very well, then! Lower him away!"

They lowered mattress and dying man to the floor. Jesus looked down at the unmoving patient, then up to the opening where staring down upon Him were the tired mother and her sons. He smiled winningly, then bent beside the dying stranger, laid lean hands on icy cheeks, and stroked the cataleptic eyes. He spoke in a profound hush:

"Be good of heart, son! Your sins are forgiven you."

A buzzing murmur raced through the audience. Bored at hearing the words of prophets thrown punctiliously at their heads, the Temple agents now sat up and gasped. Here *was* something to report to Jerusalem.

"Blasphemy!" squawked one. "Who can forgive sins but God alone? Blasphemy!"

No one replied as the dread charge, punishable by death, sounded and echoed in the room. Jesus was still bending over the sick man.

"What is it," He asked, facing the men from the Temple, "that you think in your hearts? Why do you think evil? Which is easier to say: your sins are forgiven you—or arise! Take up your bed and walk?"

He patted the cheeks of the man who until then could not budge but only feel his great pain. Then Jesus whispered slowly and deliberately:

"But that you may know that the Son of Man *has* power on earth to forgive sins, get up! I say to you, arise! Take your bed and go to your house."

Everything seemed to stand still for one breathless instant. Then in sight of all the immovable man began to move. The speechless man spoke. The first sound was a great sob of relief, a convulsion of joy that shook his whole wasted frame. Struggling up to one elbow, he cried:

"Thanks be to God!"

And hearing incoherent cries of joy from those five delirious faces at the opening in the roof the sick man put his palms on the earthen floor, forced himself to stand up, stood swaying for a moment, and then weeping in his new strength, he bent over and did as he had been bidden: he lifted up his bed and walked out of the house.

And Jesus smilingly waved His hand in farewell to the relatives upstairs before they raced after the man He had healed.

The crowds were breaking up in jabbering confusion. But the doctors of the law and the agents from Jerusalem huddled in a corner and put their heads together. The Son of Man? From where did He get that phrase? Ah! One of them remembered. The prophet Daniel had used the same pregnant words.

"I saw in the night faces, and behold, one, like the Son of Man, came with the clouds of heaven . . ."

The Son of Man! Fulfilment of Daniel's prophecy? Power to forgive sins? It was heresy. They would go back to Jerusalem and report upon this business.

Here was the first strong clash with the Pharisees; no one did the Master criticize with deeper indignation. Throughout the oncoming centuries scholars and teachers were to complain about the uncompromising severity of Jesus toward this class; yet nothing that has ever been said in their behalf has lessened the force of His indictment. Here were leaders, spiritually ill and dying, yet wielding power over the minds of the common people. He had to denounce them; His very silence would have been an endorsement of their emphasis upon wholly external practices.

The Mosaic law meant to them the observance of their multiplied regulations. Humility was rare among them; the Pharisees did not humbly and in secret try to get nearer to God; when they did good works, they let everyone know; they thought their excellence, such as they saw it, came from their own merits; they thought of themselves as God's pets in the schoolroom of life. They were arrogant scholars, and, as Jesus was to call them, "Blind leaders of the blind!"

Chapter 29 A TAX AGENT RESIGNS

ONLY a few weeks later Jesus proceeded to shock masses of the people quite as much as He had already disturbed their overlords of the Temple.

That was when He added a sixth man to His little band of followers—and chose for the honor the most unpopular man in Capernaum, a functionary everybody loathed—the publican, collector of the Roman taxes. This new disciple was called Levi, son of Alphaeus, and Jesus made his acquaintance where he sat in what was known as the "Receipt of Customs," the place of collecting tariff duties from travelers and caravaneers.

There was no personal reason for the people of Capernaum to hate a poor and good-natured man like Levi, but they did; they felt bound to despise and to detest anybody connected with taxes. In their code, it was forbidden to pay taxes to a conqueror except under protest. Technically, the taxes were paid to Jewish officers, but most certainly the monies put in Levi's hands finished up in a Roman strongbox. Annas and others of his Jerusalem cronies hired honest men in desperate need—why else would a good man take such a job?—and one of several they had employed in Capernaum was Levi, son of Alphaeus.

He seemed a mild-mannered little man as he sat there at the barrier of the frontier road, humble and acutely aware of how he was despised. In his loneliness he had become a student; it helped him in his job to speak Roman and Greek and other travelers' tongues; he was quite learned in the literature of East and West. But that did not improve his popularity. No petty torment the people could inflict upon him was considered too cruel. He was the visible agent of the taxes, so he was unclean, the butt of all.

"Robber!" the little boys called after Levi when he walked down the street, and at the supper table their fathers coupled the word "publican" with sinner and harlot master—all of a class.

Yet Levi continued to be a hard-working and conscientious man, who watched carefully over every mite and farthing, testing the true ring of dinarius and penny against a little block of marble; the Roman coins called pence, and pounds, and the talents of silver and of gold. And he remained an outcast; no one would sit at table with him; he could not testify before an ecclesiastical court; long ago he had lost all standing and all friends.

It was before the tariff booth of Levi that Jesus passed one morning and looked attentively into the sad eyes of the publican.

"Follow me!" He said suddenly.

To the amazement of all the hangers-on the publican stood up in an obedience that was instantaneous and complete. Not a moment's question! The chapfallen crowd gasped as despised Levi, son of Alphaeus, rushed from his table and calling to his assistant to take over his schedule of merchandise tolls, his careful accounts, his hoard of coins—leaving all these for someone else to attend to—without hesitation fell in step and walked off briskly with the Master.

Some of the thoughtful citizens remarked that night that while many sick persons had been healed instantaneously and sent home well and strong, no one else had instantaneously left one kind of life to take up another as simply and directly as did Levi. He was asked to follow, and he did it at once.

More, the neighbors saw how proud he seemed to be with Andrew and Philip, James and John and Nathanael that afternoon. At last he had friends! Prouder still to be told by the Master he would no longer be called Levi, but from hence he was to be known as Matthew. Proudest of all to bring the famous Jesus to his own despised house, and then to bustle out and buy provisions with spendthrift hand and scurry back home to prepare a feast; how glad Matthew was to bring in what rag, tag, and bobtail people he knew to meet and break bread with Jesus.

Who were these friends of the taxgatherer? Tramps. Alcoholics. Outcasts like himself, naturally, together with fellow collectors. And other low folk—tipsters and gamblers, hellions and good-for-nothings, furtive creatures from life's seamy side every one.

Here was room for scandal! Back from Jerusalem, to spy on Him once more, the Temple agents stood gleefully in the moonlight outside the house where the publican and his friends were eating and drinking.

As some of the companions of Jesus sauntered out for a breath of air the agents from Jerusalem accosted them. One took Andrew by the shoulder; another drew aside Bartholomew and James; the smartest of all chose Peter.

"Look here," he blustered to the big fisherman. "Why does your Master eat and drink with publicans and sinners?"

The answer came with shocking quickness. Suddenly, in the lighted doorway, appeared the lean silhouette of the teacher from Nazareth calling to them:

"They that are well have no need for a physician, but they that are sick. Go, then, and learn you this:

"I love mercy and not sacrifice!

"And I am not come to call the just but sinners to repentance."

The agents drifted off into the darkness. They would be up most of the night, trying to find fault with what He had meant.

But immediately after there came another kind of deputation from Jerusalem.

This time it was a group of followers of John the Baptist. The cousin of Jesus was still imprisoned, kept in a pit like a dangerous beast by troubled, conscience-needled Herod Antipas. A group of pallid men, with symbolic ashes worn in their uncombed hair, mourning for John's imprisonment, came to consult Jesus. They were friendy but deeply worried, even resentful men. Peter summed up for them: they wanted to know why the followers of John, men like themselves, must fast often and make prayers—but the six disciples of Jesus never seemed to fast; they ate and drank and enjoyed life.

Apparently the story of Matthew's party had been carried far and fast by these Temple visitors.

The answer should not have shocked these melancholy followers of the Baptist; not if they remembered how John himself had already acclaimed Jesus as the fulfilment of the prophecies. If Jesus were the Messiah and these six men were His chosen assistants, then His answer should be clear enough:

"Can the children of the marriage fast as long as the bridegroom is with them? But the days will come when the bridegroom shall be taken away from them; and then they shall fast in those days!"

The followers of John, still unsatisfied, went home, just as the

Temple spies returned with renewed zeal to trap the Master. Up until now He had chosen His words too carefully for them to indict Him for blasphemy. What, then? Well, among the more conservative the talk in Capernaum was that Jesus and His friends were rather loose in their observance of the Sabbath laws. There might be a real opening because disregard of the Sabbath was a heathen's offense and could also be punished by death.

Thus encouraged, the Temple agents returned to the attack on a Saturday toward the end of June in the year A.D. 28. The harvest was ripening as Jesus walked with His friends out into the open country. All around them were fields of grain called corn, not Indian maize but tall yellow wheat from which was made the good, tasty Palestinian bread. After ambling several miles Peter and John became hungry and quite casually they plucked some tall ears of wheat which they rubbed between their palms, crushing the grains and then chewing them raw. Suddenly, like jack-in-the-boxes, there popped up from the midst of the growing corn two of the Jerusalem spies.

Eyes gleaming with satisfaction, they brushed the earth from their knees and strode toward Jesus as the leader snarled:

"Take a good look at what your men are doing—that which it is not lawful to do on the Sabbath day!"

What? Nibbling a few ears of growing wheat? That is what they found fault with exactly. In the Book of Exodus, second of the Books of Moses, reaping on the Sabbath was forbidden. Unquestionably these men were reaping!

Thus the legalistic mind of a Pharisee wherever you find him on any continent, in any color, tongue, or creed, is today quite the same as then.

Like a good Jew, the Master countered question with question:

"Have you never read what David did—when he was hungry himself and they that were with him? How he went into the House of God and ate the loaves of proposition which was not lawful for him to eat nor for them that were with him, but for the priests only?

"Or have you not read in the law that on the Sabbath day the priests in the Temple break the Sabbath and are without blame? But I tell you that here is a greater need than the Temple, and if you knew what this means—*I will have mercy and not sacrifice*—you would never have condemned the innocent.

"The Sabbath was made for man, not man for the Sabbath. Therefore the Son of Man is Lord of the Sabbath also."

He had met their trivial accusation with a precedent against which nothing could stand. Again and again He was to demonstrate His complete familiarity with every jot and tittle of the Scriptures; here He had carried the argument into the very Temple which had sent them down to entrap Him.

But pertinacity is also a characteristic of Pharisees!

It was only a few weeks later, again on a Sabbath in the synagogue at Capernaum, that Jesus noticed the same foxy old faces hovering in the rear of the crowd. They were watching eagerly as a young man up front cried out to Jesus pleading that He heal his withered hand. Would the Master dare heal a man on the Sabbath? That question was in every mind in the synagogue.

"Arise and stand forth in the midst," said Jesus. The groaning man tottered forward; the Master took the withered hand, all shriveled and gray, and held it between His own strong, pale hands. By this time the Pharisees should have realized how well the Master knew the law. He was well aware that to break the Sabbath was punishable by death; so it was stated in Exodus 31:14. So once again His life was hanging by a thread as His clear challenge to His enemies rang out:

"I ask you if it be lawful on the Sabbath to do good or to do evil? To save life or to destroy it?"

Then, letting His dark gaze sweep the crowd in one magnetic glance, He demanded:

"What man is there among you that has one sheep and if the same fall into a pit on the Sabbath day will he not take hold on it and lift it up? How much better is a man than a sheep?"

His intensely compassionate eyes held them.

"Therefore," He answered himself, "it is lawful to do a good deed on the Sabbath day."

Turning to the cringing man before Him, he continued:

"Stretch forth your hand."

In another instant both the man's hands were alike; the gray and withered one restored to health, white and firm and whole as the other. The tumult of the crowd ended the services. But the Temple agents, flatulent with anger, went off to conspire with Herodians in the town. That unsavory crew of royalists did not want to free Israel; they were marplots anxious to get rid of Pontius Pilate, the procurator of Rome, and establish a descendant of Herod the Great on the throne of Judea. Here were strange bedfellows—but they were in agreement in asking one question:

"How can we get rid of Jesus and His ideas?"

The question is still being asked today.

Meanwhile Jesus Himself went into the desert alone and prayed all night.

Chapter 30 JOHN HAD TO KNOW

IN HIS prison den in the palace gardens John had heard reports of the works and sayings of his cousin Jesus; events like the healing of the withered hand and of the demoniac on the floor of the Capernaum synagogue; reports, too, of a greater wonder—the healing again, at long distance, of a Roman's servant. This miracle was performed for a centurion, an imperial officer who had come to ask help of the penniless wayfaring Jew—a spectacle that astounded the native population. Especially when the Master offered to walk to the house of the Roman and he refused, exclaiming:

"Lord, I am not worthy that you should enter under my roof—just say the word and my servant shall be healed."

"Amen!" cried Jesus to the Roman; "I want to tell you something—I have not found so great faith, not in all Israel."

And—as the tale came belatedly to imprisoned John—the dying servant became instantly and completely well, without Jesus having to go near to the house.

On this long-distance miracle the imprisoned Baptist brooded a long time. Another that made him ponder was an episode at the hamlet of Nain, where Jesus and the disciples, walking through the town gate, encountered a funeral party. A widow's son was being carried to the cemetery. Jesus stopped the procession and instantly called the dead young man back to life. This astounding fact had been witnessed by John's own emissaries.

Strange, indeed, to have power over life and death—and yet even John the Baptist was aware of doubts among his disciples; perhaps even in himself! And why not? He was himself now facing a moral choice between life and death. He could no longer rely on rumors.

"Do what I ask," he had just been told by Herod Antipas the king, "and I'll set you free. Today! But refuse—and I shall have to behead you, John. There *is* no other way; my wife gives me no peace about you."

The shallow king with the egg-shaped head really seemed to want to be John's friend. This was not mere politics on Herod's part, although he did have to take into account the continuing popularity of his prisoner. But the ascetic man from the desert not only baffled Herod but fascinated him too; the Baptist's stoutheartedness and his intrepidity were the talk of the countryside.

Just to show his kindness, the king informed the guards that John might have anything he wanted to eat. When John declined this bounty, it staggered the obese and gluttonous Herod; the Baptist sent back roasts and chops and broils and a hundred dainties from the palace kitchen. For John a few dry roots were enough, with leaves and wild honey and a gourd of water. This austerity had an extraordinary effect on the childlike Herod. Until he met John, this weak son of a strong sire had believed in nothing and in no one. All men were liars, all moved solely by self-interest; all would sell out at the best price possible. So he believed.

The more stubbornly John refused, the more the little king resolved to discover his price. Something deep within Herod Antipas was perturbed; it would mean frighteningly much to him if it turned out that after all John *had* no price. Herod could forgive himself only because he considered no man was above a bribe; no one not susceptible of being corrupted.

Late at night he would steal to the edge of the pit and look down at his prisoner. Coaxingly he would offer sweetmeats. He had platters of lamb meat, dripping with hot gravies and garnished with tasty vegetables, poked by guards under the lean nose of the fasting preacher. But all to no avail. John simply called his tormentor to repentance. And more and more the monarch listened; he dabbled with these new ideas of morality, dipping lightly but often. Finally one night the king forsook his bad-boy tricks and listened seriously as John told him that while he dallied with his inamorata, a new and mighty change was shaking the world. The Messiah had come in person, taking the body of a man. John was His announcer, His messenger.

Herod, squatting on his haunches at the rim of the dungeon, shook with laughter.

"For a fairy tale—a delusion like this—you would lose your life? Think, Baptist—don't play fool! All you need do to go free is to take back your nasty words about my marriage to my brother's wife. Go out and tell the people that my marriage is all right; that Herodias and I are not living in adultery. I will get you a nice wife for yourself too!"

Again John tried to make him understand, but Herod stopped his ears.

"No, you are fooling yourself, Baptist. I don't want to wrangle, but this man from Nazareth is not God. *You* called him that. But did *He* ever call Himself that? Did you ever hear Him say He was even the Messiah? Couldn't you be mistaken, John?"

The king's tone and manner were full of pleading; his fatuous sincerity touched John's heart. The untamed man from the Judean desert said to himself:

"Here is my chance! My followers love me too much; they are loath to leave me and become disciples of the Master Jesus. And I am no longer with them to plead to them. Here, with this guileful king who understands nothing, perhaps I can settle it all!"

And in tones unusually gentle for him John said:

"Majesty, will you permit me to consult with some of my followers about all this?"

"You have only to name them, John, and I will send for them this instant!"

That was how it was that two emissaries straight from John himself again came down to Galilee and confronted Jesus with the question they had been charged with; the answer to which would settle John's life-and-death decision:

"Are you he that is come? Or look we for another?"

With His hand moving toward a blind man's eyes, in the midst of many healings, the Master gave his answer:

"Go relate to John what you have heard and seen. The blind see. The lame walk. The lepers are made clean. The deaf hear. The dead rise again. And," he finished with an ironical smile, "the gospel is preached to the poor!"

The crowd, sick people and disciples, had heard the question and the reply. They knew about John; now Jesus established the Baptist's true position in a clear, direct statement:

"John? What went you out in the desert to see? A reed shaken with the wind? A prophet? Yes, and more. Among those born of women there is not a greater prophet than John the Baptist—but he that is the least in the Kingdom of God is greater than he."

And then He reminded them how the priests of the Jerusalem Temple had objected to John a year before as now they repudiated Himself. What did they want? John fasted and lived in wild places; Jesus dined and drank and was present at gay parties. Neither was acceptable to Jerusalem!

"It is like to children sitting in the market place, who, crying to their companions, say:

" 'We have piped to you and you have not danced; we have lamented and you have not mourned!'

"For John came, neither eating nor drinking, and they say: 'He is a devil.'

"The Son of Man came, eating and drinking, and they say: 'Behold a man that is a glutton and a wine drinker, a friend of publicans and sinners!' "

And Jesus waved good-by to John's emissaries—a salute of the hand and a rueful smile.

Two nights later Herod came again in the moonlight to look down into the pit at John. Behind the open gardens and the palm trees lay visible the wide plain and the silver-lighted highlands beyond. In the stillness of the night one could hear the babble and splash of a great fountain. The prisoner stood up briskly and politely; for all his confinement he had never known depression of body or lassitude of mind.

"Well, Baptist. Your messengers have returned!"

"Yes, Majesty!"

"With an answer?"

"Yes, Majesty."

"Then you must have decided. John, will you recant—take it all back—unsay it—about my wife and me? And go free?"

To all the king's blandishments John had but one answer:

"No!"

In saying that, he knew he was pronouncing his own death sentence. Herod uttered the ferocious oath of a weakling and strode off to the boudoir of his lady.

Chapter 31 A YOUNG GIRL DANCES

BY NOW John the Baptist had been kept in prison at the palace in outlying Machærus for so many months that his friends no longer lived in daily fear of his being put to death. There was really only one person who desired his blood: the queen, Herodias. But she had never softened her scolding hatred. Day and night she seethed with unyielding hatred that poisoned all her thoughts, ruined her digestion, and even inflamed her wartish blemish, a disfiguring defect on the temple beyond her left eye, too deep-rooted to be taken off.

On the night that John said no to the king a state dinner was being planned in the palace. In celebration of his birthday, fat and pursy little Herod Antipas had invited all the bigwigs of Galilee—princes, tribunes, important officials—to come and sup. At the appointed time they came, smiling their superior Roman smiles, flattering themselves as being sybarites and voluptuaries in a barbaric colony, making clear to one another with nudges and glances their contempt for this arrant provincial kingling, but making no secret, either, of their appreciation for his savory meats and well-aged wines.

The night was hot, moist, and still. The tall banquet hall was lit with torches and long tapers and the sultry air was thick with the smell of roasts and heady liquors. The voices of the feasters rampaged above the sinuous, devious songs of the minstrels. There was hardly one sober head at Herod's table when, at the height of the feast, the damask curtains parted and the king's stepdaughter came mincing in for the principal performance of the evening.

She was the daughter of Herodias, this Salome, and the daughter also of Philip, Herod's brother. At an early age she was already exhibiting signs of nympholepsy; she was full-bosomed and shapely, with shocking young eyes full of inviting hints.

For an instant the damsel stood poised with outstretched hands—her fingers moist with oils pressed from rare petals, attar in her hair, and the exact purpose of seduction in her brain.

The players of the harps, the strokers and incessant beaters of the drums began their rhythmic motions, and Salome in the transparency of a diaphanous robe began to dance. She moved in voluptuous measures; the lifting and weaving of her thin, infantile white arms, the promise of her educated fingers, rhymed with the stealthy insistence of her hip movements, stirred the blood.

Forward and back she moved in barefoot steps. At a final *chassé* movement, across to right and back to left, there was let loose a very hell of noise, bellows of praise, and the clapping of hands, the stamping of feet! Salome, a little scared at such incendiary success, would have run off, but Herod, who despised as weaklings men who did not suffer from inordinate desire, cast a grin around at all his guests, and made a rammish grab; then set the moist, panting young one on his knee.

"Ask me whatever you want, Salome, and I will give it to you," he whispered hoarsely. There was a long silence of lascivious restlessness in the king, of wanton ogling by the child.

What did the eldritch Salome want? Herod was never really to know. Looking at him appraisingly, like a fledgling paramour, seeing what lust was like in a king's eyes, she kept silent. That female demon, her mother, had trained her for this. Then in his ecstasy the king swore his oath aloud:

"Whatever you shall ask, Salome, my sweet, I'll give you—though it be the half of my kingdom."

Now there was an oath! Salome put her finger in her mouth. For that moment she was a giglet: a giddy little girl. Then she remembered her instructions and ran off to the queen, who waited in another apartment.

"Mother, Mother, what *shall* I ask for?"

The mother told the bacchante child quickly enough. The kingly boon must be not anything that Salome might want for herself, but what the mother desired with all her vengeful soul. The man John! The desert preacher with his pale face and cavernous eyes. That prude Baptist who had condemned her to the people for her new marriage. That insensible Baptist who, of all men she had known, was untroubled by her voluptuous beauty, unkindled by her fire. That water-splashing, locust-chewing, honey-sipping giant who would not yield to the natural passions of a man.

"John the Baptist!" Herodias commanded intensely. "Ask for his head!"

A little disappointed, now bored and languorous, Salome ran back into the banquet hall, back to the king. He chuckled at sight of her, and while the table remained under its spell he lifted her wrapped body upon his couch.

"Well, Salome, what will it be?"

"I will that immediately you give me in a dish the head of John the Baptist."

The king put the moist child down from him. His eyes were sobered with unexpected horror. A moment of pudgy incertitude and then, as he realized that his wanton vow must now be paid in blood, lust died in his soul. The Romans watched him with sheer, gloating delight; in his quandary he was making good sport for them. They made bets on whether he would dare fulfill his own oath or be forsworn before them all. How, they sniggered, would he dare invoke by murder the ill-will of the crowds who had been baptized by John? Yet how perjure the royal word? Those Romans knew that the pampered Queen Herodias, indulged in all her wishes, had long desired this very thing. And they suspected that she had coached her child in that bawdy dance and waited for this drunken opportunity. A captain, who commanded a thousand Roman soldiers, told his neighbor:

"Herod is in a box. He will be wrong now no matter what he does."

None could guess that there was something more than political concern in Herod's heart, that the conscience of the king had been beleaguered by this rugged giant from the wilderness. John was strong, where the king was weak; John believed, where Herod was always in doubt; John was positive, and Herod loved him for it.

But the king knew there was no excuse even for a reprieve, no chance for a temporary delay, and so he called for the cross-eyed steward of the feast. He regarded the servant as if he were Abaddon, the angel of the bottomless pit.

"Fetch the executioner," he said miserably, pulling a fold of his robe over his paunch. "Have him bring us here now the head of John called the Baptist. Bring it in in a dish!"

Hurrying to the prison, the executioner, shoving aside guard, keeper, and warden, woke John from a peaceful sleep. He ordered the prisoner, clad in his long, sleeveless garment of haircloth, to kneel and lay his head on a butcher block. With one expert swing the wall-eyed axman cut the head from the long, muscular neck. By the untidy hair he lifted the dripping head and let it fall in a deep dish of gold, then carried it to Herod. And the king gave it to the hands of the dancing child.

Now, as Salome started back toward the damask curtains, at her very first step the harpists smote their strings and the drummers beat with their sticks, and almost unconsciously the girl fell naturally into the old writhing of her dance. Her hips swayed again as she passed through the curtains, the lifted dish with the dead man's head held high in her little-girl arms. She laid the bloody thing at the feet of her mother and then, like a sleepy crosspatch, had to be put to bed.

John's disciples buried the headless body and, riding night and day, brought the grisly news to Capernaum.

Now, once again, Jesus retired to privacy and communion; to prepare Himself for the coming ordeal, to renew His energies; to wash the soul—for the time of the forerunner was over and His own mission lay before Him. Once again, in bleak mountains frowning above the Sea of Galilee, beyond Capernaum, Jesus stole off to be alone. All through one starlit night He remained on the dark height, alone and yet not alone, His heart opened to the infinite.

When morning came He was ready to take two radical steps.

Book Four

THE FIRST YEAR

Chapter 32 CHOSEN

THE first step was to complete the selection of His principal followers, who would be trained to carry forward His work when He would have to leave them.

Back in Capernaum He sent out Peter and James to bring to Him ten others whom He named from among the throng that helpfully and for months had followed Him wherever He went. An hour later He ranged the Twelve in a circle around Him, as they stood on an unfrequented part of the pebbly shore of the lake.

Bald and bearded Peter with his freckled nose was there, of course, and his tall brother Andrew. Near them stood the pale Bartholomew, who was also called Nathanael. Then came bright-eyed, impetuous John and his brother James, sons of Zebedee; and standing beside them bearded Matthew, the exuberant ex-taxgatherer. Muscular, athletic Philip stood with his arm around the publican's shoulder. All these had been with the Master in His recent expeditions.

The others were newcomers. They had been selected from the large group of disciples who had followed the Master around Galilee.

First there was that other, younger James. Nearly forty years later, for love of Jesus, he was to be thrown down from the pinnacle of the Jerusalem Temple, and, being seen still to breathe, was finally to be stoned to death.

Standing with the younger James was the even younger Jude, his brother; Jude, who was called also Thaddeus and Lebbaeas; Jude, who would be regarded as obscure by future generations, after being shot to death by arrows in Armenia sixty years from this June day when he was chosen.

There was also Simon Zelotes, again a brother of young James and Jude. Simon was to be crucified at an appallingly old age; some say he was one hundred and twenty-nine years old when he was nailed to an X-like cross in Persia.

Last but one of those whom Jesus now selected was Thomas, surnamed Didymus, but better known as doubting Thomas, some later day in India to be ripped with a spear and die.

At the end of the list was Judas, the son of Simon of Kerioth. His name, Judas Iscariot, meant Judas of Kerioth.

A hybrid crew those twelve! Derived from incongruous sources! Yet Jesus informed them that He had chosen deliberately, and that His official mission must begin at once, with the death of John the Baptist. In the language of that day the term apostle meant "one who is sent," and applied especially to couriers who carried letters from rulers or others in authority. Explicitly he named His Twelve as messengers. He would send them out to preach, promising that they, too, should heal sicknesses and cast out demons.

For a long time the thirteen stood in silent prayer, then started back into the town. Clearly, as they could see, He would need their devoted help. And the prospect was a little frightening; on that very day it seemed as if all the sick of the whole world were gathering in Capernaum. They came from as far as the great metropolis with its gaudy Temple, where no one, it seemed, had ever been healed; from distant parts of Judea, and even beyond; loose regiments of bedraggled men and women, streaming in from seacoast and mountains, from Tyre and Sidon, and rugged old Carmel, where Elijah had lived in his cave; farther still, from Idumea and from the outer regions beyond the Jordan. From throughout all Syria came hosts of strangers, and from the ten nearby cities called the Decapolis that ringed the Sea of Galilee.

Not without qualms the Apostles beheld the clamoring throngs. Soon it would be their job to heal such people. Life had, in so short a time, changed completely for these men. A little while ago they could have turned back, but no more. Jesus had chosen them, twelve and twelve only, as if in mystical recognition of the ancient tribes.

They followed Him, as he made His way along the shore, healing many along the way, until the press of people grew so large that once again He took refuge in a fisherman's boat. The time had come when He and His chosen dozen must put the multitudes off from them and be alone together.

After hours of sailing out of sight of the pursuing crowd they beached at a desolate part of the shore, below a towering mountain of black volcanic rock. The thirteen climbed up the steep path until they reached a shelter overlooking the inland sea and the late afternoon fog that now began to mist across the waters.

Here Jesus took His second major step.

Chapter 33 THE SECOND STEP

THE time had come to make one speech to these Twelve that would sum up all His teachings, a complete and formal statement of His message, which the Apostles would learn by heart.

For this purpose He had led them away from the multitudes to a rocky shoulder here on one side of the mountain, an isolated spot where they could be alone.

As the disciples sat on their heels in a ring around Him, He began to teach. There was never heard in this world, before that day of divine revelation, or since, a more concise or orderly statement of a universal philosophical system; nor has there ever been another such chart of human behavior. Here was all the soul needed to know of God and creation and daily life, of today and hereafter. Here, too, were the most audacious promises ever made to humanity: the good news of eternity according to Jesus Christ.

He began by telling them how a human being could be happy in his life on this earth. There were only eight rules one had to follow and one would be blessed. Not that He promised them security against the misfortunes of the world; He had no guarantee for any against pain, loss, grief, or disgrace. No such thing lay in the teaching whose revelations those Twelve were to start reverberating in every land. All that Jesus had to offer was happiness. That was a state of mental well-being by which a man could remain tranquil and yet with an eager zest for life, no matter how poignant his loss, how deep his sorrow, how excruciating his pain. Here were eight rules to keep that man serene and capable in the midst of any disaster.

The eight rules, which were to be called the Beatitudes, were simple and wise but admittedly difficult to fellow. The way to destruction was broad and inviting; the way to glory, straight and narrow. First of the rules was that a man must be poor in spirit; he must be gentle, practicing humility, not heady and proud and arrogant; if one had succeeded in some great task, he was not to sit and gloat and brag, but must go right on, planning another job, a harder and better one.

In the second rule a man must be meek; that was not to be a cringing coward but to believe in the goodness of God and in the friendliness of the universe, even when the soul is suffering and can see no reason why it should suffer; the rule meant acceptance of God's will.

To mourn, too, would be a third blessing, but happiness would come, not in feeling sorry for ourselves so much as in feeling compassion for others and trying to help them; a basic counsel implied in all the Master's teachings.

Again the dynamic follower of His message would hunger and thirst after justice and righteousness; not merely in a legal sense but in a desire to understand and follow the laws that govern life and that are part of the will of God.

We must also be merciful; so will we earn mercy for ourselves. And who shall not need it?

Those shall be happy, too, who are clean and pure of heart; Jesus promised them that they would see God. But He meant what He said in the fullest sense: purity meant more than just a lack of lust; it called for a goal, a purpose in life.

Again, those who were persecuted for the sake of justice, for the teachings He gave them—they, too, would be happy, for theirs was the Kingdom of Heaven.

"And," He finished with the last beatitude, "blessed are you when they shall revile you and persecute you and speak all that is evil against you, untruly, for my sake. Be glad and rejoice, for your reward is very great in heaven."

As there could be happiness in this world by following the eight rules, so there would be unhappiness if they were not followed.

"Do not think," He instantly answered their thoughts, "that I am come to destroy the law or the prophets. I am not come to destroy but to fulfill."

And the fulfillment as He now described it to them was like a startling challenge, dazing to conventional old ways of thinking. He recalled to them the Ten Commandments, called the Law. For example, you must not kill. Ah, but that was not the end of the matter. "I say to you that whosoever is angry with his brother shall be in danger of the judgment."

To *wish* a man dead *is* murder then? More than that! If your friend and you have quarreled, there is no place for you in church Leave the altar, fleeing your gift, and find the man with whom you have disagreed. Make up with him; be reconciled to him—then, and not before, you are in a proper state of mind to kneel before the altar of God. Agree with your adversary quickly, before things go too far.

And what of thoughts of lust? They are the same as *acts* of lust. "Whoever shall look on a woman to lust after her has already committed adultery with her in his heart."

What is a man to do, then? He is to conquer himself at whatever the cost! If his right eye is rotten, tear it out. Better to lose an eye than infect the whole body and die.

No way of ease and roses this! In a land where divorce could be obtained with communistic ease, Jesus now told them that there could be no divorce in the Christian life. He made his words plain; He said and meant that a man could have only one wife, and that to get rid of her, even if she made his life miserable or someone else beckoned him to voluptuous joy, was nevertheless to expose her to the danger of adultery.

This revolutionary command against custom was followed up by one that seemed against nature itself. To the gasping Twelve Apostles, there to learn their immortal lesson, He told them they were not to resist evil. Now there was indeed a dazing idea. Not to resist evil? No, bewildered Twelve, and bewildered posterity, you are not to resist. When you learn that force is not the answer to force, peace will come to the world; never until then. As long as attack is answered by repulse, aggression by defense, wars will never end. That is true in your private lives as well; if a man punches you on the right cheek, don't hit him back; turn the left cheek to his fist!

Audible gasps from all Twelve! For months now they had heard His merciful ideas, but nothing so radical and shocking as this calm instruction. Did they remember the old Mosaic law of an eye for an eye and a tooth for a tooth? Certainly, Master, we all remember that! But they had forgotten a potent fact: that once upon a time, and long ago, the law was not like that. Revenge was a man's own business; break his tooth and he could have your eye in vengeance, if only he was strong enough to cut it from you. Later the Mosaic law put a limit on human fury. To repay an injury, you could take in kind, but no more than equal justice. So the law was changed to put a curb on: an eye for an eye, but only a tooth for a tooth.

Now came Jesus fulfilling the old law with a new and gracious expansion. Twelve listeners, get it straight and clear: if a man takes away your coat, give him your vest as well. And if, under the cruel and oppressive laws of this occupied land, a Roman soldier compels you to walk with him a mile, carrying his shield and sword in the hot sun, go with him another mile, freely given when you don't have to.

A light of understanding was shining on the faces of the listening Twelve. Thus a man could make himself free; the giving of more than required did that—the new, astonishing, wholly Christian doctrine of the law of surplus service.

With a sense of increasing power and glory they heard Him go on to the golden rule that a man must do unto others as he would have others do unto him—an improvement over all similar statements because it was positive, dynamic like Jesus himself. They were to give, when asked to give; lend, when asked to lend; and whereas the old law allowed one to love his friend and hate his enemy: "I say to you that hear, love your enemies, do good to them that hurt you, and bless them that curse you, and pray for those that calumniate you."

Was that humanly possible? For thousands of years afterward men were to debate that amazing command. How can you love your enemies? Unfortunately, in later years, the words, translated into many tongues, were to lose the precision with which Jesus spoke that day in His native Aramaic Chaldee dialect. Jesus used two words for affection—*filius* and *agape*. In our own texts these words, widely different in meaning, were to be translated as one word—"love." So a great deal of confusion was to be caused by the injunction to love our enemies. Jesus often used love in the strong sense of the old Greek word—*agape*—a detached, impersonal, self-commanding sense of the Fathership of God which makes all people His children. Not that we are expected to feel caressing affection for our enemy, but we are to bless him, and pray for his salvation, and, forgiving his offense, leave his fate to God.

This point, because of the precision with which Jesus invariably spoke, the Twelve thoroughly understood: "Be you merciful even as your Father in Heaven is merciful."

With the same perfect clarity he went on to warn against being show-offs, especially of their good works. If they bragged of their fine deeds to excite the admiration of their fellows, then that ended it; their reward was that very admiration of their fellows and they should expect nothing further. The right hand must not know what the left hand does. Pray in secret too—in the darkness of a closed room, and not, like pharisaical exhibitionists, on the street corners, with make-up on their faces to give them a haggard look of having piously fasted for a long time. "I tell you—they *have* their reward!"

How to treat others, how to govern one's own impulses, were, as they saw clearly, the urgent parts of His teaching. This was a way of life, a pattern of conduct for all to follow. We are not to judge another; nor to condemn. If we do judge, then we, too, shall be judged; when we condemn, we insure condemnation for ourselves. But if we forgive, we may also be sure of forgiveness. It is up to each one of us, individually; we can choose what to do; we have moral freedom.

Carefully He explained all matters to them. A follower of Jesus would not criticize the small faults of others; he must be too busy correcting his own gross defects—the mote in your brother's eye, the beam in your own, springing up in this mountain sermon out of boyhood rabbinical teachings in the Nazareth synagogue. One must be careful not to waste the treasures of spiritual understanding on those unready for receiving it; pearls were not to be cast before swine. Careful, too, to recognize a false teacher, of which there would come many; wolves in sheep's clothing. As a tree is known by its fruit, so is a man known by his acts. And the false teachers will unmask themselves by their deeds.

All men were responsible for their deeds, their words, their very thoughts. Here was startling news for the twelve sobered listeners. A count was kept in eternity, a balance sheet would be ready for the final reckoning. He who did good deeds, said wise and kind words, and thought good thoughts was like a man who built his house on a rock. When storm and flood came, the house was unshaken. Those who did not follow this counsel lived in a house built on sand: "The ruin of that house was great."

This message placed an immense obligation on each of the Twelve; He stressed that point and they must all try to be worthy of it. He had chosen them because they were the salt of the earth—but if salt loses its flavor, it is useless. They were the light of the world and they must let their light shine before men, "that they may see your good works and glorify your Father in heaven."

What they had to teach was the fulfillment of the law: "Till heaven and earth pass, one jot or one tittle shall in no wise pass from the law . . ."

The whole design of a man's life should be to accumulate the treasure, not of time but of eternity. To do this he should love God and serve Him and nothing else; there could be no divided loyalty; a man cannot serve two masters. It was a basic mistake to let the exigencies of the world center on moral decisions; if God feeds the birds and clothes the flowers of the field more richly than the glory of Solomon, His earthly children should have confidence that He will care for them as well.

"Oh, you of little faith!" exclaimed Jesus sadly, when He had reached this point. "You must seek first the Kingdom of God and His righteousness, and all these things shall be added unto you . . ."

From the comfort of this great promise He passed on to others, even more audacious. To those whose lives were thus dedicated to righteousness there were these wonderful assurances:

"Ask and it shall be given you.

"Seek and you shall find.

"Knock and it shall be opened unto you.

"What man is there of you, who, if his son asked for bread, would give him a stone? If you then, being evil, know how to give good gifts to your children, how much more shall your Father in heaven give good things to them that ask Him? Therefore, all things whatsoever you would that men should do to you, do you even so to them; for this is the law and the prophets."

All these things and more Jesus explained to the Twelve as they sat around him on the ledge of the mountain overlooking the distant lake. The sun vanished behind the waters, the gloaming came and deepened, and a little scimitar moon began to rise as He told them that only by prayers could a man find the strength to live a life like that. And how should a man pray? Not with the vain repetitions that had bored and disillusioned him in his childhood, but remembering always that God the Father already knew the needs of His children and the form of their prayer therefore should be:

"Our Father who art in heaven, hallowed be thy name. Thy kingdom come, thy will be done on earth as it is in heaven. Give us this day our daily bread. And forgive us our trespasses as we forgive those who trespass against us. And lead us not into temptation, but deliver us from evil . . ."

That was the Sermon on the Mount.

Chapter 34 THE FIRST BOX OF OINTMENT

CAUSTIC remarks made publicly by Jesus about the ruling caste began reaching the ears of some of the most powerful of the wealthy faction, living close to Capernaum. A few nights later Jesus was invited to dinner at the house of a Pharisee, who had talked over the matter with cronies.

"Why not have the fellow in? Let's take His measure. He may be harmless. If He isn't, well, we'll know what we have to do!"

So the Master was summoned to sup with the rich Simon. This Pharisee had considerable curiosity, of course, about a wayside preacher reported to have magical powers. He also thought the man who voiced so much criticism of the rich might be bought by flattering hospitality and cease his most unpleasant attacks, which were unsettling to the mob. "Offer good prices and you can obtain anything," the rich man figured—merchandise, honor, or faith, if you happen to have use for such things. But in addition to his curiosity and his scheming the Pharisee's vanity made him feel that as soon as this radical from a Nazareth carpenter shop was allowed to meet him personally he would see what a nice chap he really was, and criticism of the rich would wither away. He felt himself such a wonderful symbol of his class!

But Simon, without knowing it, was letting himself in for a drastic evening.

Jesus sat down at the table, amiably composed in spite of his host's omissions of certain common acts of courtesy. There were no other invited guests, and that, in the custom of the region, was an implied insult. His choice viands were not being served this evening, and he offered none of his fine wines, nor his strong oriental brandy, distilled from the juices of the cocoa palm. Clearly the rich Simon could not bring himself to treat a carpenter as an equal. Moreover, Simon acted as if he thought his visitor ignorant of the hospitable attention any guest was entitled to. Nevertheless, Jesus was full of urbane consideration; the two ate of boiled rice, raisins, spice, and lamb meat, and they small-talked: crops promised well, but taxes were high and would go higher. There were rumors of war in the west.

Then, suddenly, Simon leaned forward, glaring over the shoulder of Jesus. Behind the divan on which the guest reclined at the meal was a sight the Pharisee could hardly believe. Crouching there was a woman with long red hair; she was wrapped in a magenta robe of perfumed silk. In soft, smooth hands she was holding an alabaster box. The Pharisee had no difficulty in recognizing the intruder; he had seen her long before, when nobody knew except the two of them.

But tonight she had no eyes for him, powerful citizen though he was, with great authority and power to do harm to such as she. All frippery and trumpery of her trade laid aside, the red-haired woman kept her bloodshot eyes fixed on this penniless, mendicant Jesus. She wept as she washed His feet. She wiped the calloused soles with her long red hair, and tenderly kissed the insteps before she rubbed them with the ointment from her box of alabaster.

The Pharisee sat back, fuming to himself:

"There, you see! This man, if He *were* really a prophet, would surely know who and what manner of woman *this* is."

Then Jesus said softly:

"Simon, I have something to say to you."

"Master, say it."

"A certain creditor had two debtors. The one owed five hundred pence and the other fifty."

"Yes, Master?"

"And whereas they had not wherewith to pay, he forgave them both."

"Yes, Master?"

"Which, therefore, of the two, loves him the more?"

"I suppose the one to whom he forgave the most."

"You have judged rightly! Do you see this woman? I entered into your house; you gave me no water for my feet, but she, with tears, has washed my feet and with her hair has wiped them.

"You gave me no kiss, but she, since she came in, has not ceased to kiss my feet. Many sins are forgiven her, because she has loved much."

And for the first time speaking to the redhaired woman He added:

"Your sins are forgiven you."

"Who is this that forgives sins also?" snarled Simon, rising.

But Jesus was paying no attention to his host. He helped the red-haired woman to her feet and gently closed the lid of her box of alabaster. Costly, that box; even more costly the ointment; all her savings must have gone to buy it.

And He said to her:

"Your faith has made you safe. Go in peace!"

And immediately afterward He, too, left the rich man's house.

Chapter 35 THE WOMAN WHO UNDERSTOOD

BECAUSE of happenings like that, the fame of Jesus was on every lip back in His home town. Cousins, uncles, and even more distant kinsfolk, all known as "brethren" and sisters, in the common usage of the time, kept running to His mother to hear the latest news.

"Mary, have you heard of the redheaded woman who rubbed your son's toes with spikenard and washed His heels with her tears?"

Or:

"Mary, do you know about the devotion shown to Him by those other women—Joanna, the wife of Chusa, who is the steward of King Herod? Or of Susannah? Or of so many others?"

If there was gossip or malice in the minds of her neighbors, Mary was still glad to hear any report from Jesus. Those women, she knew, cooked food for her son; sewed the rents in His long white robe; mended His sandals. And Mary smiled even more serenely when town gabblers told her the authorities did not like at all the way her son was encouraging women to take an interest in public affairs and to think for themselves.

The more the populace talked about the growing fame of Jesus, the more the cousins and the uncles, the brethren, felt left out of things. If Jesus had now become such a great man in the region, then why shouldn't the world learn that He had relatives, too, who were admirable in their own way? Or was Jesus ashamed of them all now that He was becoming so famous?

So a number of relatives persuaded Mary to go with them, and they walked together down into the bulging uproar of Capernaum. Because the Master had made it His headquarters, the town was having a boom. Always an overpopulated place, Capernaum was now thronged with tourists, drawn there by tales of Jesus, including thousands of sick people. Lodgings were overpriced, if and when you could find them. The harassment of those innkeepers made Mary think of long ago and far away.

In the private house where Jesus lodged the crush of supplicants from the mob milling in the road made the warm air stifling. Far back of the fringe of the crowd Mary stood outside the house, while some of her big-shouldered relations began to batter forward until they got through the door of the house into the clamoring court and, at last and breathless, stood within sight of Jesus.

"Look!" they panted to Him. "Your mother and your brethren stand without, waiting for you."

And they grinned, fully expecting that He would instantly have a pathway cleared through the hubbub and rush down the opened corridor to greet the family from Nazareth.

But Jesus, looking over their heads and past the crowd saw Mary waiting beyond. For a moment the gaze of mother and son met in tender greeting. He knew that she had trudged a weary journey to see Him here. This toiling, hard-working Mary was no longer young. And she knew full well that He must still be about His Father's business. Between them, in that protracted hail of glance and smile, there was perfect understanding. With His eyes still looking devotedly toward her, He spoke a question to the crowd:

"Who is my mother? And my brethren?"

His arms as He outflung them seemed to bless all the poor and wretched.

"Look at my mother and my brethren!" he cried. "For whosoever shall do the will of God, he is my brother and my sister and mother."

And Mary's smile to those disgusted relatives seemed to ask:

"Is it not all glorious and sorrowful and triumphant?"

Mary, the mother, who understood so much!

Chapter 36 THE TELLER OF GOOD YARNS

As HIS public speaking continued, Jesus began to prove Himself the greatest teller of good stories the crowds had ever listened to.

From the prow of a borrowed fishing ship He would often face the beach and expound His deepest ideas by simple, apt, and exciting tales. Agents and pedants from the Temple, occasionally reappearing to dog His footsteps and listen to everything He had to say, made wry faces at His habit of parable telling.

It was new. It was different. So it must be worthless! And from the point of view of an intellectual it certainly was undignified!

Besides, what *was* new about it? The very school children knew that Balaam had told parables and so had Job. The prophets had made up pointed stories to hold the attention, to make deep matters simple to peasants as well as scholars.

There were two practical reasons for His spinning of yarns. One, of course, was clarification. He was dealing with the most profound truths affecting mankind. It was too much to ask that all mechanics and fishermen should grasp abstract truths too readily. But they could grasp them when He bespelled them, telling narratives with mobile gestures and a perfect and wholly unrestrained ease of delineation—his heroes and villains and a whole great cast of fascinating characters were drawn invariably from familiar scenes; from their own daily life, the background of barns and highways. And all told with such cadence and modulation of the voice and such simple description that the characters seemed to spring up alive before them.

But if His first purpose was to clarify, it was equally true that the second purpose of His stories was to mystify. His disciples often had to ask Him to explain the meaning of His parables, and once they demanded why He often spoke in so cryptic a manner.

"To you," He told them, "is given to know the mystery of the Kingdom of God; but to the rest in parables, that, seeing, they may not see; and, hearing, may not understand; lest at any time they should be converted and their sins should be forgiven them and I should heal them!"

Amazing words, themselves harder to understand than any parable. That behind all these words and deeds of the Master was a universal purpose, beyond the grasp of men, was not yet clear to the disciples, nor is it clear to their descendants today. He had His work to do and it was the work of mercy and salvation. That work must go on, must not be interrupted before all was accomplished. In these enigmatic, seemingly hard words lay a mystery never to be fully revealed to His disciples.

These figures of His parables were everyday folk—farmers forcing the plow through stony, reluctant fields, or poorer men, planting in little gardens—all familiar sights in open Galilee. Some of His plots concerned drunken stewards and faithless servants—and who had not heard of them? He could take the profoundest truths of prophets and old lawgivers and bring them down, in terse, practical words, to the kitchen and the bazaar.

Of course He knew his material intimately; He had lived in a house so dark that a woman must light a candle in the daytime to find the silver coin that she lost; He could, when it helped the story, employ the slang of the gardener, the baker, or the builder; He knew about rotten, leaking old skins and the new bottles of the wine merchant; and the brutal tyranny of upper servants over the lower.

At times He fell back on the lore of the work He had done with His own hands. The carpenter spoke of the splinter and the beam; the strong and the weak foundations of houses; the green wood and the well-seasoned. All the teeming life about Him was material for His parables: pastures, flocks, good shepherds, and lost sheep; mountains and the hawks; how the mustard seed grows from a tiny grain, like faith; rich merchants and poor fishermen; the ingathering of corn sheaves and fruits.

The one parable of Jesus that the people remembered best was the adventures of the prodigal son. There was so much hope and promise in it. There was a tale, the like of which they had often seen acted in real life—the young man, taking what money his father had for him, and traveling off to the great city, expecting to become on his own a very great fellow before long.

But within a short time a siren wound her arms around his foolish neck and smothered his good sense in a counterfeit passion that he believed to be true love; gamblers and thieves worked with her until a whole company of city buzzards picked clean the bones of his purse—and then the young man was kicked out through the back door of the harlot's house. So hungry did he come to be that he took the only job he could find—a pig tender, an assistant to a swineherd; he even ate the husks intended for hogs.

What to do? What to do now? The miserable young man came at last to a sensible resolution. He realized bitterly enough that the lowest servant on his father's property ate better food than he did. Of course he could not ask to be taken back into his old position in the family, but perhaps he might have a job working around the place.

"I will arise," the young man decided, "and go to my father."

And now what does the ragged homebound traveler see? A hurrying figure coming toward him through the dust of the road. It is his father, who has seen him from afar and has rushed forward to clasp him in loving arms, put a ring on his finger, a robe over his cold bones. "Kill the fatted calf, for my son has come home!"

God, Jesus assured them, was a Father like that—waiting for all His sons to come home. Here Jesus reached the highest point, the grand climacteric, the apogee of His teaching.

But there was a next favorite story which He first told under most dramatic circumstances, because of a heckler in the synagogue at Bethany. At the time the vagabond Jesus had come down to Judea and was stopping at the home of three old friends of the family: two spinsters, Martha, her sister Mary, and Lazarus, their brother.

It was an exciting scene that Bethany morning: the congregation crowded the little house of worship facing the highway running from Jericho up to Jerusalem. That was a robber-infested road, dangerous to travelers, to this day as well as then—a steep descent falling from the rocky height of the capital down to the Dead Sea.

The people from roundabout that wilderness region, where John had grown up and Jesus had fasted and been tempted, loved to talk of tweedledum and tweedledee. They were a disputatious lot, relishing the subtleties of theological argument, fine points, and microscopic distinctions. Having heard how a carpenter from Galilee had worsted in debate some of the ablest dialecticians, they sensed a good show to come as they gathered to hear Jesus preach.

One, a doctor of the law, was picked by the others to be their spokesman and to challenge the speaker.

If Jesus had ever been careful in His public talks, He had dropped all caution by this time. In what He had to tell them there was nowadays every opportunity for conservatives to object. With what could seem to many only presumptuous impudence, Jesus informed them they were blessed because of what they were seeing with Him; prophets and kings had wanted to see these things and had not. To the good people of this world He promised eternal life.

In the solemn pause that followed these words the lawyer stood up. With every appearance of civility, but with a leer in his left eye, he asked:

"Master, what must I do to possess eternal life?"

Like many a good Jew before Him, Jesus countered:

"What is written in the Law? How do you read it?"

Question for question the heckler went on:

"Master, which is the first commandment of all?"

"The first commandment of all is, 'Hear, O Israel; the Lord your God is one God; and you shall love the Lord your God with your whole heart, and with your whole soul, and with your whole mind, and with your whole strength. This is the first commandment. And the second is like to it. You shall love your neighbor as yourself. There is no other commandment greater than these."

This apparently simple exchange of query and answer was of deep technical meaning to the intellectual sharks. The lawyer had asked a legal question—and a dangerous one. What he was really getting at was whether the prohibitions—there were three hundred and sixty-five specific ones, together with the two hundred and forty-eight positive commands of the law—were to be regarded as of equal value and importance; a tricky approach in a deliberate attempt to trip up Jesus and get Him into trouble with the authorities. Without hesitation the Master gave a reply that simplified man's duty to his God and his fellow man. Quoting from the Mosaic books of Deuteronomy and Leviticus He had gone back directly to fundamental laws. These He distinguished from trivial man-made observances by which the Pharisees were keeping themselves and everyone else too busy.

"On these two commandments," Jesus further told His heckler, "depend the whole law and the prophets."

But the lawyer did not sit down.

"Well, Master," he persisted, "you have said in truth that there is one God and there is no other besides Him. And that He should be loved with the whole heart and with the whole understanding and with the whole soul and with the whole strength, and to love one's neighbor as oneself is a greater thing than all holocausts and sacrifices."

Jesus nodded, but His eyes studied the man intently.

"You are not far from the Kingdom of God," He said. "You have answered right. This do and you shall live."

Now the lawyer smiled.

"And who *is* my neighbor?" he demanded sharply. By premeditation he had led the way up to this dilemma. Does the neighbor mean only a fellow Jew, Jesus? Surely you don't mean that a Gentile could also be a neighbor? Or, infinitely worse than that, a depraved, despised, unspeakable Samaritan?

"*Master, who is my neighbor?*"

From where He sat Jesus could look down the aisle and through the open door and portico out to the road beyond, the robber-infested highway. It was as if He were describing a drama being enacted there:

"A certain man went down from Jerusalem to Jericho and fell among thieves . . ."

A situation they all recognized and many had feared. Under the storyteller's spell their imagination went to work. They could see that "certain man" packing his bags for the journey, his worried wife helping him and pleading with him to wait until someone else could go with him. No, no—the business was urgent; he must get to Jericho before dawn tomorrow. And then a small, piping voice spoke up—his ten-year-old's voice: listen to the child; he knew somebody that was going on that road tonight: his chum's father.

And who might his chum's father be? What did you say, my son? Did I hear you say that your chum's father came from Nablus? Wife, explain this! A son of mine playing with Samaritan boys!

And the father became even more apoplectic when his boy wanted to know what was really wrong with a Samaritan. Why, explain to him, wife! Samaritans were all dirty and untrustworthy. Hundreds of years ago they collaborated with the Persian invaders . . .

"But, Father, is my chum to be punished for what happened hundreds of years ago?"

No more Samaritan boys for you; no son of mine may be seen playing with a Samaritan; it might even hurt me in my business. And so, having refused the suggestion of his boy, and given his orders and prayed in the Temple, the father starts out alone on the dark road. There he is overtaken by robbers, who strip him to the skin, leave him naked on the ground in the dark—beaten, wounded, and half dead.

And now the crowd was very still as Jesus told them:

"And it chanced that a certain priest went down the same way; and, seeing him, passed by.

"In like manner also a Levite, when he was near the place and saw him, also passed by.

"But a certain Samaritan, being on his journey, came near him; and, seeing him, was moved with compassion.

"And going up to him, bound up his wounds, pouring in oil and wine; and setting him upon his own beast, brought him to an inn and took care of him.

"And the next day he took out two pence and gave to the host and said: 'Take care of him, and whatsoever you shall spend, over and above, I, on my return, will repay you.' "

Here, for a moment, Jesus paused and looked from the bespelled faces of the people straight at the heckling lawyer.

"Which of these, then, in your opinion was neighbor to him that fell among the robbers?"

And looking back into the smiling face of the Master, the lawyer could answer only:

"He that showed mercy to him."

Even then he could not bring himself to use the definite but forbidden word "Samaritan." But that was what he meant.

"Go and do you in like manner!"

Chapter 37 A TIME OF WONDERS

LATE one afternoon Jesus and His group left the west side of the Lake of Galilee and sailed eastward for the desert shore, where there would be no crowds and they could all rest for a while. His resilient nature would always respond to small periods of rest. Now He was tired; soon after they shoved off He fell into a slumber peaceful and deep, as if no harm could possibly overtake Him.

But in those days, as now, the Lake of Galilee was one of the most treacherous of all earth's waters. One moment it ripples in wifely felicity and the next will foam itself into shrewish fury.

On this twilight voyage, while Jesus slept in the hinder part of the ship, His head on a lumpy old pillow, there came out of a sudden dark cloud above them a spit of forked lightning and a peal of thunder. The blow of a high wind rattled the small sails; waves splashed frothing over the bow, and water poured over the side rails.

"Master!" yelled the disciples. "We perish!"

Grabbing Jesus by the shoulders, they shook Him violently awake. As He blinked at them sleepily, the Master did what no ordinary sailor would ever do: He stood up in the rocking boat. More, He spread His hands and commanded the storm to cease, as if expecting immediate compliance—and got it. Instantly the wind fell off and the skies cleared and the little boat rode on over miraculously quieted waters.

But, He asked them, with a mournful shake of the head:

"Where is your faith? Why are you fearful?"

What could they answer? Where *was* their faith? Many times they had seen Him give movement to paralyzed legs; sight to blind eyes; health to the centurion's servant; life to the widow's son. But they had not seen enough to abolish fears for their own skins. Even now Thomas wondered: was not the vanishing storm perhaps just a coincidence?

It was not remarkable, therefore, that two thousand years later young men in universities were to smile and snort at the childish notion that man, born of woman, could, by one word of rebuke, send a tempest blowing on its way. Even those who saw it did not find it easy to believe. And they thought they had faith!

They would see Jesus go buoyantly on His way, driving out of a cave dweller a legion of devils, watching as those dispossessed and invisible fiends entered into a wild herd of swine; they actually saw and heard the pigs and hogs and sows begin to squeal and grunt and run violently down a cliff side into the lake where they were all drowned; they even saw perturbed hog raisers of the neighborhood come in a delegation and plead with the Master to depart to some other place—and still, in their hearts, they had doubts. It would take a hill called Calvary to settle those doubts. Yet others did not need so much!

For example, back in Capernaum Jesus healed an untidy woman sick with a bloody issue. For years she had not ceased bleeding; she had been dosed with the whole pharmacopoeia of her day; "had suffered many things from physicians." So great was the press of the eager crowd clustering densely around that at first the suffering woman could not get near enough to Jesus to ask His help. But she said to herself: "If I can only touch the hem of His garment, I shall be whole."

Ah, Peter—John—James—why could you not believe like this poor woman? See what happened to her now! The fountain of her wasting blood was dried up and she felt in her body that she was healed of the evil; those are the words of St. Mark.

"Who touched me?" demanded Jesus, when this happened.

The others chortled at His question. Who touched Him? In all this jamming press of people? But Jesus silenced the amusement with one flat statement: some energy had been drawn out of Him, His power had been called upon, and in all the pressure of the milling crowd, He knew! And the rebuked disciples gasped with wonder in the next confirming moment when the woman fell down on the ground before the Master, acknowledging that it was she. And He, who had asked His own disciples, "Where is your faith?" said to her:

"Daughter, it is your faith that has made you whole. Go your way in peace."

Only a few minutes before the head man of a synagogue, a Jew called Jairus, had asked the Master to come and look at his sick daughter. They had been walking toward his house when the woman was healed of the bloody issue. But now, as they started off again, a screaming man pushed his way forward and told Jairus:

"Your daughter is dead!"

The father would have fainted, but Jesus put His arm around him. The power to allay pain and jostle death itself was in His hands for brethren and pagan—but never for the unbeliever. So He whispered:

"Fear not. *Believe only!* And she shall be safe!"

Together they strode on firmly, until they came to the house of death. Already the hired minstrels had come to offer their services; they were playing their stringed instruments and singing the psalm dirges—a riot of noise and old custom.

Jesus motioned to the crowd to remain behind. Only Peter and James and John could go in with Him. On the doorstep He made a gesture toward the noisy mercenaries:

"Give place! For the girl is not dead, but sleeps!"

The hired mourners roared; already they were a little drunk; they were insolent and full of scorn. Inside the house Jesus led mother and father into the darkened room where the child lay, white and motionless. Jesus lifted up one cold, limp hand and murmured:

"Little girl, arise!"

At His words the child arose immediately. And Jesus, with the most pleased and tender and understanding smile, told Jairus and his wife to get her something to eat; any little girl, called back from death to life, would probably be hungry. He also entreated the parents not to talk about what had happened.

But the story spread like sunrise.

Chapter 38 NOT WITHOUT HONOR

By now the neighbors in Nazareth were divided about the fame of Jesus and quarreling over Him.

Had He not become too important to talk to His own mother and family?

Disgusted relatives, in spite of Mary, had spread the reproach and they found ready listeners. And others, perfectly decent folk, had the human feeling of being shut out from a recognition they felt rightfully entitled to.

And why did He hang around Capernaum? Why, if this Nazarene were now a great man, did He forget where He came from? He might help His own town a little! They were all neighbors together, weren't they? So on street corners there were arguments and scrimmages, for some would take His part; fisticuffs and knives in the alleys.

In the midst of this public unrest Jesus suddenly returned, and at once the Nazareth air grew as tense as the last moments before a thundershower. Mary's home was surrounded with people, some japing and mocking, others shouting friendly greetings. Peter and the others had to force a lane through which the Master could walk to the synagogue.

And there, once more facing the same benches where as a child He had learned the law and the prophets and the whole body of tradition, He talked about how a man should treat his fellow man.

His discourse shocked every one of them. He drove home an old teaching, but it had to do with a new situation: the racial and religious intolerance of their time. They all had racial prejudices, and it infuriated them to hear Him tell them that they must give up those prejudices: God loved the Syrians and the Sidonians too; He was God of the Gentile as well as of the Jew.

A grumbling filled the synagogue. This was not at all what most of the crowd had come for. Who was He to instruct them? Wasn't He a miracle worker? Well, what was He waiting for? Come on, perform! And they began to make shrill noises and mocking faces, and stamp their feet.

He was the son of Mary, wife of Joseph the carpenter, was He not? He had grown up with the rest of them in these very streets, praying before this very altar. Played with old companions and relatives—James and Joseph and Simon and Jude among them—and the girls of His acquaintance, too, all goggle-eyed now and giggling. Not one such girl or boy, no other citizen of Nazareth, could give a blind man back his sight, change a cripple into an athlete, exorcise evil spirits, drive out demons, or recall to life the stiffening dead. No one else pretended to do such things, either. But Jesus, now, so the tales went, had done all these things and more. Well, let's see Him do them now.

"Show us your powers, Jesus! Open the eyes of the blind, carpenter! Raise us up a corpse, Mary's son!"

Rows of impudent faces, full of taunting challenge, confronted Him from the pews. Physician, heal yourself! As great things as we have heard done in Capernaum, do also here in your own country!

And the reply of Jesus came with a forgiving sigh:

"A prophet is not without honor except in his own country and in his own home."

A prophet, is it? He really considered himself a prophet, then? At once a feeling of outrage swept through the synagogue. While they had waited for Him to perform His tricks like any conjuror with bag and stick, He would try to interpret doctrines to *them!* Not a single blind eye opened, although the place was thick with the blind this morning; not a withered hand waved and shaken until it was whole; not a body climbing out of its grave? Yet He presumed to give himself the airs of a prophet!

Loud cries of anger came from the hot-tempered citizens of Nazareth as they rushed upon Him, the whole squirming, motley crew with cut-throat eyes ablaze. They dragged Him out into the narrow street and up to the brow of the hill on which their town was built. From that great height, where often as a boy He had looked around Him at the world, they would chuck Him headlong down to the rocks.

Not one of the crowd could tell afterward just what happened. A moment He was there, the next instant gone. All they could say to the stricken Mary was that He passed through the midst of them and went His way.

Book Five

THE SECOND YEAR

Chapter 39 BARLEY LOAVES AND FISHES

THE queen had promised Herod Antipas, Tetrarch of Galilee, that, having beheaded John the Baptist, he would have peace of mind at last. He would be free, once and for all, of those gnawing doubts with which the Baptist had pricked his feeble conscience. The people, too, she predicted, would soon quiet down. But Queen Herodias was neither sibyl nor prophetess; she was wrong about both matters. The Baptist was dead, but the king could not forget him. And this Jesus, for whom John had been the great advertiser, was now making the perturbing gospel more popular than ever among the people in his domain.

Not a day passed but the king's spies brought him reports of the growing force of Jesus.

"He has multiplied His influence fifty times over," ran one communication. That estimate had to do with an experiment made by the Master when He gave many of His disciples a trial commission to go out preaching in pairs. He had also assured them that from now on they, too, would have power to cure diseases and drive out unclean spirits from those who believed.

"Heal the sick," He bade them. "Cleanse the lepers. Cast out devils! Raise the dead! Freely you have received, freely give . . ."

The intellectual skeptics at Herod's court laughed.

"How can this man give His dupes power over devils, when there are no such things as devils?" they jeered.

But it was all the more disconcerting, as duly reported to Herod, when the disciples returned full of joyous accounts of their success. Yes, all had happened as He promised. "Lord, the devils also are subject to us in your name!"

Jesus himself was full of joy at their reports, and at once thanked God in prayer:

"I confess to Thee, O Father, Lord of heaven and earth, because thou hast hidden these things from the wise and the prudent and hast revealed them to little ones. Yes, Father, for so hath it seemed good in Thy sight."

And more clearly than before, then, Jesus proclaimed Himself:

"No one knows who the Son is but the Father, and who the Father is, but the Son, and he to whom it shall please the Son to reveal Him.

"Come unto me, all you that labor and are heavy laden, and I will give you rest!"

It was hard to laugh at reports like that.

How can a poor tetrarch laugh when every day he hears that wandering up and down the roads of his kingdom there is a mysterious figure that actually does cure diseases, devilish or not? Herod for a long time refused to believe that there was such a person as Jesus; he believed the new wonder-worker was John the Baptist, risen from the dead.

Moreover, he knew that the constant occupation of this mysterious Nazarene was in preaching a radical doctrine, supplemented with healing. Through 204 cities and villages, the smallest of which numbered 15,000 subjects of Herod, through town and open country and into the Greek cities of Transjordania, the Master went, trudging with His ragged disciples—all poorly clad, poorly housed, and poorly fed—and winning the adoration of crowds by His healing and preaching.

Such a situation would be a menace to any authority!

Next Herod heard of something not only incomprehensible, but inconceivable. One could be told that it happened, but how could one think of it *as* happening?

The scene was on the northeast side of the Lake of Galilee; the time was at the beginning of April, A.D. 29, just when the paschal feast was again coming on. That day a great multitude—at least five thousand people—had followed the Master. Now evening was near and the crowds were hungry. Making a hasty inventory, the disciples found that hardly anyone had brought food on this excursion into the hills.

But Andrew, Peter's brother, said:

"There is a lad here who has five barley loaves and two small fishes. But what are they among so many?"

As the story was carried to Herod, Jesus calmly invited the crowd to sit down on the green hillside. Then He took the loaves, faced the descending sun, and when He had given thanks, He distributed to the disciples, and the disciples to the people, enough to feed the whole five thousand.

How could Herod's mind, or anyone's visualize such a happening? Yet he was informed that there were five thousand witnesses: that the Master had fed Herod's hungry subjects; and that act was enough to unsettle any king.

And then, having shown them the abundance of faith, Jesus gave the people a stern second lesson:

"Gather up the fragments that remain," He said, "that nothing is lost."

They, who had been fed with miraculous abundance, now had to fill twelve baskets with the fragments of the five barley loaves! Clearly one must practice prudence and frugality in the very presence of divine plenty.

Herod was further told that a band of revolutionaries, young hotheads, led by a principal bandit patriot who dubbed himself Jesus Barabbas, were working to overthrow the Roman colonial government by violence. They had organized a posse to take Jesus by force, make Him their leader, and constitute Him King of all Israel.

True, Jesus evaded them, losing Himself in the mountain. But, Herod asked himself, would this wonder-worker always run from such an offer? John the Baptist had been trouble enough, but Jesus might become a threat to established government itself, as politicians like to say.

It all worried Herod the Tetrarch so much that he sent his own spies out for more reports. Some of his advisers were already telling him he had better put Jesus to death before it was too late. Talk about that plan was, of course, palace gossip and soon was carried to Jesus. The Master smiled grimly and said to the talebearer:

"Go and tell that fox, behold I cast out devils and do cures today and tomorrow, and the third day I am consummated.

"Nevertheless, I must walk today and tomorrow and the day following because it cannot be that a prophet perish out of Jerusalem."

Herod Antipas rubbed his head when he heard this.

"He must mean He expects to be killed in Jerusalem," he muttered. And he never forgot those words; he passed them on, by messenger, to the Roman representative, Pontius Pilate.

Next came a story of how the disciples, right after the feeding of the five thousand, set out alone without Jesus in a boat to sail to the hinterland across the lake from Capernaum. It was dark night when, again without warning, the air grew cloudy with impending storm; high and contrary winds blew all around them, and the ship was tossed helplessly. It was the fourth watch of the night, and the frightened Apostles, blown spray in their faces, spindrift on their beards, had given themselves up for lost, when they saw the Master coming toward them. He was walking upon the sea.

Once again the wind began to veer, changing its direction, as He calmed the storm for them.

The tale was not only circumstantial; it even had its humorous aspect. For it seemed that Peter, seeing the watery promenade, suddenly lost his fear of dying in the storm and called out to Jesus—might not he walk on the water too? Certainly; come right along! For a few giddy moments Peter emulated his Master, his big feet treading the wave, his mighty bulk unsinking in the sea. Then panic came to the big fisherman's heart; losing faith, he gave a lugubrious squawk of fright and at once began to go under. But Jesus touched his hand and escorted him smilingly to the gunwale of the boat That was when they began to convince themselves that Jesus was truly a divine being, far nearer to God than they had at first supposed.

A braver man than Herod Antipas would fear a man who could walk on water.

From this and other reports the tetrarch came to see, with gloomy hindsight, that his murder of John the Baptist had served only to bring Jesus into the supreme position as leader of the moral revolution. Nothing could be more troubling. Once the disciples of John had obtained the body of the Baptist and buried it, they spread word everywhere that he had urged his followers to take up with Jesus. Until the beheading, thousands of the John people had patiently waited for the Baptist to be let out of jail. They had fully expected Herod to set him free. Far from being dispelled by John's martyrdom, they rushed to the Nazarene, adding their numbers and ardor to His following. Such a union of growing forces filled with dismay the chicken heart of Herod Antipas; night and noon he kept repeating to himself:

"John I have beheaded. But who is this of whom I hear such things?"

He decided that one day he must have a talk with Jesus. But having no more power of prophecy than his queen, he had no idea under what singular circumstances they were eventually to meet.

Chapter 40 THE CONSPIRATORS RETURN

SCARED though they were at times, as rumors and threats of police interference increased, the Twelve Apostles remained with Jesus. But many other followers, at first loud in their zeal, began to fall away. Some found the doctrine He preached, the discipline He advocated, too severe. Some were afraid of offending the palace. But the Master's increasing claims also seemed to many of them preposterous. For those were the days when He began to be most specific about His identity.

As long as He had been vague, they could interpret His words and still follow Him. When He became explicit—as He did in his famous Bread of Life oration and the whole series of speeches that followed it—making it clear that He offered Himself as the Son of God; well, then a man had to be careful! The very idea that He would be a sacrifice for their sins—no more need of burning lambs and doves—frightened them. What if Jerusalem were to hear such talk? Birds and lambs were big business in the capital.

So many preferred to stand with the powerful of the earth than with this bold, other-worldly teacher from Nazareth. But He went much further than this. Although the tragedy He foresaw was still distant, He announced the miracle doctrine of the Eucharist to them now, long in advance of the Last Supper He would eat with them. This shocked and affronted many of His followers. They could walk with Him no more, as they told Him; one after another, in scores and hundreds, they deserted. Finally He called the Twelve into private council.

"Will you also go away?" he asked them directly.

The answer of Peter was a triumph of the oriental habit of answering one question with another.

"Lord, to whom shall we go?"

And then, in faltering voice, he summed it up:

"You have the words of eternal life."

It was a serious moment in their lives; it became more serious still as the Master looked at them and replied:

"Have I not chosen you Twelve—and one of you is a devil?"

That was another question given as an answer! .

In those days their traveling was incessant. The Master's talks were delivered in synagogues all over the countryside, miracle traveling hand in hand with doctrine. The pentecostal feast of the year 29 found Him in Jerusalem, at the health-restoring pool of Bethsaida, near the sheep's gate. Here, at the basin below the Famous Five porches, He found a frustrated old cripple who for twenty-nine years had never been able to scramble down to the pool in time to be there when "the angel troubled the waters," as the people said. Yet in the capital of His enemies Jesus promptly made the old fellow well in spite of the fact that it was the Sabbath.

Under their breath the Pharisees swore at this popular mendicant; this dusty wayfarer with His burr of the Galilean dialect; this carpenter from Nazareth, whose enemies said He was illegitimate and yet who allowed it to be claimed for Him that He performed miracles! On the Sabbath too! And when this interloper comes to the Temple itself and happens to see there the ancient chap He had cured at the Probatica pool, what does the Nazarene say to him:

"*Sin no more, lest something worse happens to you.*"

And when they bait Him about that word "sin" He tells them simply to their reproachful faces, speaking as the Son of God with powers and prerogatives:

"I cannot of myself do anything. As I hear, so I judge; and my judgment is just; because I seek not my own will, but the will of Him who sent me."

Ah, the Pharisees lamented to one another, we have done wrong to allow this yokel Messiah to get as far as He has. We should have scotched Him two years ago. Here He comes, bold as you please, at the close of His second year, to preach in Jerusalem—right in the Temple! But only the lesser factotums talked so; the real rulers of the Temple authority, of course, were Annas, the former high priest, and his sons. And Annas laughed at the small fry who were afraid of Jesus.

"Messiah!" jeered the old politician. "Our roads are full of self-proclaimed messiahs. Let them all spout—it is a safety release. To shut them up because of such twaddle is to show fear. Give them rope, I say, and let them hang themselves."

The lesser officials were too aware of Annas's complete political domination openly to disagree with him. Nevertheless they put their complotting heads privately together and decided that the whole nation would be better off without such a menace as Jesus. Not only did He break the Sabbath, but He said that God was His Father. That was a hellish thing for a man to say! They would deal with this presumptuous charlatan and stop His blasphemies, one way or another, before they were through with Him, and in spite of Annas.

But because Jesus was so popular, they would have to move slowly, deliberately, and have a complete case against Him before they pounced.

So when Jesus returned to Galilee, in June A.D. 29, the Temple agents were once more on His trail. Down from Jerusalem they came to heckle at every opportunity. You, Jesus—we have watched you eat bread with unwashed hands. That is a violation. You know our observances! Why do you and your followers disobey?

First in answer that ironical smile; then:

"Well has Esaias prophesied of you hypocrites, as it is written: 'This people honor me with their lips, but their heart is far from me.

" 'In vain do they worship me, teaching as doctrine the commandments of men. For, laying aside the commandment of God, you hold the tradition of men, as the washing of pots and cups; and many other such like things you do.' "

Now that was an answer with a vengeance. It was a revolutionary challenge. In a few words Jesus had indicted Temple tyranny and futility in enforcing the letter and smothering the spirit of the law. Boldly He accused them of an organized conspiracy against the heart of the people's religion, of taxing both heart and purse, too, stripping men not only of farthings but of hope.

And such hypocrites were the critics who objected to the soil on His hands? What was true purity? Not what goes into the mouth of a man is impure, but what comes out of it—those things which come out of the mouth come forth from the heart, and they defile a man. For out of the heart proceed evil thoughts, murders, adulteries, fornications, thefts, false witness, blasphemies. *Those* were the things which defile a man!

This increasing quarrel of Jesus with Jerusalem became an absorbing topic of gossip in shops, bazaars, and synagogues. The people had long been familiar with simple disputation; they dearly loved an argument, the noisier the better. But it was with local teachers only that a poor man argued; not with scholars from the capital itself!

Furthermore, the simple home-grown debates concerned only the details, never the philosophy of the teachings. No one in Galilee had ever before dared to dispute the rightness and wisdom of ancient traditions. Many honestly found the flagrant contempt of Jesus for the ceremonials very shocking to their sense of the proprieties. All the province was soon in an uproar of taking sides. In the midst of which Jesus left them once more.

Chapter 41 TRANSFIGURED

JESUS traveled north to the seacoast town of Sidon, one of the oldest cities in the world, to rest incognito for a while. In this fascinating ancient port on the Mediterranean He would live unrecognized in a rented house and move unobserved through the hustling and colorful streets. Relaxing, He would spend long, quiet hours watching the building of mighty ships, whose tall masts and swelling prows would brave the storms of distant seas. Or He would pause at the shops of the silversmiths, toiling at resounding forges, or look down into the red furnaces of glass factories and the vats of purple dyers from nearby Tyre.

But not for long was He left in peace. One afternoon He went for a walk. A light rain was falling; the drizzle was cool to His forehead and the backs of His hands. A vagabond minstrel saw Him and named Him. Soon the rumor ran through the town that He was Jesus, the wonder-worker from Galilee. As crowds began to gather around the front doorstep, the little holiday was over.

Came first a Syro-Phoenician woman. This Gentile stood at the front door, imploring Him to heal her daughter. To the grieving mother Jesus applied a grilling test of humility and faith. He spoke to her as she was accustomed to being spoken to, reminding her that she was outcast and He a Jew: "It is not good to take the bread of the children and cast it to the dogs."

But it did not matter to this Syro-Phoenician mother if He called her one of the dogs. For she answered: "Yea, Lord, for the whelps also eat under the table of the crumbs."

He smiled with approval on this devoted woman. She told Him that her daughter was possessed by a devil or was mad. Jesus, with that same debonair smile, gentle and courteous, cast out the devil and healed the girl completely. Then, going back to Galilee, He healed a deaf man, and a blind man who came feeling his way cautiously down the street.

And then, a day later, as if to confute the skeptics who never left off mocking at the inconceivable tale of feeding the five thousand, Jesus repeated the miracle. This time not a full five thousand were fed—only four thousand famished men and women.

Again He gathered together and used up what they had—a point for all who hoped for miracles in their own private difficulties—seven loaves and a few little fishes. With that slight store He fed them all. A sentimentalist would have thought that the fribbling Temple spies—who not only tracked Him all the way north, and saw the whole thing, but who had generous helpings of the miraculous bread and fish—knowing themselves vanquished, would have repented of their grisly errand and embraced the Master. Instead, what one of them did, a bilious fellow, chronically ill from liver trouble, was to step forward and impudently ask if Jesus would please show them a sign now. With crumbs still on His fingers!

That was when Jesus told the spy and his accomplice there would be no sign for them!

So He refused! He will not give them a sign to prove He was the Messiah? Very well, then, He must be a devil. Good-by, Nazarene, for now! You think we have botched our errand? Well, you'll hear from us later.

Balked, their mission still unsuccessful, they went off to spread a story all over the province; wherever they went they defamed and slandered Him with the same line of propaganda. Jesus was not a prophet; not even a charlatan, a pretender to medical knowledge; He was ridden by a devil! These undeniable powers of His were black magic, straight out of hell.

Soon the tale of what the Temple agents said of Him came back to the Twelve.

"Whom do the *people* say that I am?" Jesus asked keenly, as they sat one day near to the springs of the Jordan; the sound of the water pouring out from the mountain's hip was like a song.

The fervent John, and James, Andrew, and shy, diffident Philip told of strange tales that were believed. Some of the people thought He was John the Baptist, head back on his neck, cadaver out of the grave. Others thought He was Elias, or some other prophet of olden time, reincarnated to call Israel back to first principles.

"But whom do *you* say that I am?" Jesus persisted.

Often His profundities blurred their thoughts and obscured their understanding, but this was a question they felt ready for. There was a moment's silence, then vast Peter stood up and hoarsely cleared his throat.

"You," declared Peter, lifting his beard and forcing back his mighty shoulders, "are the Christ, the Son of the living God."

"Blessed are you, Simon Bar-Jonah!" exclaimed the Master. "Because flesh and blood has not revealed it to you but my Father, who is in heaven. And I say to you: that you are Peter, and upon this rock I will build my church and the gates of hell shall not prevail against it. And I will give to you the keys of the Kingdom of Heaven. And whatsoever you shall bind upon earth, it shall be bound also in heaven; and whatsoever you shall loose on the earth, it shall be also loosed in heaven."

Not one but was deeply affected, not only the disciples but the Master. He charged them with the utmost secrecy. Now was not the time to insist bluntly to the public that He was the Christ. The mere assertion would call down upon themselves the full weight and ferocity of Jerusalem. He would surely be made a prisoner before He had delivered some of His most important coming utterances. Oh, the Temple would make Him prisoner anyway soon enough.

Calmly and with a certitude that overawed all protest he forecast on that calm summery afternoon the coming struggle and its outcome. Not one of the Twelve could ever argue afterward that what happened in Gethsemane and on Golgotha was a surprise to him. Jesus foretold it all several times; already it was clear to Him how He must go to Jerusalem and suffer many things and be put to death.

"Lord," groaned Peter, feeling, in the new authority he had just received, strong enough to protest, "be it far from you! This shall not be!"

Not alarm, but an instinctive awareness of danger flashed into the Master's face as he heard Peter's words; goodhearted Peter, so lacking in intuition.

"Go behind me, Satan!" whispered Jesus, looking directly at His friend, as if He were casting out a devil. "You are a scandal to me, because you like not the taste of things that are of God but the things that are of men."

Peter bowed his shaggy head. Five minutes after having been called the foundation of the church he had been called Satan by the Son of God. Like the good man he was, he prayed for grace.

Another apostle, Judas Iscariot, turned to one side, as if he would walk away. An underbred fellow, that Judas; with a gauche manner, awkward, even boorish, he seemed almost blatantly disinterested in the dreadful prophecy the Master was making for Himself. The eyes of Judas were turned to look off, as if his interest were caught by a scene below, a Roman funambulist, a performer on a tightrope, giving a roadside show.

Meanwhile, as if prodded on by some deep necessity, Jesus told them flatly that the Kingdom of God was near at hand.

"There are some standing here that shall not taste death till they see the Kingdom of God."

Not know death? Yet Peter died. So did John and James, and all the Twelve. For twenty centuries afterward men would argue about that declaration. Ecclesiastics and theologians and masters of exegesis would set up a score of theories and probabilities and deductions.

Yet only a few days later the prophecy came true. Peter and James and John came to that state of grace, miraculously, instantaneously, and with an exaltation that probably surpassed any other single human experience. That was when they witnessed the remarkable phenomenon on the top of Mount Tabor.

Mount Tabor rises at the northeast edge of the valley of Esdraelon. It is not a great mountain, not so high, for example, as Mount Hermon with its lingering snows, farther to the north. But Tabor is a holy mountain because, on its rounded summit, within sight of Jesus's own town of Nazareth, occurred the miracle of the Transfiguration.

To this day no one knows what really happened there. Jesus never explained the mystery. It was six days after He had predicted His crucifixion that He led His three close friends up almost to the very peak. Near by was a stream, and they could hear the babble and the rippling sound of flowing water. When they were quite apart to themselves, Jesus knelt down on the stubble and dried-up grass and began to pray, and the others knelt with Him. Presently Peter and James and his brother John became aware that something extraordinary was happening. Some inexplicable access of power had suddenly taken hold of the Master. He was not now as He had been even five minutes before.

The first great, overwhelming fact that His three friends had to grasp was that *the shape of the Master's countenance was altered.* That, and a moment later the equally visible and undeniable fact that His garment became white and glittering.

The robe that Jesus wore that afternoon was the robe of a teacher of Palestine, long and flowing, and no matter how clean in the morning, it was bound to be stained by dust before He had walked far. But now the raiment, for all its frazzled hem, was pure and glittering, as if woven not of common cotton and wool, but fashioned of an incomprehensible substance, soft and shining. White as snow, that raiment now, whiter than any fuller's earth can make cloth white; any launderer or bleacher of cloth with all the soaps and clays and scrubbing brushes.

"He is being transfigured before us," Peter said in a hoarse whisper.

And now two others suddenly appeared and began talking with Jesus. The Apostles knew, without knowing how they knew, that they were present at and witness to some peculiarly important moment, some vast and significant interruption to the normal course of natural law, some instance of infinite rarity when two worlds are in contact and the dead mingle with the living in felicitous communion.

More, the three fishermen standing on the mountaintop not only saw the Master with Moses, the great leader dead all these vanished centuries, and Elias, long-buried prophet, but they heard them talk, listening to what they talked about.

It was too much; the other world will always be too much for mortal eyes and ears. Their minds grew dense, their eyelids heavy, and they fell asleep. . . .

Waking, they were just in time to see the close of this strange experience. As the Apostles rubbed their eyes, not knowing how long they had slept, light was shining around their beloved leader. They saw the two celestial visitors retreating, walking off as it were, not into space but into some unknown dimension—figures that presently disappeared.

"Master!" came Peter's mighty basso, "it is good for us to be here. Let us make three tabernacles. One for you. One for Moses. One for Elias."

And in sheer exuberance he grinned, as Luke pointed out later, "not knowing what he said." Before he could go on, a fog fell upon the scene, its damp embrace seeming to hide them all from the world, and they heard a voice:

"This is my beloved son; hear Him."

The three Apostles now were so scared that they fell face downward on the ground and stayed there until Jesus touched them and told them to get up.

No more voices then! No more shining figures. Only Jesus smiling and binding them to secrecy.

Now the favorites, Peter, James, and John, had secrets which the other nine must wait to learn—secrets which the favored three themselves did not understand.

The obligation of silence had been laid in frightening terms:

"Tell the vision to no man till the Son of Man shall be risen from the dead."

In their uncertainty the three fishermen quizzed Him in private. What did He mean—when He was risen from the dead? If all that they had seen meant that He was, indeed, the Messiah, what about the old prophecies which had promised that before the Messiah appeared, Elias would be reborn on the earth? How about that? The answer was staggering. The very people who had taught the old prophecies, the scholars who stood by the letter of the law, had not recognized that the spirit of Elias, the prophet, had been revitalized in the ministry of John the Baptist.

Again Jesus repeated His prediction that He was to die a violent death. His persecution would come from the very people who should support the truth but would not.

No words that He spoke, no deed He would do would soften their hearts. And the three remembered how once, when He was about to heal a young man who had attacks which made him foam at the mouth, bite and tear and bruise himself, the scribes and the scholars had gone to the sick boy's father and tried to keep him from the Master. Better to have a dumb spirit, they advised; better to be an epileptic than to be healed by such as He! The father was greatly disturbed, but he loved his son so much that he could manage humility of which the skeptics were incapable:

"I do believe, Lord. Help my unbelief!"

And of course the boy was healed because father and son had faith like a grain of mustard seed; if you had such faith as they had shown, you might say to this mulberry tree, be you rooted up and be you transplanted into the sea, and it would obey you!

The time was not far off, He constantly assured the Twelve, when He would be buried and rise again. Then the Apostles began to gossip and bicker among themselves. He would take on His kingdom when He rose again, and the whole world would have to recognize His power! And when that time came, they, the Twelve, would, of course, have very important positions. Before very long they were thinking about who would be the *most* important, which is a way human beings have of making dunces of themselves, even when they are close to God and on the way to being saints.

Surely they would all sit somewhere quite near the throne of God. But in what order of precedence? The disciples, like wives of cabinet officers and ambassadors, began to be excited about protocol. On the way to Capernaum one day soon afterward they disputed among themselves with some heat.

When they were all in the house at Capernaum, Jesus, who had arrived before them, calmly asked:

"What did you treat of on the way?"

They did not want to tell Him what they had been talking about but He beckoned the whole Twelve to the back yard and when they had squatted around Him, He went on:

"If any man desire to be first, he shall be the least of all, and servant of all."

And as they looked away, with good reason to feel sheepish, He called to a child playing in the doorway and drew him to His embrace. Then, holding on to him, He turned intently from face to face, and taught them with simple directness:

"Unless you be converted, and become as little children, you shall not enter into the Kingdom of Heaven. Whoever, therefore, should humble himself as this little child, he is the greater in the Kingdom of Heaven. Whosoever shall receive this child in My name receives Me, and whosoever shall receive Me, receives Me not, but Him that sent Me."

Chapter 42 TRIBUTE TO CAESAR

NEVER were they allowed to feel safe any more. Go where they would, spies from the Temple were at their heels. The Jerusalem agents were still baffled by the Master's adroitness in avoiding open blasphemy but still hopeful of tripping Him. After two years, during which Jesus had been preaching north and south, they had failed, but their optimism was tireless.

One day, when they were quartered at Peter's house in Capernaum, the spies came, following a pair of taxgatherers and a Roman officer, wearing a baldric loop across his breast to hold his sword—all full of crafty smiles and palm rubbings.

"Well, Simon, does not your master pay the diodrachma?"

"You'll see," answered Peter with a scowl, and strode into the house. The whole question of taxes to a foreign power made the gorge rise in any patriot. And there were so many taxes! No end, it seemed, to the misery. In every Roman province the conquered people had to pay two direct and inescapable taxes—poll and land. The poll tax was a property tax, distinct from the ownership of farms and houses and building lots. If you were a farmer, one tenth of your wheat and one fifth of your wine and fruit were taken for Caesar. On top of these taxes were piled every new and clever and outlandish trick those in power could devise, or the publicans could think up. As if the Temple tithes were not enough, the people must also pay the highway tolls, the house rates, the excise taxes, crown taxes—all very much as poor creatures of governments and politicians have been doing ever since.

More than once Peter had wondered whether he was not, by paying taxes to the representative of Rome, also committing a grave offense against the religious law of Israel, which, as far as the populace was concerned, was the only true law.

And resentful Peter also knew, as he stormed into his house, that these scoundrelly *publicani*, as the Romans called their native collectors, would often lend money to impoverished fellow Jews who found themselves unable to pay. By this act of hypocritical kindliness they converted a public obligation into a private debt, on which they could charge usury as interest.

Such practices had heaped hard times upon Palestine. From broad fields the unhappy farmer would be reduced to a small farm, that is, from a plow to a spade—yet he still could not pay, and so he would lose his second, his smaller farm. Eventually he would become another of the thousands of beggars like those who still hold out their scrofulous hands to tourists in Nazareth and Cana and Tiberias and at all the gates in the wall of Jerusalem. Others might flee into the mountains, becoming bandits or revolutionaries, or both —raiding towns, inciting mobs to rebel, and raising doubts even in the minds of cowards.

"Is it lawful to pay tribute to Caesar?"

One day soon the Temple spies would force Jesus to declare Himself on that poignant issue. But today they had to content themselves with payment in money, which is its own answer.

For reasons of His own, apparently, Jesus chose to delay the inevitable clash; He greeted Peter, as He stomped into the house to seek in the little hoard of the family for tax money, and knowing all the while there was not enough there.

"What is your opinion?" Jesus asked Peter. "The kings of the earth, of whom do they receive tribute for custom? Of their children, or of strangers?"

"Of strangers," Peter replied with bitter certainty.

The nod of Jesus was enigmatic.

"Then the children are free!" He exclaimed. "But that we not scandalize them, to the sea and cast in a hook; and that fish which shall come first up, take; and when you have opened its mouth, you shall find a stater."

A stater? A piece of money—in the mouth of a fish?

"And give it to them for me and you," finished Jesus.

You are not a fisherman, nor am I. Yet you have taxes to pay and so have I. Are we then to hope for gold pieces in the mouths of lake trout? No! No! What are we then to do? We are to stop scowling, stop worrying, go on working—if you are a fisherman, *fish!* The needed money will come from your own labor—and trust the benevolence of our loving Father, who has promised to provide for all needs of the faithful.

The money was put in the taxgatherer's hands, the debt was paid, and the disgruntled spies from the Temple sought comfort at the tavern.

Two long years, and they had not trapped Him yet.

Next year, they promised themselves, would be different! The members of the Sanhedrin, Supreme Council of Israel, were already getting worried. Something was bound to happen.

That was not the opinion of these frustrated detectives alone; it was shared by a few men in the Council itself—liberal rich men who found some merit in these new doctrines being taught by the Nazarene leader.

That was why a visit to Jesus was secretly arranged for one of these rulers with vision. He came and walked with Jesus in the countryside one night.

The stranger was a little man, richly dressed and with carefully trimmed beard, who introduced himself as Nicodemus, a member of the Sanhedrin. He came by night, he explained, because he could not afford to be known as an associate of the man who had created such a tumult of criticism. But Nicodemus, before he came, had informed himself of some of the history of this wayfarer. He got directly down to business.

"Master," he said, "we know—some of us—that you are a teacher that comes from God. For no man can do these signs which you do unless God be with him."

Jesus waited thoughtfully. He knew what Nicodemus was after. This wealthy man of good heart wanted to know the essence of Jesus's teaching. Jesus gave it to him directly:

"Unless a man be born again he cannot see the Kingdom of God."

Nicodemus looked startled. These were strange words, hard to understand. All Israel was waiting for the Kingdom of God, for the Messiah who would throw out the Romans and re-establish the independence of the race, but how could a man be born again to see that happen? Said Nicodemus:

"How can a man be born when he is old? Can he enter a second time into his mother's womb and be born again?"

Jesus smiled and insisted:

"Unless a man be born again of water and the Holy Ghost he cannot enter into the Kingdom of God. That which is born of the flesh is flesh, and that which is born of the spirit is spirit. Wonder not that I said to you, you must be born again. The spirit breathes where he will and you hear his voice but you know not whence he comes and whither he goes. So is everyone that is born of the spirit."

Nicodemus sighed and shook his head.

"How can these things be done?"

As Jesus talked on, really giving this earnest man a panoramic statement of the plan of salvation, Nicodemus began to realize a part, at least, of the enormity of this teacher's claim. Jesus was calmly, quietly informing him that He, the Nazarene, was the Messiah, the bringer of the spirit for which all the race had been waiting for a thousand years.

"For God so loved the world that He gave His only begotten son that whosoever believes on Him shall not perish but have everlasting life. For God sent His Son into the world, not to change the world but that the world may be saved by Him. He that believes in Him shall not change, but he that does not believe is already changed becaused he believes not in the name of the only begotten Son of God."

Nicodemus went away very thoughtfully.

Book Six

THE THIRD YEAR

Chapter 43 YOU MUST HAVE A DEVIL

THE real danger to their safety began to be visible at the Feast of the Tabernacles. That was a great holiday; the popular proverb declared: "Who has not seen this joy of the Feast of the Tabernacles has not seen the glory of Israel."

Together the thirteen started the dangerous journey to Jerusalem. All the long way hostility seemed to meet them. The spies from the Temple had been very busy spreading their canards. A few of the disciples traveled on ahead, and two kept coming back to tell of animosity sowed in people's minds.

In Samaria, where once they had been well received, they found a new coldness; when they visited here before they had been coming from Jerusalem; now they were going toward it, and the Samaritans hated Jerusalem and all travelers who went that way. James and John became purple with fury when they learned that there was no room to be made for them at the inns. In their rage, they were ready to have fire and brimstone fall upon Samaria and scorch it off the face of the world.

Jesus shook His head sadly. These disciples! When would they understand that He came, not to destroy, but to save?

Before they were even halfway to Jerusalem new spies met Him, demanding that they stand and be questioned. The knowledge of Jesus, the resourcefulness of His learning, and His instant access to all the vast body of the law amazed them to the point of exhaustion.

"How does He know, never having been trained as our rabbis are trained?" the inquisitors groaned.

Jesus blandly explained to them that He brought not His own doctrine but the law of One that had sent Him into the world. The Temple provocators worried about that "One," especially when speaking of His divine mission. Jesus went on quietly to ask why they wanted to kill Him.

"You must have a devil, Jesus; who wants to kill you?"

They did, and they knew it, and Jesus knew it; the struggle would not long be delayed. In dialectic too swift and keen for their denial He held up their criticisms to ridicule. Why did He heal the sick on the Sabbath? That, again! Well, it was lawful to circumcise on the Sabbath, because by circumcision a man was improved; yet they would criticize Him when He improved not a part, but the whole man on the Sabbath?

The boldness of such attacks astounded the agents. Already a case of blasphemy might possibly be made against Him—if they could prove that He represented Himself to be of divine origin. Only, it did not seem to them too precise a case as yet because the people knew He was so poor. Even the most stupid man would not expect the Messiah to be born poor and humble! So they hurried back their reports to Jerusalem, upon which the high priest in the Temple turned lavender with ire.

This current high priest, whose name was Caiphas, was the son-in-law of the powerful old politician, Annas; only because the daughter of Annas was his wife was Caiphas high priest. He was a large, handsome coxcomb of a man and not very clever.

At first even Caiphas was not inclined to take Jesus seriously, any more than was Annas later on. But in October A.D. 29 the people of Jerusalem were already talking about the workingman from Galilee as if He were the most interesting person in the world—far more interesting than any of the underground revolutionary leaders. Some enthusiasts even then openly declared they believed that Jesus of Nazareth was the Messiah, the Christ. As they argued:

"When the Christ comes shall He do more miracles than this man does?"

That kind of talk did begin to trouble Caiphas. His quarry was very adroit; there was no evidence against Him yet on which to found a case, although he so often came close to it. But Jesus threw the Temple into an intellectual panic when they learned He had told His followers that He would be with them for only a little while and then would go to the One who had sent Him:

"You shall seek me and not find me, and where I am, you cannot come."

"What is this saying?" they asked one another. "Where will He go that we shall not find Him?"

"If any man thirst," Jesus was telling the public, "let him come to me and drink. He that believes in me, as the Scripture says, out of his belly shall flow rivers of living water."

The Temple agents lifted their ears at the boldness of this indelicate self-assertion. Voices in the roadside crowd were shrill:

"This is the Prophet indeed."

"This is the Christ."

"But was the Christ to come out of Galilee?"

"No, the Christ was to be born in Bethlehem."

"Jesus *was* born in Bethlehem!"

By this time even the tireless agents of the Temple were wearing down. When they came to report to Caiphas, the high priest, their voices were trembling.

"Never did man speak like this fellow," they gasped.

Caiphas was outraged.

"Are *you* also seduced?" he stormed. "Has any one of the rulers believed in Him? No! Not one of us. Or of the Pharisees? No! But this multitude—*bah*. They don't know the law. The crowd is accursed . . ."

Nevertheless, it was at this time that one of their own, one of the rulers as they liked to be called, actually did say a good word for Jesus. He was Nicodemus, the aristocrat, who, muffled in a great dark hood, had once talked by stealth with Jesus at night, to learn His doctrine. Now he accused the others of the Sanhedrin of malice. Said Nicodemus:

"Does our God judge any man—unless He will hear him and know what he does?"

Upon which the aristocratic fellow judges of the Sanhedrin cried at Nicodemus:

"Are you also a Galilean?"

And left him standing alone on the Temple steps.

All this was heating up as Jesus and His followers drew near to the city, and the crowds on the road thickened until it was like a marching army. At the suggestion of Jesus the disciples entered Jerusalem alone. His time was not yet come when He should enter with them, provoke a demonstration, and so cut short His active ministry, in which so much was yet to be done. However, He did enter the capital that night alone, and in secret He moved among the throngs.

Meanwhile, the Apostles, mingling with them openly, heard more talk of their Master than of anyone else. He was the famous legend of the hour. Although here in the capital the opposition of the priests was well known, many dared to say a decent word for Him. Everywhere He was discussed with the utmost seriousness; was He a new revolutionist, a man sent from God, a risen prophet? All the old familiar questions.

"And where is He?" asked some of the Eastern pilgrims.

No one knew.

"He is a good man," one bold spirit dared to say.

"No!" cried others. "He seduces the people."

"No!" cried still others. "He is the Messiah!"

The crowds flowing into the city hired quarters in tents, because the feast commemorated the long nomadic years when their ancestors lived in shelters made of goat skins. It was always celebrated on the fifteenth day of the seventh month, about the time when the harvest was brought home, so it was also known in Jesus's day as the Feast of the Ingathering, a very happy time.

The Apostles stayed that night near to the Temple, which was illuminated. For the whole night dancers with torches were performing in the forecourt, and the air was sweet with the harmonies of dulcimer, cymbals, and trumpets, and drums played by an orchestra of Levites. When dawn came, the crowds would follow the priests to the Pool of Siloam, and from the pool water would be drawn up in a vessel, not of mere lead nor even of silver but of pure and shining gold. Afterward the water was poured out on the high altar of the Temple.

Meanwhile, as Jesus slept on the Mount of Olives, to the east of this city, His enemies in a huddle behind the Temple sat up to discuss ways and means to take His life. Finally one bleary-eyed conspirator had an inspiration.

"If you will listen to an old man," he wheezed, "I can tell you how to trip this fanatic into His grave—and all quite legally too."

They listened and rejoiced at his cleverness. Here was a plan that looked like a certainty. And so simple! Thus the next morning, when Jesus walked calmly into Jerusalem, with polluting exhalations rising from its filthy streets, and appeared in the Temple, returning to His speeches, a band of Temple guards were busy elsewhere on business of the high command. From out of the snarled traffic of some hideous bystreet they lugged a woman from an adulterous bed. She was the bait for the trick they meant to play.

As Jesus sat in the Temple, teaching busily, a delegation of men suddenly appeared with the adulteress by the arm. They shoved her in the open space between Him and His listeners and one guard stood forward as interrogator. He spoke with deep respect, suave, indignant, and with every appearance of sincerity:

"Master, this woman was even now taken in adultery. Now Moses in the Law commanded us to stone such as she. What do you say?"

This kind Jesus from the Bethlehem stable, this healer of the sick —was He likely to order the woman to be stoned to death? They knew it was not in Him to do it. Yet, on the other hand, if He told them they might disregard the Law, He was also guilty of a crime that called for death. Oh, here, now, was a most cunning trap!

Jesus's eyes went from face to face, His gaze straight and full of question. He did not seem to notice the sniveling prisoner. Clearly the man who was her partner in adultery had not been detained. Having looked at all the guards and Temple scholars one by one, eye to eye, the Master leaned forward on His knees and with the nail of a lean brown forefinger wrote in the dust.

There were those who said afterward that what He wrote was a list of women—intimates of the members of this outraged delegation.

When Jesus looked up again over His shoulder, He said calmly:

"He that is without sin among you—let *him* cast the first stone."

And stooping down again, He resumed His mysterious writing in the dust.

The trick had failed! For each man there knew about the improprieties of the others. And they could all read the writing in the sand. And so they hurriedly went out, beginning with the oldest man.

The woman lay there, groveling on the stone pavement, abjectly prostrate. Jesus sat back, relaxed, and smiled at her—such a tender smile as she had never hoped to see on any man's face. His head a little to one side, He asked:

"Woman, where are those that condemn you? Has no man condemned you?"

"No man, Lord."

"Neither will I condemn you. Go!"

And she was almost out of earshot when He called after her:

"*And*—sin no more!"

Chapter 44 A REAL INVESTIGATION!

This episode of the harlot and the guards excited such hilarious appreciation in Jerusalem that Jesus became more than ever an issue, not only in homes, taverns, and outside doorways of the synagogues, but in the highest councils of the Temple.

The rulers now determined to make a thorough investigation of His next miracle and to expose it as a fraud. They did not have long to wait.

On the Sabbath day after a long argument in the Temple Jesus went walking with the disciples down one of the coiling, twisting streets when He came upon a blind man. Seeing the pitiful figure, some of the disciples halted the Master for a question. Probably this mendicant, who had never seen anything in his life—blind before his first cry—was the victim of the disease of a dissolute father. That was why the disciples asked him:

"Master, who has sinned—this man or his parents, that he should be born blind?"

The answer which Jesus gave was bewildering:

"Neither has this man sinned, nor his parents; but that the works of God should be made manifest in him."

Not waiting for more questions, He spat on the dusty ground and then, bending over, kneaded the wet dust into a kind of clay which He spread on the blind man's eyes. And He whispered:

"Go—wash in the pool of Siloam."

Off went the trusting blind man, thumping with his stick, and Jesus resumed His stroll. But it was not long before they heard a hullabaloo in the streets behind them. Here came the blind man again, having done as he was told; now he returned, romping down the highway, seeing the world—the blue sky, the white clouds, the sun, the streets, the houses, the people, the smiles on children's faces. And people ran with him, jabbering:

"Is not this he that sat and begged?"

"He is like him, but—"

The beggar looked back over his shoulder, shouting scornfully:

"I *am* he."

They clamored around him:

"How were your eyes opened?"

And the man said:

"That man called Jesus . . ."

So! But the Pharisees had been telling the people they were not to believe in that man called Jesus. Plainly the thing to do was to take the former blind man and show him to the Pharisees. What would they have to say to this?

The answer of the Pharisees was typical of all the Pharisees in the world then and ever since. Having heard the facts, they shook their heads. Here was a very serious offense indeed. Jesus could not possibly be a man of God and for the same old reason—if He *had* healed this blind man, He had done it on the Sabbath. Therefore He had broken the law of Moses.

But a few of the rulers were more impressed. Timidly one asked:

"How can a man who is a sinner do such miracles?"

About this point they began to squabble among themselves. Finally they turned on the beggar and put the question squarely to him:

"What say you of this man that has opened your eyes?"

The beggar answered doggedly:

"He is a prophet."

By this time the Pharisees had recovered from their first shock and retreated to firmer ground. They were certain the whole thing must be a fraud; of course there had been no healing—the man had never been blind in the first place. Most likely he was a sensation-monger as well as a liar. But suddenly an old man and an old woman were shoved forward by the crowd. They were the beggar's father and mother. The Pharisees had to ask the old couple:

"Is this your son who you say was born blind? How then does he now see?"

The old man and the old woman said they certainly knew this man was their son *and* that he was born blind.

"But how he now sees we don't know. Or who has opened his eyes we don't know. Ask our son; he is of age. Let him speak for himself."

Their simple declaration left the Pharisees in such a quandary that they wanted to end the interview as quickly as possible. So they recalled the beggar and gave him some sound advice. Perhaps he had been a little blind; if now he had his sight, let him give glory to God.

"Don't you know this man Jesus is a sinner?" they nagged him.

But the beggar answered:

"If He be a sinner, I don't know. But one thing I know—that once I was blind and now I can see."

It was a long, tough day for the Pharisees!

An even more desperate clash between Jesus and the Temple was to come soon afterward on the question of His authority.

Who had told Him He could teach the people?

Who had appointed Him?

Plagued with these questions, the Master told them plainly that He was in Palestine to do the will of the heavenly Father, adding boldly that He and the Father were one.

So carefully phrased were His assertions that not even then could the Temple make out a case of presumptuous blasphemy against Him. Yet the claim He then made to divinity was clear. He alone could fully know the Father; so He informed them. None except the Father could fully know the Son, either. That was an assertion of infinite at-oneness between the two. Staggering declaration! Even more staggering was the profundity of concept, the precision of utterance, when He hurled at them the statement:

"*Before Abraham was made, I am!*"

Why all this disputation? Partake of universal beauty and wonder with me, you unhappy people; in one instant I shatter all the ideas an ordinary man has about time and space and sensibility; in another instant I give you welcome to eternity.

"Come unto me, all you that labor and are heavy laden and I will give you rest.

"Take up my yoke upon you and learn of me, because I am meek and humble of heart and you shall find rest to your souls.

"For my yoke is easy and my burden is light."

For such words, in spite of all the power and antagonism of the Temple, the people loved Him.

Chapter 45 THAT BETTER PART

It was about this time that Jesus found Himself scolded by one of the best friends He had in the world. That was Martha, the sister of Lazarus and of Mary, who lived in Bethany.

For a long time the four had been good friends. At the very outset of his ministry Jesus had met the gentle, shy Lazarus, who took Him home for supper one night and introduced Him to his sisters. Ever since that night they had all adopted Jesus into the family. Whenever He came near Bethany, which is only a few miles from Jerusalem, He must stay with them. It was in the synagogue near their home that Jesus had engaged in that breathless colloquy with the heckling lawyer and silenced him with a story destined for immortality—the parable of the Good Samaritan.

But there was a difference in the relation of Jesus to each of these three vivid personalities. Lazarus himself was a retiring, self-effacing man who never once dreamed that he was to be an instrument of universal power, an experiment in love and death. Mary was a thoughtful and dreaming girl whose brain was clear, curiously insatiable, full of a great yearning to know and to understand. Her sister Martha was quite the opposite: the busiest housewife in Bethany—and the most respected. She scrubbed and swept and dusted and washed and ironed and baked and roasted and basted and tasted and poured forth her abounding energies in performing all the duties a woman was expected to perform.

One day Jesus came to stop at their home. In the cool shadows of late afternoon He sat in the dooryard, talking of profound matters with Mary, the thinker and dreamer, who sat listening. Her eyes on the Master's face, she asked many questions, while from within the house came an increasing clatter of plates and pots and jugs—it was, somehow, a very noisy kitchen this day.

Suddenly Martha, red-faced, hands dripping wet, breath panting, appeared angrily on the doorsill. She spoke with labored politeness. It was wonderful out in the front yard; she could feel the coolness now, but she could not understand why her sister Mary should sit at ease on the front stoop with their illustrious guest and chat while she baked and stewed in the hot kitchen and got the supper ready.

She, too, would like to have sat and talked, but somebody had to get the meal.

"Martha, Martha," Jesus answered, "you are careful and troubled about many things. But one thing is needful: and Mary had chosen that good part, which shall not be taken away from her."

Now what was Martha to gather from that? She was very puzzled, as she turned her back on her guest and her sister, to retire to the kitchen and go on with her cooking. Her face was very red, her heart very sick.

She felt virtuous about doing all that drudgery just to give Him the right kind of meal. Certainly both wanted to put a good table before Him. Both wanted Him to be comfortable, well fed, the food savory, the dishes shining, the linen crisp and clean. But it was Martha who must see to all that, and in return she heard those strange words as she came back to the kitchen wiping her hands, confusion in her eye.

What could He have meant? Was honest labor being rebuked? Was this shiftlessness of her sister the good part which was not to be taken away from her?

Here was a riddle for all the good Israelitish wives and daughters. They had no voice anywhere except in the kitchen; they were like house slaves. No woman had ever appeared in those casual roadside debating societies where Christ and His disciples matched wits with argufiers of all sorts. In those days men believed that woman's place was in the house. She was expected to be careful and troubled about many things—but never about ideas. Women were workers, not thinkers; practical, not speculative; drudges ministering to the physical wants of man.

Martha knew her duty and she did it—with the self-righteousness that is found sometimes in such good housewives. And Martha resented any other woman—but most of all her own sister—who wanted to discuss philosophy with a man. No woman, before that Mary, had ever been allowed to do such a thing.

Jesus was opening the door to Mary, the modern woman, when He encouraged her intellectual rebellion.

He said that she had chosen the good part in taking an interest in matters which men had, until then, appropriated to themselves. It was an important matter that He settled on the doorstep in Bethany. Today all the women of the world have chosen that good part, and it shall not be taken away from them.

Chapter 46 THE DINNER TABLES OF THE MIGHTY

THOSE were busy days, filled with many healings—including two blind men from Bethany, who howled down the dusty road: "Have mercy on us!" and ten lepers who were all made clean at one stroke. Only one of the ten gave thanks for deliverance from the loathsome disease, and he was a Samaritan!

Once more, in defiance of the Pharisees, Jesus restored another patient on the Sabbath; openly, in front of all, on the floor of the synagogue. This poor woman was very ill; her body bent inward so that she was bowed together, head and toes nearly touching; she had not been able to look upward at all for eighteen years. By laying His hands on her, Jesus straightened out the contorted body; she was a well woman on the instant. Yet——

"Master, we would see a sign from you!" the hecklers told Him again.

Aristocratic scholars from the Temple and the Pharisaical rabbis from the neighborhood synagogues no longer hid their fears of His effect on the common people. Enemies of various kinds were drawing together against Him in a conspiratorial unity of alarm.

If they could have read the future (they who could understand neither present nor past) they would have known that the very answer of Jesus was, of itself, a true sign, although He scorned to tell them so. There was a gleam in the dark eyes as He replied:

"This generation is a wicked generation. It asks a sign, but a sign shall not be given it, except the sign of Jonah, the prophet.

"For Jonah was in the whale's belly three days and three nights. So shall the Son of Man be in the heart of the earth three days and three nights—and behold a greater than Jonah is here!"

They could not, of course, penetrate this sign, this precise prediction of His three days in the tomb. But the Pharisees knew they were getting nowhere with Him; the chief counselors decided that their agents sent out to ensnare Him had not been very clever. Wiser heads were needed now.

That was why, on a twilight walk from the synagogue at Bethany, Jesus was stopped by a rich old Pharisee who invited Him to dinner. Here was news! True, Jesus had been entertained by rich men before this, and others had come stealthily, after nightfall, and kept their visits secret. But never before had Jesus been given social recognition so near the capital.

The Pharisee who invited Him, a tall, sallow man with the cold eyes of an undertaker, never did cease regretting it for the rest of his natural life—because things went wrong for the host from the moment Jesus entered the house. It began when the Pharisee noticed, to his shocked dismay, that Jesus had not washed before dinner.

Now, while the Pharisees knew little enough about sanitation in the time of Jesus, since the time of Moses they had had the good sense to wash faces and hands before they took food in their fingers. It seemed a perfectly fair question for the Pharisees to ask Jesus why He did not wash; He who had made cleanliness the very life of His teaching and whose first sacrament was baptism. Jesus had been teaching in the synagogue on the Jericho turnpike; then, jostled by a stinking, unscrubbed mob, He had walked across the stony hillsides to keep His dinner appointment. He entered the burgher's house and sat down at table without asking first for a basin of water and a towel.

The Pharisee did not mention the omission. He merely thought about it. What he did not realize was that he was in the presence of one from whom no thought could be concealed. It was not merely that Jesus knew what the Pharisee was thinking about washing before meals. He knew the whole psychological history of this Pharisee; and why he had invited a wayside teacher in to dine. That old Pharisee also thought—just like the rich man in Galilee, human nature seeming the poor thing it sometimes is—that Jesus would be flattered by the invitation. A wandering visionary, with no home of His own, a man with no position in the community whatsoever—such a poor creature might be expected to feel a sense of great social elevation. That would soften Him up, making Him ready to be wheedled. A table heaped with good food, delicacies a poor man never tasted, goat skins puffed with European wines from Samothrace and Naples and Rome—soon the vagabond would be heady, giddy, talkative—He would say too much; why, they might even be able to nab Him before the dessert.

Jesus knew that was how the Pharisee thought and how he had planned his evening. When the Master entered the house, He did not wash for the single reason that He had no intention of remaining there to break bread with this old schemer. Instead, the dinner still untouched, He seized the occasion to give His host and other guests a lesson they would never forget. He began by directly answering His host's discomfort because He had not washed: in quiet voice He stated simply:

"You Pharisees make clean the outside of the cup and the platter. But your inside is full of rapine and iniquity. . . .

"Hypocrites. Because you are like whited sepulchers, which outwardly appear to men beautiful but within are full of dead men's bones and of all filthiness."

That was a dismaying beginning for an evening meal. The shocked silence was broken by one of the other guests, a scribe who knew every jot and tittle of the law; one, though, without much humor, for now he spoke up in a tone of pained protest:

"Master, in saying these things about Pharisees you reproach us, the lawyers, also!"

Did He? Most certainly He meant to!

"Woe to you lawyers also! Because you load men with burdens which they cannot bear; and you yourselves touch not the packs with one of your fingers. You have taken away the key of knowledge; you yourselves have not entered in, and those that were entering in, you hindered."

After that outspokenness Jesus arose and went quickly out of the house. That same night a second council was convoked in Jerusalem. The lawyers and the Pharisees came together in what was like an ecstasy of hate. They must not have a man at large, saying things like that! There must be some way found to catch something from His mouth by which they might accuse Him.

As a practical result of their convocation they decided to make another try. If He blaspheme in front of expert witnesses, they might be able to indict Him. So for the third time Jesus found Himself invited to a rich man's table. On this night Jesus observed all the amenities. He washed His face and hands and reclined on a couch at the ruler's table. Suddenly, through the open door there staggered a man with dropsy—an accumulation of water in various parts of the body. No one said anything as the dinner was interrupted by the silent apparition of this suffering man, but all the other diners looked at the Master. Would He forget that this was the night of the Sabbath?

Sensing the familiar trick, Jesus looked around at all of them—

the lawyers, the formalists, the Pharisees to whom the slightest dereliction in the strict observance of the Sabbath was a mortal sin—and He asked them a question:

"Is it lawful to heal on the Sabbath day?"

He got no answer. But He waited for none. He turned to the sick man and made him well, and sent him away.

"Which of you," He then asked, "shall have an ass or an ox fall into a pit and will not immediately drag him out on the Sabbath day?"

The silence was still acute. By this time, because of news of the healing, the house of the Pharisee was surrounded by a multitude. Jesus left the table, turned His back on the supper guests, and, standing in the open doorway of the rich man's house, He began to speak with supernatural eloquence and power, delivering the greatest of His parables—for that was when He told the story of the prodigal son.

This exhortation to the multitude in front of the Pharisee's house was almost as moving as the Sermon on the Mount. With supreme earnestness and poetic eloquence, He talked to them of God's forgiving way with sinners, of the virtue of humility, and the abominations of pharisaical pride. This was a time when He served notice that no man could serve two masters and explained the necessity of renouncing all to follow the way of Christ:

"If any man come to me and hate not his father and mother and wife and children and brethren and sisters; yes, and his own life also, he cannot be my disciple. And he that takes not up his cross and follow me is not worthy of me."

Well, that was the third time the Pharisees had Jesus in to dinner. They would never ask Him again.

Chapter 47 URGENT TEACHING

Beyond Jordan, in the country across from where He was baptized, Jesus retired for a while to talk over the future with the Apostles. There was now an urgency in His attitude; He told them the time was short before He would close His earthly mission, to bring forgiveness to the world.

This pardon of God to a man, based on how that same man pardons his fellows, was the peak of His teaching, and it reached the peak of expression in this region near where John had first proclaimed Him three years before.

There was so much He had still to impart, and the human limitations of His chosen Twelve were sadly visible, yet they were the men who must carry forward the work when He was gone. To them He emphasized major problems—the sex life, marriage and divorce, celibacy and virginity. Whom God had joined together, He told them again, let no man put asunder.

But was celibacy ever to be recommended above marriage? Only for those who choose to be free of family ties and obligations, and the tyranny of the senses, in order to carry on the Master's work:

"For there are eunuchs who were born so from their mother's womb; and there are eunuchs who were made so by men; and there are eunuchs who have made themselves eunuchs for the Kingdom of Heaven.

"He that can take it, let him take it!"

Then He turned and held out His arms to mothers and their children. His face glowing with love for all the little ones of earth and their mothers, He turned to the same disciples to whom He had explained virginity, marriage and divorce, and with little boys and girls climbing all over Him, He smiled at their confusion. Peter! James and John! You are trying to chase these children away, as if they were a nuisance and a disturbance; listen:

"Suffer little children to come unto me and forbid them not, for of such is the Kingdom of God. I tell you, whoever shall not receive the Kingdom of God as a child shall in no wise enter into it!"

More and more He taught of the particular care God has for every living individual:

"Are not five sparrows sold for two farthings and not one of them is forgotten before God? Yes, the very hairs of your head are all numbered."

Thus He emphasized the uniqueness of the individual, and they loved it, though little comprehending the literal import of His words. But two thousand years later, in the laboratories of modern criminologists, the spectrograph and spectrophotometer show us that the hair on every mortal head is different from all others; and, more, that each individual hair is "numbered," is different from any other hair on the same head! Not only are there no two thumbs or fingerprints alike in all humanity, but even the lines and whorls and loops and corrugations on the hoofs of cows and bulls and the feet of dogs and cats are all unparalleled. It is science today that shows individuality to be of persistent uniqueness in God's world, just as Jesus taught it.

Science was to learn that not one man's sweat was like another's; you could break it down into its chemical elements, and find an infinite diversity in mere drops of perspiration. Let the killer leave but a stain from moist finger tips on the lace collar of the woman killed and he can be convicted by it.

Every part of me and you is intrinsically and unmistakably you and me; the combination and proportions of your phosphorus and calcium and all the rest of you are unique. That immense importance of your uniqueness, and mine, your individuality, your immortal soul was what Jesus was trying to bring home to the people:

"Yes, the very hairs of your head are numbered . . . you are of more value than many sparrows."

In those days, too, He began to promise them the coming of the Holy Ghost, which was the good spirit, the comforter, or paraclete, always to be guide and counselor to every Christian, after Jesus was gone. If they were ever brought into court, they were not to be afraid of how or what they should answer; the inner voice of the Holy Ghost would let them know in the hour of trial what they should say. They need not fear hunger or homelessness; they must put their confidence in His promise of this help to come.

Jesus seemed to be more deeply concerned than ever with the relations of the poor and the rich; of capital and labor; the responsibilities of workman and millionaire. A brightly dressed, golden-curled young man rushed up to Him one day on the open road and gasped:

"Good Master, what shall I do that I may receive life everlasting?"

"Why do you call me good?" Jesus waited a moment for the young man to get his breath. "None is good but God alone." Jesus was well aware this baffled young man was no more than a curiosity seeker; he had no real faith in Jesus or His divinity. "Then why call me good? You know the commandments: you shall not kill; you shall not commit adultery; you shall not steal; you shall not bear false witness; honor your father and mother."

"But, Master, all these things I have observed from my youth. What else shall I do?"

And again the smile of Jesus was rueful.

"One thing is wanting unto you. If you will be perfect, go sell what you have, and give to the poor, and you shall have treasure in heaven; and come, follow me."

The kneeling man stood up. His face was stricken, tragically full of regret. He went away sadly. He was very rich; he had great possessions.

Looking after him, seeing his sorrow, Jesus remarked how hard it is for a rich man to enter the Kingdom of God; harder than for a camel to pass through the eye of a needle. Yet, He added whimsically, with God all things are possible.

But no sooner had the rich man gone off than the Apostles picked up that promise about treasure in heaven.

Peter cleared his throat.

"Master, *we* have left all things and have followed you. What, therefore, shall *we* have?"

Smug and self-righteous as he was at that moment, Peter spoke only fact. He and the others had certainly left house and nets and ships, brothers and sisters, father, mother, wife, children. The reward, they had thought, was well worth the price—life everlasting. But after hearing that talk with the golden-curled young rich man, there was a large question in their minds. They had given up their all for the rest of their lives. What about the Jacob-come latelys? The people who had enjoyed a full worldly life and then, just shortly before they were going to die, joined up in the movement of Jesus? Would these late arrivals get as great rewards as the others, who had served a lifetime; had borne the heat and burden of the day? That didn't seem just—for the late ones had much more to repent than the original followers.

Yet Jesus was constantly preaching forgiveness—not once, not seven times, but seventy times seven; and endlessness of forgiveness. How about those who asked forgiveness at the eleventh hour? Did they share equally in the great rewards to come? And even though He told them a parable of laborers in the vineyard, there was still a growing riddle in their souls.

He saw their plight clearly; in the little time that was left He would try to buttress their faith. But in the midst of their counsels there came a call to Bethany, back to the house of Martha and Mary.

Chapter 48 COME FORTH!

As ALL the world knows now, but few cared then whether they knew it or not, Lazarus was the brother of Mary and Martha. By hired courier the sisters sent an imperative message to Jesus:

"Lazarus, he whom you love, is sick."

But to the consternation of the Twelve the comment Jesus made seemed almost casual:

"This sickness is not unto death, but for the glory of God; that the Son of Man may be glorified by it."

Now the sisters had not misrepresented the facts. Jesus did love Lazarus; He loved all three of that family as personally as He had ever loved any other mortal, except His mother. All the more surprising that He seemed to dismiss the desperate message while He lingered; He even seemed to dawdle for two whole days, nor would He budge from the town where the message had found Him.

The earthbound Twelve Apostles applauded His behavior, although they completely misconstrued it.

"Good thing He stays here! Sensible!" they said among themselves. "To go back to Bethany, so close to Jerusalem, would be like walking into the den of a bear. By now the Temple is so stirred up, they would be bound to do Him mischief. They might even hire a killer to put Him out of the way. Or even massacre the whole lot of us while we sleep. The Master is right: it is all very sad about Lazarus, of course—every one of us loves Lazarus—but it is much more prudent to stay right here and be safe!"

Upon which Jesus suddenly told them He was going on to Bethany. They bitterly protested. What could He be thinking of? Only a short time before, when He was there, agents of the priests tried to stone Him. Why go back? His only answer was:

"Lazarus our friend sleeps; but I go that I may awake him out of sleep."

"Lord," protested the disciples, "if Lazarus sleep, he shall do well!"

Then the kindly smile faded from the lips of Jesus and He spoke to them sternly:

"Lazarus is dead."

That was mournful news. It was true that they had all loved Lazarus. It was heartbreaking to think of their friend as dead. Yet even more shocking, fuller of heartbreaking bafflement were the next bewildering words of their leader:

"Lazarus is dead. And for your sakes I am glad that I was not there—that you may believe. But let us go to him."

Then up spoke Thomas, whose other name was Didymus, in Greek, "the twin." Thomas Didymus was an early exponent of the scientific spirit; his hardheaded insistence on facts made the others call him Doubting Thomas. Doubter he was, a man slow to make up his mind, one truly born with a thirst for honest inquiry and one who dearly loved a fact—yet once doubts were resolved, his loyalty was simple, fixed, and unshakeable. Although in this sudden resolution to go into danger Thomas foresaw nothing but disaster, he wheeled on his companions and snapped:

"Let us also go! That we may die with Him."

Their hearts were heavy, but they backed up Thomas, all of them, from John to Judas.

The house of Martha and Mary was crowded with mourners, friends and relatives and professional weepers and groaners hired for the occasion, according to custom; criers and breast beaters, who created a frantic disorder night and day.

As soon as she was told that Jesus was coming, Martha ran out to meet Him. Mary remained at home. Both women were in agony of sorrow and disappointment: Mary withdrawn to herself; Martha, the forthright practical one, rushed out.

"Lord," she exclaimed bitterly on confronting Jesus at the edge of town, "if you had been here, my brother had not died."

The redness of grief streaked her gaunt face and quivering cheeks. Then, recalling herself, she bowed her head submissively and her lips trembled:

"But now—also I know—whatsoever you will ask of God, God will give it you."

Jesus put His hand on her shoulder and whispered:

"Your brother shall rise again."

But Martha frowned, because even then she did not trust herself to believe or hope.

"I know that he shall rise again—in the resurrection at the last day."

Jesus had to force her to look at Him; made her eyes meet His own as He said:

"I am the resurrection and the life."

A hush fell on them all at these fateful words.

"He that believes in me, although he be dead, shall live. And everyone that lives and believes in me shall not die forever. Believe you this?"

"Yes, Lord! I have believed that you are Christ, the Son of the Living God, who are come into this world."

By the look in His eyes she felt forgiven and released. She gathered up her skirts and, turning, rushed back to the house and called her sister Mary:

"The Master is come and calls for you."

Mary did not wait. Now she, too, ran out of the house, down the stony hillside. Everybody in the house followed her; they were in a tumult; what had happened? Perhaps Mary was going to the grave itself to weep and pray. If so, she must not go alone!

Mary did not care who was following. At first her heart was lifted up, like the heavenly gates and the everlasting doors in the psalm, just because Jesus had sent for her. But as she ran on, the memory of His absence at a time when they needed Him most, when they sent for Him and He hung back when He might have answered—the resentment welled up in Mary, so that when she came to Him, although she fell down at His feet, she, too, reproached Him.

"Lord, if you had been here, my brother had not died."

She wept, and all the others that had followed her wailed with her.

"Where have you laid him?" Jesus asked patiently.

"Lord, come and see!" shouted the mourning relatives.

Jesus wept. The sight of the Master in tears as they trudged all together once more into the Bethany hills made many a woman speak behind her hand to a neighbor:

"Look how He did love Lazarus!"

"Ah, yes, but——"

"But? But what?"

"Could not He that opened the eyes of the man born blind have caused that this man He loved so much should not die?"

Now they were come to the grave of Lazarus; it was a tomb, really a cave, dug down out of the slant of a rocky hill and reached by going down a set of three stone steps and crossing two large flagstones. A boulder stood before the entrance of the sepulcher.

Jesus said:

"Take away the stone."

Let him who has an ear hear that! Remember all that you see here now, Apostles!—miracle of reassurance for you when you shall need it most, from one coming desolate Friday until its Sunday.

"Take away the stone," said Jesus, but the practical sister Martha, notwithstanding all the faith she had professed, had to protest:

"Lord, he has been in the tomb for four days. By this time . . ."

"Did I not say to you, that if you believe, you shall see the glory of God?"

Sweating, gasping, and feeling they were doing a mad thing, the relatives shoved away the stone. And Jesus, going to the edge of the steps, looked up at the sky and spoke:

"Father, I give thanks that you have heard me. And I know that you hear me always, but because of the people who stand about, have I said it; that they may believe that you have sent."

There was a moment of critical silence. The spring winds blew sweetly on their faces and the smell of the tomb was crossed with the odor of wild flowers. Then Jesus cried in a loud voice:

"Lazarus! Come forth!"

And he that had been dead, the buried Lazarus, did come forth. He came of his own motion, revenant under his own propulsion, though he was bound, feet and hands, by the white winding sheet and his face tied around with a napkin under his chin. Jesus said to them:

"Loose him and let him go."

And Lazarus embraced his sisters.

Chapter 49 A POLITICAL SETBACK

From a political point of view, the raising of Lazarus was a handicap.

To bring back a dead man to life in the very shadow of Jerusalem's walls was bound to fill the capital population with awe and therefore further anger the priests. True, this was not the first dead person Jesus had brought back to life, but the miracle of the house of Jairus had been performed in a northern province; from such a distance rumors of miracles were not taken too seriously. But not so with Lazarus, who lived right next door. Plenty of people in Jerusalem could swear that Lazarus had actually died and had been buried in his tomb. Now, with their own eyes, they could see him walking around again, living as usual.

No wonder Caiphas, the high priest, found himself suffering from gas pains after every meal. Caiphas had run the Temple from the year 18, and always he had been a jumpy, apprehensive man. But now he was becoming sleepless–a victim of insomnia because too many people were beginning to believe the Galilean miracle-doer really was the Messiah.

That was more than a nuisance in the high priest's comfortable scheme of things–it was potential ruin. The Nazarene *must* be stopped.

After all, the Temple scouts had been dillydallying with the fellow for nearly three years, and with no results. How far must He be allowed to go? Not until the raising of Lazarus from the dead had Caiphas realized the depth of the peril. If a determined majority of the people were to come to believe in Jesus, before long they could –and very likely would–turn out of authority scribes and politicians, Sadducees and Pharisees, concessionaires and all their rackets. The sacrificial fires would go out and the altars smoke no more, which would mean no more booth-selling of lambs and doves, the end of money changing and simony, good-by to the juicy traffic in sacred things.

Hardly a rich man in Jerusalem whose pocketbook would not be affected by such a turn in the popular will. If the people believed in Jesus, they would throw out the men who exploited their hopes and fears. When *that* happened, the Roman officials, up to the mighty Pontius Pilate himself, would say to the high priests and all the interlocking directorates of the Temple aristocracy:

"Since you cannot control your people any more, we won't make any more deals with you; we must do business with this newcomer who has the support of the people; we will make our arrangements with Jesus!"

No, that would never do! As Caiphas realized the situation, he stroked his long and perfumed beard and murmured to his anxious comforters:

"It is expedient that one man should die for the people–not the whole nation perish."

How truly he spoke he did not know!

Caiphas was in a hurry to settle Him, but Jesus needed time to complete His instruction of the Apostles. So He retired to a retreat His enemies did not know, to a place called Ephraim, a tiny and remote brown mud village in the desert, fifteen miles to the northeast of Jerusalem.

There Jesus taught His Twelve at length, making a third prediction to them of His death and resurrection. Six stages He counted out for them: betrayal, the sentence of the court, the handing over to the Roman governor, mockery and humiliation, crucifixion, and the final triumph. Here He became most precise, calmly preparing His friends for what was to happen when He would be mocked and scourged and spit upon.

"The Son of Man shall be betrayed to the chief priests and to the scribes and to the ancients; and they shall mock Him and spit on Him and scourge Him and kill Him; and the third day He shall rise again."

Chapter 50 THE GREAT FEAST

IT WAS now the time of the Passover, the greatest of all celebrations in Israel. From the sea and from over the caravan routes of mountains and deserts, by ships and camels and walking barefoot, travelers by thousands and scores of thousands turned weary and sweaty faces toward Jerusalem. No matter how tiring, they must make the journey, for the Pasch was coming: the great Passover feast commemorating the night when the Lord, smiting the first born of the Egyptians, passed harmlessly over the houses of the children of Israel. All devout souls who could possibly do so wanted to make their way to the Temple at Jerusalem. For seven days they would join in the prayers, offering up the paschal lamb in the traditional sacrifice and eating the unleavened bread.

Soft spring lay over that hard city on the great height. Time for the cuckoo to sing and new little flowers to bloom. Time of the racing of the sap and a sense of resurrection in human bodies and thoughts, when life renews itself.

Jesus and the Twelve were also going up for Passover in Jerusalem. The Apostles were boyishly excited by the great crowds; somehow the explicit prophecies made by the Master of blood and death soon to come had failed to weigh upon them. They were humanly giddy in the midst of great events. Actually when the Master had foretold His death, they could not bring themselves to believe it. He had always shown such resistless power! Was He not the Christ? How, then, could He be harmed? They simply couldn't accept it.

So it was without any feeling of deep melancholy that they started out making a long loop down the mountain paths, in a detour to the southern road.

Soon some of the Galileans recognized Jesus and clustered around Him; another miracle, please, dear Master!—here are two blind men. And when sightless Bartemaeus was made to see, the crowds intensified until the road was choked. That was when the Master noticed a little man swinging perilously from the topmost bough of a sycamore tree.

This swinging dwarf of a man was dangling a few yards back of the customhouse, and on that office door he cast, now and then, a wary eye on his balsam tax cash.

In those days the Romans controlled the balsam trade, getting a royalty from plantation owners on every shell. The balsam trade was a busy one and kept many workers employed; all around the city were plantations. The field hands would hack at the back of the trees with jagged stones and then would hold a handful of wool near the open wound and catch the bleeding drops of sticky white juice. This would be squeezed into a mussel shell where it would harden and the shell would be its container. All over the world went the balsam shells, to be sold to those who believed the odor would cure headache. That was one reason why the Romans had set up their special customhouse here on the frontier of Judea.

And that was why they had a little hunchback, a misshapen man named Zacchaeus, to be their taxgatherer here.

The townspeople called Zacchaeus a scoundrel. Like Matthew, the saint, he was lower than low in his neighbors' eyes, not only because of his deformity but because he collected the tribute money imposed upon his own people by conquerors—and made a good profit for himself on the transaction. He was very rich.

Nevertheless, Zacchaeus wanted to see Jesus. He beheld the mob come plunging ahead of the Master, down the road in a frenzied swirl of burnooses and dusty robes and rushing through the city gates, shouting and singing in fine, excitable mood. The hunchback was in a panic. He *had* to see this teacher of whose doctrines he had heard; he had been told that another despised taxgatherer, Matthew, was one of the Master's closest friends. Maybe the Master would deign to notice him too!

Did any man ever feel more inferior than Zacchaeus? He was so small, his body so badly made, that he was almost a midget; he was a tax man, and no one would have anything to do with him. Only in this stranger from Nazareth did he see any promise of human warmth and understanding—and now that Jesus was about to pass right in front of him and his customhouse, he feared he would not get even a glimpse of his hero, because the crowd was so large and Zacchaeus was so small. That was why the hunchback scrambled up into the branches of the sycamore tree—a medium-sized, bushy green tree that swayed crazily under his monkey-like movements of arms and legs; and through the damp, flat leaves he thrust a bearded face to look down the squalid street for the man he had heard would be a friend to anyone.

Jesus looked up and saw him there, in his brocaded silken cap, imported from Ctesiphon. Zacchaeus turned pale but the Master waved His hand and called:

"Zacchaeus! Hurry up and come down! . . . *Come down*, for this day I must abide in your house!"

The Master in *my* house! Jesus *my* guest!

A savage, delirious tumult of joy was in the taxgatherer's heart. The malformed little millionaire tumbled down from the last branch of the sycamore tree; he ran with pounding feet down the avenue the crowd opened up for him; he cried and laughed. And Jesus laid His hand on the shoulder that came barely to His waist and they walked on together, while the crowd murmured and whispered.

For now the people were as shocked in their way as so often the Pharisees and the Sadducees had been shocked in theirs: the Master was going to be a guest of a wretch like Zacchaeus, he who wore the great glittering beryl ring, a gift from Herod the Great himself. In the doorway of the house of the rich taxgatherer the Master, inspired with His theme, told the gaping spectators the parable of the Ten Talents; and thus let them know that to be diligent about one's business and thereby to earn a profit was not dishonorable. That night, when salvation came to the house of Zacchaeus, there was song and celebration under the roof.

On the following night Jesus slept in Bethany, closer by a day's journey to Jerusalem. But He did not bide in the house of His friends, Mary, Martha, and Lazarus; instead He chose to put up at the house of a man called Simon the Leper—one of those healed by Jesus. While He was in Simon's house, on that Saturday, the first day of April in the year 30, Martha served the supper and Lazarus sat at the table, with just as good an appetite now for his sister's cooking of braised lamb and garden vegetables as if he had never been laid in his cerements for three days in the family vault.

Mary, the other sister, was mysteriously absent.

Suddenly she came through the doorway and knelt at the feet of Jesus. Like the harlot back in Galilee, Mary carried in her hands an alabaster vase. In it was a pound of spikenard, a very expensive ointment; the sisters had used up their savings to buy it for the burial of Lazarus. Silence fell as the guests watched Mary. She knelt and lifted one foot of Jesus and began to rub instep and toes with the ointment. Both feet she massaged with the sweet-smelling paste and then, again like the other woman up north, she dried off the feet from heel to toe with her long dark hair.

Finally in the same critical silence she poured some more of the ointment on the top of the Master's head and rubbed it in with strong, slender fingers. The room was filled with the odor of the ointment.

And Judas was whispering to Martha:

"What a waste of this ointment! It could have been sold for three hundred pence! It cost much more than that, when it was bought originally for your brother Lazarus, who, as things turned out, did not need its sweet smell. You sisters could have sold it all and given the money to the poor!"

The onlookers imitated the Pharisees now, muttering together and turning dark glances toward Mary, with her extravagant alabaster vase in her hands; darkest glances of all came from Judas. For a long time Judas Iscariot had been the treasurer of the Apostles; he kept the purse and doled out the money, and of him John later said that he was a thief at heart and cared nothing for the poor. Judas would actually have snatched the box and what was left of the ointment from Mary's hands had not Jesus seen this bogus zeal for what it was and intervened.

"Let her alone," He commanded, "that she may keep it against the day of *my* burial."

Then, as shocked silence fell, He continued:

"Why do you trouble this woman? She has wrought a good work upon me. In pouring this ointment upon my body, she had done it for my burial. What she had, she has done. She is come beforehand to anoint my body. The poor you have always with you, but me you have not always. I tell you, wherever this Gospel shall be preached in the whole world, that also which she has done shall be told for a memory of her."

And indeed after nearly two thousand years, in which it has been told day after day, here it is being told again!

On the day after Mary anointed the feet and head of Jesus, He walked with His disciples from Bethany up the stony road to Jerusalem. It was the Sunday before the Pasch or Passover and all the high roads were thick with pilgrims, noisy with their psalms.

Yet what began as a pilgrimage—for Jesus and His friends going into the city to join in celebrating the Passover—ended in what can be called nothing less than the most remarkable triumphal march of all time.

Chapter 51 PALM SUNDAY

THE legions of the Caesars, tramping under arches of victory, were meaningless beside this sudden and miraculous triumph. One instant Jesus was one among a hundred thousand pilgrims; then, before any of His disciples could realize what was happening, the same Jesus was isolated, singled out, for the adoration of the people, the target of deep-toned amens and shrill hallelujahs!

Yet it all came about so simply. They started early on that Sunday morning, passed through the hamlet of Bethanage, and paused at the foot of that green Mount of Olives, Olivet as the Christians call it, place of a garden where He was to meet agony, and from whose topmost point He was to say farewell to the world.

Now at the base of the Mount Jesus paused; called two of His disciples and gave them curious orders. They were to press on to the next little town, really a suburb of Jerusalem, and in the village they would find, tied to a hitching post, the colt of an unbacked ass, foal of a beast accustomed to the farmer's yoke, yet no man, woman, or child had ever ridden this youngster donkey. The two disciples were to loose the ass and bring him back to Jesus; if anyone tried to stop them, they were merely to say the Lord had need of the animal's service.

And so it all turned out! The two disciples, not a little upset by their errand, did not remember that the prophet Zacharias centuries before had written:

"Tell ye the daughter of Sion. Behold the king comes to you meek and sitting upon an ass . . ."

They found not only the colt but the mother who foaled him standing hitched, their owners lounging near by. The disciples unhitched the young beast and gave their ready-made explanation to the startled owners. No objections! The words of Jesus, repeated to the farmers, was somehow all that was necessary; the disciples came back leading the dumb beast by a short tether of leather thongs.

Jesus and the other disciples were surrounded as usual by a multitude, but at sight of the donkey some curious sudden resolution seemed to seize the crowd. They gave a great shout. Between them where they stood at the foot of Mount Olivet and the great city lay a gorge, the gulley called the Valley of Gehenna, a place of abominable memories. All the pilgrims must descend into that valley and then climb the steep paths on the other side in order to get up to the Jerusalem gates—and journey's end. Yet suddenly, now mysteriously, inexplicably, the tramping hordes of pilgrims stood still, milled about, and, as if moved by a common and overmastering purpose, made a vast human barricade around the tall, bearded figure with His friends in long white robes on the green hillside.

The convoy of the two disciples was greeted with shouts and cheers as if, without being told, the crowd not only knew the unbacked colt was for Jesus, but also remembered that an ass's colt was the royal equipage, full of symbolism for the kings of Israel.

Lurking agents of the Pharisees, always near, did not miss the significance of the unridden ass, fulfilment of old prediction. They watched with narrowed eyes what followed—the general, spontaneous adulation of the multitude. When had such extravagant devotion been seen before in all Judea? The mob gone wild over this one man; the garments of the disciples laid over the ass's back for Him to ride upon, and the people, catching the contagion, throwing down their clothes to the dust before the four feet of the beast. They cast their robes for Him to ride over, while others turned to cutting down boughs from the trees of balsam, acacia, and tamarisk, and green branches of the palm trees. Running far ahead of the popular rider on the donkey's back, they strewed the ground before Him with their greenery, with bouquets and nosegays and wild flowers.

The Pharisees not only saw all this but they had to listen to the shouts of witnesses avouching a great miracle to the pilgrims and strangers; yes, sure they knew the man Lazarus; yes, they had seen him dead and wrapped and yes, by the eternal God of Israel, they had seen the cadaver called out of its grave and turn again into a living human being.

And then thousands of men and women began to shout with joy, joining the voices of the Apostles, and crying:

"*Hosannah! Blessed is he that comes in the name of the Lord.*"

"*Hosannah to the Son of David!*"

"*Blessed be the kingdom of our father David.*"

"*Blessed be the King that comes in the name of the Lord.*"

"*Peace in heaven and glory on high.*"

"*Hosannah in the highest.*"

Those words were enough to strike terror to the heart of any privileged caste. Why, they were saluting and adoring and praising hosannas to this man; they were calling Him king. He had the mob under a spell.

They thought of Him not only as a real king but as one with unearthly supernatural powers; an angel man, a God man—they believed it all! Of course then He could do with these people whatever He cared to do. At any moment He could turn loose these mobs against all organized authority, against the Roman governor and the Temple priests, break down all supremacy, all power, set up Himself as ruler and king indeed.

Such a sight, such a prospect, such a danger was intolerable to fanatic Pharisee and greedy Sadducee alike. A spectacle like this, of unbridled and fantastic trust and devotion, called for action. The priestly authorities looked at one another with pale, blank faces. The whole world is gone after Him!

Now the procession was climbing up, very near to the city with its long, curving walls of tawny stones; its tower forts and tall, armored gates. The sight of it, the nostalgic boyhood memories, the certainty of what was now at hand, brought tears to the Master's eyes. Weeping over Jerusalem, "the place of peace," Jesus cried:

"If thou hadst known, even thou, at least in this thy day, the things which belong unto thy peace! But now they are hid from thine eyes.

"For the days shall come upon thee, that thine enemies shall cast a trench about thee, and compass thee round, and keep thee in on every side.

"And shall lay thee even with the ground, and thy children within thee; and they shall not leave in thee one stone upon another; because thou knewest not the time of thy visitation."

It was as if He could see into the future, see the distant armies of Titus in their encampment forty years later on Mount Olivet; the fire and the sword that fell upon Jerusalem and made sure every word of His prophecy, so soon to be one of the awful facts of history.

On He moved amid that sudden general ecstasy of love and utter trust. Through the city gate, where mobs of the narrow streets came spilling and mingling with the arriving crowds of pilgrims who escorted Him. Who comes? This is Jesus, the prophet; from Nazareth of Galilee! The blind and the maimed followed Him as close as they could until He reached the courts of the Temple, and there, in the very shadow of the altar of the Most High, He healed them.

And children, flocking near, took up the refrain of their elders: "Hosanna to the Son of David!"

"Do you hear what these brats are saying?" screamed the scandalized theologians and the scribes.

"Yes!" agreed Jesus. "Have you never read: 'Out of the mouths of infants and sucklings you have perfected praise?' "

Ah! They knew what that meant—a prophecy of old David about the Messiah! Was that not blasphemy enough? No, for He had still merely quoted a text; they could not arrest Him on that.

But it could not be allowed to go on much longer!

Chapter 52 THE GREAT CLASH

THE whole Temple—court of the strangers, court of the women, the inner court, even the high altar, the very sanctum sanctorum itself—echoed with the full-throated clamor of His followers.

Even the Gentiles, who did not celebrate the Passover, came as near as they could to see the wonderful prophet. With many questions they plagued Philip, who came from Bethsaida, where there were many Gentiles and Philip, who was a little shocked, turned to Andrew. They talked it over.

Was this Kingdom of God a blessing only for Israel? Or could even the Gentiles also be saved? Peter and Andrew left no doubt in the minds of the stout, dark-curled Gentile strangers; the message of the Master was for everybody. For that fact, if for no other, He was to die. And some asked: "If you think He is going to die, why doesn't He try to escape?"

"And what shall I say? Father, save me from this hour? But for their cause I came unto this hour."

So Jesus spoke, most distinctly, in the Temple.

Did all who were there hear, at the same instant, a sound of thunder? Many were to swear that what they heard was actually a voice; John, who was an ear witness, declared it was the voice of God; a repetition of what he had heard three years before on the farther bank of the Jordan, when that other John baptized Jesus. Then the spirit of God descended in the form of a dove; on this, the original Palm Sunday, there was no bird from heaven, but instead that thunderous voice, as loud, as reverberating as a long peal of thunder, a cosmic voice, breath of the universal, answering the prayer to glorify His name:

"I have glorified it and will glorify it again!"

In the fear that caught them all, whether they thought it voice or thunder, Jesus quickly explained:

"This voice came not because of me but for your sakes. Now is the judgment of the world; now shall the prince of this world be cast out."

Summing up the full historical importance of His mission, He added, referring specially to the brutal death already planned for Him:

"And I, if I be lifted up from the earth, will draw all things unto myself."

The Temple scholars and theologians, the ancients as they were sometimes called, because of their wrinkles and long beards and their reputation for wisdom, kept after Him with crafty questions. They even joined one day with a shrewd group of Herodians; working together they cooked up a new stratagem.

"Tell us," they demanded, "by what authority you do all these things. Who is it that gave you this authority?"

Now this was nothing more nor less than a new change on the old effort to trap Him into blasphemy. So sure He seemed of Himself today in the face of so much popular applause, they reasoned that perhaps He would become heady and forget to be careful. If He answered, as they hoped He would, that He was the Christ, then they would have Him, hip and thigh.

But Jesus, shrewdest of all debaters and dialecticians, countered with a demand to be told whether they thought the baptism of John was from heaven or not. This was an adroit maneuver. They knew, as well as did He, that in public memory John, the beheaded, was now more popular than ever, a venerated martyr. If the priests were to say: "John's baptism was from heaven," the next question would be, naturally, "Why didn't you believe him, then?"

But to say otherwise—to maintain that John was merely a man, never a prophet—would have been too dangerous; the old priests might be roughly treated by the crowd. All they could answer was that they did not know.

This equivoque set the crowd grinning and chuckling so that the Pharisees had to return to the attack, this time trying to upset Jesus by posing another dangerous political and social question: Should a good Jew pay the Roman taxes? That was a real poser! For if Jesus said no, He would be guilty of treason. Pilate would polish Him off without ceremony. But if He said yes, all Palestine would be offended.

Jesus called for a penny and pointed to the image on the coin; the profile *in rilievo* of Augustus Caesar.

"Render unto Caesar the things that are Caesar's"—and so with that astute answer, another trap failed. Even His enemies were ready to concede their admiration for the skill by which He demolished that craftily prepared piece of heckling. But while He was on the subject, Jesus denounced to their faces the scribes and the Pharisees for also laying insupportable burdens on the shoulders of the people.

Immediately these daring words reverberated all over the city. They were carried quickly to the luncheon table of Caiphas, the high priest. How the dandy Caiphas writhed! For his friends and partners to be called publicly and in so many words the devourers of widows' houses—which he and most of the associates undoubtedly were! Jesus mocked their vanities, their sitting in the seats of honor, and getting bows from the poor men in the market place, and sewing bands on their robes with long, fancy fringes. They raked in the money and goods of the poor with their tithes, but forgot law, judgment, mercy, and faith. Serpents! Generation of vipers! How would they flee from the judgment of hell?

This was the strongest lashing the Master had ever given His enemies, a castigation in the very shadow of the altar of their magnificent Temple; He was ruining them in the eyes of a believing multitude enchanted by His every word.

And even as He was speaking, He pointed to the dark, bent figure of a little woman creeping toward the money collection box; she dropped two brass coins into the treasury. Who got the widow's mites? Caiphas and his great father-in-law Annas and their elegant crew—they would get the widow's cash and all the other mites and pence and farthings and pounds that fell into the Temple money boxes. So Jesus told the crowd that this poor woman had cast in more than all the others, for the others had given of their abundance but she of her want, her undeniable human misery. Looking round Him at the Temple, majestic in its gifts and wondrous stones, glittering gilt and tessellated pavements, He warned them again that the days of the Temple were counted; not a stone would be left on a stone.

Again He warned of the future. Let all who loved Him watch out for those who would come, quoting Him, preaching in His name, but really serving evil. There would be wars and seditious nations rising against nations; kingdoms arrayed against other kingdoms; famines and terrors which would be only the beginnings of sorrows. But those who believed in Him should not be frightened, though the end was not yet in sight. For the good news must be preached to all nations.

He did not try to belittle the peril of His followers. Those who loved Him would be unmistakably marked for persecution. When the police laid hands on them, however, they were not to be frightened, and, in panic, try to think what they would say in court on the day of trial. He would give them a mouth! And out of it wisdom to confound their adversaries. Nor would all their foes be strangers. They and their descendants through centuries of the future would find themselves, because of their loyalty to their faith in Him, betrayed by friends, by their own brothers even, and by their parents.

"In your patience," He advised them, "you shall possess your souls."

That day He prophesied at length and with great explicitness. Not only did He forecast the woe that most certainly did fall upon Jerusalem only a few years after He departed, but He went on to define the nature of the end of the world itself.

". . . And upon earth, distress of nations . . . men withering away for fear . . . and then they shall see the Son of Man coming in a cloud . . . and the stars of heaven shall be falling down and the powers that are in heaven shall be moved. . . ."

Before that great day of the Second Coming of Christ they could be sure that hypocrites who quoted Him solely to serve evil would appear in greatest profusion. Very clever and deceiving men they were certain to be; they would be doing miracles of themselves, showing signs and wonders of accomplishment anyway—clever almost enough to deceive His most pious followers. They must be very watchful.

And how soon would He come this promised second time? Ever since that day of prophecy in the Temple, loving disciples of the Master have been asking the same question with increasing anxiety. And for two thousand years, as still today, all of us must be satisfied with the answer He gave them:

"But of that day and hour no man knows, neither the angels in heaven, but the Father alone!"

Because of the need for vigilance, He told them a story of wise and foolish virgins invited to participate in receiving a bride and bridegroom. Only five of the virgins thought to bring oil in their lamps; the five others, the foolish virgins, forgot to be ready and were left behind when the great time came. For this event of the second coming was far more than a mere ceremony or celebration: it would be literally and finally the day of the Last Judgment.

Chapter 53 THE POLITICAL BOSS

THE next day was the day before the Pasch; the celebration of the Feast of the Unleavened Bread would begin at sundown on the fifth of April, A.D. 30.

In strict accord with the Mosaic law, as stated in Exodus 12:18, the ceremonial paschal lamb must be slain on the fourteenth day of the first month in the evening. According to the Jewish reckoning of a day—from 6 P.M. to 6 P.M.—the actual day of the Pasch was reckoned from one evening until another. However, in this year of 30 the Pasch happened to fall on Saturday. To avoid violating the stringent Sabbath rest, many of the Jews transferred the slaying of the lamb to the evening of Thursday.

Strangely, that fateful morning when Jesus resumed His preaching in the Temple there were no spies waiting to debate with Him. Why had Caiphas called off his crew? Had he other plans in mind? As a matter of secret fact, for some days the high priest's agents had been paying increasing attention to the disciples rather than to their leader. Later one of these spies talked confidentially to the high priest.

"We are almost ready," Caiphas exclaimed. "There is only one more big hurdle. That's my father-in-law, Annas."

And to himself he added: "Father-in-law won't like this. He never likes any of my ideas. But this one cannot be allowed to fail; I've got to make him see it our way."

Caiphas was very much pleased with himself. He had found one of the Twelve who would sell out. He had never known any man who did not have at least one disloyal friend. . . .

Annas was now a very old man but he was still the political boss of Jerusalem. Of the sixty families in the Temple aristocracy, his was the richest and the most powerful. For years—as far back as that long-before day when Joachim had pointed him out to Joseph—Annas had served his people as high priest. When he felt he had held the post long enough, he passed on the fringed blue robe and stately headdress to his eldest son, and then, in turn, to six of his other sons. Now that his own seed was used up, his son-in-law Caiphas got the job—he was the visible authority, under the God of Abraham, of Isaac and of Jacob, but he was also privately under the firm governance of Lord Father-in-Law!

Not seven sons nor son-in-law, all ganged together, could ever be a match for Annas. Even now, when he was in his eighties, and secretly considered a dotard by his family, they stood in mortal fear of the slight figure with the oblong head on the lean corded neck. There was something awesome in the long wisp of white hair that dangled over the pale green glimmer of his left eye. Annas had a sharper brain than his relatives and he was not nearly so greedy. All that they possessed he had given them; even the little wisdom they knew he had taught them.

In no one except himself did Annas believe. The god he worshiped at the Temple was a respectable and convenient bugaboo to keep the lower classes in check. The people must be led by an elite class, men of superior managerial talents. Of such men Annas was, beyond question, the best example in Palestine.

His agents still sold the people the doves and lambs to burn on the altars of sacrifice to keep God in a congenial mood. His bankers still changed the Roman money used in ordinary commerce to the coinage of the Temple with a large gain in the transaction. Annas saw no immorality in such business. Keep the people poor and full of fear and they will believe. Otherwise they will start movements for their own improvement and no good can come from that.

Right now there were men storming through Judea and Samaria and Galilee preaching revolution against the Romans. Annas took an annoyed view of such crackpots. Only yesterday he had ordered the arrest of a leader called Barabbas, who had stolen money to finance an insurrection to free the people. To temporize with such movements was sheer, downright nonsense.

No man to make an enemy of, this Annas, son of Seth, whose name meant "Grace of Jehovah." He was the most superb intelligence among the ruling class in Judea. Calm lived in his bosom; he had no hatreds and no grudges, and knew neither remorse nor fear —a dangerous personality. He had been born to money, he had married money, and he had cultivated money because he early learned its power. Annas was owner of vast property; he had no friends except among those who also owned property and a great deal of it. The Temple Sadducees were cautious men, well pleased with their way of life, suspicious of change; conservative men and proud of their ancestry—they wanted no social traffic with anyone placed outside themselves in these important particulars.

True, the radicals continually charged that Annas and his friends had betrayed the people. Some of the Pharisees joined in the accusation. But such Pharisees were a motley crew of lower-class, overpious, fanatical demagogues. Their dislike left Annas untroubled. He considered himself the actual king, master of the people, and they, in turn, called him "the most fortunate of the human race." He smiled, disdaining to dignify an insult, when occasionally some impudent rebel mourned aloud at a crowded bazaar:

"Woe is me on account of the race of Annas; woe is me on account of their serpent's hiss!"

Fearing neither radicals nor Pharisees, Annas had taught his sons and son-in-law that everybody in the world was a hypocrite and a liar, and could be bought at the right price.

It was a dark spring evening. Pontius Pilate reckoned it as in the seven hundred and eighty-third year of Rome and the twenty-sixth year of the reign of Tiberius Caesar. The people of Israel called it the fourteenth Nisan. We would call it Thursday, the seventh day of April, in the year of our Lord 30.

From his window Annas could hear a distant noise; Jerusalem, already crammed with hundreds of thousands of pilgrims from Judea, from Samaria, from Galilee and from Perea, was still receiving more from distant parts of the Roman empire, pouring through the gates.

Windows shut against the blatant clamor, Annas was sitting loftily by a fire of coals. Against the high red wall opposite him in his private chamber stood a younger man, gorgeously attired and with an elaborate black beard. He was Joseph Caiphas, bending toward his father-in-law and fixing him with a myopic squint. As the old man warmed his fingers the son-in-law said:

"I know you want to go to sleep, Lord Annas, but my business simply will *not* wait!"

Annas sucked his last tooth. White wisp across left eye, head turned to one side, he seemed hardly to be listening. Actually, he was hankering childishly for the silly notes of the cuckoo bird; for in Palestine, from April until June, it is harvesttime, and that is when the cuckoo bird sings. More, because this was the eve of the Feast of the Passover, which comes following the full moon, Annas was remembering other such festivals of the past, when everything was younger and not so tiresome. Although his loins were withered, hands slightly palsied, the soul of Annas felt younger than ever tonight. He tugged at his ramlike little beard and his face was bleak and mystifying.

"What kind of business then?"

And the old man added to himself: "You popinjay! Your very name Caiphas means depression. And how you depress me, with your silken beard that reeks of perfume, and your resonant voice that is always just teetering on the edge of a belch. Those cowlike eyes and loud tones would make you a political candidate anywhere."

"I think the fate of this nation may hinge on what we do tonight," announced Caiphas with a solemn shake of his head.

"The nation has withstood many other nights. Are we at the crossroads again?" jeered Annas, who hated rhetoric. "Why tonight?"

"Because unless we settle this fellow Jesus He will ruin us all."

Annas sneezed, helped his nose with his fingers, and demanded: "How can I possibly be ruined by a wayside tramp?"

Caiphas threw up his hands.

"Just consider, Lord Annas, what He has been able to do in three short years. A Galilean mechanic—probably illegitimate, if one is to believe what one hears--three years ago began to talk to whomever would listen to Him. Today the whole world is listening!"

"A big audience!"

"Our whole world here about, I tell you, is filled with lying reports that He is a prophet, with a great new message which proclaims the dignity and importance of the individual soul, and dangerous rubbish even worse than that—and that He can perform miracles!"

"Don't they know miracles don't happen any more?" Annas sniffed again.

"They believe," pursued Caiphas, parting his beard, "that Jesus drives out devils, makes crooked legs straight, gives sight to blind eyes, and even brings the dead back to life."

"And I still want to know why do you bother me with such nonsense, Joseph Caiphas?"

"Last Sunday, the tenth Nisan, while you were away, He rode into Jerusalem, with twelve of His followers trailing behind Him. He was seated on a Babylonian ass! As if, by our traditions, He considered Himself a king, a judge, or a prophet. How do you like that?"

Annas stuck out his chin and seemed to swallow something with difficulty.

"Why didn't you order the man arrested then and there?" he asked querulously.

"Because this is feast time, and Jerusalem is full of pilgrims—two hundred thousand and more . . ."

"Rabble! Just rabble and scum!"

"Yes, but that is the danger—the rabble love Him. The scum love Him. They might easily revolt. The poor are all for Him. The desperate turn to Him. I tell you," Caiphas finished bitterly, "the whole world has gone after Him!"

Annas lifted his old arms in a mock helpless gesture.

"Joseph Caiphas," he barked, "what is it you want to do with this Jesus?"

The high priest rose and strode over to the old man; he placed white, puffy hands on the iron shoulders.

"I want to arrest Him—and then summon the whole council!"

"On the eve of the feast?" gasped Annas, as if his ears lied.

"I want to arrest Him tonight, Lord Annas," Caiphas replied with a gaunt nearsighted look. "His influence has reached a point where we should not hesitate any longer."

"Arrest Him! Summon the whole council! Nonsense! For what?" barked Annas, waving his hands as if to cast folly into the stove. "The man thinks He is the Messiah? Well, what Galilean does not? Messiah! I'm sick of the word. Jeremiah and Isaiah made a lot of trouble for us, let me tell you, when they promised us a messiah! Insurrections! Revolts! Zealots! That fellow Jude of Gamalia! After a madman like that Jude, you worry about this mild Jesus? I tell you, He's only *another* Messiah! I do hope, my boy, you are not taking your position as high priest too seriously."

The old man's scorn failed to shake Caiphas. With a deep breath he returned to the attack.

"I have to make you see that this is a *different* Messiah," he said sternly. "One with ideas about the rich and the poor not to my liking—nor to yours, Lord Annas. He says the Gentiles are just as good as we are . . ."

On the old man's firelit face there came and went a puckering twinge of malice.

"Quite mad, no doubt! Quite mad!" But his covert satire was lost

"But, my dear Lord Annas, He goes further than that!"

"I detest your rhetorical pauses. Be specific. What else?"

"He says that family loyalty, too, is nonsense."

"Family loyalty? Well, there may be something to his point of view!"

"Because, He said, everybody who believed in Him was His mother and His father."

Annas laughed in a soft humming tone.

"There!" he crowed. "I said so. The fellow is crazy."

"A dangerous craziness, then. Jesus is against our entire economic system and intends to destroy it. He denounces the rich. He sets class against class. Already His teachings are affecting some of our own young men—members of our Sadducean families actually joining His group. They are traitors to their class and they admit it and laugh at their fathers for telling them so."

The wrinkles deepened on the dried-apple face of Annas.

"He talks to the people and after He goes away they begin to ask questions," Caiphas continued. "Such as why the poor do not have the same civil and political rights as the rich. Why our Sadducean families have so much to eat and the others have so little. He tells them all men are equal in the sight of God. He tells our young men they have to choose between riches and God Almighty —He wants them to give their inheritances to the poor and follow Him!"

"Well—this *is* news!" muttered Annas.

"He teaches that misusing riches is the most dangerous of sins, because it gives one man tyranny over his brothers. He wants every man to love his fellow man as his own brother. He shakes His finger in our very faces and only the other day He said, 'Woe unto you, scribes and Pharisees, hypocrites! For you devour widows' houses.' "

"He *is* provoking class hatred, that is clear!"

"Why, Lord Annas, Jesus is making it so that any man in Jerusalem with two pairs of sandals begins to feel ashamed of himself when he passes a barefoot beggar."

The glimmer in the old man's eye was turning into an incalescent gleam.

"Why was I not told of this before?"

"You have been away for two months. Besides, we waited until we were ready to lay the whole matter before you," Caiphas explained hurriedly. "But not all the Sanhedrin has been idle. An inner group has had Jesus watched for two years now. We've held meetings for the last six months to find a way to deal with Him. And would you believe it, at the conventicle we held on the Feast of the Tabernacles, one of our own group actually defended Him there!"

"Was it not Joseph of Arimathea?" asked Annas quickly.

"No, Lord."

Annas sucked his tooth again.

"Then it *must* have been Nicodemus. I know my crowd. Never mind how I guess. Go on. When did you meet again?"

"About six weeks ago, when there was a wild tale in circulation that Jesus had raised a man named Lazarus, over in Bethany—raised him from the dead."

"You have indeed kept this all very secret," complained Annas petulantly.

"We thought it best to work in the dark," admitted Caiphas with satisfaction. "We did not ourselves appear in the matter. We allowed the scribes and the Pharisees to bicker and debate with Him, but we of what some insist on calling the Caiphas group were always on the watch to catch him."

"In what crime?"

"Blasphemy—and, if possible, in treason."

Annas's slow smile was shrewd and a little tragic. He understood the deadly strategy. The old political boss was not a bloodthirsty man, but he was beginning to suspect that perhaps his son-in-law was not alarmed without cause.

"You have not heard what happened in the Temple," pursued Caiphas, ready to play his winning card. "Did you know that this harmless Galilean fanatic, as you called Him, entered the Temple, kicked over the tables of our money-changers, and drove our dealers out with a whip?"

"Attacking our dealers?" Annas was instantly scandalized.

"He said, 'Make not my Father's house a place of merchandise.' "

"*His* father's home? And He scourged our changers!"

"Did I not say so?"

"And people are listening to this man, you say?"

"They greeted Him with palms last Sunday, and called hosannahs to Him. There is not one of the inns in Jerusalem tonight where they do not debate if He is or is not the Messiah, the Christ!"

"Tell me just what happened there at the Temple!"

"He was teaching, but all the while, out of the corner of His eye, He watched the people going up to change their money at the tables of our bankers. My spies told me everything: how His eyes glowed darkly and how He played with a loop of ropes in His hand, picked up idly in His walk. Slowly He moved through the throng of buyers and sellers, watching the profits made on the sale of sheep and pigeons. Then His hands moved swiftly. With incredible dexterity He fashioned for Himself a whip out of those cords, a scourge, and suddenly He let fly with that whip. He flailed the backs of our money-changers, and turned over their tables so that the money spilled and ran tinkling over the marble floor. This sudden move of His so startled the crowd that they fell back and left Him standing, breathing heavily, face moist, strong hands lifted, and His voice deep as He told them in a voice full of scorn and anger:

" 'It is written: "My house shall be called the house of prayer to all nations." But you have made it a den of thieves. Take these things hence and make not my Father's house a house of traffic.'

"No one challenged Him, no one laid a hand upon Him. He walked out of the Temple back to His lodgings. His disciples were frightened, let me tell you. They expected trouble. And they are going to get it. . . . Oh, and one thing more! He told the people there was no need for them to buy doves and lambs—Jehovah required no sacrifice on the altar. He, Himself, would be the sacrifice for them all. *Wah!*"

"*Wah!*" rumbled the echoing Annas. "When the feast is over, then we shall go after Him, Caiphas."

"Lord Annas, we can't wait that long—not another day, even. The mobs might rise up and rescue Him."

"We must raise our own counter-rabble!" decided Annas suddenly.

"To denounce Him?"

"Of course! For blasphemy! And treason. The first to worry the poor pious fools of the Pharisees. The second to worry Pilate."

"Lord Annas," exclaimed the high priest, with a noisy exhalation of his breath, "you understand at last!"

For the first time since his son-in-law had arrived, Annas rose from his chair. His oblong old face, that had been so animated, was suddenly as unmoving as a mask, unlighted with the glow of thought; a lantern whose candle had blown out.

There was in this moment an inexplicable fear in Annas. He knew his son-in-law to be a thoroughgoing scoundrel. Here Annas was, for the first time, giving up his own judgment to Caiphas. There was something terrifying in that simple fact. The white and wrinkled visage was without expression and the humming voice seemed to creep from the stiff lips:

"You don't believe this Jesus has any real miraculous powers, of course? Any gifts our learned scholars have not yet discovered?"

"Why do you jest with me. Lord Annas?"

"Something makes me hesitate to enter on this business. So hurried an arrest—a trial under conditions unprecedented in all our history . . ."

"But Lord——"

"Peace! My practical good sense tells me I am justified in agreeing to your plans. It is only inside of me . . ."

"Your soul?" mocked Caiphas, white teeth shining through his beard.

"If I believed in a soul, that would, no doubt, be it. Yet look at it this way, Caiphas! I sincerely believe that with fanatical crowds, commoved and unsettled, cheering on a revolutionary leader in the streets, the patriotic folly of our people may lead them to excess. It could easily happen at any time during the next few days. Pilate would then have to order Roman troops to take action. That would certainly mean resistance, riot, bloodshed, death! It might also increase the restrictions laid upon the whole people by the Romans. Is it not logical to act to prevent that, Caiphas?

"Furthermore, I am anxious to show the Roman authorities how sincerely I want to co-operate. And so——"

"And so, Lord," urged Caiphas, "we can convince the full council that it is expedient for them that one man should die for the people and that the whole nation perish not."

"You have made definite plans, I suppose?"

"I don't have to tell you that the practical and legal difficulties were enough to discourage even a man of action like myself. Getting the court to agree to assemble in the dead of night—and to keep their clacking tongues quiet beforehand—that in itself was no simple task. But they realized now there is an emergency!

"Arranging for witnesses is not proving to be easy, either, let me tell you. No one seems to want to talk against Jesus. I have worked harder on this . . ."

"But what about ratification?" interrupted Annas. They both knew perfectly well that while the Sanhedrin could pronounce the death sentence, before it could be carried out Pilate, the Procurator, had to agree to it. "Can you secure Pilate's approval of the death sentence in time? You must kill this man before the crowds find out what you are doing! If you don't . . ."

"I know, Lord. We *are* doing this against the wishes of our people. There *may* be mobs rioting to save Him. The whole plan is carefully laid out up to the door of Pontius Pilate . . ."

"And then?" Annas's voice, harsh and guttural, was like the croak of a raven.

"And then we all draw back. We leave Pilate to you. You are the one man in Judea who knows how to handle him."

The flattery was not lost. The face of the withered little man flushed and his quivering fingers spiraled through his scanty beard.

"So," he sighed benignly, "you set out to save the nation and wind up by asking me to save you from your own folly. Very well, since it is necessary, I will do it. Send out and arrest Jesus!"

The high priest lifted his large soft hands.

"Sorry, Lord Annas. We don't know where to find Him tonight. He constantly eludes our spies, as if He were a sorcerer with power to change His shape, or disappear. But if you will permit, there is a man outside . . ."

"An informer?"

"One of his own men. He will talk only to you."

"Do we really need him?"

"Those who could tell us where He hides for the night all seem to be His friends," answered Caiphas, with an exasperated air. "Only this one man seems to be amenable."

"Well," sighed Annas, "it is sometimes necessary to make use of traitors, but they always turn the taste of a decent man's spittle. Send in your man."

And Joseph Caiphas, going to the outer hall with bumptious stride, called softly:

"You may come in, now—Judas Iscariot."

Chapter 54 THE UPPER ROOM

At sundown of that same day thirteen men met to celebrate the Passover in a great gray hall, an upper room in a house on Mount Zion, northeast corner of the height of Jerusalem.

In the tall-roofed chamber with heavy beams holding up the ceiling the only furnishings were rattan divans and a long oaken table, on which tall candles were burning. The flickering flames played upon the sturdy figures of the Apostles and repeated them in distorted shadows against the unwindowed walls.

During the afternoon their sacrificial lamb had been properly and ritually killed in the forecourt of the Temple sanctuary; soon, now, the roasted carcass would be eaten, when the day of the Pasch was legally come; with the twilight came a new day, beginning when the sun went down—an analogy full of hope.

Now they were all gathered here in this room as by a kind of miracle. They had not known where to turn or how to proceed when the Master called to Him Peter and John and told them to arrange matters.

"But where?" mumbled Peter in his always exasperated and impatient voice.

The answer was casual, but specific:

"Look, as you go into the city there shall meet you a man carrying a pitcher of water; follow him into the house where he enters. And you shall say to the goodman of the house: 'The Master saith to thee, where is thy guest chamber where I may eat the Pasch with my disciples?' And he will show you a large dining room furnished and there prepare."

Every word of which came true immediately. Now here they were assembled in that same goodman's upper room, all twelve, with only the Master yet to appear.

In spite of the warnings Jesus had given the Twelve, none of them realized, or was willing to believe, that this would be their last meal together. They were still too earthbound and too worldly to grasp, as they would later, the great historical realities of the drama in which they were actors, playing, as a group, a major role.

At such a tragic time, while they were still a good long way from being saints, and while waiting for the Master to join them, they began arguing among themselves all over again about priority. In spite of previous rebukes, they argued once more which of them would be the greater, which would be the closest assistant to the Master, in the glory of the future.

Perhaps, too, they counted on the fact that if Jesus heard about it, He would forgive such weaknesses in His chosen ones, because He really loved them, knowing that men must be lovable—if at all —not because of the absence of defects, but because of the presence of merits. John once said of Him: "Jesus, having loved His own who were in this world, loved them until the end."

But the Master did not permit this inexcusable bickering on such a solemn occasion to pass without a final admonition.

In the very midst of their squabbling He suddenly appeared, wrapped in a long blue cloak, at the doorway. Their sudden silence was again that of back-yard children, discovered in some naughtiness. This time Jesus did not admonish them in mere words, but in unmistakable action.

His garments laid aside, He stood facing them with only a towel wrapped around Him. In the unbroken and bewildered quiet, undisturbed by so much as the clearing of a throat, Jesus poured water from a pitcher into a basin. Then He knelt at the foot of His strongest and strangest disciple.

"Master," gasped Peter, "do you wash my feet? No! No! *You must not!*"

Jesus, on His knees, looked up at the great, heavy-handed fisherman.

"What I do, you know not now—but you shall know hereafter."

Peter's face suddenly turned a deep maroon and he shouted:

"You shall *never*, *never* wash my feet!"

The disciples were thunderstruck at Peter's vehemence. But the Master's warning voice was as calm with him as it had been with the storm over the Lake of Galilee.

"If I wash you not, Peter, you shall have no part with me."

Peter gasped and glared hopelessly around him, then bowed his head and groaned:

"Lord, not only my feet—but my hands and my head."

Turning next to John, Jesus washed the calloused feet of that long-tramping apostle. Twenty-two feet He washed, laving, rubbing, and drying toes and instep and heel with the towel with which He had girdled Himself, and at last He came to Judas.

Some in the room had already noticed that a strange mood had fallen on the treasurer and keeper of the bag. Tonight the son of Simon Iscariot seemed afflicted with melancholy; there was in him none of the love-feast spirit which should dominate the meal. Pale, glassy-eyed he sat, limp and yet fixed; the crown of stiff red curls did not move, nor the hairs of the curly red beard turn even an inch; the brooding eyes, so intensely small and so black, had lost all familiar gleam and authority; it was as if Judas were looking upon some dire vision, visible only to him.

Jesus got up, carried His basin, and knelt to Judas. As He methodically washed the treasurer's thin, long feet, He said:

"He that is washed needs but to wash his feet but is clean wholly. And you are clean—"

He paused and looked up straight at Judas.

"—but not wholly!" He added, with a sigh. He finished the business of the washing, threw out the water, and put on His own garments.

Then He sat at the table surrounded by the twelve familiar faces.

His arms were opened, His hands lying, palms up, unmoving on the snowy napery. His eyes were lowered and He looked at no one. To His right sat the pale-faced John, his cheek almost touching the Master's shoulder; and farther to the right, baldheaded Peter, absent-mindedly sharpening a long knife against the tip of his horny thumb. Near him, Andrew and Zelotes. To the left were bearded Matthew, and Jude Thaddeus, the oldest man at the Last Supper; curly-haired, black-bearded Thomas, doubting churl but a loyal and faithful man nonetheless; James the Greater, of long and powerful physique; beardless Philip, almost feminine in his gentle aspect; Nathanael Bartholomew at the end of the table, with James the Lesser—and finally, on the opposite side, as if set apart from all others, Judas Iscariot.

"With desire," Jesus told them, "I have desired to eat this pasch with you before I suffer."

He made the words as emphatic as He knew how.

"For I am telling you that from this time I will not eat it till it be fulfilled in the Kingdom of God!"

And going straight back to the argument which He had begun, with the washing of their feet, He asked:

"For which is greater, he that sits at table or he that serves?

"But I am in the midst of you as he that serves; and you are they who have continued with me in my temptations. And I dispose to you, as my Father disposed to me, a kingdom, that you may eat and drink at my table in my kingdom."

After a long silence He lifted His voice in one of the psalms of David, which all sang feelingly. A cup was passed and blessed: "Blessed be Thou, O Lord, our God, Thou King of the world Who has created the fruit of the vine!" Each had his portion, then, of the bitter herbs, endive and lettuce, dipped into a compote of almonds, nuts, and figs. By the color of these fruits they were reminded of the bricks, which their ancestors had to make without straw.

With this bitter dish they again ate the bread of misery, the Mazzoth to remind them of the hasty flight out of Egypt. Then they ate the Easter lamb, and drank a third cup, which, as good and religious Jews, they all knew to be the cup of blessing.

It was then that Jesus lifted up His hands.

"Know you what I have done to you?" He asked them. "You call me Master and Lord. And you say well, for so I am. If I then, being your lord and master, have washed your feet, you also ought to wash one another's feet. For I have given you an example, that as I have done to you, so you do also. I say to you, the servant is not greater than his lord.

"I speak not of you all when I said you are clean now. I know whom I have chosen, but that the Scripture may be fulfilled: 'He that eats bread with me shall lift up his hand to betray me.' At present I tell you, before it comes to pass, that one of you that eats with me shall betray me."

These sudden and completely shocking words of the Master resounded frighteningly in the dining room. This was the first time He had ever said anything like that. The Twelve had not had the slightest hint of what was coming. Jesus had seemed to trust them all completely; showed suspicion of none, not in all their three years of journeying through Palestine. The charge of treachery stunned them.

True, the old religious books were full of prophecies that the Messiah would be sold out by one of His friends. True, too, they believed Jesus was the Messiah. But never, never, had they actually brought the old prophecies home to themselves; as for the betrayal, even if they had remembered the predictions, they would never, for a moment, have believed that the forecast of treason was meant for one of the Twelve.

Their faces were full of sorrow as they pointed fingers to their own breasts, looked imploringly at Jesus, and one after another, man by man, asked Him the same question:

"Is it I?"

"Is it I, Lord?"

"Who is it?" shouted Peter, glaring around at them all.

And John, who loved Jesus intensely, was even at that moment leaning his head on the Master's bosom; the young disciple gently echoed the fisherman's voice:

"Lord. who is it?"

"He it is to whom I shall reach bread dipped," Jesus answered. "He that dips his hand with me in the dish, he shall betray me."

They were like frozen men, unable to move, as the Master dipped a morsel of bread in the dish of lamb and gravy and then very quietly held it out toward Judas.

The voice of the treasurer trembled as he croaked:

"Is it I, Master?"

"You have said it," answered Jesus. Even then He could not keep the pity from His eyes. "That which you do, do quickly."

As John wrote later, Judas received the morsel of bread and gravy and then fled from the room; the door slammed heavily behind him.

"And," John added, "it was night."

Even now the disciples found it hard to take in. True, Judas, son of Simon, was the least popular among them, but who could believe he would sell his Master's life? Such a thing still seemed beyond belief. As they looked at the door, closing behind the escaping Judas, they told themselves, with the same fatuity with which good men always doubt the existence of abomination, that Judas must have been sent out on some business mission. After all, he held the purse; perhaps Jesus had sent him off to buy supplies for the festival day, or on some urgent errand to give money to the poor.

But when Judas was gone from the candlelit refectory, Jesus made no further reference to him. Instead, He took the bread, and broke it, passing a piece to each of the eleven, as he said:

"Take you and eat. This is my body."

They ate. Then He filled with wine the chalice, one of the liturgical cups of the paschal rite, as Melchizedek had once offered a sacrifice of bread and wine in the very beginning days. And now Jesus gave thanks and passed the chalice of wine to the eleven, saying:

"Drink you all of this. For this is my blood of the new testament which shall be shed for many unto remission of sins. Do this for a commemoration of me."

And they all drank of it—all except Judas, who had gone, but who was still crouched on the stairway outside listening to the great new rite, the way in which a man becomes one with God—and he knew that for him it was too late.

Chapter 55 THE PARTING

THIS was the time of the real parting between Jesus and those who loved Him in this world.

What He said to His faithful eleven, after that first communion, was a farewell, not merely to them, but to Mary and to His friends in Bethany and to all those, born and unborn, who would love Him and keep His ways.

"Little children," He told them softly, "yet a little while I am with you. You shall seek me, and as I said to the Jews: 'Whither I go, you cannot come,' so I say to you now.

"A new commandment I give unto you: that you love one another—as I have loved you, that you also love one another!"

And, as often before, He told them they would be ashamed of Him, but now His forecast of this odious act was not in the indeterminate future—but tonight!

They would be ashamed of Him within the next few hours, but after He was dead and buried, they would find Him waiting—there and then He made a post-mortal appointment, a rendezvous after death in Galilee!

And now He made to Peter a most extraordinary statement. Here, in the upper room, was bald and bearded Peter with the freckled nose; Peter, the rock on which Christ would build the church secure against the gates of hell; Peter, to whom Jesus now said:

"Simon! Simon! Look, Satan has desired to have you that he may sift you as wheat.

"But I have prayed for thee that thy faith fail not, and thou, being once converted, confirm thy brethren."

Peter looked wildly insulted. That Satan desired him, he well knew. That the Master prayed for him was a great blessing, although Peter felt he could defeat the devil by his own strength, if he needed to. But to be told that he would someday be converted . . .

Peter coughed and grew red in the face at the thought.

"Lord," he said, as if he might even reprove the Master, "I am ready to go with thee both into prison and to death."

Jesus looked at him compassionately. Prison? Aye, the Mamartine in Rome would be one of his prisons. Death? Upside down on a cross, Peter, at your own humble request, because you will not feel worthy to be crucified head side up as was the Master. Peter! Peter!

"I say to thee, Peter, the cock shall not crow this day till thou three times deniest that thou knowest me!"

Peter roared a protest. So did all the other disciples. But Jesus held out His arms to them, even while Peter was shouting to the rafters:

"Although I should die together with thee, I will *not* deny thee."

A grim silence settled upon them as He turned and motioned them back to their divans. Once He had told them to go without scrip or purse and shoes; now there were to be changed conditions and new orders; let them carry money and weapons; a man could sell his coat to buy a sword. "For the things concerning me have an end."

They showed Him two swords and He said they were enough.

Speaking in a whisper, He gave them His final charge:

"Let not your heart be troubled. You believe in God, believe also in me."

They sat, listening intently, yet not understanding that God Himself was with them there. Much must be done before the full truth would come to them, the mystery of Father, Son, and Holy Ghost, all three but one divine reality. But in only a moment Jesus was to make a clear statement on that point.

"In my Father's house there are many mansions. If it were not so, I would have told you; I go to prepare a place for you. And whither I go, you know, and the way you know."

He paused because He could read their hearts. That brave, flinty old skeptic, Thomas, with the cast in his eye, leaned forward.

"Lord, we do *not* know whither thou goest and how can we know the way?"

To which came an immediate answer that men have been quoting ever since, for two thousand years:

"I am the way, the truth, and the life. No man cometh to the Father but by me. If you had known me, you would, without doubt, have known my Father also. And from henceforth you shall know Him, and you have seen Him."

Did He mean what He seemed to be saying? The question burst from Philip:

"Lord–show us the Father and it is enough for us."

Jesus waited a moment, as if He were looking backward three years into mortal time, when that Andrew, sitting there on the other side of the table, had brought to him a shy young friend with the Greek name of Philip. That thoughtful youth had been escaping Bethesda because of its brutal wickedness. That same Philip had brought Nathanael into their party. Yet listen to Philip now:

"Lord, show us the Father and it is enough for us."

"Have I been so long a time with you," sighed Jesus, "and have you not known me? Philip, he that seeth me, seeth the Father also; how sayest thou, show us the Father? Do you not believe that I am in the Father and the Father in me? The words that I speak to you, I speak not of myself. But the Father, who abideth in me, He doth the works."

There they had it, full in the heart. He was not merely a reincarnation of some old prophet, or the new messenger of the Lord; not merely a messiah to lead the people into a new dream of peace —He was in Himself God, one with the Father Almighty, the Master of heaven and earth.

Only now, an hour from Gethsemane, twelve hours from Calvary, could He tell them this. Had He said it to them before, they could not have lived with Him as disciple and Master; they would have been crushed with awe. At last they had been told the full, paralyzing truth. But much more must come before they would fully believe.

At that candlelit table in the upper room God sat with them now.

"If you shall ask me anything in my name, that I will do.

"If you love me, keep my commandments.

"And I shall ask the Father, and He shall give you another comforter. He may abide with you forever.

"I will not leave you orphans; I will come to you . . .

"If any one love me, he will keep my word and my Father will love him, and we will come to him and will make our abode with him.

"But the Paraclete, the Holy Ghost, whom the Father will send in my name, He will teach you all things, and bring all things to your mind, whatsoever I shall have said to you."

Peter gave a great sigh of relief. His brain had been dizzy with his worries. How was he to remember all the wisdom of the Master, not one word of which was yet written down? Now he knew. The Comforter would come. The Holy Ghost from heaven would be the guardian of the church he was to found. The Holy Ghost would bring it all back to mind. A load was lifted from the heart of the tormented fisherman. He turned again to hear the Master's farewell:

"Peace I leave with you; my peace I give unto you; not as the world gives, do I give unto you. Let not your heart be troubled nor let it be afraid. I am the vine, you the branches; he that abideth in me, and I in him, the same beareth much fruit.

"If you abide in me, and my words abide in you, you shall ask whatsoever you will, and it shall be done unto you. This is my commandment, that you love one another as I have loved you. Greater love than this hath no man, that a man lay down his life for his friends.

"Arise! Let us go!"

And one by one they followed Him to Gethsemane.

Chapter 56 THE BARGAIN

SALLOW-FACED Judas slouched through the door at the farther end of the red-walled apartment and approached the two elders with graceless steps. All his life, in all that he did, there was a boorishness, an awkwardness in Judas, a maladdress and a roughness that gave to his whole manner an uncouth swagger. He was a red-bearded man with tough curly hair, thick with ringlets, and his eyes chronically swollen. The movements of his body were quick and jerky, as if his strength lay not in muscle and sinew, but in an abundance, a very torrent of nervous energy. His straw sandals squeaked on the marble floor as he made a stiff, perfunctory bow to Annas.

"Peace be with you," said Annas softly, and Joseph Caiphas bowed his head; he had retired into shadow.

"Your name, my son?"

"Judas, son of Simon."

"Where do you come from?"

"Kerioth."

Annas scribbled on a piece of parchment with a goose-quill pen, and while continuing to write, pursued his examination. His next question was asked with the utmost casualness:

"How long have you been a friend of this Jesus of Capernaum?"

"Jesus of Nazareth, Lord—I have been His friend for three years."

"How did it happen that you, a good man from Kerioth, took up with one of these wild Galileans?"

"I believed in Jesus," replied Judas.

"Believed what about Him?"

"Everything."

A flash of anger came into the old man's bright eyes; then he clucked his tongue and exchanged a rapid glance with his son-in-law.

"Then why do you offer to betray Him, now, in His hiding place for the night?"

"Understand me clearly," exclaimed Judas in a voice deepening with indignation. "I am not a common informer. What I do, I do—and why, is my affair and I do not wish Him to come to any harm."

Old priest and young priest remained silent.

"You do not intend any harm to Jesus, do you?" persisted Judas.

"Do you doubt the mercy, the justice, or the wisdom of the judges of Israel?" demanded Caiphas.

"No. I believe in the Sanhedrin as the true judges of the Lord."

The eyes of Judas were filled with a flickering light as he said these words.

"I believe," said Annas acidly, "that you are a revolutionist. Do you know that I could send *you* to prison?"

"No, Lord Annas! You have no evidence against me."

"I found evidence enough only yesterday against a conspirator called Barabbas! Another fellow trying to stir up trouble and bring us all to ruin. You have been foolish, my son, if you have harbored thoughts of revolution. What did you do all these three years with Jesus?"

"I carried the bag; I was His treasurer; that is how much He trusted me."

"Did you have much money to handle?" asked Annas.

"A few pence at our most prosperous time. We trusted to God for what we ate and where we slept."

"Are you sure Jesus didn't keep some back for Himself?"

"Yes, I am sure of that!" shouted Judas. "How can you——"

"Judas!" snapped Caiphas. "You forget yourself."

Judas stopped his mouth with the palm of his hand, then bowed low.

"I am truly sorry," he muttered. "Please forgive me. I must try to forget Him and all His works. I was under His spell—that was it—and now the scales have fallen from my eyes and I see Him as He really is. He charms you, and the thoughts He puts into words sound wonderful. But these are violent times, and He talks soft words. If anybody slaps you on a cheek, turn your head around so he can slap the other one. Give in to everybody. Never resist anybody."

"I think I begin to see," interrupted Annas. "You thought the important thing was for Him to rally our people. Well, He had his chance. He had it last Sunday, when He rode into this city and the whole multitude fell at His feet, with hosannahs and acclamations. Why, He could have done anything to that mob that He wanted. What *did* He want?"

"Nothing. He was preaching some pacifist madness about the Kingdom of God. He needs to be placed under arrest——"

"Protective arrest—for His own good?"

"Yes, Lord," agreed Judas.

"Another question," went on Annas in a musing tone. "Did you ever hear your Jesus attack—the priesthood?"

"Yes, Lord."

"The details on that, now, please."

"You will do Him no real harm or punishment, Lord? He is at heart a good man."

"We went over that before. How did He attack us?"

"Lord, He has told more than a dozen parables that would blast you all out of the Temple."

Annas sucked his tooth noisily as he turned blankly toward Caiphas. "Then Jesus *is* a dangerous man," he grunted. "You have done well to come to me."

He seized his pen.

"Who are the principal supporters of this fellow?"

As Judas began to enumerate, Annas wrote down the names of sixteen persons: the eleven other Apostles and Mary, the mother of Jesus; Mary, the wife of Cleophas; Salome, the wife of Zebedee, Mary Magdalene and Joanna, the wife of Chuza, who was Herod's steward. These, Judas declared, together with Mary and Martha of Bethany and their brother Lazarus, formed what might be called the inner group of the followers of Jesus; they were His friends and confidants.

"But does He not hobnob also with men of a much higher social class?" asked Annas.

"Why not? While they have not openly avowed their membership, they are strongly sympathetic. They are Joseph of Arimathea and the counselor Nicodemus."

"You were right, Lord Annas!" exclaimed Caiphas savagely. "And I never once suspected either of them."

"They have a right to their opinions, son-in-law. Now, Judas, one thing more and we shall be finished. I believe you told the high priest that tonight above any other time was the best to take Jesus. Why was that?"

"Because it is the only time He would let you take Him."

"Riddles again."

"No riddle—a simple fact, Lord Annas. Jesus could escape from your guard, disappear before your very eyes if He had a mind to. I saw Him do that when the mob tried to kill Him in His home town of Nazareth. The man is invulnerable, He is not capable of being wounded or seized if He does not wish to be. But He expects to be taken tonight."

"And why no miracles tonight?" requested Annas with sarcasm.

"Because He believes He must die. He keeps saying He must die to save the world. Take Him now—while He is in that mood—and He will not resist you—so you," Judas added with heavy mockery, "will be well off."

For a moment Annas and Caiphas talked together in low tones. Annas suddenly stood up.

"Listen to these special instructions. Get for us their certain plans for where they will spend tonight. That is important, my son—we must not take this man until Jerusalem is asleep, and we must be through with Him before Jerusalem wakes up."

"No harm will come to Him?" reiterated Judas.

"Leave everything to us—and hurry."

"What I do, I must do quickly."

As Judas lifted his head, he heard a clink of silver. Annas was bent over, trembling hands held up near the flame of the candle; Judas saw that the old man was counting out money.

"I am not doing this for hire!" he blurted out.

The old man glanced at him witheringly.

"Hire? Hire a patriot? Don't be foolish, Judas. But I have had too much experience in life ever to take anything for nothing. Tomorrow you will not come back to me with new demands—you will be paid off now. Thirty pieces of silver!"

The coins clinked in the palm of Judas. The false apostle put it idly in his bosom, bold eyes searching the red walls, as if he expected to see the hand of the Lord writing there to rebuke his perfidy.

"Hurry!" said Annas. "Or you will be late."

Judas stalked out.

Chapter 57 A VISIT TO PILATE

THE conspirators, Annas and Caiphas, knew they had to hurry. The difficulties confronting them only strengthened the resolve in Annas to obtain the death penalty for Jesus, and to be satisfied with nothing less.

Now that the old leader believed in the real danger of the situation, he was far more stirred than Caiphas, although outwardly still calm and lordly. No one knew better than Annas what the consequences would be to him, to his family, to his class, if Jesus prevailed. It would mean the ultimate eclipse of the Temple aristocracy. The idea of a workingman, a carpenter, coming to Jerusalem with such a program and with power over the imagination of the people was infinitely more disturbing than a messiah of the kind the malcontents desired. A military messiah Rome would know how to answer; he might be disturbing for a while, but any uprising of the people would speedily enough be crushed.

Jesus came preaching something else: a revolution in the heart. The sooner they killed that, the better.

But Annas was resolved also that the illicit plan must be put through with the utmost appearance of legality.

"Thank God, Pontius Pilate is in residence at the palace," said Caiphas.

"Pah!"

Annas spewed Pontius Pilate out of his mouth with his spittle.

"Lord Pilate will go along with me, I dare say. You make sure of your witnesses, Caiphas—men who will testify to the blasphemy."

The heart of Annas was elated now; even at his extreme age he relished politics, intrigue, secret action. Obstacles had always hardened the resolve of Annas; in the excitement he forgot his weariness and felt young again. He tasted victory in advance.

It was nightfall when Annas set forth upon his errand. Boys with torches went before and behind his litter as he was carried through the narrow, crowded streets. The old man hated the bustle and confusion of holiday times; he was glad that it was but a short way to the castle of Antonia, where Pontius Pilate stayed when in town.

The crowds made way for the party as the bearers carried the mighty Annas past the bridge that led over the little valley of the cheese-masters, and higher up the Temple hill, scene of the old man's activities through a lifetime. Dimly he could see the great Temple in the deepening night: the forecourts rising, one over the other, like terraces, and beyond, at the northwest corner, a glimpse of the green stones of Pilate's castle. Threatening sign of the might of empire, it rose upon a steep rock, fifty cubits high. Tonight, because of the festival, a double garrison of alerted Roman troops was stationed in its walls and barracks; Pilate had sworn the people should never riot again while he governed Jerusalem.

Annas came to the castle with an imprecation in his heart. He, an aristocratic Sadducee, playing hand in glove with Pilate, actually hated the Empire with a passion greater than Pharisee or revolutionist. For one detail of oppression he hated it most of all. As a symbol of their power, the Romans kept the sacred robes of the high priest in the castle and would lend them back to the Jews only on state occasions; tomorrow Caiphas might wear them for the Passover, but then he would have to give them back again to the foreign master. That detail of infamy was an excruciating symbol of subjection.

Also Annas was well aware how deeply Pilate hated all Jews, avoiding every possible contact with them, even while living among them and governing them; he would certainly not be pleased at this late call by Annas. But this errand was an urgent political consideration, by which the old man knew he could justify the intrusion and hold Pilate's ear long enough.

The litter bearers were halted at the gates of the Praetorium by imperial guards. To a lowbred churlish guard Annas barked out his name and mission; the Roman gave him surly glances but pulled a chain which produced repeated clanging of a distant bell, and when another guard came, turned in his name. Presently they let him pass.

Annas was in the castle of Antonia less than half an hour, but when he came out, his eyes held the gleam of a man who has won.

"When the case of Jesus comes before Pilate, the Nazarene will die," he was thinking. "And that will be the end of it—He will never be heard of again."

Chapter 58 WE ARE READY

BY THE time Annas reached home, a crowd had gathered before his front door. Rough-looking men stood idly talking together, like laborers waiting for a foreman to come and give orders. Which, Annas reflected with satisfaction, was exactly what they were—laborers, hired mobmen, shouters, screamers, fist-shakers, noisy professional pickets who would rail against any person or any cause—for pay. Tonight Caiphas would be their foreman.

Caiphas had worked swiftly. Not only had he assembled these hirelings to give tongue at the proper time, and sound as if they were the voice of all Judea, howling for blood, he had also assembled a troop of Temple guards, sentinels without weapons. These were men of the priestly classes, very important, too, and they let you know it by the way they swung their shoulders as they walked and the scornful way in which they looked past people in trouble. Their duties were to guard the Temple and maintain order; they had already been greatly reproached for not having prevented the disastrous scene in the Temple, when Jesus overturned the tables and whipped the money-changers.

The priests charged that if these guards had been attending to their business, such a thing would never have happened. But the Temple militiamen replied that they *had* been attending to their business, and faithfully—they had charge of the singing and the instrumental music: the lyre, the dulcimer, the horn, and the sounding brasses; they had to see that the Temple was kept clean; that the building was kept in repair; and arrange for the buying of supplies, the sewing and embroidery of the priestly robes. They must also supervise the preparation of the vessels, the utensils, and the stuffs used in the ceremonies, and the endless washing and dryings and safeguards against defilement. So many technical points had to be observed that the guards spent their whole terms learning the rules and instructing the novices who would succeed them.

Presently they would be joined by Roman soldiers with armor and swords, who would give empire authority to the arrest.

"You have acted quickly, Caiphas," said Annas, when once again the old man and his son-in-law stood face to face in the room with the red walls.

"Better than you realize," replied Caiphas, showing teeth through his beard. "I have sent personal word to every single member of the council, telling them all that the Sanhedrin must be prepared to meet tonight and to stay in session until the case of this fellow is disposed of. They will recognize how serious the emergency is in the way I worded the call. Meanwhile, Judas is back."

"Judas?"

"Judas Iscariot, Lord—the man who will take us to Jesus. He has learned exactly where to lead us."

"Then are you ready?"

"At once!"

Chapter 59 THE DARK GARDEN

IT WAS well after nine o'clock and quite dark when Judas, ready for his traitorous job, emerged through the back doorway of the house of Annas and descended to the alley. Loitering before the steps was the posse of the Temple guards; though forbidden to carry arms, they had picked up staves and cudgels. Standing off from them were the six Roman soldiers with an officer; they carried lanterns and torches, clubs, and staves.

Judas turned his back on them, stalking around a corner into a jagged and poisonous-smelling little street. Not a sound was heard, except the shuffling feet of the men, the clank of armor, and the lonely howl of some faraway dog. The course they followed was zigzag, a series of short, sharp detours; the streets were all rough and full of holes, so the marchers made haste slowly. Pale in the light of harvest stars loomed the Temple; then around a last reeking corner the men came to a passageway cut in the southeastern angle of the Temple wall and began the hazardous descent of a flight of old stone steps falling sharply from the upper city to a locked gate below.

At this ancient portal, near to the pool of Siloam, the Roman officer talked with the gatekeeper and made arrangements for opening up and admitting the party when they returned with their prisoner. On a promise of scourging, the terrified gatekeeper agreed to keep his gate open and his mouth closed.

Meanwhile the imperial soldiers, facing the wall, grumbled to one another.

Why this crawling through the dark in force to catch one man? They had heard tales about their quarry. Report said the Nazarene possessed mysterious powers; He could walk on the sea, the winds of heaven performed His bidding, and once He had fed forty thousand hungry people with one basket of loaves and fishes and everybody had a bellyful. This wonder-worker and all His familiars were said to lie hidden in some dark garden outside the city wall. What might He be doing even now in that garden? Witchcraft? Spells, conjurations, devil praying? Why must they be sent after such a magician in the dark? Would not daylight have done as well?

Judas heard them talking among themselves and quietly reproved them. Jesus had never harmed anyone. He was not a sorcerer. The disciple reassured them, coaxed them to follow him as he led the way through the gate and still farther down, until they reached the brook Kedron that flows between Jerusalem and the Mount of Corruption. Once, in this dark valley, the god Moloch had been worshiped in human sacrifice.

Having passed beyond the mystical murmur of the brook, they hastened on toward the Mount of Olives.

But the soldiers continued to grumble—they were brave men, but who would not be anxious about a fugitive with such powers as those?

Well, Judas assured them they need not fear Him tonight. Jesus, he reported, was actually waiting for them to come and get Him in a farmyard, an oil press called by some the Garden of Gethsemane. It was really a series of gardens within enclosing walls—a place He had often visited before, but never so late. On any other night by this time He and His followers would be at the home of friends, like Mary and Martha and Lazarus; with them and their neighbors Jesus and His men stopped often.

But tonight He and eleven followers were late out of their beds.

What were they doing in the Garden? Judas did not know. It did not matter anyway, he expostulated, again and again, as he trudged beside them. The silver coins in his bag made a soft, jingling noise as he walked. Nonsense! Nonsense! And Judas sighed heavily as he led the long and mincing column of men who swung their hissing torches and walked like women, not to stumble over the stones.

Presently Judas called softly and lifted his hand, and they halted at a high hedge, which served as a wall that completely enclosed the area.

Now most of the party knew where they were. This was the farmyard with the oil press—a dark patch of olive trees in a familiar triangle between the most-traveled footpaths over Mount Olivet and the highroad to Bethany. Not a native in the city but had heard the ribald jokes about the top of the hill where Solomon once built houses for his heathen wives.

A little doorlike opening had been cut in the hedge that otherwise completely enclosed the olive garden. Judas waved back the guards while he leaned in and peered. Miraculously the darkness seemed to soften then, as if the stars grew brighter. With narrowing eyes Judas searched among gnarled and hunchbacked trees of immemorial age; his long, shrewish nose took in the soft orchard smell of ripening fruits and the damp sweetness of night greenery. And the peaked ears of Judas reported the deep sound of the wind, soughing and murmuring through those ancient olive boughs.

But where were the eleven and the Master? Dimly, Judas began to make them out. That vast hunk of man sprawled on the grass, his head on a rolled-up cloak, was surely Peter, snoring. The slim form yonder by the pavilion platform was John, also deep in slumber. Other dark smudges under the trees were unrecognizable, but Judas counted eleven, all asleep. Their leader was invisible.

Judas would have entered then and brought the guards with him, but he was stopped by the sound of a familiar voice at prayer. He stood listening. Somewhere off in the deeper foliage there, where he remembered a white boulder half buried in the earth, Jesus of Nazareth was on His knees. Judas could hear the suffering voice:

"My Father! If it be possible, let this cup pass from me!"

The nostrils of Judas twisted in disdain.

"Afraid?" he murmured. "He is afraid! He is praying to be let off—to escape——"

But Jesus was not done with His praying.

"Nevertheless, not as I will, but as you will."

Then Judas was startled—because of that double wishing prayer to God; that ambivalence in Gethsemane. The Master wanted life, yet if the Father to whom He prayed insisted, knowing what was best, then He would obediently take death. The contradiction stirred a deep resentment in the listening Judas. This humbleness was unbecoming to a man. At the altar, from ancient times, the people had struck the best bargain they could. Do this for me and I will do that for you, O God! So the patriarchs and kings and prophets had tried to do business with the infinite. But Jesus did not seek to force His will; He sought instead, and Judas was astonished by it, to come to an understanding of the will of God, that He might obey it.

The silence after the prayer was touched by a low swishing sound as by a trailing garment brushing the grass. Out of the dark and walking by starlight the white figure of Jesus appeared, moving toward a sleeping disciple. Judas could see Him clearly now—tall, robed, walking barefoot across the chilly field. Jesus bent over the snoring man.

"Peter! What! Could you not watch one hour with me? Watch you and pray that you enter not into temptation. The spirit indeed is willing but the flesh is weak . . . Sleep, now, and take rest. It is enough! The hour is come! Look, the Son of Man shall be betrayed into the hands of sinners. Rise up. Let us go. He that will destroy me is at hand."

Then He reached forward His foot and with the bare toes gently joggled Peter's shoulder. The fisherman grunted, rolled over, and then sat up violently, his round face and pug nose and blinking eyes turned upward.

"It is enough, Peter. The hour has come," Jesus said simply.

Peter scrambled to his feet and bared his knife.

Judas waited for no more. He laid a hard, damp hand on the wrist of the leader of the band, and whispered:

"Now is the time. Let us go in and take Him. You will know Him sure—He will be the one I will kiss!"

The sound of rough voices and the clank of steel, the sight of the fires, brought all the drowsy disciples to their feet. They blinked at the frightening torch-lit scene, shining with the cold brilliance of armor and swords.

Judas strode forward until he stood directly in front of Jesus.

"Hail, Master!"

Jesus moved toward Judas and seized Him by the shoulders. Then the arms of Christ drew Judas to Him and the disciple kissed the Master on the cheek. At the signal, the Roman soldiers came forward, weapons in hand. But Jesus did not at once let Judas go. He held him tightly, His cheek laid against the tough ringlets, eyes lifted, as if asking a favor of the invisible. Then at last He released him, and as Judas stood back, the prisoner brought His hands together and held them out as He approached the Roman captain.

That was more than the panic-stricken Peter could bear. The knife he had toyed with at the supper table gleamed in his hand—a knife with a blade five inches long, for gutting fish. This uplifted, the stalwart Peter sprang at the officer; there was a moment's tussle, a disorderly struggle, and then the ironic voice of Jesus:

"Peter, Peter, put up your sword!"

And Peter's fishing knife fell at his feet.

A little soldier from the Temple scurried forward with a handful of ropes and began to tie the wrists of Jesus. That action was like a warning to all the other disciples, who had been watching in startled dismay.

This sudden invasion of men in armor and others armed with cudgels and staves filled them with fright. The torches burned like small new worlds fuming in a dark universe. Voices rose in brawling question. Peter and all the others were overwhelmed with fear for their own safety. Stampeded, like wild creatures, they scampered off into the night. One, wrapped only in a linen cloth, was seized by a guard, but he tore himself free, leaving the garment in the soldier's hands; naked, he vanished among the trees. Leaping the hedges and running as fast as legs would carry them, they left Jesus, the captive, alone.

Chapter 60 THE PRISONER

As he waited for the prisoner to be caught and brought before him, Annas, the most powerful man in Israel, felt depressed. Already he foresaw certain trouble; no matter how many "messiahs" they exterminated, the troubles of the people continued to create the need for salvation.

The old man glared hopelessly around his grand salon and then, rising from his stool, walked slowly toward the steps of his dais. Wearily he mounted the platform and sat in the imposing chair, as the door was flung open and the captain of the guard stood at attention before Annas.

"Lord," he said, "we have done as you commanded. We have taken the man prisoner. Behold Him at the door—Jesus of Nazareth!"

The prisoner was shoved forward so that, in a circle of light from the hanging candelabrum, He came in full sight of Annas.

The political boss of Jerusalem was instantaneously jolted at his first sight of the captured Jesus. He blinked and looked again. No outer detail seemed important—this tall, fettered man in the white robe and sandals; what was it in Him that was so jolting, like to a blow over the heart? It could not be the prisoner's luxuriant brown hair and untrimmed beard; most peasants and mechanics so wore their hair. It could not be the white turban wound loosely around the head, for that was the national headdress, and the white turban of Jesus fell at the side, as did most of the turbans in that place and at that time, down to the shoulders and over the tunic; and, as did His fellows, Jesus fastened His turban under the chin with a cord. But the sharp eyes of the old politician did notice that the blue inner robe of the prisoner was all of one piece and without a seam. The garment had been given to Jesus by one of those women along the way who had been grateful for His message. That night He was also wearing a blue tallith, a loose-flowing mantle over His shoulders; at its four corners were blue fringes.

By the looks of Him He was just an ordinary man with sandals dusty from long tramping on the open road. Yet Annas sensed, nevertheless, that his prisoner was not ordinary at all, but most extraordinary. How was that? Whence that remarkable quality of separateness and power which Annas immediately felt in Jesus? Where did it reside, and how did it visibly express itself?

Was it in the bright glory of His large eyes, set so wide apart, like His mother's? Some inner energy of incalculable force looked out of those large and patient and unfailingly interested eyes, of one to whom God was an overpoweringly intimate and personal experience. They spoke of an intimate understanding of the nearness and goodness of the heavenly Father; a kind of unendurable ecstasy prolonged through life. It was as one who knew, moment by moment, this deep and rich experience, that Jesus walked into the red-walled room of the home of Annas; as one who felt no humiliation, though His wrists were bound with leather cords that cut into His flesh.

Feeling himself in the presence of a mystery, Annas promptly declined to take any stock of it and fastened his gaze approvingly on the bound wrists of Jesus, but even so he was already aware of an uneasy suspicion that you cannot tie up infinity with a string.

The prisoner looked around calmly. All these men, hirelings, hirers, judges, believed that the Lord God Almighty, the God of Israel, of Abraham and Isaac and Jacob, was really a glorified member of their caste; the land-owning, slave-owning, mortgage-foreclosing aristocrats represented here. As Jesus regarded Annas and Caiphas in that moment, He seemed to say:

"Joseph Caiphas, you are the high priest of the Temple and you and your ancient father-in-law sanction the oppression of the poor. You have helped the people to forget the eighth-century prophets; I would call the people back to listen once more to the thunder of those voices."

There was in that long glance of His from the face of Joseph Caiphas back to the face of Annas almost a bemused compassion for the political and judicial problems that confronted them in their conspiracy against Him.

Annas, letting the silence stretch almost unendurably, seated himself again with determined aplomb, to listen to the reports. It was good news that the prisoner's band of followers had deserted Him and fled. That promised well; the fickle populace, too, might not resent His death so much as had been feared. Where were His supporters now? Annas sucked his tooth with satisfaction. He had no suspicion of the presence in the doorway crowd of two of those very Galileans. One was a stout fellow, woolen robe belted with a frayed old cord; beard turning white, pate turning bald; a rough and fusty fisherman with freckled nose and lacking in city manners. He was Simon called Peter, but Annas did not know about him. Close by, but ignoring Peter as if the two had never met, was also another fisherman, John, one of the sons of Zebedee—a young man with anguished face.

Annas beckoned impatiently for Judas, hovering in the rear.

"You promised there would be no resistance," he said with some choler. "What happened about the soldier's ear, Judas?"

Judas lifted weary shoulders and shrugged.

"That was just Peter," he groaned. "Crazy Peter who always

loves to swagger and show off, no matter what happens. It was Peter that resisted arrest; he should be punished, too, Lord, even more than your prisoner here, for Peter is a very violent man."

"Was there an ear cut off?"

"An ear?"

"That is what I asked you. Was there an ear cut off, or wasn't there? I have been just told children's tales about an ear restored again on a soldier's head. Will you answer?"

All along Annas had merely been tolerating Judas, but now he had had enough; he was in a heat of temper.

"I know not about the ear, Lord. There was a good deal of excitement and shouting at the time. Perhaps so! But Jesus can do more wonderful things than restore ears when He wishes to."

The glance of the sharp old eyes leaped quickly to the prisoner. But Annas did not prolong his scrutiny. Something in his every glance at the captive face disturbed him. Perhaps it was the tranquillity of Jesus, so composed, so at peace; the line of great decision on the kindly mouth was upsetting too; there was in it no impertinence and no overconfidence; nothing unfriendly or suspicious, but it was the reflection of a great inner serenity, a sense of grace and power that—under the circumstances—was hard to contemplate.

Annas made a churlish clearing of his throat and clapped his hands together. His withered body seemed to grow taller as He resolved not to be outstared by his prisoner. Let the fellow realize he was brought first before Annas because Annas was the most important man in Jerusalem, the behind-the-scenes power, the uncrowned king of Israel—and the multitude who had begun to murmur that their Nazarene was "King of the Jews" must soon hear of this proud, responsible moment; all the hardened arteries and clogged veins of the old man glowed with a reborn physical warmth and sense of power.

"Jesus, you are called a blasphemer!" began Annas; he held his wrist tight against his ribs as he pointed to Jesus. "Are you a blasphemer?"

The ready smile of Jesus had in it no complaisance or appeasement. He looked about Him, comprehension without mockery in His glance. When He spoke, His voice was calm and unshaken; there was in His well-mastered tones the country accent of a Nazarene:

"I have spoken openly to the world. I taught in the synagogue and in the Temple, where all the Jews come together—and in secret I spoke nothing. Why do you ask me? Ask them that have heard me!"

A reluctant glitter of admiration came into the scornful eyes of Annas. This self-assured prisoner was shrewd—not one to be caught easily in a snare. Promptly He had just taken His stand as an innocent man, squarely on His rights and privileges as a citizen, living under the law of Moses—Annas and his crew would have to prove those charges by witnesses in a court of law; that was the technical, legal meaning of Jesus's answer.

"I see!" murmured Annas, milking his beard. "You demand proof? Very well, Jesus of Nazareth, I hold you for trial. For immediate trial. Blasphemy!"

A noise ran through the mob listening at the open door, a noise running back through vaulted sides of the courtyard to the open steps that led down to the street. From Judas came a strangled cry, and he grabbed at the cloak of Annas.

"Blasphemy! You would try Him for such a crime!" he protested. "No, you promised——"

A guard clapped a hand over the mouth of Judas. His tortured eyes sought the face of Jesus; but the soldiers had turned Jesus around and were already escorting Him out to the next stop on His dark journey.

Chapter 61 DENIAL

FROM the hands of Annas, Jesus was led directly to the home of the high priest which adjoined the Temple. The journey, which on foot took less than twenty minutes, was made in silence, commanded by the guards; at that hour it was like the very belly of darkness, and the narrow, coiling Jerusalem streets were deserted. Except for the hired mob, and Judas and the Roman soldiers, almost no one saw the dismal procession on its way to the judgment.

Outside the priest's front door they waited for orders from Caiphas—the mob surging around Jesus who, wrists bound, stood erect between two soldiers. Not once did the luminous dark eyes turn; had He looked left, He might have seen a stout figure warming tough old hands nervously above a pan of coals. Peter!

But Jesus did not see Peter then, nor did He look to the right where, among the moist dark faces of hired disturbers, He might also have seen the young and distrait face of John.

Peter was still warming his hands when a young woman carrying a bucket stopped suddenly before him. The girl's name was Huldah and she was one of the favorite servants of Caiphas; she studied Peter with slow recognition.

"You!" she said, something spiteful in her voice.

"I?" answered Peter in a worried tone.

"You. You were also with Jesus, the Galilean."

"I don't know what you are saying," stammered Peter, uneasy at a lie.

"You *were* with Him," Huldah insisted, stamping her foot.

"Woman, I know Him not," said Peter, and shook his head. He moved off, hoping to lose himself in the crowd, but before he could go two steps, another maid joined Huldah, crying shrilly:

"Surely he is one of them. He is a Galilean himself. Even the way he talks gives him away."

Then Peter uttered an oath and swore:

"I don't know this man you are talking about."

The lying words had no more left his lips than there came a lull in the clamor of voices and Peter heard the shrill crowing of a cock. And when Peter turned he was looking into the eyes of Jesus, and it was the compassion in those eyes that made the fisherman weep bitter tears. Not reproof, but the full understanding of a loving heart. The sound he heard when the cock crowed no more was the gentle chuckle of God!

Chapter 62 THE JUDGES

The prisoner was kept waiting outside the Hall of Judgment while the crowd inside watched the space between two monoliths at the entrance, where they knew He must very soon appear.

The high vaulted basilica of the council chamber where the trial would be held was lit with hundreds of oil-burning torches set in niches cut in the walls. An enormous auditorium, built of great marble pieces, it was called the Hall of Hewn Stones, or Lishkath Haggazith, and was regarded as the national shrine of Justice.

By eleven o'clock that Thursday night the majority of the seventy judges were in their places; Caiphas had worked busily enough. The roof echoed with the low drone of their voices—chatter subdued by the solemnity of a capital occasion. Turbaned, barefoot, and cross-legged asquat embroidered cushions, they were ranged in a deep hairpin design, a living letter U. And the judges, rubbing finger tips, shaking heads, rolling eyeballs, spreading hands fan-shape, shrugging shoulders, scratching buttocks, all were whispering energetically, speculating on the suddenness of their summons and the anxiety that must have driven Annas to sanction such an unprecedented move. Was it because he feared the powers of magic with which the prisoner was said to be endowed?

At the bottom part of the U sat a blotch-faced old functionary who was called the Nassi, chief of the assembly. Like a meditative patriarch, he was conferring with the gorgeous and blooming Joseph Caiphas. In ceremonial garments, the high priest was now a sight to strike almost any prisoner with awe. Annas, his father-in-law, was not yet visible.

At either tip of the human hairpin were stationed rows of little men with inkhorns, quills, and strips of parchment; they would record what was said and done. Beyond the scribes were three rows of younger men: blackbeards, but few graybeards, for these were only learned novices. If one of the squatting judges were to fall ill, or become paralyzed or die, an understudy from the row of young substitutes would take the vacant cushion and the trial would go on.

All of these various ranks of men made up the Sanhedrin, most potent ecclesiastical and secular assembly convoked now to try, under the code of Moses, one accused of being a false prophet.

They were learned scholars and of true character; among them were schoolmasters and lawyers; Pharisees, too, fanatics who would make every breath a man drew subject to some new and capricious twist of scriptural interpretation, but they would be equally meticulous to see to it that any prisoner got a square deal. For among them, Pharisee, Sadducee, all, there was not one judge who did not accept his responsibility, or who carried it lightly. These were counselors who could not be threatened or influenced by outsiders, but only by their own prejudices and fears. Theirs was the highest of all honors, a place in the Sanhedrin, and they had obtained it only by a lifetime of hard work and sacrifice. As a man is acquainted with his own fingers they knew the law; from memory they could cite precedents and decisions of countless judges who had gone before them, together with all essential passages of Scripture. They were schooled, too, in science—medicine, chemistry, astronomy; and they also had to be familiar with the condemned practices of the black magicians, the soothsayers, and the necromancers. All spoke the language of Roman, Greek, and Egyptian as well as certain dialects of neighboring countries. They were supposed to have a spotless moral reputation, and many of them did.

They were, of course, rabbinical logicians and apt in dialectics. Finally, not one of them had ever followed at any time in his life a trade, an occupation, or a profession by which he had earned an income.

The scope of this court had no boundaries within the range of morals and dogma and human behavior. In its humanity, the detachment of its attitude was oddly objective; an intellectual determination to be scrupulously just. Since from the court's verdicts there could be no appeal, the sacred duty lay on the conscience of every judge to protect the interests of those on trial. Their oaths bound them to be actual attorneys for a prisoner. They must interpret the law in his favor whenever that was possible; it was their explicit duty to look for extenuating circumstances.

Since, then, the whole judicial scheme of Israel was designed to make it impossible to convict an innocent person, these judges, if they respected their oaths tonight, would have to acquit Jesus. Annas knew that, if Caiphas did not.

One might be certain they would think a long time before they beheaded Jesus, or strangled Him, stoned Him or burned Him, or hung Him on a cross. In a dozen regulations their own laws stood between Jesus and a sentence of death—especially one great and favorable point, that, in criminal procedure, was a final check on injustice called the "antecedent warning"—a safeguard for a prisoner unequaled in any other court of law, before or since. Under its provisions no man accused of a capital offense could be convicted unless it were also proved beyond contradiction that he had been warned in advance; had been told that, for what he was about to do, he could be put to death. Even more than that, it was required that the offender must have then replied that he did realize he was about to commit the crime, was fully aware of its penalty, and that he meant to do it anyhow.

How could anyone ever be sentenced to death under such merciful latitude? How, above everyone else, could Jesus of Nazareth be convicted?

Through a small door to the left popped suddenly, like a breeze of authority, the little figure of Annas. Promptly on the midnight bugles he came, the crabapple face pale in the fluttering torchlight; the wisp of white hair greased and pushed back. Solemnly the little man marched to the table where stood Caiphas, arms folded in magnificently pretended repose. Briefly Annas spoke to his son-in-law, then made his way to a reserved cushion and sank down upon it with a painful little grunt. Everyone knew that now the trial could go on.

Without delay Joseph Caiphas strode forward with a grand sweep of arms and robes and took a commanding position. He spoke in serious, even gentle tones:

"I ask for silence! I ask for attention! I ask for truth and justice!"

In a low, responsive murmur came the chorused answer:

"So mote it be!"

Upon which Caiphas, turning to the great doorway, called out:

"Jesus of Nazareth, stand forth!"

Chapter 63 ON TRIAL

AT THE top of the great stairs the figure of the prisoner appeared between two vast marble pillars. The guards stood back and let the whole assembly get a look at Him. Seeing Him this second time, Annas was jolted harder than before. The impregnability of that alert and tranquil countenance tormented him, not because the old one did not understand, but because he was beginning to suspect that he understood too well.

The prisoner's calm humility was enough to pierce intellectual pride. In one straight glance Jesus seemed to survey the whole entrenched and greedy power which here was marshaled against Him. His head slightly tilted, He might have been listening to echoes of the long-ignored voices of the prophets and seers of the people.

The cackle and gabble of conversation dwindled as guards led Jesus forward. It was just a few minutes past midnight. Now, in the bright torchlight of the huge chamber, they sized Him up with the most intense curiosity, and wondered at His calm. Did not this man realize His peril?

He realized everything. He knew this court, with its full and legal quorum assembled illegally in the night; its powers and unbounded jurisdiction; its ideals and its frail humanity; and imbedded in that humanity its fears.

And now Caiphas stood up in the middle of the hollow of the U. On his head the high priest wore a turban of blue enwrought with gold, and across his chest was the brass plate of his office glittering with twelve precious stones. His flowing robe was also of blue, but his girdle was of scarlet, purple, and gold, and out of his sleeves fluttered the pure white linen of his sacerdotal underwear. Of the whole court only he wore sandals, but you could barely see them for the gaudy fringes of his robe embroidered with crimson pomegranates.

Before the trial began Caiphas prayed with theatrical intonations and histrionic pauses; he should have begun by making the morning sacrifice, but he skipped over that detail. He merely lifted up his hands and brought palms together just below the last ringlet of his redolent beard, and a silence fell as the intoning voice fairly crooned up to Jehovah. Caiphas, addressing the God who, as a pillar of cloud by day and of fire by night, had led the Israelites out of the bondage of Egypt, now entreated this same light to shine on the deeds done here at this trial; that the elders, the priests, and the scribes might know the truth and judge justly.

The prayer, as Nicodemus said afterward, was much too long. As it was finished there was the uneasy rustling of men seizing a little opportunity to settle themselves, clearing of throats, coughings behind the hand, brief whisperings, neighbor to neighbor, and finally a full, expectant hush.

Caiphas gave a signal and the guards shoved Jesus down the last two steps, into the hollow of the great U surrounded by His judges.

"Let every man know of what this Jesus of Nazareth stands accused," resumed Caiphas. "His crime is blasphemy. For that crime He is now to be tried. He is accused of having used certain words, of having said certain things. If these charges are true, if the witnesses agree, then He is guilty not only of sacrilege, the most abominable crime, but also of that charge which has been forbidden since Moses gave us the law—the crime of sorcery. Let the witnesses be called."

First there was brought in a tall, gaunt, hungry man with eyes that peered from under red lids in unaccustomed wonder at all this height and depth of room, this display of torches and candles, this splendor of wardrobe, this unaccustomed glory in the dark hour of morning. Caiphas caressed his beard as he asked the first question.

"What is your name?"

"Ben Jezrel."

"You have promised to tell the truth. You have not forgotten the commandment?"

Ben Jezrel put his hand under his right thigh in token that he had spoken the truth and answered:

"I remember: 'You shall not bear false witness against your neighbor.' "

Crossing his hands, the high priest began the recitation of ritual words required by the code:

"Forget not, O witness, that it is one thing to give evidence in a trial as to money and another in a trial for life. In a money suit, if your witness-bearing shall do wrong, money may repair that wrong. But in this trial for life, if you sin, the blood of the accused and the blood of his seed, to the end of time, shall be imputed unto you . . . Therefore was Adam created one man and alone to teach us that if any witness shall destroy one soul out of Israel, he is held by the Scripture to be as if he had destroyed the world, and he who saves one such, it should be as if he had saved the world—for a man from one signet ring may strike off many impressions and all of them shall be exactly alike, but He, the King of Kings, He the Holy and Blessed, has struck from His type of the first man the forms of all men that are living, yet so that no one human being is wholly alike to any other!

"Wherefore let us think and believe that the whole world is created for a man such as He whose life now hangs on your words!"

Caiphas waited for a moment and then began the formal questioning:

"Did you actually see and hear the prisoner commit the crime with which He is charged?"

"Yes."

"Did you caution the prisoner of the gravity of His offense?"

"I did."

"And he persisted?"

"He did."

"Did you warn Him of the punishment to which He would be liable if He were convicted of the offense?"

"I did, sir."

"Do you think He was aware of the serious nature of His crime?"

"I am certain that He was."

"Now, what were the words you heard Him say?"

"I heard this man say these words," Ben Jezrel testified: 'I will destroy this Temple that is made with hands and in three days I will build another not made with hands.' "

A murmur ran through the elders, the priests, and the scribes. Had this Galilean dared to say such a thing? Would He deny it?

Caiphas turned toward the prisoner.

"Well, Jesus of Nazareth, what have you to say to this that you have heard?"

There was no answer.

"Do you deny the testimony of Ben Jezrel?"

Jesus, wrists bound, face untroubled, stood mute in the great lighted hall. To remain silent was His legal right.

"Do you admit that you said those words?"

Still no answer. Caiphas turned, with a long sweeping grimace that encompassed the whole court. His shrug seemed to say to them: "You see how it is? We have a stubborn, stiff-necked prisoner here." But he scrupulously refrained from saying any word detrimental to the accused. Instead, he dismissed Ben Jezrel with a toss of his hand.

"Bring on the second witness."

The second witness was Isaac ben Marath, a good man from King David Street, a poor merchant in beans and barley but one who, nevertheless, gave up his tithes to the Temple three times a year.

"Well, Isaac ben Marath," began Caiphas, "tell us what were the words you heard spoken by this man?"

And Isaac ben Marath answered:

"I heard Jesus of Nazareth say: 'Destroy this Temple, and in three days I will raise it up.' "

"You may go!" said Caiphas, turning with triumph to the whole court, right and left, seeming to say: "Well, judges, you have heard the necessary two witnesses. Does not their testimony agree?"

As if in answer to that unspoken question, one of the most respected members of the court, Joseph of Arimathea, brought his knees together and stood up with an agility surprising in so elderly a man.

"The witnesses do not agree!" Joseph sternly declared. "If you think they do, you are very much mistaken. The first witness testified—I have written down very carefully what he said—that this prisoner, Jesus, had uttered these words: 'I will destroy this Temple that is made with hands and in three days I will build another not made with hands.' That is one accusation we have heard.

"But the second witness said something entirely different; he attributes to Jesus an entirely different statement which was, according to him: 'Destroy this Temple, and in three days I will raise it up.' "

A new murmur ran through the court, some saying one way, some another. They no more agreed among themselves than had the witnesses. But Joseph went doggedly on.

"In the first instance," he argued, "Jesus is accused of announcing His intention of destroying the Temple and then restoring it by sorcery. In the second instance He is quoted as promising to restore the Temple if someone else destroyed it. Which, then, did He actually say? Certainly one of these witnesses must be wrong, and our law says that at least two witnesses must agree!"

Caiphas, looking imploringly toward his father-in-law, had received an almost imperceptible signal. He gave vent to a deep breath of outraged annoyance, and answered:

"Very well; there is no need to argue the point. Let us hear from another witness."

Now Jacob, the corn seller, was a man Caiphas felt he could rely on, and he was there to be used in an emergency. Willingly Jacob slapped his thigh for the oath, answered the ritual questions, and was brought promptly to the point: he *had* been there in the Temple and he *had* heard what Jesus said.

"What, then, did He say?"

"He said," replied Jacob, ruffling a somewhat tattered beard, "these exact words: 'I am able to destroy the Temple of God and to build it in three days.' "

Again Caiphas turned to the Sanhedrin with a vindicating smile. But now there was a deeper murmur, and Joseph of Arimathea was again on his feet.

"This," cried Joseph, "is confusion piled upon confusion. Here we have a third testimony and what we call a vain, useless one. This third witness now quotes the prisoner as saying: 'I am able to destroy this Temple.' This is not what the others said; not the same thing at all. The first testified to a threat—the third to a mere boast.

"Which is it then, threat or boast? Or was it anything at all? A man's life hangs on the answer. Our law requires that the witnesses must agree together. Three have already disagreed. Caiphas, you have produced no case against Jesus of Nazareth!"

"In all three testimonies," replied the high priest, in a shrill voice, "the witnesses agreed in one essential point: they all say three days, do they not? Is not that agreeing together?"

Joseph smiled disdainfully.

"That is reasoning for a Roman, but not for a Jew," he replied. "I remind you again, Lord Caiphas, this man is on trial for His life. He is entitled to every protection the law affords."

"Certainly you are very active on His behalf," observed Caiphas with an acid glance.

"It is my duty and yours to be active on His behalf," Joseph returned. "No, Caiphas, as I told you before, you have not made out a case against this man. Furthermore, I see a witness over there anxious to be heard. Let us hear him."

Caiphas turned brusquely. Standing near to the prisoner was a stout, pale man, eyes shining with extraordinary brilliance.

"I asked," he faltered in a nervous voice, "that the questions be put to me. I have already been before the Committee."

With patience that lacked all grace, Caiphas applied the ritual to the stranger. His name was Benjamin, also of King David Street.

"Well, Benjamin, what have you to testify here?"

Benjamin sank to his knees, picked up the dusty robe of the prisoner, and kissed its hem.

"I was blind," he said. "He put some clay on my eyes after mixing it with His spittle and when He took the clay off, I was healed."

Caiphas shook his finger in the face of the witness.

"Get up!" he barked. "You are not here to tell fairy tales! What do you really know?"

"One thing I know," reiterated Benjamin. "Once I was blind and now I can see."

There was a hush in the trial room; something in the manner of this witness filled them with belief. They turned to look at Jesus with new interest. Could it be possible . . .

Caiphas lifted his well-tended hand and guards hustled the witness off.

"There is no value in such an interruption," he complained angrily. "No value whatsoever. We are not here to decide whether this accused man is a physician or is not a physician. The question is clear enough: is he, or is he not, a blasphemer?"

"You have yet to prove it," said Joseph.

A vociferous shout from the assembly reinforced the objection. Caiphas saw then, if he had not realized it before, that not he nor his great father-in-law, nor anyone else, held the ancient tribunal of Israel in his pocket. These judges were not to be ruled except by law.

As the confusion grew, another of the judges, Nicodemus, stood up from among the elders and clapped his hands for a sign that he wanted to be heard.

"Mark you this, my lords," Nicodemus declared. "If you attempt to limit the blasphemy charge against this prisoner to the subordinate charge of prophesying, how can you ever prove the man a false prophet? You can't possibly do it until the Temple *is* destroyed. If, then, Jesus of Nazareth fails to rebuild it in three days, then and then only is He proven to be a false prophet. That is the law, my Lord, and we are bound by it."

And as Nicodemus sat down, Joseph of Arimathea rose again.

"My lords," he said, "I propose that we dismiss Jesus of Nazareth here and now, and let Him go His way!"

As Joseph of Arimathea sat down, he saw many approving headshakes. As yet there was certainly no majority for conviction. Only momentarily disconcerted, Caiphas again lifted his ringed hand, Annas having just left his side.

"My lords," began Caiphas, "it is true that under our law the least discord between the evidence of witnesses is held to destroy its value in so solemn an issue as we are now trying. However, this does not mean that the entire case against this prisoner can be thrown out on merely technical grounds. Moreover, we have more evidence to bring. I charge, that this man claims to be the Messiah all Jews have waited for, the Christ. That is His abominable crime and now He must answer for it."

"Wait!"

Both Nicodemus and Joseph of Arimathea were on their feet, clamoring to be heard.

"You are changing the very ground of the accusation during the course of the trial!" shouted Nicodemus. "That is unjust. I believe it is illegal."

Before Caiphas could attempt an answer, old Annas rose again and took over. Very straight he was, in his physical slightness, standing in that vast public chamber, the incarnation of the elder statesman, the voice of authority and experience.

"Let us hear no talk of injustice in this honorable court," he began crisply. "Nor of illegality. We are here to exercise our best talents in trying a man accused of the worst crime we know—blasphemy. The accusation that the prisoner pretended to be the Messiah is merely a further count in the indictment. It *is* fair. It *is* just. It *is* legal. Caiphas, your witnesses!"

No one cared to challenge this opinion; Annas was their supreme, most respected, and powerful adviser.

The new witnesses were called: Simon, the web-toed watchman from the Porch of David; Ezra ben Tobeth, the one with the sweet singing voice; and Chalis of Bethany, a neighbor of Mary and Martha. They slapped their thighs, or raised hands, according to preference, and to them were put the regulation questions. Then they gave their evidence.

And more than before it became clear that something was amiss.

For Simon testified that Jesus had called Himself the Son of God, but Ezra swore he had called Himself the Son of Man. And Chalis declared that he had once heard Jesus ask His disciples how public men called Him and what they said of Him; Chalis had overheard Him inquire if men thought He was the Christ.

Caiphas was in the same dilemma as before; beads of angry sweat glistened on the cheeks of the high priest and rolled down to dampen the ringlets of his whiskers as he bowed to consult Annas.

"Joseph of Arimathea is right," the old man whispered. "You have not been able to prove a case against Jesus. And yet, my Lord Caiphas, having gone this far, you have *got* to prove a case against Him."

"And quickly too," added Caiphas, "or someone will say it is time to end the trial and go home."

"Nicodemus is getting ready to do that now," said Annas. "He is the kind of man who likes to make a speech. He will offer some quillet of a technicality, because that is what he is, a quibbler on small points, subtleties, and nice distinctions. Hang and burn such a man! But let him talk! By the time he finishes and sits down, I will have thought of a plan."

Chapter 64 PROVE IT!

NICODEMUS was demanding to be heard.

"This case," he argued, "has fallen apart; it has collapsed. Nothing has been proved. It is already an hour after midnight. How long, then, are we to be kept out of our beds? I, for one, want to go home!"

There was no mistaking the approval that ran murmuringly through the rows of judges; they agreed with Nicodemus.

"What should have been done here tonight," resumed Nicodemus, "is plain for everyone to see. This prisoner should have been defended much better than He has been. What if He did say He was the Messiah? Can we disprove it? His claim raises an issue of fact; it is not, of itself, in my opinion, a blasphemy.

"Oh, my Lord Caiphas, so many questions needed to be asked to lay a firm foundation for the defense of this undefended Jesus. Do we find anywhere in our history an account of any time when God appeared on the earth in the form of man? If we do"—and here Nicodemus slowed down and repeated with emphasis—"if we do, then how can we know that He will not do the same thing again? How *can* we know?

"No, no, Caiphas, please—I have almost finished. I insist that at the finish of this parade of witnesses, with tales that did not hang together, what, pray, is the final result? Clear as the daylight which will break before long Jesus remains an unconvicted man. I say that we should set Him free and then we can all go home to our beds where I, for one, at my age belong."

Chapter 65 THE AFFIRMATION

HAD the vote been taken then as Nicodemus sat down, the judges might have acquitted Jesus and set Him free.

Caiphas and Annas knew that, but the long speech of Nicodemus had given the old politician just the time he needed to meet the situation. Now Caiphas, schooled in whispers by his father-in-law, stood forth to play a new and desperate part.

Erect in his gorgeous robes, pre-eminent in the midst of the silenced and watchful tribunal, the high priest raised his right hand, two fingers pointing to the ceiling. They all knew—elders, priests, scribes, and prisoner as well—that Caiphas was about to put to Jesus the most solemn of oaths known to the Mosaic code—the adjuration, the oath of testimony. But on what point?

Ah, here it was that Annas had perfectly discerned the true character of his captive. Son-in-law would fail; no, he had already failed to prove the charge. But by a deep instinct the experienced Annas knew that the charge was true, nevertheless. This man did believe He was the Christ. Believing that sincerely, would He ever deny Himself?

Why, then, they could make Him commit the abomination of blasphemy in the very hearing and sight of the whole court! Watch and see. This, Caiphas, my sweet-reeking son-in-law, is how you must go about it:

"Jesus of Nazareth," cried Caiphas, in a resounding and orotund voice, "I adjure you, by the Living God, by the Almighty, that you tell us if you be the Christ, the Son of God."

In the silence then a man might have heard the fall of snow. Every person knew what this question meant. Caiphas had done more than put to Jesus the most solemn oath known to the Hebrew constitution; for such a question, silence itself was an offensive answer. Caiphas was playing his last card with this man who had not spoken since the trial began. As a pious and law-abiding man, Jesus now *had* to reply.

His answer came, clear and bold:

"You say that I am."

You say that I am! To the ears of the judges there was nothing evasive in the answer. It was idiomatic, not equivocal. By the custom of their speech, it meant "I would not presume to contradict you."

But Caiphas was not to be satisfied by that reply. He repeated the challenge:

"Jesus of Nazareth, I adjure you by Sabaoth—the unnumbered host of heavenly angels—by the gracious and merciful God, that you tell us if you are the Christ."

Again the crystal-clear voice:

"You have said."

Triumph rejoiced the bosom of the prosecutor; actually, the prisoner had already committed Himself. "You have said" was the traditional form in which a cultivated man would reply to a question on a grave or sad matter; courtesy forbade at such a moment a direct "yes" or "no."

"Jesus of Nazareth, I adjure you, by the long-suffering and compassionate God, that you tell us if you be the Son of God!"

And then Jesus answered in a voice clear and ringing:

"*I am!*"

It was as if lightning had struck in the Hall of Unhewn Stones. Caiphas himself turned pale. Here was triumph beyond his dreams! Before the whole court, just as Annas had schemed, Jesus had committed the very offense they had failed to prove against Him.

Caiphas took full advantage of the moment. He uttered a loud cry and fell back as Jesus went on speaking in the same calm tones:

"Nevertheless, I say to you, you shall see the Son of Man sitting on the right hand of the Power of God and coming in the clouds of heaven."

Caiphas was backing away from the prisoner, he was turning like a dervish in long circles and tearing at his own robes as if he would rip them into rents and slits and tatters. So the law required any priest to behave when blasphemy was uttered in his hearing. He must rend his garments. But the high priest, being a frugal soul, did not tear them beyond repair. And all the while Caiphas kept crying in hysterical tones:

"He has blasphemed! He has blasphemed! What further need have we of witnesses? Behold, now, you have heard! He has blasphemed!"

Then suddenly, coming to a dramatic pause, he asked in a husky whisper of the court:

"What think you?"

And from most of the scribes and priests and elders came a shout:

"He is guilty!"

The faces of the judges were pale and covered with sweat. They knew the stern duty that now lay upon them. Again they cried:

"We ourselves have heard it from His own mouth. He is guilty of death!"

Their minds were made up and their task was almost done. But even now the fate of Jesus was not fully decided.

Caiphas faced the judges.

"My lords," he said, "up until now I think I have been very patient. Although some of these interruptions tonight have begun to make me a little suspicious. What is behind this business? Is it not possible that there is a conspiracy afoot with some designing persons, setting these men on to save Jesus for His real work, which is to stir up agitation against us and bring on a revolution? I keep my tones moderate, my lords, but only with some effort, for mine has not been an easy task. I say that now we must seize our problem, grapple with it, and settle it."

From all parts of the smoky auditorium came strident voices.

"Question, question! Let us decide! Put the question!"

The voting began.

The particularities of the voting were observed to the last ancient landmark, let it never be reported to the people that Jesus of Nazareth, or anyone else, was unfairly tried. The final speech of Caiphas was scrupulously fair: he admonished them to render an honest verdict in the secret places of their hearts where thoughts and actions were clear to the Most High.

Beginning with the youngest, a course followed only in trials for life, and advancing to the eldest in strict rotation, the high priest solemnly posed the question to which there could be but one of two answers: yea or nay.

The reason for the younger men voting first in capital trials was that justice again demanded safeguards; if the older men voted first, their very acts or their words, explaining their votes, might influence less mature minds, men merely in their late forties. So the youngest voter present was the first called to vote for the acquittal or conviction of Jesus.

His vote was for death.

Each judge, on hearing his name called, scrambled up from his bright silken pillow, stood erect, and spoke his verdict. Some made little speeches to explain the vote; this course was followed almost invariably by the dissenting friends of Nicodemus and of Joseph of Arimathea, and by some others too.

Caiphas did not expect a unanimous verdict; more, he did not want one. Opinion was against all judgments speedily or unanimously voted. Such a verdict could invalidate itself. The legal theory was that if the accused had not a friend in the court, then the element of mercy was not in the hearts of his judges and so they had to let him go. A minority of two votes, at least, would be necessary before they could convict Jesus. He could even be acquitted by a minority of one. Such was the law.

So the voting went on with yea, yea, yea, and for a long time no nays at all. But Nicodemus and Joseph of Arimathea were not parliamentarious, and so they voted in strong, loud voices for acquittal.

"Barbeli of Nehan?"

"Yes."

"Andrew of Dazar?"

"Yes."

"Gamaliel of Bethany?"

"Yes."

In the very midst of the solemn voting a man came rushing down the great stairs, straight at Caiphas. The fingers of his left hand were contracted as if they would tear out the heart of the high priest; the right hand held up a bag.

"Judas Iscariot!" cried Caiphas. "What do you here?"

"I declare," cried Judas, "that this man you are condemning to death is innocent. You promised me otherwise than this. Here is your money."

And Judas cast his bag on the floor; the string was loose, the mouth gaping, and pieces of silver rang sharply on the stone slabs and scattered gleaming like little living things in all directions—one rolled to the very heel of Annas.

"Judas, get gone!" cried Caiphas, advancing with a threatening air. "Guards!"

"High priest," cried Judas, "I repent myself of what I have done. I have sinned in betraying innocent blood."

In the silence that followed Judas turned agonized eyes on the calm face of Jesus, but several judges called to him.

"What is your mistake to us?"

"Look you to it!" answered another.

From the throat of the lost apostle came a broken cry. He rushed up the steps and out of the Hall of Hewn Stones and the crowd parted to let him pass into the deepest darkness of the morning hours. Flying, when no man pursued him, Judas rushed into an open field where he would find a rope and a tree. There he hanged himself and dangled publicly until his body swelled up and burst. . . .

Meanwhile the balloting resumed and presently was finished. Caiphas once more faced the tribunal.

"My lords," he said, "there is a minority of two for acquittal; all the rest are for conviction. That settles our work for now."

Chapter 66 PILATE'S FIREPLACE

IN THE dark and early chill of Friday, April 7, Pilate was waiting. Because of what was going on in the Hall of Hewn Stones, he had to remain up all night in his gloomy reception hall. He must be ready for the official hearing he would soon be called upon to give the Nazarene prisoner. By now the first and second sessions of the Sanhedrin had been held; messengers had been keeping well informed the brusque Spanish giant, called by the people Lord Pilate; reports of all the legal quibbling over small points while a life hung in the balance; he even knew about the insults and mockery of those who stood in a sniggering and drunken ring around the prisoner during the intermission between the hearings.

Pilate felt a persecuted man himself. The Roman governor, a warrior and a most distinguished soldier, hated the mean fate that had sent him to rule a poor colony like Palestine. In the present turmoil he knew that while he was facing a local situation, it nevertheless had explosive political aspects, dangerous to his own interests.

Unhappily for him, Annas and Caiphas held him actually at their mercy. One more complaint to Rome, one more uprising in Palestine, and he would be out of the imperial favor. His position enraged him; if he could help Jesus, he would, just to frustrate Annas.

He wanted to leave this empty chamber and go to the beautiful Claudia Procula, and all the boudoiresque joys the thought of her instantly conjured. His wife would not likely be asleep; she suffered from insomnia and then read far into the morning hours in books that Pilate found to be silly bores. For example, what did Procula see in that man Horace—Quintus Horatius Flaccus? Yet night after night she had her favorite girls read from his long scrolls. And Julius Vergilius Maro she enjoyed, too, and even Publius Ovidius Naso, although it had been forbidden to read his books ever since Augustus banished him in the year A.D. 8. That was partly because Ovid's *Ars Amatoria* was considered a direct challenge to the imperial policy of moral reform. Why should Procula read such deadly dull books? The only volume Pilate and Procula could enjoy together was the eloquent history written by Titus Livius, who had been a friend of Procula's royal grandfather.

Only the night before Procula had wakened from a troubled sleep and told Pilate of a dream. She had been dreaming of Jesus. To Pilate's amazement, she knew something of the doctrines taught by that wayside wanderer. How had she ever heard of the man? Well, she had once been visited by a messenger from the household of Herod of Galilee. She had talked with Herod's servant? Aye, Lord Pilate! A man? Nay, Lord Pilate, a serving maid called Joanna, who was a devoted follower of Jesus. Well, what had Procula dreamed of this Galilean? Pilate's wife capriciously, or at least suddenly, decided not to tell. She assured him he would never understand.

That was it. There was always something where they thought he did not belong or fit in. Something in life slipped past him, unseized, like a springtime eel. He did his work, which was to fight, to govern, to administer, to report—to see that the great plain of Hauran sent on its vast wheat to make the Roman bread; he did everything practical that was to be done, yet other people found values in life that he missed.

Take these natives, for instance. They all loved something invisible; and that was a love that kept them true to one another and charitable, meanwhile holding a sustained and bitter aversion to all his attempts to win their respect. Here in Palestine, his wife was his only consolation, and now because of these stiff-necked people he must give up the idea of seeking her out; must leave his fireplace; must go face Annas whom he respected but distrusted, Caiphas whom he despised, and Jesus of whom his wife had dreamed an untold dream.

The air of the dark house before dawn was damp and cold as a dog's nose. Pilate shivered a little as suddenly he heard a tantara sounded on a Flemish horn; a quick succession of brassy notes, signal that Annas and his prisoner were at the gate.

Chapter 67 CLAUDIA'S DREAM

KNOWING travelers today, when they go to Jerusalem, spend a thoughtful hour in the Convent of the Sisters of Zion. They turn to the staircase leading from its chapel and go down nineteen centuries. Under the foundations of the chapel are the flagstones of the old Roman street before the palace of Pilate, great flat slabs of limestone and granite, rutted with grooves worn by chariot wheels and lacquered smooth by long-stilled bare feet.

To stand there in the dimmish light and feel the reality of those flagstones is like an exercise in evocation. All of the modern piled-up city of Jerusalem overhead fades out like an unsubstantial vision and in its place stands the gate of the Praetorium. The mob is there, the hired and drummed-up mob whose purchased fists are lifted and whose scurrilous voices snarl in the dark. They follow after the guards making clear the path of a majestic little man with the wisp of white hair over his left eye—Annas, the tireless old boss of Jerusalem.

With Annas comes his son-in-law, lifting his rent robe of blue so that its fringes will not trail in the dust. Behind these two, in a ring of soldiers, the condemned prisoner.

They pull a long cord and a bell rings. Annas knew what would happen: Pilate was coming out to them instead of asking them inside. In their earlier confab the procurator had agreed that he would hear the case out of doors, beyond the gates of the Praetorium, as a concession of Pilate to the religious immunities of the people. Because this was the Passover feast, they had a ceremonial objection to entering the domain of a Gentile; they would have to purify themselves, and there would not be time for that before the feast. To enter a pagan's house meant contracting impurity for seven days.

Annas and Caiphas stood a little to one side—Annas rubbing his long nose reproachfully and Caiphas playing with his beard. They were making room for the prisoner, who was pushed forward so that He stood with them before the still-closed gates.

The prisoner had been ill-used, one could see that. One tanned cheek, gleaming in the flickering torchlight, showed a red splotch where someone had struck Him; His left eye was bruised and the skin under the lower lid was turning color. Loosely around His throat hung a napkin knotted at the back; it had fallen there from His eyes; they had blindfolded Him, as loafer after loafer struck Him, crying: "Prophesy, now! Who is it that struck you?"

His beautiful seamless robe was stained with phlegm where many had spat upon Him. Yet the open eyes were still serene; one soldier said to his wife later on that nothing could disturb the man's composure; they had pushed Him by the shoulders while He was blindfolded, buffeted Him back and forth, spun Him around, and mocked Him with blasphemous oaths, yet He seemed preserved by some inner force, some grace that rose above the buffoonery and actually brought it to an end. They soon gave up their sport because, with such a man, it wasn't fun.

His hands held before Him, still knotted at the wrists, He kept His eyes on the gate, and while they were waiting, for Pilate took his time about it, a few yellowish streaks appeared in the eastern sky. As if the fragile glow were a signal, there came a rumbling of wheels and rusty chains, the screak of hinges, and the Praetorium gates fell inward.

There was Pilate sitting in his chair of ivory and bronze on the high platform.

Jesus, bound and delivered, lifted His keen face to meet His new judge. Pilate, well robed against the morning chill, cast Him a brief but appraising glance, then stopped; the official's first startled feeling was one of recognition. Where had he seen this man before? He had an insane impulse to lift his hand in the salute and greet Him as a friend. That was why he turned away so hurriedly from the prisoner to the villainous faces of the mob—swarthy faces, bearded, pock-marked, scabby, with eyes diseased from their mothers' wombs and hands ready for anything.

The procurator heard the low hurly-burly of their mutterings and then, shaking himself free of foreboding, he turned to Annas with a cynical expression and asked for the indictment.

"What accusations do you bring against this man?"

Caiphas gave a pompous, even impudent answer; he felt no need to truckle to Pilate.

"If He were not a malefactor, we would not have delivered Him to you."

But Pilate had formally demanded the facts and so Annas continued:

"We have found this man perverting our nation and forbidding to give tribute to Caesar and saying that He is Christ the King."

This man with His wrists bound, in this soiled robe, and His lacerated face—a king? Perdition! These people had never seen a real king! Thus thought Pilate, who had twice broken bread with Tiberius. He chuckled to himself and leaned down toward Annas.

"Take Him, you," he suggested, with a lenient clearing of his throat, "and judge Him wholly according to your own law."

But Caiphas shouted back angrily:

"It is not lawful for us to put any man to death. You know that."

Of course Pilate did know that. Their elaborate process had been no more than a sort of magistrates' court held to establish a *prima-facie* case; or even less than that, these elders of Jerusalem had acted as a grand jury and all they could do was return a true bill.

Pilate turned to the accused and with a wry turn of his mouth, which showed a broken tooth, he suddenly roared:

"Are you the King of the Jews?"

Jesus returned his smile and answered:

"You say it."

Again Caiphas stepped forward and lifted his forefinger warningly.

"We know this man to be the son of Joseph the carpenter, born of Mary, but His followers say that He is the son of God and a king."

Again Pilate chuckled.

"Tell me how I, being a procurator, can try a king?"

Caiphas, having no sense of humor, protested:

"*We* do not say that He is a king, but they say that He is."

Pilate looked down at Jesus, and this time it was a long scrutiny of the wavy brown hair that fell about the shoulders, the forehead without a line in it, the dark eyes luminous and wide apart. The bruises and blood gave Pilate the creeps. All his life he had missed something, a mystery forever eluding him. Now did he see it, like a bright and wonderful light, in the face of a condemned man? Now, if he had found it, must he kill it?

Pilate made a brusque motion; the prisoner was to go inside; Pilate would talk with Jesus alone.

What did this mean? Here was a most unlikely surprise! Annas and Caiphas were well aware that Jesus was a charmer. The procurator might be talked out of doing his duty. He could not be ignorant of the doctrines of Christ, His reputed miracles and His much-beloved character. Pilate was showing far too much interest in the prisoner.

The big, heavy-breathing official, with his clinking bracelets and perfumed armpits, led the way boldly inside to the same fireplace from which he had just been called. He kicked a second chair toward the hearth and with a rough, almost threatening motion of his arm, bade Jesus be seated, facing him. One was the judge and the other the condemned prisoner, and yet now the expression on Pilate's face was that of man to man.

"Are you," he repeated with a gleam of amusement that emphasized their privacy, "the King of the Jews?"

Jesus, back and head erect, leaned forward, palms on knees; Pilate was conscious of the intense personal magnetism in the great eyes. In that moment of deepening attraction a soldier appeared between the drapes of the farther door and gave a salute. He brought Lord Pilate a perfumed note from Procula. Scowling, the Roman read what his wife had written:

"Have nothing to do with that righteous man; for I have suffered many things this day and dreamed a dream because of Him."

That dream again. Why should she dream so powerfully of Him? Pilate was known as a uxorious man, foolishly and extravagantly devoted to his wife. But he had not expected tonight that she would try to interfere in the conduct of his office, a thing she had never bothered to do before in all the time they had spent together in this frontier outpost. She was a Caesar's granddaughter, born with an instinctive respect for the Roman law by which he must try this man. The moment Procula interfered, Pilate stiffened and was chilled with resistance. No woman could tell him what to do.

At once he began to think of the counts against the prisoner. He was said to be a seditionist. By all reports He stood for demolishing established social ideas; a rebellion, after which a new sovereign would take over, a God-anointed king with his throne in Jerusalem. Did Procula expect her husband to encourage that? Now the governor looked at Jesus with a restive eye, while his thick fingers tore the letter. Messianism, that was what it was! And messianism meant anarchy and treason—a terrible thing in this spot of infection in the empire. The heart of Pilate hardened.

This fellow, he thought, was closer to torture than He probably realized, for all His composure and with that disturbing glow in His large eyes. Wonder if he really knew what crucifixion meant? First came the scourging, the flagellum. That was as terrible as the crucifixion it preceded; the whip was tipped with nails and scraps of bones, and it was wielded by soldiers with the arms of weight-throwers. Why, if Pilate were to turn this man over to the whippers with the flagellum He would probably never live to be crucified; He would die from the stinging torture of the forty blows.

If He did survive that horrible pain, would He have the strength to carry His own cross? That was the way the plan was ordered; if you were sentenced to be crucified, you had to carry your own cross through the streets, through the gates, and outside the walls to a hill where the capital sentence was executed. The prisoner had to watch all the preliminaries: the hole dug for the foundation, the laying down of the cross and then he was spread on it, stretched and wrenched to fit, nailed to its crossbars by his hands, to its centerpiece by his feet.

Pilate's eyelids narrowed as he thought of all this. A nasty way to die—you were nailed up there in an unnatural position, your body in a fearful tension, and the slightest movement of any muscle brought anguish. And the thick spikes hammered through the hands and feet, the open wounds quickly inflaming, the overburdened and swollen blood vessels, the long-drawn-out agony, and the horrible raging thirst.

What penalties to inflict deliberately on this gently serene man, with His lustrous eyes and their candent light, and the lean, strong hands on His knees! He was all right now, except for one bruised eye and the red mark on the left cheek and the spittle on His gown. All right now. And yet what could happen to Him in a very little while, if Pilate so decided! That was the way Annas and Caiphas and their troublesome crew wanted him to decide.

The Temple aristocrats would all like Pilate better if he condemned this Nazarene straight to the cross. What the people would think, the people who had trudged after Jesus for three years down dusty roads and over weary hills; who had seen Him heal their lepers, give sight to their blind, and bring back their loved ones from the grave—the poor men and women and children whom He had fed and whose hearts He had uplifted with hope, what they would think was not hard to foresee, either.

There had been hosannas on Sunday!

But now it was early Friday morning. All those who welcomed Him with waving palms were asleep. Only the hired crowd of the high priests stood wakeful on the paved stones beyond the palace gates.

"Are you," Pilate repeated truculently, all chuckle gone from his voice, "are you the King of the Jews?"

"Say you this of yourself?" asked Jesus calmly. "Or did others tell it you concerning me?"

"Am I a native?" barked Pilate. "Your own nation and the chief priests delivered you to me."

He was startled at the aptitude with which Jesus had met the first question. The prisoner had demanded that Pilate make clear his own position. Was it that he was searching into the political side of this problem, which would be a proper position for a Roman judge? Or was he concerned with blasphemy, a charge of no importance to Rome but abominable in the eyes of Jerusalem? In effect, Jesus was asking Pilate: "Do you ask me this, fearing that I am an earthly pretender to an earthly crown and hence an enemy of Caesar's empire, or do you want to know if I claim to be the Messiah?"

Pilate's answer was thus most explicit when he scornfully shouted: "Am I a native?" No, he was not; he was a Roman conqueror and very wary of any radical with kingly pretensions. He was there to stifle insurrection.

Then Jesus replied with final explicitness:

"My kingdom is not of this world."

In those seven forthright words Pilate had his reply; yet it was hardly the answer he wanted. It would have been all right if only Jesus had been willing to utter a simple one-word denial. But He had preferred instead to speak of "my kingdom." The words irked the governor; a kingdom was a kingdom, and what other world was there, except this one? How can anyone have a kingdom without being a king? Hadn't Jesus already convicted Himself?

Jesus, in His quiet voice, was explaining:

"If my kingdom were of this world, my servants would certainly strive that I should not be delivered to the Jews, but now my kingdom is not from hence."

Pilate's blue eyes blinked as he grated in hard repetition:

"What I want to know is—are you, then, a king?"

To this question Jesus made an answer for the ages:

"You say that I am a king. To this end was I born and for this cause I came into the world, that I should bear witness to the truth. Everyone that is of the truth hears my voice."

And Pilate, hearing His voice, feeling the near presence of that mystery that had eluded him for so long, leaned forward, swarthy hands seizing the arms of his chair, all mockery gone, and asked in a deep whisper:

"What is truth?"

Pilate was not jesting, but he did not stay for an answer. He read it in the eyes of the prisoner. He rose from his chair, bent over Jesus, and said pleadingly:

"Do you not hear how great testimonies they allege against you? Look in how many things they accuse you. Do you answer nothing?"

Jesus answered nothing. Pilate threw up his hands.

"You don't answer me? Don't you know that I have power to crucify you—as I have also power to release you?"

Then Jesus answered:

"You should not have any power against me, unless it were given to you from above. Therefore, he that has delivered me to you has the greater sin."

Pilate's eyes gleamed with the joy of a wholly irrational relief. This man understood. Why, He even forgave! He was reassuring Pilate that He really did appreciate the difficulties of his position. Pilate would do anything for a man like that!

It was no longer for Procula's sake only, it was for the sake of the prisoner Himself that Pilate would try to free Him. Brusquely he ordered Him to walk before him down the long, shadowy corridors that echoed to the flap of his Roman sandals; Jesus's feet were bare and made no sound upon the floor. Past the torches of the guards they marched, the accused and the judge, and out again into the open courtyard.

Chapter 68 THE DRUNKEN KING

AT THE appearance of Jesus the crowd roared and laughed and made mewling sounds like alley cats. But at the sight of the representative of Caesar they were instantly quiet. Jesus stood again, with thonged wrists, at the foot of the platform and near to His accusers, Annas and Caiphas.

Pilate sat out of doors in his ivory and gilded bronze chair. This was a defiant moment in his life. His simple, uncomplicated brain was whirling with discordant arguments: what Procula dreamed and what Annas had already reported to the Emperor about the procurator, and the blessed light in the eyes of the condemned man. He kept them waiting for his decision as he groped for words.

How would he defend himself, if he made the wrong decision and Rome called him on the tapis? He knew the law; had to know it. The statute that was operative in this case was the Lex Julia Majestatis, which had become the law in 48 B.C. Anyone who offered a claim of being equal to the king committed treason and was open to a sentence of death; the Twelve Tables of Rome, originally written in blood, gave sanction to the most horrible punishments the mind of frightened rulers could conceive. If what Jesus had said constituted high treason, there was no greater crime known.

Pilate, by the gods, make up your mind! In your heart of hearts, do you really believe Him guilty?

Well . . .

And still the restless mob waited and still Pilate hesitated. What was it Jesus had answered in there? "*My kingdom is not of this world.*" Then it was clear that Jesus fully recognized the temporal majesty of the Roman law. It was as if He said: "Lord Pilate, if I said my kingdom were of this world, you would be right in condemning me. But I do not say that. Mine is a kingdom of the spirit."

Well?

A lawyer would probably have said that Jesus offered a confession and avoidance. At least Pilate reasoned it so. Then is Jesus guilty or not, Pilate? The minutes are slipping by. Without a glance at Annas or Caiphas, nor yet at Jesus, Pilate stood up and announced:

"I find no cause in this man!"

They were thunderstruck! No fault in Jesus at all? That judgment can't be final! Yes, it was the finding and order of reversal of the case which had come to the procurator on appeal. The shrewdest lawyer in the Sanhedrin would have to concede that Pilate had done his job. He had held a hearing and had decided that, in his judgment, the verdict of the trial court was not in accord with the law and the evidence. Therefore Jesus had been illegally convicted and must now be discharged from custody. The hearing on appeal was ended, the verdict pronounced, and it was "not guilty."

Roman jurisprudence had done its task; it had acquitted Jesus Christ.

"He stirs up the people!" gasped Caiphas, his flushed face visibly paling in the creeping light of dawn, while behind him the hired mob began obediently to rumble: "He stirs up the people, teaching throughout all Judea, beginning from Galilee to this place . . ."

"Galilee?"

Pilate's hoarse voice broke in on what promised to be a harangue. "Did you say this prisoner came from Galilee?"

"It is so!"

Pilate smiled affably. Already he had seen a riot beginning in front of his palace. Now he experienced a vast sense of relief, for if Jesus came from Galilee, then He was really not Pilate's problem after all; it was a question of jurisdiction; it was Herod's problem, and Herod was even now in Jerusalem! The princeling who ruled as tetrarch over Galilee could take over the responsibility of deciding this case. What a fortunate solution! Especially as there was no love found or lost between Herod Antipas and Pilate; this courteous gesture in protocol might put an end to an old animosity.

"Take him to Herod!"

Annas grumbled and Caiphas roared, and his mob roared with him, but to no avail. This time Pilate stood firm. The ivory chair was carried inside, the gates of the Praetorium were closed. Pilate proceeded to drink two goblets full of red wine poured from a stone jug with a wide handle and a narrow mouth. There was nothing else to do but to turn about and march through the dark streets to the palace of Herod. As they marched on, in grim silence, Annas and Caiphas did not talk. They had been outfoxed; Pilate's position was politically sound; they could not complain, for what he did was legal.

Of course it was nothing more than a trick by which Pilate was trying to extricate himself from a dilemma. The lawyers would insist that Jesus was being charged with what was called continuous sedition. True, the crime was first committed in Herod's Galilee, but it was continued in Judea, and that was where Jesus was arrested—at the very gates of Jerusalem. The procurator was lawyer enough to know that he had full jurisdiction, if he cared to use it. But he had stunned the priests with an apparent insistence on scrupulous observance of legal details.

However, Herod Antipas was nobody's fool either. He, too, had a legal turn of mind, when it was necessary. Once before he had executed a prophet. The name was John the Baptist, and like skunk spray the odium of that beheading had clung to him ever since. Would Herod see through Pilate's transparent trick?

On this morning when Pilate tried to leave Jesus on his doorstep Herod Antipas was staying in the ancient Jerusalem castle of his family, the Asmodean palace on the height of the Xystas, just opposite the Temple. There at dawn sat Herod under festoons and decorative garlands, still carousing before the remains of a gluttonous meal littering a tablecloth slopped and stained with wine. The tetrach was wrapped in a white robe fringed with gold. Around him a group of yawning, half-naked girls pretended still to be enjoying his company; a fat one with a ring in her nose belched rhythmically every two minutes and with each eructation Herod Antipas, "the little Antipater," threw back his head and cackled.

The girl had just belched, and frowzy Herod was again cackling, when suddenly they heard a noise at the outer gate. A snuffling page boy, ill with a head cold, bowed prostrate before the Tetrarch of Galilee and told him the news: a detachment of Praetorium soldiery was arriving outside! With them came Annas and Caiphas, leading a condemned prisoner.

That, Herod told himself, was an extraordinary state of affairs. Who was the prisoner? Jesus! Not Jesus of Nazareth! Well, who could tell what would happen next? This Jesus, who had the reputation for being so gentle-spoken, so full of loving-kindness for everyone, had once sent a bold message to Herod Antipas and the tetrarch, who, unfortunately, had a vulpine face, had never forgotten it:

"*Go you and tell that fox, Behold I cast out devils.*"

Herod, a typical Oriental, who lived fatly and for the full pleasure of his passions, had been of several minds about Jesus. Ever since he had dallied with decency over the rampart of the dungeon of John the Baptist he had been haunted by the spirituality of the prophet he had slain. Like Pilate, like Tiberius, like all men whose lives are lived for pleasure and power, Herod envied the man who could do without these. For a while he was afraid of the very name of Jesus because he believed the prophet from Nazareth was really John the Baptist, risen from the dead. However, his advisors had assured him that this was not so, and Jesus Himself had never made any such claim.

Next the stories came to Herod of the miracles Jesus performed. The idea of any magical feats stirred Herod like a boy going to the circus. Could this Jesus do the Hindoo rope trick that caravan travelers reported was done in India? Could He make ivory balls disappear under cups, flowers bloom from a seed under a shawl? Could He make voices come from hidden corners where no man was?

Besotted as he was that morning, surrounded by bottles of cholagogue and purgative and sobering-up doses he had learned in Rome, Herod Antipas still remembered the answer he got to those questions. This Jesus differed from all other magicians in one important particular: He did not give exhibitions merely to excite wonder and awe; His strange powers were devoted to helping others, and for this help He made no charge. That puzzled Herod Antipas. John the Baptist had been another who would take no fee. What kind of fellows were these prophets?

For a long time Herod had wanted to see this wonder-worker perform, and now here He was, early in the morning, sent to him by his old antagonist, Lord Pontius Pilate. Anything could happen in this foolish world! As the fat girl belched and winked one bleary eye, dull and dimmed, Herod Antipas slapped her thigh, and, cackling with glee, bade them bring in the Master.

But Jesus was a great disappointment to Herod Antipas.

The debauched tetrach, looking upon this subject Galilean, immediately wanted to see thaumaturgic signs and wonders. He gave a ribald grunt. Show me some tricks! Come on, magician, and do something! Even the watching Annas and Caiphas were outraged at his alcoholic frivolity. Why would not a ruler behave like a ruler? They listened while Herod tried to joke with the prisoner, cajoling Him to do just one miracle. Jesus would answer nothing.

Then the priests went to it, and had at Herod Antipas. With savage emphasis in their charges, they told the tetrarch of the three-fold allegations: causing sedition among the people, refusing tribute to Caesar, and claiming to be Messiah, King of the Jews. Their vehemence brought Herod to his political senses. With a lopsided look at the priests, he gave a vast shrug and slapped his belly. King of the Jews! *Wah!* Hail, King!

Fat, slovenly, and uncertain in the fumes of his wine, Herod, squatting on his haunches, made a mock and wobbling obeisance:

"Hail, King! Slaves, bring me a royal white robe! Not that one. Not good enough for a king like this. Hail, Wonder-Worker King! Where's his robe? Haven't you fetched it yet? Give me now. *Wah!* This is a royal robe all right. Look, King! That's yours! Mighty fine too. Put it on! What? You stand stiff and straight and look me in the eye and neither answer nor plead for mercy? You're like your cousin, then! Like John the Baptist. I cut his head off! And they put it on a plate! Salome danced with it. No more of that. I won't cut your head off, Jesus!

"Hail, King! Ha! Ha! How goes it with you, King, old King, old King, old King, hey, boy! Your head stays on for me. If it comes off, let Pilate take it off—not I. Once was enough for me. Back with you! Soldiers! Salute and bow to the King of the Jews, and take Him away. I thought He was a magician. *Wah!*" . . .

The captive Jesus was led to the door in the white robe of mockery, when Herod Antipas, suddenly grown serious, staggered to his feet.

"Wait! You remember me three years ago—I wanted to kill you then. You called me an old fox and you said I couldn't kill you, because a prophet must perish only in Jerusalem. How could you read the future like that?"

The door closed. The prisoner was gone. But He left Herod Antipas as frightened as Pilate. Indeed, the very next day Herod had a heart-to-heart talk with Pilate. There had not been cordial relations between them for a long time, but after the troubled night they both had known because of Jesus, the Tetrarch of Galilee and the Procurator of Judea became friends.

Chapter 69 CRUCIFY HIM!

Pilate had been talking with his wife. He knew what the returning clamor in the outer courtyard meant. Messengers swifter than the tired feet of the priests raced back to the palace with word that Herod had not risen to the bait; he returned the prisoner with his compliments. Whatever the crimes of Jesus, they were committed in Jerusalem and therefore under Pilate's jurisdiction. The problem was back in the procurator's hands and it was even greater than before; now he had talked with Claudia Procula.

Never before had Pilate seen that sophisticated Roman lady of the court so much in earnest about anything. To kill Jesus of Nazareth, she told him, was unthinkable. Exaggerated as such a thought must seem, still Pilate had got from her the feeling that if he failed her in this, life between him and his wife would never again be the same. That was a dismaying thought to Pilate. From Toledo to the Tigris he had never touched her like; he was a rough, uncomplicated man, and she was the sum of his pleasure.

Yet what must the governor do now? He had to find a way to acquit Jesus and still not incur revenge from a frantic priesthood. Again he sat in his fancy chair and confronted the pale, bruised prisoner. Serene as before He was, even in the new royal robe of white with golden fringe which Herod had draped over Him in drunken mockery. The faces of Annas and Caiphas were pale and haggard with the long labors of this night and morning; their conspiring, their illegal trial, their running from the Temple to Pilate and from Pilate to Herod and now back again had tried the smooth legs and swollen the fat ankles of Caiphas; he seemed even more tired than his aged father-in-law.

Pilate rubbed his fingers over a pan of smoldering charcoal on a tripod beside his chair. He turned from Jesus to Annas, and then, hoarse voice edged more than ever with impatience, he pointed out to them that although the prisoner was a Galilean, nevertheless Herod Antipas, the Tetrarch, had refused to do anything with Him. As for himself, he could only repeat what he had said before:

"I find no cause. You have presented to me this man as one that perverts the people, and behold, I, having examined Him before you, find no cause in this man in those things wherein you accuse Him. No, nor Herod either. For I sent you to him, and behold, nothing worthy of death is done to Him. I will chastise Him, therefore . . ."

"Good!"

He could see some of their faces now. Greek sailors with bearded mouths, gold bangles in their ears, and their long arms around unkempt slatterns and blowzy women, drunk on blackstrap wine; gamblers with old blue scars on their necks, blacklegs, cheaters at dice, with their sluts from the town bagnios, beldams and hags. One old vixen kept shaking a scrawny fist while she whistled through her teeth.

"And then I shall release Him!"

Release Him! A yawp of fury came from the mob. To heal more blind men, raise up more supporters, preach more perversions of the established order—release Him? Caiphas turned quickly and spoke two words into a dirty ear lowered to his beard. The words ran quickly to the very core of the mob and there rose a sudden piercing cry:

"Crucify Him!"

From one, then from a dozen came the uncouth cry. Soon it was a rhythm and a chant—"Crucify Him! Crucify Him!"

Pilate's shaggy brows went up. Had he heard aright? This prisoner was supposed to have enemies in the Temple but friends in the streets. That cry for crucifixion came from the gutter. To flog Jesus would be almost to murder Him. They all knew what official chastisement meant. That ought to satisfy the most bloodthirsty among them. To let Jesus live—that would be keeping his word to Procula.

Although he knew that blatant, noisy, blustering mob for what it was, nevertheless the situation was intimidating. Such hate, real or acted, could be contagious. A riot could easily be in the making. Nevertheless, Pilate was not ready to admit defeat.

The idea in Pilate's mind to get his prisoner off was like a fear gnawing at his brain. He still had one untried idea. Forcing a conciliatory smile and rising, ignoring the priests, he talked for the first time directly to the people.

In Jerusalem, he reminded them, they had a custom which he had faithfully followed: on the Feast of the Passover the procurator could set one prisoner free, with a full pardon. The crowds had only to shout the names of their favorites and he whose name got the loudest noise he would set free. Now Pilate, making a last effort to keep his promise to his wife, put two names before the mob—this prisoner of Nazareth and the other, the notable revolutionary leader —Barabbas!

He was truly a seditionist, was Barabbas, and in his conspiracy to overthrow the government by violence he had already committed murder.

"Will you," asked Pilate, pretending to make light of the whole charge, "that I release to you the King of the Jews? Whom will you that I release to you—Jesus Barabbas or Jesus Christ?"

Then, obedient to signals from Caiphas, the crowd screamed:

"Away with this man! And release unto us Barabbas!"

By this time there were honest voices as well as hired that took up the bellowing. Barabbas had his own friends in that crowd; the clamor was deafening:

"Away with this man! Give us Barabbas!"

Arms outstretched, Pilate strode forward and tried to plead with them, but they drowned out his words; they took up a rhythmic chant, and it swelled, as guards beat the paving stones with their spear handles and a drunken woman clapped a pair of cymbals.

"Crucify Him!"

"Crucify Him!"

"Crucify Him!"

Pilate raised his hand furiously in an imperial gesture and there was a sudden awed silence.

"Why, what evil has He done?" he roared indignantly. "What evil has this man done?"

Instantly their reviling voices bellowed again in the same final bitter reply:

"Crucify Him!"

"Crucify Him!"

"Crucify Him!"

Pilate flung himself into the ivory chair. He gave an exhausted growl and made a sign. The crowd screamed with joy as Jesus was led off to His fate.

It was then that the guards took Jesus and beat Him within a gasp of His life. This was not being birched like a schoolboy, nor merely thrashed like an ordinary malefactor—they flogged Him with a whip made of three leather lashes, to the flaying ends of which were stitched those bits of metal and bone. With forty blows they scourged

Him, and when it was done Jesus was so weak that He had barely strength to stand. His body was covered with wales and stripes and welts; He had been drubbed within a few breaths of His life.

But He must continue to stand, for they had still more to do to Him.

Over His back, streaming from the blood opened by the counted lashes, they laid again His own robe. Two idle soldiers had plaited wild thorns that grow in scraggly hedges around the farms to keep out fox and wolf. On His head they pressed this crown of thorns.

It was in the court of the governor's palace that this pain and mockery were heaped on Jesus. Pilate meanwhile had returned to Claudia Procula, who reclined in her bed, pale and reproachful. He told her brusquely what had happened; from the courtyard the jeering voices reached their ears:

"Hail, King of the Jews!"

"They give Him many blows!" wailed Procula. "Yet He makes no outcry!"

"True, they strike His head, and spit upon Him——"

"I warned you to have nothing to do with that just man!"

"You told me more than that," snapped Pilate. "You told me you had suffered many things all day because of a dream concerning Him."

He bent over, but she thrust him away. He rose with an oath.

"Very well," he snarled. "I will go out and try again."

Once more the prisoner and His judge stood before the mob. This time Jesus was on the platform beside Pilate as the governor squirmed in his ivory chair. The face of Pilate was tired and worn, and his eyes had a hunted look; the face of Jesus was bloody.

"Behold," Pilate began, trying to put a note of reasonableness and casual common sense into his voice; "behold, I bring Him forth unto you that you may know I find no cause in Him."

The purchased gangs looked at the beaten Jesus, face and hands bloody, wrists knotted and stained crimson, new scars on His face, but with shoulders up and straight and the eyes and posture serene in indestructible composure. The crown of thorns gave to His face a dignity and not the clownish buffoonery they had expected.

In the silence Pilate spoke, as a man speaks when he thinks he is clinching a deal:

"Behold this man!"

Then he lifted his powerful thumbs to his ears as the shriek and roar of their voices deafened him:

"Crucify Him!"

"Crucify Him!"

"Crucify Him!"

Pilate screamed back at them:

"Take Him, you, and crucify Him, for *I* find no cause in Him."

Here Annas stepped sternly forward. He was not going to let Pilate escape his proper responsibility. He pushed back the forelock wisp of gray hair from over his left eye and cleared his throat and spoke in crisp, authoritative tones:

"Lord Pilate, we have a law—and according to the law, He ought to die because He made Himself the Son of God."

And a new shout went up:

"Crucify Him! Whoever makes himself a king, speaks against Caesar. If you release this man, you are not Caesar's friend!"

Over and over again the mob chanted those desperate words. They struck to the depths of Pilate's little soul. Yet, even so, he persisted still. He stood beside the object of all this fury and, forcing himself to jest, as if to ask the whole race if they were in fear of this bedraggled figure, Pilate roared:

"Behold your king!"

No, they would not join in his laugh. He could not cajole the hirelings, paid to be implacable. They yelled:

"Away with Him! Away with Him! Crucify Him!"

In a panic of forced jesting Pilate cried:

"Shall I crucify your king?"

"*We have no king but Caesar!*"

Pilate heard that shout—and lost. Beyond that phrase he could not go. Those words were the frontier line past which no politician could advance; not if he cared for his own skin. Pilate had done all that he felt he could do. Had he done more, he would have had a different name in history.

Somewhere in his soul he knew that the beautiful mystery had escaped him again and now forever. That was why he called for a basin. A negrillo paddled forward on deformed feet, carrying a golden bowl in his dark, apelike arms. The lustrum, ceremony of purification! In front of all of them, he, a Roman, washed his hands. And as the waste water dribbled down, and drops of it on the black hairs of the back of his hand glistened in the faint light, he lifted his face sidewise to heaven and cried in a broken voice:

"I am innocent of the blood of this just man."

As he motioned to the soldiers to take Jesus off to His crucifixion, the voices of priest and hired mob joined in one last cry:

"His blood be upon us and upon our children."

Here the mob, hired by scoundrels, in an excess of malice uttered fateful words which for untold centuries were to plague and vastly injure the lives of innocent people. The words they screamed in that awful hour were often to be misconstrued, so that generations of decent people were to be unjustly stigmatized. The conspirators who hired this mob to hunt the prisoner of Pilate had loosed a whirlwind of injustice and misunderstanding.

So the long trial was over at last. Barabbas, the revolutionist, was released to the people. Jesus was condemned to be crucified, all very legally, by Pilate, who made no further objections to the wishes of Annas and his son-in-law. Jesus was started again on the trek to Calvary, and Jesus Barabbas, gray-haired, dazed, strode off with his supporters, his bewildered inkberry eyes not noting the woman in the dark blue cloak who stood in the shadow of the wall weeping and remembering Samuel, her husband's friend.

Mary had seen him. She had seen it all.

Chapter 70 THE DOLOROUS WAY

THERE was a yellowish creep in the east that slowly took the place of the pale rose of dawn.

The start of His journey home--after His incarnation, perfectly lived--was at the barracks where they had beaten Him, the guard-room of the castle of Antonia. There Pilate had turned Him over, and from there He descended the broad stairs in the unfamiliar yellow light of a strange dawn. He came down the steps almost unnoticed, while the crowd turned in an ecstasy of welcome for the revolutionist that Pilate had just set free--Barabbas, striding, cocky, curly head twisted to one side, laughing with an I-told-you-so smugness, accepting the raucous welcome as a tribute no more than his due. In the jaundiced aurora Barabbas took the center of the stage, while Jesus, going on down, came to the second station of His journey—to a place at the bottom of the steps where the cross was waiting.

It was a crude thing of wood, blackened and smelling of creosote and tar, the centerpiece rounded and large as the mast of a small ship, and the horizontal bar of a long beam split in half and fixed firmly with two bolted iron clamps—not much of a carpentry job; the workman from Nazareth could have made a better one than that. There was a huddle of men there, not soldiers, but servants and artisans who had fetched the cross, dragging it by a chain. One who gave the orders and acted like a gang boss came up to the two soldiers who guarded the bleeding and beaten prisoner and said what must be done. The fellow must kneel in the street. A part of the crossbar would be hooked over His shoulder. Then He must stand up again with the weight of the cross on His back and He must put one foot in front of the other, dragging it alone, down the stinking, festering streets, scarcely pausing at the narrow turns, and never to pause, never to wait, never to catch His breath. This was a slave's punishment—two thieves shared His fate, carrying their crosses in the same procession.

No greater humiliation could be inflicted on a man. He must carry His own cross to the place of execution; drag His stake and crosspiece, emblems of guilt, of pain, of ignominy.

At that part of the narrow street where today there is a broken column set in the stone wall Jesus tottered, swayed, and fell, but they yanked Him to His feet again and pushed Him on. A child rushed by, trundling a hoop, belaboring it with a pointed stick and never noticing what was passing by. Only a few minutes later Jesus saw in the crowd that lined the street the face of His mother; Mary was watching there, by a blind alley that was filled with dirty, neglected, and wretched children holding to her skirts.

How she had got there, all the way up from Galilee, what impulse urged her, no one knew. But Mary, who could not get into the trial, stood in the street and watched, as, bent and breathing hard, He pulled His cross along.

Their eyes met, and all the years were in their glances. Then she was lost to His sight as the howling tatterdemalion mob clotted around Him. Once more there came a dizziness; He was about to fall again. A murmur of chagrin ran through the gang that followed. It began to look as if that beating had been too severe. Hereafter the soldiers should be warned about such excesses. They had beaten more than half the life out of Him; if the guards were not careful, He would die right here, collapsing under the cross at the busiest crossing in Jerusalem. Then there would be no crucifixion; no long-drawn-out death on the cross to watch intently; the people would be angry if cheated of the most interesting part of the whole show. Was this what they had stayed up all night for?

The guards felt that they knew what the public wanted.

They would not run any further risk of killing Him prematurely; when they saw how little strength was left in Him, they drafted a man from the onlookers to help out. The chosen man's name was Simon, a pilgrim with his two small sons, Rufus and Alexander, from the beautiful city of Cyrene, in upper Libya, where a Jew was a man as good as anybody else among the Gentiles; where he held equal citizenship with the Greeks who founded the town—and the synagogue stood side by side on terms of equality with temples of pagan gods. One minute before he was drafted Simon was an unknown molecule swimming in the vast bloodstream of the human race. Suddenly a guard pointed a finger, snarled an order, and the burly Cyrenian, seething with his bad luck, ceased to be a gawping spectator from a distant city and became immortal. Simon the unknown Cyrenian bent to help Jesus carry His cross, his two little boys following him in tears. When he straightened up he had become a figure in history.

He had done no crime; his pleasure was spoiled; it was an aching nuisance to take such a load—and the way to the hill of Golgotha was still a long one—but because of that half hour's unpaid toil Simon won immortal fame.

Now, as he moved onward with Jesus, the noise of the crowd took on a different note. The riffraff and the hirelings were no longer alone. Word was going through the awakening city; news of what the Sanhedrin and Pontius Pilate had done together flew from doorstep to upper window and along the domed rooftops; the women heard of it first, and they came running out to see if it were true. There is a legend that as Jesus and His unwilling helper Simon came by the house of a girl named Veronica, she rushed from her doorway and wept at the sight of Him; she bathed His sweating face with her veil and the tradition seems deathless that an image of His face was imprinted on the silken meshes of her scarf.

Through the gate called Porta Judiciaria by the Romans He passed outside the wall of the city, into the open country and within sight of a gloomy hill. There the women of Jerusalem surged into the road, elbowing aside tramps and drunkards, pickpockets, thieves and cutthroats, and all the savage crew that followed the cross. Unafraid of them, or of the priests who hired them, these housewives, daughters, and widows fought their way to the Master's side, bewailing and lamenting Him.

The countenance of the Master cleared, and His eyes took on new strength as He cried to these decent women:

"Daughters of Jerusalem! Weep not over me, but weep for yourselves and for your children. For behold the day shall come when they shall say, Blessed are the barren and the wombs that have not borne and the paps that have not given suck. Then shall they begin to say to the mountains: Fall upon us; and to the hills: Cover us. For if in the green wood they do these things, what shall be done in the dry?"

In the woeful day of destruction before long to dawn on Jerusalem many were to remember those sorrowful words.

Even with the strength of Simon the Cyrenian—who suddenly found himself taking a mysterious liking to this convict and carried the cross with an inner and utterly inexplicable satisfaction—Jesus felt His knees buckle under, and for the third time He fell down. But His tormentors were not so worried now. Here was their destination; He had only to lug the cross up that final stretch of steep hill and there He would be!

Calvary!

Golgotha, the natives called it, meaning the place of the skull. See, two other felons, also soaked with sweat and blood after their flogging, come dragging their crosses, too, from around the turn of the outer wall. Two thieves also going up today. It promised to be a really interesting exhibition.

Chapter 71 FINISHED!

It was high noon as workmen arranged the crosses on the ground.

The three condemned prisoners stood together—Dysmas and Gestas and Jesus, while the soldiers shoved back the crowd and the common workmen disposed the crosses on the ground near the holes and heaps of fresh earth.

High noon, and the sun brightly shining on bay trees and laurel over yonder, but on the four edges of the world clouds were gathering. In spring is it not unusual for clouds to begin gathering on the four horizons all at once? Few noticed the dark ring around the lower part of the sky. They had other things to look at: the three crosstrees laid out now and ladders being bolted and braced, and men with hammers and spikes and other men with spears goading each prisoner to lie down on his cross.

It was a quick business; the three victims were tired out, inert, incapable of resistance. They stretched Jesus out on the prostrate device, fingers in His armpits and palms forcing down His thighs and holding His head in the middle of the crosspiece, and they held Him so while they hammered huge pointed spikes through His palms—then nailed His feet to the main piece. Up now, hoist high, and dump the foot of the cross in the open hole.

So, there, and at last, the will of Annas and Caiphas was fully done. Jesus was crucified between two thieves, the three gaunt crosses with their suffering human beings uplifted upon them making sharp, bleak silhouettes against the paling sky.

One would have thought, then, that with this finality malice would wither, but it was not like that.

At mocking Pilate's orders—strange commands of a strange man who meant the priests to be confronted with a reminder—a sign was nailed up on the cross over the head of Jesus, an inscription in three languages: Latin, Greek, and Aramaic:

"Jesus of Nazareth, the King of the Jews!"

When he heard that this was being done, Caiphas was uncontrollable. In spite of the pleadings of Annas, who wanted now only to get to his bed, Caiphas had himself carried in a litter back to the palace where Pilate was having a meal that was both breakfast and lunch.

Caiphas came storming into the small blue-walled room with the fireplace, where Pilate received his visitors.

"Why do you do such a thing as this to us? Don't write 'King of the Jews'; if you must write anything, write, 'He said, I am the King of the Jews.' "

Pilate snorted at Caiphas and a leer twisted his thick, loose-formed mouth. He was through yielding to this popinjay.

"What I have written I have written," said Pilate, and stalked back to his wife.

"I feel like a vaticide!" he was reported to tell his wife. "I have killed a prophet."

"Perhaps," lamented his wife, "you are a deicide—perhaps you have killed a god."

"But who," cried Pilate, the born interrogator, "can possibly kill a god?"

"That," his wife answered, "is your only hope!"

On the hill of Calvary the crowd of watchers was growing constantly, in a vast half-moon of concentrated attention before the figure on the central cross.

Jesus, turning from the tapestry of faces, murmured to the sky:

"Father, forgive them, for they know not what they do."

Forgive them? All? Where were His friends? Where are you, Peter? The rock on which I shall found my church and the gates of hell shall not prevail against it. Is that you, back there? Peter! Ah, bold, baldheaded fisherman, with your human nature you suffer for me so; the full price must be paid now.

But *is* that you, Peter? Where is John? John, the well-beloved; John, who, at our Last Supper, laid his head on my breast and wept? Where is John now? And Judas! Judas not here to see what his treachery has brought us all to? Judas is in the potter's field, after hanging from a tree. Is that what is to be seen, so far, far off on the road to Bethlehem, where Mary's son was born?

And all the others, where are they? The nine other Apostles. You ran away! Why did you run away, James and Thomas and Bartholomew and all the rest of you? For your lives you ran, scampering off in the dark rows of olive trees in the Garden of Gethsemane; scattering down the deep slopes of Olivet to the grand highway and off to the road that leads back to Galilee—back home.

Why did you nine forsake? That is so clear to see now. You never completely believed in Jesus. You wanted to believe; you persuaded yourselves that you had accepted the idea fully and with no reservations, but in your heart of hearts you never, for a moment, believed that I and the Father are one. The soldiers came and took me. Why did I not release Myself as I had done before?

Because you feared that you would share this fate of mine, up here on the cross, crucified. You, too, might bleed and die. But the day is almost here when you will have such faith that fear will no longer matter.

"I thirst," said Jesus.

So the monstrous-conscienced guards prepared for Him a cup of wine mixed with myrrh and gall and bile. He would not drink it. His last cup on this earth was the chalice of the communion at the Last Supper. The leering fools who had mixed up the filthy mess could not force it down His throat, so there was nothing left for them to do but to spill all of it on the ground.

Calmly He hung there, suspended, as the guards who had nailed Him up threw dice for His robe which was without seam, woven from the top throughout. They had taken all His garments and divided them into four parts—one for each soldier. But when they looked at that beautiful seamless robe one of them proposed: "Let's not tear it. Let's cast lots for it, whose it shall be."

It was while the soldiers were throwing the dice that Jesus looked down and saw that He was not alone. Moving slowly forward through the crowd, coming ever closer to the cross, were three women—three Marys close at hand. Mary, His mother, stood at the foot of the cross. And Mary, the wife of Cleophas, His mother's sister, knelt beside her; Mary of Magdalen, out of whom he had cast seven devils, was prostrate on the earth.

And who standing beside His blessed mother? John! Yes, it *was* John! John, the well-beloved disciple. This was why you hovered on the far outside of the crowd; you were waiting to bring Mother here.

With a sudden access of strength Jesus called out in the premature gloaming that was creeping in:

"Woman, behold your son!"

With infinite tenderness He had called to her; and then, turning to John, the drops of sweat glistening on His neck and forehead and cheeks, He summed up all the concern and compassion in His heart in these words to His dear follower:

"Behold your mother!" And from that day on John would be like another son to Mary. But his devotion was a symbol of a greater service, for Jesus had spoken to mankind, had showed all living the symbol of motherhood.

The slowly darkening indigo sky was losing its deep violet blue and turning to black. The agony of the gentle prisoner, the memory of His good works, the wailing of the women all helped to change the mood of the watchers. Twice He had spoken from the cross: once to pray for the soldiers even at the very moment they were enforcing the tent pegs through His hands; and again when He spoke to His mother. The compassion of the suffering man moved the people to a dangerous sympathy, so back came the priests with their troupe and they began to jape:

"He saved others; let Him save Himself if He be Christ, the elect of God."

They waggled their hands and fleered and blasphemed.

"*Wah!*" they cried with oriental frenzy. "You that destroy the Temple of God and in three days build it up again. Wah! Save yourself! Come down from the cross!"

And even Caiphas, standing with the silent Annas and some of their cronies of the Temple priesthood, spoke out of the side of his mouth:

"Others He saved; Himself He cannot save."

One of the scribes answered:

"If He be the King of Israel let Him now come down from the cross and we will believe Him. He trusted in God; let Him now deliver Him, if He will have Him."

But there were some who noticed that as the darkness deepened a small light shone behind His head, and that it grew more luminous as death came ever nearer.

So the priests talked away among themselves, feeling very safe, as the soldiers offered Jesus a sponge soaked in vinegar, because He had said He thirsted; while the soldiers tormented Him, the mob railed, and the women of Jerusalem mourned and the blood flowed slowly, trickling down from pierced hands and feet.

One of the robbers, Gestas, took up the cry from the onlookers and spat it out with blood and foam at his mouth:

"If you be the Christ, save yourself—and us!"

But Dysmas, on the right-hand cross, called back to him:

"Neither do you fear God, seeing that you are under the same condemnation. And we, indeed, justly—because we receive the due reward of our deeds. But this man has done no evil."

Then, turning his head toward the Master, he said with pleading sweetness, amazing in so rough a voice:

"Lord, remember me when you shall come into your kingdom."

The eyelids of Jesus flew up, the eyeballs rolled back, and He smiled. It was a smile of blood and sweat, but He called out boldly, in His old clear, strong voice:

"So be it, I say to you—this day you shall be with me in Paradise."

The storm was gathering its darkness now; the air of the black sirocco was getting murkier by the minute with a wrack of clouds and dark floating vapor scudding across the sky. There was a low, rolling sound of thunder, a rumble swelling to roar and crash over the heads of the people. As the rain came, many scattered, but others remained, to miss nothing. Even the most vociferous of the paid mob began to feel a germ of fear. The sun was lost behind the thickening nimbus overhead and there was a low and constant murmuring among the people. Tumult and panic were ready to break out into mob madness. This, they began to fear, was no ordinary storm; this was not the familiar black sirocco which came to Jerusalem each year at the beginning of April. This was a brooding, deepening, lightless storm of sinister intensity.

It was close upon three o'clock in the afternoon, when, for the fourth time, they heard Jesus speak:

"*Eloi, Eloi, Lamma sabacthani!*"

Had they heard clearly? That strange mixture, that sentence, a compound of Hebrew and Aramaic Chaldee? Some, far in the back, thought that in delirium He was calling on the prophet Elias. And some of the mockers again brought the vinegar sponge and stuck it on a long reed, and thrust it up at Him, while they cried:

"Let be! Let us see whether Elias will come to deliver Him!"

But Jesus had not called upon Elias. His mother knew and understood. So did all good and pious people gathered there, and even the hypocrites, if they remembered their Scriptures.

What Jesus had said was:

"My God, my God, why have you forsaken me?"

Standing near the foot of the cross, Caiphas, hearing those words, gave a hoarse chuckle of delight. Seizing his old father-in-law's withered wrist, he rejoiced:

"Hear that, Lord Annas? His followers will never be able to live down those words. First He says He is God, then He asks Himself why He has forsaken Himself. Pretty comic, don't you think?"

There was a terrible peal of thunder. But presently Caiphas heard the voice of Annas, despondent and disheartened:

"You complete and utter ninny and fool!"

"Lord Annas, did I hear you . . ."

"You did. You are high priest, Caiphas, but you do not even remember your Scriptures. Especially the Twenty-second Psalm, which begins: 'My God, my God, why hast thou forsaken me?' and goes on to prophesy perhaps what happened here today—even to the parting of his garments."

"Father-in-law, you're not going——"

"I am going home," sighed Annas, and turned his back on his son-in-law.

And Annas might also have reminded Caiphas that the very next Psalm declared the Lord as the Good Shepherd: "Even though I walk in the dark valley I fear no evil; for you are at my side!"

With an unearthly smile down upon His mother and His other loved ones, Jesus had spoken the words as King David anciently predicted; without further protest He let the vinegar from the sponge pour down into His parched throat and He spoke the sixth time from the cross:

"It is consummated."

Caiphas then knew what that meant. The whole body of prophecies of the old prophets had been fulfilled; his own prophecies as well. They had said that the Messiah would be born in Bethlehem, the city of David. There Jesus had been born, and in a stable, as also prophesied—all the long story was full of milestones, verifications, credentials, from the old prophets that He, Jesus, now in His pain and humiliation, was the promised Messiah.

"It is consummated!"

Having said that He took a deep breath and spoke out softly, spoke as Mary remembered He would often speak when He was a boy, falling off to sleep, on His bed in Nazareth—softly and with a tone of surrender and relief:

"Father, into your hands I commend my spirit."

And bowing His head, He gave up the ghost.

Thus it was that Jesus of Nazareth died, about four o'clock in the murky air of Good Friday afternoon, April 7, A.D. 30.

Men told strange stories afterward: tales of how the veil of the Temple was torn into two pieces—the rainbow veil that hung at the Holy of Holies and hid the innermost altar from the eyes of all except priests, rent and ripped, from top to bottom, although no man's hand had touched it. Tales of a trembling of the earth and rocks crashing from hillsides; graves ripped open, their white domes splitting wide. All this was talk behind the hand, because the priests would retaliate on any of their own who had a sympathetic or significant word to say about this execution.

Those at the cross who loved Him beat their breasts and sobbed. The Roman officer who had given all the orders for the execution of the death sentence turned his back on the women and gagged. Perhaps it was the earthquake that weighed the man down, or perhaps the darkness. Or it may have been the face of Mary. Then, cleaning his mouth with an oblong of silk, he turned to one of his lieutenants and gasped:

"Indeed this man *was* the Son of God."

Chapter 72 WHY DO THEY NOT CARE?

THE old man Annas sat in his great room and fanned himself. A small lamp on the table at his right hand raised a flickering light to his little goatlike face and the wisp of tired white hair hanging over his left eye. On the divan sat his son-in-law Caiphas with the voluptuous perfumed beard, a bulk of shadow against the lesser darkness of an open window.

"It is hot tonight," complained Annas. "We are going to have a torrid summer. I know the signs."

"Did you not understand me just now when I told you this town was in an uproar?" asked the high priest of Jerusalem primly.

"You know very well it is the Feast of Weeks, Caiphas. The city is simply crowded again, full of visitors."

"Full of Christians," reported his son-in-law bitterly. "I cannot seem to make you realize. You are getting more obstinate all the time. Seven weeks ago I had all I could do to make you act against that impostor, Jesus of Nazareth. And now——"

"And now," Annas broke in with his humming voice, "the followers of your executed impostor are back in town and only this week they made three thousand converts!"

"Five thousand!"

"They seem very confident of their faith."

"The danger of revolution is even greater with Jesus dead than alive," complained the priest.

"Are you sure that He is dead?" asked Annas lightly.

"You saw Him die."

"No, I did not wait. But, Caiphas, what *do* you suppose happened to His body?"

"It was buried. And there's a pretty story too. Do you know where they laid that cadaver? In the tomb that Joseph had built for himself!"

"Joseph? Of Arimathea?"

"Exactly. One of our own kind, but a traitor to his class. He went to Pilate and asked permission—and got it. He worked fast, and was able to observe the ceremonial law before sunset, and he had help—help from another traitor."

"Nicodemus, no doubt," chuckled Annas, with an obscene roll of his pale blue eyes.

"Yes, it was Nicodemus. Two substantial men like that extending charnel hospitality to the remains of a felon, winding the body in the traditional cerements, eight feet long; anointing the body with embalming spices, as our ancestors learned from the Egyptians. They had women with them, too, silly women who believed in Jesus. *Wah!*"

Annas lowered his fan, folded his arms, and gave a toothless grin, barely visible in the dark.

"Is the scoundrel's body *still* in the tomb?" he asked softly.

"No!"

"No?"

"*No!*"

"It is not?"

"No, I said."

"It is gone?"

"Yes!"

"But where, Caiphas? You have suddenly become quite monosyllabic."

"It was stolen."

"I see. Why did not Joseph and Nicodemus see to it that the golal, the great stone, was placed securely against the tomb?"

"That was done, but . . ."

"And weren't there guards?"

"I believe so."

"You *know* so. You yourself specifically asked Pilate to put them there. Then how could anyone have stolen the body?"

"Wah! I don't know," groaned Caiphas. "I wish I did."

"Caiphas," Annas advised, "calm yourself. Have another drink of cool and sweetened water and listen to me. I have not been so indifferent as you think in this business. I selected my own representatives to investigate. It is a fact that the tomb of Jesus now has no corpse in it."

"Those scheming disciples . . ."

"Stole it? No. They might well have tried to, but no! They had no opportunity. But *suppose* they had done so. Where have they hidden the remains? I employed the smartest spies in Judea, experienced in espionage. They mingled with these apostles pretending to be true believers. We got nowhere. It is still a fact that the remains of a criminal, who was put to death, have disappeared under your very nose. Now you tell me the body has been stolen. What else *could* you say?"

"You begin to talk like one of them," murmured Caiphas.

"No. I am merely trying to be factual and objective, as always. There are several possible reasons for that tomb being empty. Suppose, for example, the body was never put in there at all. Suppose that Joseph of Arimathea and Nicodemus did not trust you. I happen to know they never have. They may have feared that you would send vandals after that body, for fear the faithful followers of this man would continue to visit the tomb and make it a shrine. They may even have been afraid that you would use His body for dog meat, Caiphas. So Joseph and Nicodemus may have removed the body to another, more obscure, secret tomb."

"I shall face them."

"You need not trouble. I have already talked to them. They did nothing of the kind. They were too scared!"

"Pilate, then?"

"What should the Procurator of Judea care about a convict's corpse? He did his best for Jesus as long as he could."

"Then where can it be, Father-in-law?"

The laugh of Annas was low and chuckling.

"Don't you know? The Christians say He has risen from the dead, in three days, on schedule, as promised! And it is supposed to promise a similar grace to all His followers—a palingenesis, a rebirth into a higher life."

"Do you think you have to remind me of what the Christians say!" exclaimed Caiphas, with a tremble in his voice. "Peter the fisherman, ana James and John, the sons of Zebedee, and the whole crew of them are standing on our street corners, preaching these insane lies—'*Jesus is Christ, the son of the Living God! He rose from the dead! We have all seen Him! We have all talked with Him! Here, ask Thomas Didymus—he was the skeptic, he saw the wounds of the nails in His hands and feet and put his own hand into the wound in His side!*'

"That is the sort of talk they are blabbering all over town. They even call to me, as I stand listening at a little distance off, and ask me if I have gone to the tomb to see for myself; and why don't I call the gardener and ask him what *he* knows about it."

"Well," snapped Annas, "why don't you?"

The fact was that Annas had done just what he now advised his son-in-law to do. He had talked with the gardener, and with the Roman soldiers, and even with Christian witnesses. Out of the minor disagreements, the divergencies in detail, even the apparently irreconcilable differences, there emerged in all essential substance accounts that were impressively the same.

Annas had not wanted to believe any of them, yet these witnesses were not liars; he could see that.

They reminded the old politician that Jesus was crucified on Friday, which was the parasceve, the eve of preparation of the Sabbath, and, more than that, on this occasion also, the night before the Feast of the Passover. It would be an affront to the people, both in their Sabbath devotions and their celebration of the Pasch, to leave meanwhile the three bodies beginning to putrefy on their crosses. So even the priests had gone to Pilate that day—only a short while behind Joseph of Arimathea—to ask that the legs of the corpses be ceremonially broken and the bodies pulled down and taken away. To this request Pilate also gave consent, and sent soldiers to finish the job.

These guards broke the legs of the two thieves but they did not touch the legs of Jesus. But one of the soldiers—Longinus was his name—opened up His side with a thrust of his spear, and testified that blood and water flowed from the open wound. Many of the followers of Jesus also believed that the spear pierced His heart.

When their work was done, Joseph of Arimathea showed the guards his writ from Pilate, by which they must relinquish to him the remains of Jesus. There was no difficulty about it; the two thieves were tossed into a common burial pit, but the body of the Nazarene was given to the two daring aristocrats who risked the condemnation of all their friends to do this service.

Joseph and Nicodemus freely admitted to Annas just what they had done. The garden in which Joseph had made for himself a sepulcher hewed in stone was quite close to the hill of the crucifixion. There the two rich men carried the body and Nicodemus opened a bag and took out a hundred pounds of an ointment made of myrrh and aloes. Joseph had brought fine linen and so, while the two Marys helped, they laid Him away.

"It is queer," continued Annas in his humming voice as he reviewed the testimony; "the guards say there was an earthquake. Some talk about an angel with shining face coming down and the soldiers falling unconscious with fear. Anyway, a woman came into the garden. Her name was Mary, she came from Magdala, and she used to have a dubious reputation. Before dawn—her grief for this Jesus was poignant quite evidently—she came to the tomb with more spiced ointments for the corpse. It was still dark at that hour, but she could see well enough to be both astonished and terrified. She ran back into town to tell this new leader of theirs—I've talked with him; a fiery fellow who won't back down—Peter of Capernaum. She told Peter that she feared robbers had stolen the body of their Lord!"

"Rubbish!" grumbled Caiphas.

"Most mysterious rubbish! Pretty soon there were two other women called Mary in the garden. One was His mother, from up in Nazareth, and the other His aunt, the wife of Cleophas. They, too, were astonished when they found the stone gone. Now, Caiphas, as one man tells the story, they found two angels in the tomb. I do not know what an angel looks like, so I find it hard to visualize."

"Why try? Isn't this whole conversation a waste of time?"

"That," said Annas, "depends entirely on how much of it you are going to be able to grasp. I hear, too, that they found a young man sitting on the right side of the tomb, as one enters the place. The young man, who was wearing a white robe, told them not to be frightened; I think I have the testimony of what he said here."

Annas picked up a thin scroll lying on the Athenian stand at his left hand. He flipped it open, clucked his lips twice, and then read:

" 'You seek Jesus of Nazareth who was crucified. He is risen! He is not here! Behold the place where they laid Him. But go, tell His disciples and Peter that He goes before you into Galilee; there you should see Him; as He told you.' "

"And I suppose," said Caiphas with a leer, "you sent agents into Galilee!"

"I am sorry to say I did not. I did not believe, when I first heard these stories, that there could be anything to them."

"Lord Annas!"

Caiphas stood up and assumed a dramatic pose.

"Do you mean to sit there and give me to believe that you do put any belief in them *now?* Are you going to tell me Jesus of Nazareth *did* rise from the dead?"

"I don't know," grinned Annas uncomfortably. "I wish I did, but I don't. I don't know."

"You know that such a notion is mad," Caiphas retorted coldly.

The old man tugged at his dangling wisp of white hair and his smile became glacial.

"Hear it all and judge for yourself. If nothing else, it will have the interest of a curious tale. The women went back and told Peter, whom I mentioned, and another, younger disciple—a decent enough young man called John. I heard them tell the story—to me—and I cross-questioned them severely. No, I could not make a breach in either man's testimony. Both men ran to the tomb after hearing the story from the women. Hard as they found it to believe—in fact, they didn't believe it at first any more than you or I did——"

"Do," corrected Caiphas.

"Nevertheless, they ran to the Porta Judiciaria as fast as they could. John peered into the tomb and saw the linen cloths and the face napkin lying loosely on the shelf where the body had been. Then he waited for Peter. He was not ready to tell me why, but I think he was just plain scared, as any man might well be. These disciples think their Jesus was a God, but they themselves are very ordinary fellows, believe me. Then along came Peter, puffing from the run."

"Never mind the descriptive passages," pleaded Caiphas sourly. "I know you are a frustrated poet. That is what made you such a successful politician. Have I much more to hear?"

"Peter," repeated Annas implacably, "was puffing heavily. He did not loiter at the door; not Peter. He plunged right on into the sepulcher; he, too, saw the loose grave clothes and the napkin that had been about the head of Jesus wrapped up and put carefully in a separate place."

"So what is the point of all this miracle story, Lord Annas?"

A warmer light came into the bleak eyes of the old man.

"The point I make to you is a point in logic, a point in sheer reason, my son-in-law. Let us overlook or, if you prefer, dismiss all the arguments and look only to the salient facts. They say that Jesus appeared visibly to Mary Magdalen. We need not discuss that. I am also told that you tried to bribe the soldiers——"

"I?"

Caiphas picked up his skirts and again stood dramatically erect.

"You, yes! Sit down. You have bribed before, as we both know.

"Caiphas, you tried to bribe the soldiers to say that robbers took the body, and that the robbers were His disciples. Silly that you should expect soldiers of the Roman legion to report to Pilate such a self-incriminating tale as that the body was stolen right under their eyes. They took your money, of course—and I know you interceded for them at the palace—but the story, Caiphas, is against good sense. Never mind!

"There is a little village called Emmaus, about seven miles from Jerusalem, and there is a repeated report that Jesus appeared and ate with a family there."

"What rubbish, rubbish, rubbish——"

"It is not so easy to jump on the next report. That is when He is said suddenly to have appeared in the midst of His friends, right here in Jerusalem. He nearly scared them into sickness. Have you read the account of what they all testify He said to them? Listen:

" 'Peace be to you! It is I! Fear not! Why are you so troubled and why do thoughts arise in your hearts? See my hands and feet, that it is I myself; handle and see; for a spirit has not flesh and bones, as you see me to have.'

"He showed them the wound in His side," Annas went on. "He ate with them. He bestowed on them some mystical blessing of the Holy Ghost, whatever that may be; the whole business is beyond my comprehension. But it did have something to do, Caiphas, with the forgiveness of sin."

"That," said Caiphas, "was blasphemy *again!*"

Annas chortled.

"He seems to go right on committing that sin," he mused in his humming voice while Caiphas swore humorlessly.

"But there was one remarkable circumstance which we must never forget," the old man continued. "One of their members—Thomas Didymus by name—was absent at this visitation. The others told him all about it but doubting Thomas shook his head. He refused to believe any of it."

"The first Christian with a grain of sense," said Caiphas.

"The first true scientist, perhaps. Anyway, Jesus returned to confront Thomas, the skeptic, with His hands—the apostle saw the holes in the palms left by the tent pegs and the wounds in His feet; he put his own hand into the open wound in Jesus's side, where the spear of Longinus had pierced it."

"And what did Thomas say then?" asked Caiphas, beguiled in spite of himself.

"He said, 'My Lord and my God' and then Jesus said, 'Because you have seen me, Thomas, you have believed. Blessed are they that have not seen and have believed.' "

"But that," cried Caiphas, "denies rationalism!"

"Exactly!" said Annas, and laughed to himself, long and silently, like a very foolish—or a very wise—old man. "And I, for one, am glad of that much—I never like those pessimistic ideas."

Both knew that it was not necessary for Annas to complete the story; each had tried to sift it down to its realities. They had heard the reports of the appearance of Jesus to His disciples by the Sea of Tiberius; and of how He had appeared to others on a mountain in Galilee. More, they had heard over and over again the story, incredible to them both, of how Jesus had gathered all His loved ones around Him on the top of Mount Olivet, had promised them—"Lo, I am with you always, even until the consummation of the world"—and then had visibly departed heavenward until He was hidden and lost in clouds.

Now, in the moist warmth of the torrid night, Annas and Caiphas sat together in the dark, remembering so much of this man whom they had ordered killed yet who still could plague their peace of mind.

"The reason I came here tonight," explained Caiphas, "is that we shall have to agree on a strong policy."

"You still want action? More action?"

"Yes."

Annas clucked his tongue and lips together.

"But I thought you had already started on this sort of thing without bothering to consult me. Haven't I heard that you had a young man named Stephen brought up on charges? Wasn't he a follower of Jesus? Did you have a lot of trouble with him?"

"We condemned him, too."

"Yes, and you stoned him to death, and the followers of Jesus now declare that he is a martyr—the first from among themselves."

"Perhaps he will not be the last."

"But has it occurred to you, Caiphas, that this brave death contradicts all that you had to say earlier this evening? Would any man be willing to die—in a heroic, glorious martyrdom like this—for some conjurer's trick involving the stealing of a corpse in a hoax, a sham? No! He was one of the men present when they say Jesus showed them hands, feet, and the wound in His side."

"I still don't see——"

"Probably you never will. But I shall try to give you a gleam of light. On the night we killed Him, you remember that two of His disciples followed Him into Jerusalem but one of them denied Him three times and both kept themselves hidden. What happened to the other nine? They couldn't get away fast enough. They went back to Galilee where they came from, and glad enough to get there. Why? Because they were afraid. They had pretended all along to themselves that they believed He was the Messiah—and maybe they did—but when they came to face danger they lost faith and ran."

"Cowards as well as fools!" fleered Caiphas.

"But what makes them brave now?" asked Annas sternly. "How is it a man can die so willingly? All the others, preaching today on the streets of Jerusalem, know that their ultimate fate is violent death. They know what they stand for and what you stand for, Caiphas, and they know this world will always be a place of fear, of want, of war, of all kinds of suffering, as long as those two conflicting points of view exist. The world will be a better place, Caiphas, only when their side wins. And they *will* win. We can only kill them; but they can conquer us.

"Why do they no longer care whether they live or die? Because they have seen their leader rise from the dead; they expect to do the same; to them, now, life and death are mere words for temporary things and do not really matter. Since the resurrection, that is what it means to be a Christian."

Again there was silence except for the droning of the insects.

Sobered Caiphas was thinking of that uncompromisable conflict.

"Lord Annas," said Caiphas, "the tales of rising from the dead are comical. The views taught by the followers of this man are not comical—they are subversive."

Old Annas sucked on his noisy tooth.

"Very well," he said. "Do as you will do anyhow. But Caiphas, these roots are deep and spreading. Before you get through—God only knows! I have a horrible feeling that we have blundered. History may blame us. Worse, history may blame all our nation, all Israel, for the guilt that belongs so much to you and me and our rich and powerful friends—who were afraid of the truth."

"What is truth?" Caiphas was sarcastic. "Pilate asked *Him* that. Do you know the answer?"

"No. But now I believe it is truth itself that we nailed to the cross and then buried—and truth, as usual, rose again."

Annas chuckled softly.

"I am old and sleepy," he muttered. "Good-night, Caiphas." He moved toward his bedroom.